SACR

S0-ATJ-076

Sacramento, CA 95814
09/16

PRAISE FOR
THE NOVELS OF LEXI BLAKE

"A book to enjoy again and again . . . Captivating."
—Guilty Pleasures Book Reviews

"A satisfying snack of love, romance, and hot, steamy sex."
—Sizzling Hot Books

"Hot and emotional."
—Two Lips Reviews

Ruthless

LEXI BLAKE

BERKLEY BOOKS, NEW YORK

BERKLEY

An imprint of Penguin Random House LLC
375 Hudson Street, New York, New York 10014

RUTHLESS

This book is an original publication of Penguin Random House LLC.

Copyright © 2016 by DLZ Entertainment LLC.
Excerpt from *Satisfaction* copyright © 2017 by DLZ Entertainment LLC.

Penguin supports copyright. Copyright fuels creativity, encourages diverse voices,
promotes free speech, and creates a vibrant culture. Thank you for buying an authorized
edition of this book and for complying with copyright laws by not reproducing, scanning, or
distributing any part of it in any form without permission. You are supporting writers and
allowing Penguin to continue to publish books for every reader.

BERKLEY® and the "B" design are registered trademarks of Penguin Random House LLC.
For more information, visit penguin.com.

Library of Congress Cataloging-in-Publication Data

Names: Blake, Lexi, author.
Title: Ruthless / Lexi Blake.
Description: Berkley trade paperback edition. I New York, New York :
Berkley, 2016. I Series: A lawless novel ; 1
Identifiers: LCCN 2016025595 (print) I LCCN 2016026305 (ebook) I ISBN
9780425283578 (paperback) I ISBN 9780698410305 ()
Subjects: I BISAC: FICTION / Romance / Contemporary. I FICTION / Romance /
Suspense. I FICTION / Romance / General. I GSAFD: Erotic fiction. I
Romantic suspense fiction.
Classification: LCC PS3602.L3456 R88 2016 (print) I
LCC PS3602.L3456 (ebook) I DDC 813/.6—dc23
LC record available at https://lccn.loc.gov/2016025595

PUBLISHING HISTORY
Berkley trade paperback edition / August 2016

PRINTED IN THE UNITED STATES OF AMERICA

10 9 8 7 6 5 4 3 2

Cover design by Sandra Chiu.
Portrait of businessman by Peskymonkey / Getty Images;
Cityscape by Evgeny Dubinchuk / Shutterstock.
Interior text design by Laura K. Corless.

This is a work of fiction. Names, characters, places, and incidents either are the product of
the author's imagination or are used fictitiously, and any resemblance to actual persons,
living or dead, business establishments, events, or locales is entirely coincidental.

Penguin
Random
House

I would like to thank my amazing editor, Kate Seaver, and the entire Berkley staff for helping me make this transition. I kind of like not having to make all the decisions. I would also like to thank my staff: Kim, Riane, Stormy, and my amazing husband, Richard.

This book is dedicated to my agent, Merrilee Heifetz, who took a chance on me when no one else would. It took us a while to get here, but I'm so glad I had you with me for the ride.

Prologue

R iley Lawless sat in the chair they'd offered him, but he wasn't alone. There had been only two chairs in the small office at the police station and there were four of them, so he'd settled Mia in beside him.

Four of them.

There used to be six.

"I'm tired, Riley. When can we go home?" Mia asked, her blue eyes wide.

Riley exchanged a look with his oldest brother, Drew. What was he supposed to say to that? He still couldn't believe what had happened himself. How was he supposed to explain it to Mia? She was barely six. They'd had a Barbie birthday party for her two weeks before. She'd worn a princess tiara and opened her presents with a grin that showed her first missing tooth. Their dad had forced them all to attend. Three boys amid a sea of six-year-old girls.

Where was his father now? He didn't understand anything.

Brandon looked to Mia with tears in his eyes. "I don't think we get to go home ever again, Mia."

Drew put a hand on his brother's shoulder. "We're going to be okay, Bran."

Riley wasn't sure how that was possible. Had it really only been two hours before? Had it really happened at all? Maybe he was dreaming. His mind drifted back.

The sheets tangled in his feet as he tried to sit up. Confusion. There was a crackling sound he didn't understand. He fought his way out of the sheets and sat up in bed. The computer he shared with his brother was still on, the green light of the screen illuminating the room. Riley rubbed his eyes.

Something was wrong. He could smell smoke.

The light on the computer died suddenly and so did the one on his small fish tank.

Bran?

His brother was on the top bunk. Riley scrambled up the ladder that connected their beds.

Bran, wake up.

There was a pounding on the door to his room and he thought about all those horror movies he wasn't supposed to watch but he did when he was at Tommy Ferguson's house because Tommy's mom always took a sleeping pill and then nothing would wake her. Bran sat up, and Riley could see him even in the darkness. He reached for Riley's hand. Bran was only eight. Riley had turned twelve months before. Riley gave him a squeeze. Bran was his responsibility.

Hide. Get in the closet and hide, Bran. I'll deal with what's happening.

That crackling sound was so much louder, but nothing was as loud as the door exploding as it was kicked open. Riley tried to cover his brother's body with his own, his heart pounding.

An eerie red light filled the room and smoke came pouring in. In the midst of the haze, a tall figure appeared.

Drew. He was carrying Mia and his face was smudged with dirt. His voice was husky, older than normal when he spoke.

Come on. We've gotta move. I think the back stairs are still clear. If not, we're going out a window. Move it. Now.

What's happening? *He didn't understand.*

The house is on fire. We have to go.

But Mom and Dad? Shouldn't their dad be the one ordering them around?

Drew shook his head and Riley realized the world had flipped and he didn't recognize where he'd landed.

He took Bran's hand and followed his brother.

"Don't think about it." Drew looked down on him, bringing Riley back to reality. The grim expression on his face made him look so much older than fourteen.

"I want Daddy." Mia started to cry.

Drew immediately picked her up, settling her against his lanky frame. "I'm sorry, Mia. But it's going to be all right."

Riley wasn't sure how. He got to his feet. "I'm thirsty. They said there was a water fountain outside."

"Don't be gone long," Drew said in a voice that let Riley know he was in control.

Riley didn't really want a drink. He was fairly certain he was going to throw up.

A man and a woman, both in blue uniforms, sat at their desks talking. The rest of the building seemed almost eerily empty. "Poor kids. Their dad tried to kill them all. Did you know he'd locked all the doors and propped them closed from the outside so the kids couldn't get out? The bastard wanted to make damn sure those kids died with him. Found the window he used to get back inside, but the kids wouldn't have found it because of how he lit the fire before he offed himself."

"Yeah, well, I heard what he did to his wife was even worse," the female officer replied with a shake of her head. "They don't know if there's enough of her left to identify. What a way to go."

Riley felt his stomach turn. They were talking about him. They were talking about his dad. His mom.

They were really gone. His dad, who played ball with him and never got mad even when Riley interrupted his work. His dad worked a lot, but he always smiled when one of them entered the room. He would grin and thank them for the interruption because work was boring but his kids were fun. That house had been filled with his dad's unique energy.

"He didn't kill her." His father would never hurt Mom. He loved her.

The two officers looked back, and he saw a nauseating sympathy cross their faces.

The female officer immediately crossed the space between them. "Honey, you need to stay in the captain's office. I promise a very nice lady is going to be here soon, and she's going to take care of you."

"Drew and me will take care of us." He didn't want some random lady. He wanted his mom.

"No, honey." The woman shook her head. "You don't worry about that now. It's going to be all right."

He turned to go back into the office before he heard them whispering again.

"Damn, I hate that they're going to break those kids up," the man said in a hushed voice he probably thought no one would hear.

Break them up?

"They don't have any family. No one's taking in four kids."

Riley slammed into the room, his heart in his throat.

"They're breaking us up." He couldn't lose them. He couldn't lose his brothers and his sister. Mia was so young.

Drew's eyes closed, and when he opened them again, there was the same steely glint in them he got when facing down a pitcher in a baseball game. "No matter what happens, know that I will find a way to see you, Riley. I won't let any of you go and when I'm old enough, I'll come and get you."

But that could be years.

Bran and Mia were sitting together, slumped against each other. They were asleep and Riley wished he was. He wished this was all a bad dream.

"They say Dad killed Mom."

"No," Drew said sharply. "That's a lie and you never believe it. No matter what they say. Dad and Mom were murdered."

"By who? Who would want to kill them?" It didn't make a lick of sense.

Drew shook his head. "I don't know, but I will find out. I saw some of it. I tried to tell the cops, but they don't believe me. They think I'm a kid who doesn't want to believe his dad could do something so evil."

"He wouldn't." How was his dad gone? Where had he gone? Riley didn't understand. He didn't understand anything at all.

Drew put a hand on his shoulder and in that moment, in the dim light of the office with silence all around them, Riley could see his father in his brother's face. "One day when we're older, we'll find them and we'll make them pay. I'll make them pay."

The thought gave him strength. It was better than thinking about what he'd lost. "No. You were right the first time. We'll make them pay. You and me and Bran and Mia. We'll make them hurt."

The door opened and an older lady with a briefcase strode in. She started talking about temporary housing and grief counseling. She began to gently broach the subject of foster care and how difficult it would be to place the four of them together.

But Riley just looked at Drew.

And knew one day they would be together again. After all, they had a job to do.

One

"M r. Lang? Can I get you anything? Anything at all?"

Riley Lawless looked up at the pretty blond receptionist and got the distinct feeling she really meant what she'd said. She was staring at him like she could eat him alive.

"I don't think we have time for what she has in mind," he muttered under his breath. Drew chuckled beside him, lounging back.

Riley shook his head because his brother was right. He needed to focus on one thing and one thing alone, and that was making an impression on Ellie Stratton. "Thank you, but I think we're fine."

The blonde blushed and handed him her card. "If you change your mind, Mr. Lang."

She walked away, her sky-high heels clacking against the marbled floors. It had been years since Riley had started using the name Lang professionally, and he still wasn't used to it. They'd decided on the name to give him distance from the Lawless history. He and Bran went by their paternal grandmother's maiden name so they wouldn't be easily associated with Drew. He still hated not sharing a name with his parents.

He had a bunch of very official documents proclaiming him to be Riley Lang, but that didn't make him forget that he was a Lawless.

"I do not get that. I'm obviously more attractive than you. How do you get all those women?" Drew watched the receptionist's very nice ass sway as she walked back to her desk.

Riley snorted. They had this discussion at least once a month. "You scare the hell out of women. It's like they can sense the predator in you."

Drew gave him a smile. "See? I can smile. I'm utterly harmless."

It was Riley's turn to laugh. "Dude, even smiling you look like you're ready to hunt someone down. You need to take after me."

"So I need to be a brainless himbo?"

"Yeah, tell that to Harvard Law. No. You need to look friendly. You need to look normal. Normal men don't look like they'll sprout claws and fangs at any given moment." His brother got more than his fair share of female attention, but years of growing a company and raising his siblings had killed any light in Drew's eyes. Riley straightened his tie and put on his game face.

When the mission required man candy, they went with Riley. He was the charming one, the one who had figured out how to shove down all the dark stuff and give people what they wanted. Drew was too predatory, and Bran . . . there was always something dark bubbling under Bran's surface. Women seemed to be even more wary of Bran.

So Riley was the go-to guy when a little seduction was needed.

"Are you ready?" Drew's eyes were on the hallway that led back to the two executive suites. Riley was certain Drew knew the whole layout of the office, though he hadn't been inside it before. Drew never left anything to chance. Anything.

"I am." He was ready to meet Ellie Stratton. Daughter of Phillip Stratton and business partner of Steven Castalano.

Phillip Stratton and Steven Castalano had been involved in their parents' deaths. They were murderers, and finally they were going to pay. Unfortunately, Phillip Stratton was dead.

The sins of the father were about to be visited on the daughter's doorstep. Ellie Stratton would have to pay her father's debt.

"Here we go." There was a wealth of satisfaction in his brother's voice as Steven Castalano strode down the hallway.

It made sense because this was the beginning of a game Drew had been working on for twenty years. It was a game Castalano wouldn't know he was playing until he'd already lost.

"You the lawyers?" Castalano didn't waste time on politeness. He was a man past his prime, and the photos Drew had of him hadn't done his florid face justice. Craggy and lined, his face bore the marks of long nights spent partying. According to everything they knew about the man, his love of women and booze had cost him two marriages and the majority of the fortune he'd come into exactly two months after Benedict Lawless and his wife had been murdered. Riley wondered if wife number three knew the truth about her husband's cash. Castalano had made his money the old-fashioned way—he'd murdered and stolen for it.

An IPO had been much more important to Castalano than a good man's life.

Yeah, that was going to cost him, too.

Riley got to his feet and put out a hand. The thought of touching the man disgusted him, but he was willing to do just about anything to get his foot in this particular door. "Riley Lang. This is my associate, Andy Hoover. I thought we were meeting with Ms. Stratton."

Castalano studied them through narrowed eyes. "Yeah, well, I always like to know my enemies." He stopped on Drew. "You look familiar."

Drew looked most like their father, though not a single one of the kids was a carbon copy. Drew and Mia had inherited their father's sandy hair coloring and blue eyes while Riley and Bran had darker hair and green eyes.

It was more likely Castalano had seen one of the few photographs reporters had managed to take of the infamous Andrew Lawless, reclusive billionaire software developer. At the tender age of twenty-three, Drew had built the firewall system almost every corporation now used, including StratCast. Drew had used the money to put them all through college, and he'd used the teeny-tiny backdoor he'd left in his software to spy on his enemies—starting with Castalano.

Drew remained perfectly cool. "I've been told I look an awful lot like that actor who plays Thor. I promise not to throw a hammer your way, though."

No, Riley was sure Drew would much rather use a knife on the man. Or leave him to burn to death. Like Castalano had left their father.

Castalano shrugged. "Right. I appreciate that."

"And I thought this was a friendly buyout." Riley was ready to do anything to turn his attention away from how familiar Drew looked. They'd done their level best to keep his profile as low as possible, but a few shots had gotten out.

"It is," Castalano assured them. "The company is in good hands with Ellie, but I need a comfortable retirement. It should be an easy transition, but I want to ensure everything is done properly and aboveboard. That's why we're getting two sets of sharks involved. I mean lawyers, of course. I don't want anyone to be able to challenge Ellie for what's rightfully hers. She's been through a lot in the last year, and I don't want this to be stressful for her. My own lawyers will be here this afternoon, and I wanted to warn you, I'm paying for the best."

He wasn't. He was paying for a middling firm because according to the information they'd accumulated on the man, he was damn near broke. This man had killed Riley's father over a public stock offering, made millions of dollars off it, and then wasted it on booze and hookers.

Riley was going to make sure he didn't make millions more. And he intended to make sure StratCast was completely ruined at the end of this game. The company had been founded with blood money, and he was going to bring it down. "Well, I'll consider myself warned."

Castalano's eyes narrowed. "Here's another warning. Take care of

Ellie. Like I said, between her father's death and the divorce she went through, she's had enough to deal with. This was her idea to hire you. The attorney who had represented her dad retired recently. He recommended you. I've never heard of you."

Her father's attorney had happily given in to their blackmail scheme. Once Robert Danford, Esquire, had realized they had evidence that he'd cheated his partners out of more than a million dollars, he'd smiled and agreed to everything Drew asked for.

They already had so much blood on their hands.

"I assure you, we'll do everything we can for Ms. Stratton," Riley replied.

"She's special." Castalano sighed and for a moment looked like he gave a shit about something. "I want to make sure she's solid. Ellie got screwed over in her divorce. Her good for nothing husband took half of everything. She had to spend a ton of her own cash to buy the stock he got in the divorce so she could keep her shares. Everything Ellie has is tied up in StratCast and it's going to stay that way until we get through this buyout. She loves this company. Make sure no one can take it from her."

Ellie Stratton? Castalano seemed awfully concerned for her. He wasn't a man who cared about his fellow employees. So maybe there was another connection between them. Was it possible she was sleeping with her elderly business partner?

"We'll make the deal airtight." And then they would tap the first domino in their chain and watch it all fall down.

"Hello, I see you've met my business partner." A soft feminine voice caught his attention.

Riley turned and got his first glimpse of Ellie Stratton. Pictures didn't do the woman justice. In her pictures she was serious, even somewhat severe. She'd had them done to go out with newsletters and in business journals. He'd found her to be a bit boring, a couple of pounds overweight.

Those extra pounds were in all the right places. Ellie Stratton had that brownish-blond hair color that looked dull in photographs because no picture could catch the subtle variations of color that the midmorning light could. Her hair was down, flowing past her shoulders. Blond and chestnut and sable strands vied with a few shades of mahogany. She'd ditched the severe suit she wore in pictures in favor of a wrap dress that clung to her curves. No panty hose. Her legs were round and feminine, descending to four-inch heels that would look nice wrapped around his neck.

Where had she been hiding that rack?

His brother cleared his throat, a sure sign that Riley was fumbling the ball.

"Ms. Stratton, it's a pleasure to meet you." He was going to have to figure out how to handle her. He needed to get close, to gain access to the building and the offices and, more importantly, to the data Drew hadn't been able to find. He needed access to everything StratCast had to offer, and the closer he could get to Castalano, the better.

Revenge was only one part of their plan. Justice was another.

He held out his hand and she took it. She had a firm grip, but when she was about to pull away, he placed his other hand over hers, trapping her. He looked right into her eyes. They were brown with flecks of gold in them. Pretty eyes. Another thing she tried to hide in those business pictures. She wore glasses, likely trying to make herself look serious. "I want to assure you that we're here for you and you'll be satisfied with our services. We're dedicated to our clients, and I'll make sure this buyout runs as smooth as clockwork."

Her eyes widened and he saw a flare of awareness go through her.

It was a revelation to meet her in person. It was likely difficult to be the female boss in a male-dominated industry. She would have to hide her femininity, to cloak it in a coat of chilly intellectualism in order to be taken seriously. It was obvious that she felt at home here in her own office.

In the real world, she likely had very carefully placed walls.

Poor Ellie. He was going to have to break them down.

She smiled at him, and it turned her face from serious to stunning in a second. When Ellie Stratton smiled, it was like someone had turned a light on in a previously dark room.

"Thank you." She seemed to realize what she'd done and pulled her hand out of his. Her cheeks had a pretty blush to them. She was divorced, according to the dossier their security firm had worked up on her. He would know more this afternoon when Mia got back from Dallas for their briefing. "I'll be honest, I'm actually quite happy to have found a new firm. My father's lawyers were oh-so-stuffy. I'm not sure they knew what to do with me."

Castalano smiled her way. "You're a force of nature, sweetheart. They should let you do what you do."

She smiled for the disgusting old man, and Riley felt his heart rate tick up. "You're too nice to me, Steven. And not everyone thinks the same way you do."

"Then they can take a long hike," Castalano said with a smirk. "You're going to do great here. And don't worry about the lawyers. This will all work out. I promise."

"It's only a formality." She stepped back and nodded Riley's way. "If you'll follow me, we can get started. Steven, if you'll excuse us. I hope your day goes well."

Castalano suddenly seemed bright. Well, as bright as his craggy, florid face would allow. "It's already wonderful, Ellie. I'm going to grab my clubs and meet my friend at Chelsea Piers for our weekly session. You look like you're in good hands with these two. See you later, dear."

She gave him a wave and then began walking toward the executive wing. "If you'll follow me, gentlemen. I was so grateful you could take me on. I know it was short notice, but I'm very appreciative."

Riley walked slightly behind her and wondered if she knew how the dress she was wearing clung to her backside. She had a spectacular ass. Little Miss Prim and Proper turned out to be someone entirely different than he'd thought, and she had some serious junk in her trunk. What had seemed like a mission of sexual martyrdom suddenly looked like something else entirely. He might very well enjoy the next few weeks.

"Come on, brother," he said quietly. "Let's get this thing started." They'd waited twenty years and it was finally here.

Drew was watching Steven Castalano walk away, and there it was—that dark, predatory look that scared all the women away.

His brother turned and joined him. Drew's eyes found Ellie Stratton's backside. "Hmmm, that's unexpected. You sure you want to take point on this?"

Oh, his brother wasn't going to take over. Not now that they'd discovered the mission might be so very pleasurable. "I think we should stick with the plan." He looked forward and Ellie had stopped, looking at them with expectation in her eyes. He remembered that she'd made a statement. One he should reply to. "We were more than happy to have the business, Ms. Stratton."

She shook her head, nose wrinkling. Yeah, even that was cute. "Ellie, please. I'm not very formal."

"Ellie, then. And you should definitely call me Riley." He followed her, suddenly optimistic about the next few weeks.

That was totally professional, Ellie. You damn near melted at your new lawyer's feet. Way to make an impression.

Why had she chosen this week to debut the new her? She was going to throttle her best friend. Lily had been the one to convince her to toss out all the black she had. Black business suits, she'd found, covered up the fact that she wasn't a teeny-tiny size four, like the rest of New York. Lily had been the one to convince her she could be sexy and it wouldn't hurt her professional image.

Lily didn't have to deal with Lawyer McHottie and his drop-dead-gorgeous friend.

Who the hell went to law school when they looked like that? Riley Lang and the other dude—whose name she'd forgotten because looking at Riley Lang apparently made her drop a couple of IQ points—should be on a billboard in Times Square selling menswear. Or anything else. What they shouldn't be doing is using their what she was sure would be rock-hard abs to pound out a buyout deal between her and the man who'd been her father's partner for years.

"I hope you found the place all right. Did you take the subway? The street can be pretty trafficy at this time of day." Wow. That made her sound smart.

She could hear her father. *It doesn't matter that you graduated at the top of your class at Wharton. If you act like a moron, you'll be a moron in their eyes. No one will take you seriously. You'll be nothing but a nice set of tits and a fat ass to them.*

Her father had really wanted a boy.

She didn't dare look back. The last thing she wanted to see was her new lawyer and his superhot associate laughing at the dowdy businesswoman.

Professional. She needed to be superprofessional. That was the only way a woman at her level could be. And that meant not putting *y*'s on the end of words, because whimsical didn't play in the business world.

"It was definitely trafficy." Riley Lang was suddenly right beside her, his long strides easily allowing him to catch up to her. "We happily took the subway. After all, where else could we get our morning started off right with a homeless man's recitation of Britney's '. . . Baby One More Time'?"

She couldn't help but smile because she actually knew what he was talking about. "That would be Oscar. We like to call him the Ninety-sixth Street Crooner. He's gotten very modern. Sometimes he sings One Direction. He dances, too, but that can get ugly. Not very coordinated."

His grin ticked up a notch, showing off the most adorable set of dimples. "I'll remember that." He gestured to the windows. "You have a hell of a view."

They were walking by a bank of windows that showed a spectacular view of the Upper West Side. Riverside Park was in the distance, followed by the Hudson. She'd often stood at those windows as a kid and dreamed about working here one day. Standing there, overlooking the city, made her feel twelve feet tall.

Riley's hot but really intimidating associate walked beside him. The man had to be six and a half feet, with sandy hair that contrasted with sapphire-blue eyes. He was a striking man who looked like he should be off playing linebacker somewhere, but it was Riley's lean body and softer good looks that called to her. Not that he was really soft. It was simply that he was standing beside a lion. The associate looked like he might kill someone and soon.

"Thanks." She had to remember her words around him. Like a toddler. That was how much he disconcerted her. She wasn't sure she liked the feeling and decided that she would utterly ignore it. He was a lawyer. She needed a lawyer. She'd argued that they could use the same counsel, but Steven had vetoed the idea. Just because this buyout was a friendly one, he'd explained, it was still a delicate business matter that required solid legal advice to make it run smoothly. "My father and Steven bought this space about seventeen years ago when they founded StratCast. My office has the same view. If you'll follow me."

If Riley Lang was as good as he was supposed to be, StratCast would be all hers in a matter of weeks.

She wondered what else Riley was good at. Sex. She was thinking about sex. Lily would be thrilled that she even had a libido. Since she'd divorced Colin, she'd put her entire sexual being into the deep freeze. Not that there had been much of one to start out with. Lily kept trying to set her up with guys she thought could defrost her. Ellie had been hiding behind work.

And that was exactly what she was going to do now, because if she couldn't handle Lily's cop, bank teller, or that writer guy who she was fairly certain simply wanted a free meal in exchange for dating her, then she really couldn't even consider fantasizing about the Greek god Riley Lang. He would make a good one. He would be the god of justice, balancing the law and truth and wearing nothing but a toga that would slide down his hips, almost revealing what was hidden underneath.

"Did you want to go to your office?" The deep voice of the associate pulled her out of her daydreams. What was his name again? She'd seen it on her appointment book but couldn't for the life of her recall it now.

She stopped. God, she'd walked right past her office. She felt her cheeks stain with embarrassment. She was acting like a teen at a boy band concert. There was nothing to do but blaze right through. She gave them what she hoped was her most professional smile. "I thought it would be better to conduct this meeting in the conference room. It's not far."

Riley was staring at her as though he knew exactly what she was doing. A smile curled his ridiculously sensual lips up. "I would prefer your office, actually."

The guy who looked like a sexy human lion nodded. "Definitely your office. We need to explain how we work things, and it would be best to do that in the most intimate of settings."

Intimate. He probably meant the smallest space possible, but her brain went to a bedroom. Her bedroom.

She shook it off. She wasn't sex obsessed. Normally. Hell, she was the girl who could go a year and not mind. She strode back to her office and opened the door, gesturing them inside.

"This is nice," Riley murmured as he walked past her.

He even smelled good. Sandalwood. It must have been his aftershave. Whatever it was, her body reacted to it. Damn Lily. She'd told Ellie the dress looked amazing, but she hadn't mentioned the material was so thin her nipples poked out. "Thank you. It was my father's before he retired. I haven't done much to redecorate. I haven't had time."

That wasn't the real reason. Her father's office was masculine. It made a statement. The officers of the company, and the entire board of directors, were made up of fifty-year-old and older males. Until she could start breaking that glass ceiling and hiring more women, it was best to play their games. The minute she owned the majority share of StratCast, there were going to be some changes for the better. She was going to bring the company into the twenty-first century. Kicking and screaming, if she had to.

She reached for her sweater, drawing it around her frame and hiding the fact that her nipples looked like they were stuck in a snowstorm.

Unfortunately, she was fairly certain it was heat and not cold that was making her nipples go all crazy.

"Feel free to have a seat. I'm going to turn the air up a bit. It's chilly in here."

Riley and the lion stood, watching her.

"I thought it was rather warm myself," Riley murmured as she turned the thermostat up. "How about you, Andy?"

Andy. That was his name. It was a very fifties-sounding name for a lion. Maybe he thought if he had a defenseless-sounding name, he could hide the fact that he looked so damn brutal.

"I don't notice things like that," Andy said, setting his briefcase on her desk. "Should I start, or do you want to?"

She moved back to her desk. Her father's desk. When she had the cash, she was going to strip all the dark wood away and open the place up, making it lighter, brighter.

She'd been in the dark for far too long.

"Did you get the contracts I sent you? We don't really have to go over them right now. I thought this was a brief get-to-know-you meeting. I haven't taken a look at the contracts yet." She'd thought she had a little time, and she'd been dealing with other problems.

"Oh, we have the contracts. You don't need to read them," Riley explained as he opened his briefcase. "That's what we're here for. Andy, feel free to begin."

She would still read them, but she hated all the legalese. She was much better at dealing with people. Her father had always told her that she was soft, but even he had admitted she got more work and better ideas out of the employees than anyone else.

What would he do if he knew what she planned on doing to his company?

She hadn't breathed a word of it to anyone. Not to her father before he died. Not to Steven Castalano. Not even to her lawyers. She knew what they would say. Eventually she would bring them in, but when she did she would have all the power and no one would be able to stop her.

She'd known exactly what she was going to do the minute she'd realized her father was a monster.

Andy pulled a small device out of his briefcase and began to run it over her bookshelves.

"What is he doing?" Ellie asked. The last thing she'd expected was that the lawyers would want to peruse her collection of business books.

Riley sat down in the chair across from her desk. "He's checking for bugs."

She got the feeling he wasn't talking about cockroaches. She felt her eyes widen and her jaw drop a bit. "Why would someone be listening in on me?"

It was ridiculous. And slightly embarrassing since sometimes when she worked late and no one was around, she turned on the music and sang while she worked. She was pretty sure she did not sing as well as Ninety-sixth Street Oscar.

While his associate made a thorough sweep, Riley shuffled through some papers, seeming to search for the right one. "This is a multimillion-dollar deal. We have to take security very seriously."

Thank God. He was being a paranoid weirdo. "I know this is a lot of money on the line, but it's also kind of like a family business. Steven wants to sell his half of the company to me. He always planned to when he retired. He has a son, but Kyle is not the business type and honestly, they're not close. He didn't even know about Kyle until he was already in high school."

"Yes, you're talking about Kyle Castalano. Mr. Castalano's illegitimate child," Riley said, not looking up from his notes.

That came off a little judgey. And there she went again. "Kyle's a good guy. He just came up rough, and Steven is trying to do right by him. I'm hoping they can get closer once Steven's retired. Look, Mr. Lang."

His eyes came up, staring at her. "Riley."

Next time she hired a lawyer, she would make sure he wasn't so gorgeous he flustered her. "Riley, I understand that you're some sort of a shark. I've heard you're in-house counsel for 4L Software. I know you're used to working with paranoid people."

Riley laughed. "I assure you, Mr. Lawless is one of the least paranoid people I know. Everyone really is out to get him. He's quite an asshole."

"He also has ears everywhere," she heard Andy mutter under his breath.

4L Software had revolutionized Internet security. She was completely fascinated with the head of the company and his reputation for being a complete recluse. But this wasn't the time for gossip.

"I'm simply saying, I'm not on the same level as Drew Lawless. You can relax. This is a mutually beneficial deal. I really just need you to look over the paperwork and let me know if it will hold up." Maybe she'd made the wrong call. When she'd realized her father's personal attorney was closing up shop, she'd called the number of the man he'd recommended. She hadn't realized how high-powered he was until she'd already made the appointment with him. She'd had the head of StratCast's legal department look over the contracts, but she'd been convinced she needed an outside opinion as well.

"I don't ever relax, and if I'm your attorney, I won't let you, either. You need me for far more than the buyout contract. Now let's talk about what I can provide for you," he offered. "I want you to consider me a general in the war you're about to find yourself in. Your general."

"This isn't war, Mr. Lang. I need a lawyer to make sure the transfer of all assets is handled in a smooth manner, and after that I need you to basically oversee the legal department." She'd read over his employment demands. They seemed a bit steep to her for what she needed him to do. "That's why we really should negotiate some of the finer points of your contract as well. I thought we might go over that."

"Of course, Ms. Stratton, though you do understand that dealing with the preliminaries of the buyout is my way of showing you how helpful I can be, so why don't we get right to it?" The smile on his face was gone, and he slid a stack of papers her way. She recognized the contract. From the flurry of sticky tabs denoting pages Lang had comments about, it looked like the man had a lot of problems with it. "This current contract will very smoothly transfer all intellectual property rights for the new cooling system straight to Mr. Castalano."

She felt her jaw drop. She suddenly couldn't get those contracts in her hands fast enough. "What?"

The new cooling system currently in development was supposed to double the running time of computer batteries and reduce overheating by two hundred percent. It was the jewel in StratCast's current development crown. It was also a project she'd been shepherding.

"You heard me correctly. He's trying to walk out with your biggest project in his back pocket. It's buried on page seventy-nine as a part of his retirement package." Lang sat back, crossing one leg over the other. "Andy, did you find anything?"

Andy placed a tiny disk on her desk. "That is a listening device. It was under the frame of your Wharton degree, so I think we can safely say it's recent or you would have found it when you moved into this office. I've disabled it, but they'll know we have it. The rest of the place is clean, but I'll teach you how to use this device to make sure anyplace you have private conversations is bug-free."

She stared at the tiny bug. Someone was listening to her? Steven? She couldn't believe it, but then there was the issue of the contract. How could he try to do that to her? "I don't understand."

It made her sick to her stomach.

"Ms. Stratton, this is business, and business at this level is always war." Riley shrugged as though finding a bug in a client's office was no big deal. "Now they'll know we know. They'll know that you are no longer unprotected. In some cases I would have left the bug in place and used it to our advantage, but you are right about this being fairly straightforward, and we need a show of strength."

Had Steven done this to her? Had he been listening in on her conversations? She knew he had a reputation for being ruthless, but he was a man she'd called Uncle Steven for most of her life. He'd been sitting by her father when she'd graduated from Wharton. He was the man who advised her.

The ground seemed to be shifting under her feet. She counted on Steven, and now she had to question everything he said and did.

She had to try not to cry. God, she couldn't cry. "He's the one who insisted I get outside counsel."

"Perhaps he intended to try to pay me off. Or send you to another lawyer. Or this could all be a mistake. Perhaps his own lawyers are being too aggressive and he doesn't understand what they're asking for. I don't know. All I can tell you is the clause is there and we're not going to agree to it."

She forced down the pain the betrayal caused her. Yes, it was buried, but he had to have known she would find it. Perhaps he was uninformed. Maybe. "No, we can't agree to that."

"I've made notes on the contract," Riley said, his voice softer than before.

She looked up, and the lawyer was looking at her with sympathy in his eyes. That was the last thing she needed. She hardened her resolve. "Let's go over them."

"Ms. Stratton . . . Ellie, why don't you take some time and read through them. You could probably take the afternoon off. I understand that what we've pointed out to you is probably quite disturbing. It's easy to see you're unsettled."

Weak. She looked weak. She schooled her expression. If there was one thing a woman at her level wasn't allowed to do, it was show any weakness. It was better to be the bitch than show any softness. "Not at all. I'm perfectly fine. Now obviously I won't sign away rights to what will be the company's most profitable development. How do we counter? Should we counter?"

"Oh, we're going to counter. I've hired a firm that will help us with information gathering about your opponent. I'm meeting with them after we leave here. McKay-Taggart is one of the world's leading experts on security and intelligence."

She'd certainly heard of them. They were all ex-military or CIA agents who handled twenty-first-century security problems. God, it boggled her mind that she needed a firm like that to look into a man who had treated her like family.

"Excellent." At least it seemed like Riley had a firm grip on the problem. Though she was embarrassed by her naiveté, she seemed to have made the right call by bringing them in. "I'm going to spend the afternoon firing the head of my legal department. He okayed this deal."

It would be fun. She would have him escorted from the building. She really hoped he gave the big guards trouble.

"I would advise against that." Andy took the seat beside Riley.

That wasn't what she wanted to hear. "That man went against the best interests of this company."

"Until you buy him out, Castalano is the company. He can outvote you. Your father left you in a perilous position. He left your sister some of his stock."

She still shuddered at the thought. Her dad had left Shari a voting share of StratCast. Shari didn't have a brain in her head. "I vote my sister's shares. Don't worry about dealing with her."

Riley's brows climbed up as though he was confused. "From what I understand, she recently sold her stock."

"What?" For the second time that day, she felt her stomach take a deep dive. Shari only owned five percent of the company stock, but that voting share was something Ellie counted on. "Who? Who did she sell it to? Why wouldn't she tell me? I don't have control without that five percent."

He held a hand up. "You can easily build a coalition. I can help you with that. Your sister sold the stock to an individual. I haven't run that name down yet. It won't matter if you successfully buy out Castalano."

He had her paranoid. She needed to calm down.

Riley closed up his briefcase and looked down at the Rolex on his wrist. "As to firing the head of your legal department, in this case, it's better to go with the devil we know. You can fire the man after we finish the deal. I would actually advise you to fire anyone who you suspect was loyal to Castalano, but we're getting ahead of ourselves. This is going to take a while. I need to go and meet with Taggart. What do you say I pick you up for dinner at eight and we can talk about what he discovered?"

Dinner? With him? That seemed like a bad idea. A really bad idea. "I think we should probably meet back here at the office."

"Where someone planted a bug to listen in on you?" Riley asked, standing and giving her a bland smile.

Put like that, it did seem like a bad idea. "All right. Um, let me give you my address."

The blandness was suddenly gone and there was a certain heat in his eyes. "Don't worry about it. I think I can find you. Eight o'clock."

He turned and walked out, Andy hard on his heels.

The minute they left, it felt like Ellie could breathe again.

Then she caught sight of the defunct bug, and her stomach was in knots. How had everything turned upside down over the course of one morning?

"Ellie? Are you all right?" Her assistant walked in with a mug in her hand. "I saw the male models walking out the door and decided you could use something to calm your nerves. They looked intense."

Lily Gallo was her personal gal Friday and all-around best friend.

Ellie's father had advised her not to hire a friend, but they'd been close since college and she wasn't sure what she would do without Lily. Sometimes Lily was all she had.

"My sister fucked me over."

Lily set the mug down. "That is her way. You no longer have a husband, so she can't be sleeping with him. What did she do now?"

"Sold the stock Dad left her."

Lily's eyes went wide. "That bitch."

It felt like more of a betrayal than Shari having an affair with Colin. After all, Ellie loved the business more than she'd ever loved Colin. "It gets worse. It looks like Steven is trying to walk away with the cooling system."

Lily slumped into the chair in front of her desk. "No. Oh, Ellie. I'm so sorry. And that's not tea. It's vodka and cranberry. Like I said, I thought you would need a drink."

She took a long sip. This was why they were such a great team. Lily always knew what she needed.

Business is always war, Riley had said.

"You want to split this up with me?" She handed Lily half the contract.

Lily might not have graduated from Wharton, but she had a hell of a business mind. "Yep. Let's go over this with a fine-tooth comb."

Ellie took a deep breath and forced herself to focus on the contract in front of her.

It looked like it was time to join the battle.

Two

Riley walked into the cool confines of the office building that served as their New York headquarters. It had a very lovely-looking nameplate on the outside that proclaimed it to be the home of Lang and Associates.

There was a perfectly manicured and coiffed receptionist who would explain to any and all who wandered in that Lang and Associates was very exclusive and not accepting new clients.

The truth was Lang and Associates was just Riley Lang, and he only had one real client.

And one fake client, who might mean the end of his law career. He'd gone to law school because Drew needed a lawyer he could trust. There hadn't been any thought in Riley's mind to do anything else. He didn't know what he would have done, had he been given the choice. He'd been focused on helping his family. Now he was licensed to practice in two states. Texas, where the firm's main office was located, and New York, where so many parts of their game needed to play out. If Ellie Stratton pushed at the end of their game, she could likely get him disbarred. But then he'd known going in that revenge was worth any price he had to pay.

So why had seeing her start to cry hit him so squarely in the gut?

"Good afternoon," Drew said to the receptionist as they entered. Gayle was good with calls and handling wayward members of the public who happened to wander in. She was also excellent with any number of weapons. She'd served her country in Iraq and came highly recommended as a bodyguard. "Good afternoon. They're waiting for you in the conference room."

Riley had noticed she rarely used their names. Likely because it was hard to keep up with all the aliases. "Thanks, and if Ellie Stratton calls trying to get hold of me, tell her I can't be interrupted and I'm looking forward to seeing her tonight."

"Of course." Gayle nodded and went back to her computer screen. He'd always wondered what she did during the long hours she put in. It certainly wasn't typing up documents for the boss.

He did everything on his own because he trusted no one.

Drew slapped his back as they walked past the secured door that led into the office that wasn't really an office. "You afraid she's going to cancel your date?"

He didn't bother with correcting his brother. It wasn't really a date. At least it wouldn't be to Ellie's mind, but he intended it to end that way. The safest way to ensure he got what he needed from her was to secure her loyalty. The easiest way to secure her loyalty was to become her lover. "I'm not going to allow that to happen. Besides, calling it off at this point is merely a sign of her embarrassment. She got very emotional when I pointed out what was happening with her sister and Castalano. It would have more to do with that than any issue with me. She was definitely attracted to me. That office was not cold."

Ellie Stratton was turning out to be quite different from what he'd expected her to be. Having made a case study of her father for years, he'd expected Daddy's Little Girl to be a lot like the man himself—cold, distant, intellectual. He'd expected any beauty she had to be aesthetic only. He definitely hadn't expected a warm sensuality that clung to her. He hadn't counted on her smile to be so damn inviting.

Or her nipples to look so ripe and round under that dress she'd been wearing.

He'd steeled himself to do his duty. Now he wondered if his duty might not be fairly pleasurable.

"Maybe she was actually attracted to *me*." Drew pushed through the double doors that led into the conference room, where it looked like everyone had gathered.

"No. It was definitely me she wanted." He didn't like the flare of jealously that snaked through him at the thought of Ellie flirting with his big brother.

Yeah, he certainly hadn't expected that.

They opened the door to the elegant conference room with a view of Central Park. It was the kind of conference room that impressed people, which was exactly why they'd bought the space. It was one more set in their well-thought-out play. When they were done here, they would sell it again and he would go home to Austin.

It appeared they were the last to arrive, but then Drew always liked to make an entrance. The whole group was sitting around the conference table. Bran on one side, with Mia and Case on the other, their hands entwined.

"Mia, Case, I'm so glad the two of you could make it." Drew held out a hand to the massive, stone-faced dude their sister had recently married. "I hear you had some trouble in Dallas. I'm sorry to take you away at such an awkward time."

Case stood and gave Drew's hand a manly shake. "Anything for Mia's family."

Mia grinned and hugged Drew. Of all the siblings, she seemed to be the only one who had come out of foster care with all her sweetness intact. She'd been adopted by a couple within months of their parents' deaths, and they'd given her the stability she'd so desperately needed.

If only they'd been able to do the same for Bran. They'd attempted to take him in, too, but the judge they'd dealt with for Bran hadn't been so friendly to the two women. They'd lucked out with Mia's adoption. The judge thought a boy couldn't be raised by a lesbian couple.

Politics had fucked them all over.

"And awkward doesn't cover it," Case Taggart said, his voice deep. "My younger brother came back from the dead. It happens more often than you would think. Especially in my family. Anyway, I didn't want to let Mia come up here alone. She gets into trouble when I let her roam free-range. We've got a few days before we're needed back in Dallas. My oldest brother sent along a report."

His oldest brother was Ian Taggart, a legend in military and intelligence circles. Riley had met a lot of scary dudes in his life, but Big Tag, as they called him, was the scariest. He still had trouble reconciling his smart, funny sister being madly in love with the brother of Ian Taggart.

Family, though, did have its uses.

"Let's hear it. I want to know everything." He sank into his chair and nabbed a copy of the report. "Ellie Stratton isn't what I expected. I've read all the reports on her, but none of them prepared me for the fact that she's nothing like her father."

Drew took the chair next to him. "She looks nothing like her father and she appears much friendlier, but we have no idea what she's involved in. Don't judge the book by its very curvy cover."

"Wait," Bran said with a frown. "She's hot? She doesn't look hot in the pictures. That's not fair. I get the Wicked Witch of the West and he gets some hot chick? I want a do-over."

Drew's eyes narrowed. "There are no do-overs."

"I don't think it's fair. I think we thumb-war. Best two out of three gets the hot chick." Bran held up his hand, thumb out like when they were kids.

Sometimes Riley's brother was an idiot. "Dude, I took StratCast because I'm the one who managed to get the law degree. You want to spend seven years studying business law?"

Bran made a vomiting sound. "I just don't know why I have to sleep with the dragon."

"No one expects you to sleep with Patricia Cain," Drew said patiently. "She's thirty-five years older than you and I haven't said a thing about you being the one to go in. I haven't made that decision yet."

Bran ran a hand over his torso. "All the cougars want a piece of this. She won't be able to help herself."

There was a snort from the end of the table, and Riley realized Bill Hatchard was here. Hatch. He'd been their father's best friend. An alcoholic asshole whom Drew had forced to become someone after he'd aged out of foster care. Drew had found Hatch, used him to get his siblings under his care. In return, he'd rewarded Hatch with millions from 4L Software.

Hatch reached out and slapped the back of Bran's head. "One of these days you'll read some of the reports I send you. You'll be lucky if I don't forbid you to be anywhere near that assignment. I'd do it myself if she didn't know what I look like."

Hatch had to stay out of sight. He knew every single one of their targets because he'd been in business with them. When they'd murdered Benedict and Iris Lawless, Hatch had found the bottom of a bottle and not left it for years. It was still a struggle to keep the man sober, but he was brilliant when it came to business.

"Can we get back to the problem at hand?" Drew asked, turning back to Riley. "Why do you think she's nothing like her father?"

He slid his brother a long glance. "A number of reasons, but one stands out. She was truly shocked that Castalano would pull that move on her. And she was shocked that someone was bugging her office. I would bet the thought would never occur to her. Did you plant one of ours?"

Drew nodded as he flipped through the file. "Of course. And I gave her a device that will detect anyone else's. She'll never find the one I planted. I'll give you several for you to plant at her house if you make it back there this evening."

"Oh, I'll make it into the inner sanctum." He didn't intend to be left at her doorstep, and then he would plant the devices they needed.

In her bedroom. He was the snake in the grass who would plant listening devices that would capture her every word. Including his conversations with her, and he intended those to become intimate.

For the first time since they'd decided on this plan, his stomach flipped at the thought.

He had to remember that she was a means to an end. She'd lived a damn near perfect life at the expense of his family. She'd had the best private schools, the finest care, and all because her father had murdered his.

She'd lived the life he should have. More importantly, that Drew and Bran and Mia should have lived. He needed to always remember that. Ellie Stratton had lived a perfect life on the backs of his siblings' pain, his parents' death.

It didn't matter what had happened to him. That was nothing. He shoved the pain down. What mattered were his brothers, his sister. They counted.

They meant more than some passing attraction to a woman he should hate.

Why had her smile been so fucking sweet?

"I'll get it done. We'll get what we need. Is there any way she could figure out you're the one buying up StratCast stock?" It was a worry in the back of his mind. "We told her about her sister's five percent. She might start investigating."

Drew's eyes rolled as though the question was far too silly for him to answer. "I didn't buy it at all."

Of course not. Drew would never get his hands dirty when someone else could do it.

"*I* bought it," Hatch offered. "And before you freak out, know that I bought it under a couple of shell companies that 4L owns." Hatch was in his customary half suit. That was what Riley called it. Hatch would wear the slacks and dress shirt. He donned ridiculously expensive Louis Vuitton loafers, but he wouldn't be caught dead in a tie or jacket. "Everything's going exactly as we planned. Her sister ran out of money. We were there to supply her with some."

What he wasn't saying was they'd been the ones to make sure Shari Stratton got into trouble. Hatch had sent some of his associates to a nightclub Shari frequented. They'd gotten close to her and ensured Shari spent way too much and owed some nasty people money. She'd quickly found herself looking for something to sell, and one of her new friends suggested the stock.

They left nothing to chance.

"We'll spread it out," Drew explained. "I want to avoid FTC regulations until the last possible moment. Ellie Stratton needs to have nowhere to go. She can't see that this deal is not going to go through. That's why we're here. We're going to make sure Castalano doesn't get the money for his half of the company before we can take over and ensure he never sees a dime. I want her to have no safety net when I walk in."

Case turned Drew's way. He was the only one in the room who hadn't been planning this revenge for years. "And what do you plan on doing with it if you do take over?"

Riley had been afraid Case would be difficult. He was the all-

American, upright soldier who seemed to do things simply because he thought they were the right things to do. He needed to put this in terms Case could understand.

"Whatever we need to. Look, we're not planning to bankrupt Ellie Stratton or throw all her workers out on the street, but you should understand that this is war," he began. "We didn't start it. Castalano, Stratton, and Patricia Cain started it twenty years ago when they murdered our parents over money. So money and business are the field of battle. Have you ever taken out a bridge so the enemy can't follow you?"

"Of course," Case replied.

"StratCast is a resource they can use. We're going to take away all their resources, and they'll find themselves with no way to avoid justice." Bran sat back in his chair. "We move in, gather the evidence we need, and salt the earth as we retreat."

"If we merely found the evidence against them, they would use their wealth to circumvent the system," Drew continued. "They did once before. I don't intend to allow it to happen again. I need to separate Castalano from StratCast. That doesn't mean I'm going to punish everyone who works there. If I can help them, I will. Tell me something, Taggart. Do you understand the concept of revenge? Has anyone done something so unforgivable to you or your family that you would stop at nothing to make him pay?"

Taggart's eyes went stone cold. "Her. Yes, I will make *her* pay."

Mia's fingers tangled with his, bringing him back from wherever dark place he'd gone. "This isn't about revenge. Not really. It's about justice. We're going to bring our parents' killers to justice. Unfortunately, Drew's right. If we leave them enough money, they'll buy their way out. I think we should find a way around hurting Ellie Stratton. She seems so nice. She's really kind and funny. Y'all would like her."

Every eye in the room swung to Mia.

Bran leaned forward. "What did you do, Mia?"

His sister sighed and flipped that sandy blond hair of hers over one shoulder. "What I'm trained to do. I got to know my subject."

Mia was an investigative reporter. She liked to get up close and personal with the people she wrote about. As in all things with Mia, that could get dangerous at times. In this case, it was dangerous for all of them. Mia could be a loose cannon. Riley had been in the same group home as Drew. They'd leaned on each other and gotten Bran out as soon as they could. They'd all grown up, fed by the need for revenge.

Mia was different. Mia believed in justice. She could bring everything down around their heads if she wanted to.

Case's eyes narrowed as he stared at Mia. "I thought you said you were having coffee with a friend."

She shrugged and gave her husband big doe eyes. Yeah, he could have told Case she'd been pulling those since she was about two years old. "Baby, I did have coffee with her and she did become a friend. She's really nice. She's not at all like you would expect some killer's daughter to be. She's having trouble with her ho-bag sister."

"You're going to kill me one day, Mia," Case said under his breath. His arm slid around the back of her chair, pulling her closer to him. "I swear, it's the only time I haven't had eyes on her the entire time I've been in the city. I had a conference call with my brothers. She did that thing where she waits until the last minute, just before I have to take the call, and ducks out on me."

Bran stared at their sister. "Ho-bag? Is that a technical term?"

Mia nodded. "It is when your sister is the reason your marriage broke up. She's dating Ellie's ex-husband. Bet you didn't know that."

They hadn't gone into the sister's life in much detail. He'd had McKay-Taggart focus on Ellie. They hadn't put anyone on the sister or the ex. Maybe that had been a mistake. "No, we didn't. We only knew she'd blown through the money her father had left her. We ran financials on her and found out what clubs she liked, but I hadn't heard about an affair with her brother-in-law."

"The dossier on the ex-husband mentioned that we believed he'd been unfaithful, but he was discreet," Case said. "You didn't want us to get too close or we could have figured that out."

"The good news is Mia doesn't charge by the hour." Drew sat back. "Maybe it's not such a bad thing. You could befriend Ellie, maybe give us valuable intelligence. I'm going to assume you know her routine by now."

"McKay-Taggart sent an agent up here for a couple of weeks," Case offered. "We did a complete study of Ellie Stratton's habits and schedule. It's all in the report. During the two weeks we followed her, she spent most of her time at work. When she wasn't there, she was usually alone at her apartment. She went to a movie with a friend. Lily Gallo. Also her assistant at work. She had a single date that didn't seem to go well. And she had lunch with Castalano's son."

"What didn't go well on the date?" He was definitely interested in not making the same mistake.

"She got a phone call and left in a hurry," Case explained. "I suspect she had a friend call to save her from a bad date. Other than the dangers of Internet dating, she lives a very quiet life. She doesn't have a gun registered with the state. No record of any kind. Even though her divorce was acrimonious, there were no domestic calls while it was going on. I would say the risk of her being dangerous is minimal."

Mia nodded. "And he gets shot a lot, so you should listen to him."

"I do not get shot a lot. It was twice, three . . . fine, I get shot a lot," Case conceded. "I'll try harder to dodge the bullets next time, but most of the recent bullets I've taken have been aimed at you, princess. Don't you forget it."

His sister's lips curled into a secretive smile. "I know. I owe you. Big-time. You keep on collecting, big guy."

Drew shook his head. "No sex talk. It makes me sick. Do all the couples shit on your own time. To me, you're still six and in pigtails."

"She looks hot in pigtails," Case said, then turned a nice shade of red. "Sorry. We'll keep that to ourselves. Back to the point at hand. Her husband cleaned her out in the divorce. No prenup and she was the breadwinner. She's got absolutely nothing of real value with the exception of her StratCast stock. Even her apartment is mortgaged. She took her inheritance and put it all into the company."

"Who gets the stock if she dies before the sale of the company?" Drew asked.

Bran chuckled, though it wasn't a particularly pleasant sound. "Her business partner. Castalano gets everything. He has to pay any heirs she has fair market value for it, and he has the option to choose to waive the clause. It was built into their partnership all those years ago. Kind of wish Dad had that clause. At least we would have gotten some cash."

That was Bran. He could smile all he wanted, but the bitterness always came out in the end.

"Why did he allow the stock to go to her after Stratton died?" Drew asked.

"He didn't have the money to pay her fair market value," Mia replied. "He looks good on paper, but he's got cash flow problems. Lots of them and lots of debt. I had a forensic accountant pull all his personal financials. They're working to do the same with Patricia Cain. One thing is interesting."

"I find it all interesting," Drew murmured.

"Phoebe Murdoch, the accountant at McKay-Taggart, was able to work wonders. It's all very complex and they have various companies they work under, but one thing ties them together," Mia explained.

Years of working as a journalist had honed Mia's senses, so when she got that look in her eye, Riley listened. He leaned in. "Are you telling me you found proof?"

Mia took a deep breath before speaking. "I'm telling you that three days before our parents were murdered, Stratton, Castalano, and Cain all sent fifty thousand dollars to the same unmarked Swiss bank account."

Riley felt the hair on his arms stand up. Proof. They'd searched forever for it.

Bran's eyes widened. "That's amazing. All we need to do is prove the bank account was owned by the hit man."

Mia held a hand up. "Wait. There's more."

It was a huge leap forward. He couldn't understand why his sister looked so grim. She'd done an amazing thing, something they'd been trying to do for years. "We figured out a long time ago that an assassin did the deed. Drew even recognized the man. Bran is right. If we can figure out a way to tie that bank account to the assassin, we've got them."

Case pulled out a photo. "Yes, we've ID'd him as well. His name is Yuri Volchenko. He was a paid hit man who worked often with several criminal organizations. I'm sorry to report that he was killed five years ago, likely by the same people he worked for."

Drew brushed that off with a wave of his hand. "It doesn't matter. The money does. Riley, could you convict off what we have?"

He had to shake his head. "It's good, but we need to tie the money to the assassin and then prove that all three of them gained financially. But again, some of this is circumstantial. With a decent lawyer . . ."

"Four." The word dropped from Case's mouth like a mini bomb, exploding and forcing everyone's attention right to him.

"What do you mean four?" Drew asked.

"He means we've talked to people who knew Volchenko. My husband here has some interesting family connections. Volchenko's asking price at the time was two hundred grand. And this was not a man who handed out coupons. We've also confirmed that two hundred thousand dollars was delivered to his bank account that day," Mia said. "The trouble is the final fifty thousand was delivered from a bank in the Caymans. From what I can tell, it does not belong to Stratton, Castalano, or Cain. The account was opened the day before the transaction. Closed the day after."

Riley felt his head nearly spin. "So after all these years, you're telling me there was a fourth person involved?"

"Yes, and we think the only way you'll find that person is through Castalano or Patricia Cain," Case explained. "We'll keep digging from my end. Our tech people are already looking into Patricia Cain's business dealings. We'll have everything ready in a few weeks. We need to get some information in order for Phoebe to report on Strat-Cast's actual business accounting, but then that's what Riley's supposed to get us. Once we have that, she can do her job."

"Riley should have that to you in a few weeks." Drew's jaw was a tight line, a sure sign big brother was unsettled by the latest bit of news. "And as for the other, we have to consider that Castalano might try to kill Ellie in order to take her stock."

"We don't have any indication of that." Mia shook her head, ever the optimist.

"It's how this guy works," Drew insisted.

"Why try the contract thing, then?" Bran asked. "If he's going to kill her, why attempt to take that technology with him? I would think he would keep it quiet that he wants the tech."

Riley shrugged. "Could be he's hedging his bets. Or he could use it as a tactic to drag things out, give him more time. He doesn't have the money to pay the sister if Ellie dies. We know he's killed before over a company. He would do it again."

"If you really think she's in danger, I say we talk to her," Mia said. "We tell her what's happening and we ask for her help."

Sometimes his sister was so naive. "Yes, she's going to help us take down the company she stands to make millions from."

"Maybe she's smart and she can find another way," Mia shot back.

"Or maybe we stick to the plan because we're closer now than we've ever been," Hatch said suddenly. "Mia, I know you want the world to be all sunshine and roses and shit, but the truth of the matter is we stand to lose everything we've built if Ellie Stratton discovers our plan and has time to counter our moves."

"She isn't the one who killed our parents." A sheen of tears covered Mia's blue eyes. "She was only seven when it happened."

"It doesn't matter," Riley insisted. Mia didn't understand. Mia had been raised by a loving couple who unfortunately planted some very weird ideas of equality and justice into her head. "She's the only one who can get us what we need."

He and Drew and Bran had gone without. Without each other. Without food at times. Without any fucking hope. The one thing that had gotten them through was the idea that one day they could make it right. Or if not right, at least even.

It wasn't fair that sweet Ellie Stratton might bear her father's burden, but then Riley had discovered the world wasn't fair a very long time ago.

Drew pinned her with that fixed stare Riley had come to dread long before. It meant Drew wouldn't be moved. "I need to know if you're in or out, Mia. If you're out, then feel free to return to Texas. It seems you've found a new family."

Mia went red and Case started to stand up.

"You want to push her like this, you're going to go through me, Lawless. You understand?" Case said, his eyes narrowing.

Mia immediately reached for his hand. "It's all right. Case, it's all right. Sit down, baby."

"They don't get to talk to you like that. No one does," Case insisted.

"Let me explain." Drew seemed to calm a bit. "If you don't want to be a part of this, go back to Texas. It doesn't mean you aren't my sister. It simply means we'll do this on our own. I love you, Mia. But this is going to happen."

Mia leaned in and spoke softly to her husband. He visibly calmed and took a deep breath.

"I'll wait for Mia outside. Let me know if my firm can handle anything else for you." The big guy strode out.

Mia's eyes narrowed. "Don't upset him again. He's been through enough. Now you want me to spill some blood or something to prove I'm a Lawless? I think I should stay in and watch every single one of you. I love you, too, brother. I love you enough to stand beside you, but don't expect me to keep my mouth shut when I see you doing something wrong."

"I don't need you to be my conscience," Drew insisted.

"Oh, trust me, you do. You all do. And don't act like I haven't done my part. If you didn't have me, Bran would still be in college. Riley would still eat like a five-year-old. Drew, you would never have gotten 4L off the ground because you would have named the company after a dinosaur or a superhero, and Hatch would still be sleeping with skanky hookers."

Hatch nodded. "She's right about that. I now sleep with strippers. It's an entirely higher class of women."

Drew frowned. "I actually still think MegaRaptor Software would have worked. It screams *strength* to me."

His sister was right about some things, and he was proud of the way she stood up for herself. "It screams *nerd*. And I still eat like a five-year-old. Mostly. I work in a salad every now and then. She's definitely right about Bran. He was shit at algebra."

His younger brother rolled his eyes and flipped him off. "I only took it twice."

Mia gave them all a satisfied smile. "That's because I convinced your professor to let you do extra credit in exchange for a write-up in the paper. That pushed you over the edge and into that sweet,

sweet D. So you all need me. And be nice to my husband. He's had a rough time and he's still here trying to help us out."

Drew stood and walked over to Mia, enveloping her in a hug. "Case is a good guy. A scary guy, but a good one. I'm sorry. We're all on edge because it's so close now."

Bran stood up and joined them. "It'll be over soon and then we can . . . hell, I don't even know what we'll do, but we'll do it."

"I say strippers for everyone after we put this thing to bed," Hatch said, joining the group hug.

Riley pushed his chair back and stood. Mia was at the center. He put his arms around Drew and Bran. "We'll be able to get on with our lives. And I'll take that stripper and raise you a high-priced call girl. Mia, don't even. You have no idea what a well-trained pleasure consultant can do for a man's stress."

Mia's head came up, her eyes twinkling. "I know what a six-foot, five-inch former Navy SEAL can do to a woman's clitoris."

And the moment was over.

"Mia, please," Drew said.

"If Riley can talk about random hookers, I should be able to talk about the beautiful lovemaking between a woman and her newlywed husband. I was raised by two women who had zero interest in dick. It was really surprising to find out how good it felt." Her lips curled up. Yes, she enjoyed teasing her brothers.

"No more talk," Drew insisted. "I'm getting a beer."

Hatch sighed. "Thank God. It's almost three. I was about to go into withdrawal."

"I'm going to visit the ladies' room. Let Case know I'll be right out," Mia said, heading for the hallway.

Riley followed his brothers and Hatch out the opposite door and found Case looking out over the Upper East Side, his arms crossed over his massive chest.

He really hoped this wasn't going to cause problems for his sister.

She seemed very happy with her former Navy SEAL turned security consultant/private investigator. "Hey, Mia's visiting the ladies' room. She'll be out in a second. I'm sorry you had to see that. Our family, well it's complex."

Case didn't turn his way, still staring outside. "All families are complex. I worry that's what you're not taking into account. It's where you'll have problems on this op."

"Op?"

Case finally turned, smiling slightly. "Sorry. My brother runs his company like we're all still in the military. Operation. Mission. It's what you're embarking on. You'll run into trouble because you're not counting on complexity."

"I think I understand the complexity. We've been planning this for decades. The business moves started years ago. I know the legal ramifications of every step we're going to take." It rankled that the pretty-boy soldier thought he couldn't handle it.

"I wasn't talking about the individual moves. Though the fact that you're treating this like a chess game makes me more certain this is going to go poorly. These are people, not chess pieces. Your whole family believes Castalano and Cain are purely evil. You can't view them that way. Yes, they did something twenty years ago that was evil, but a lot can happen in two decades. You have to take a fresh look at them. Strip away what you think you know about them. Figure out what they want, what truly motivates them."

"Money." He'd always known that. Even as a child he'd understood his parents had been murdered over cash.

"That's the simple answer, and people are rarely simple. They grow and change over time, and what they were twenty years ago may not be the same today. Trust me, change can happen in much less time given the right circumstances. Hell, sometimes the people we're closest to change and there's nothing we can do to bring them back."

He wasn't sure what Case was talking about, but it didn't seem the man wanted to go further. He went silent and Riley sought to fill that empty, uncomfortable space. "Don't worry about us. You handle Mia. Protect her."

"I will. She's precious to me, but you're precious to her," Case replied. "Be careful with Ellie Stratton. Is there any way you can get what you need without getting into bed with her?"

He should have known he would get this from the Boy Scout. "Don't worry about her."

"I wasn't. I am worried about you. I know you all think I'm just a guy with a gun, but there's actually a really good brain behind all this beauty. I've been watching you for a long time. I do know what you want."

That didn't prove Case was smart. Anyone who got close to him realized what he wanted fairly quickly. "I want revenge."

"More than that. That's what you've been taught to want, not the need that fills the core of you. You crave constancy. You want someone who'll take care of you. Not because they have to. Because they want to. Because they can't quite bring themselves not to. You want someone who'll put you first, and the woman who does that . . . well, either she'll get lucky and you'll accept it, or you'll tear her apart because you won't believe her."

His brother-in-law had apparently read too many pop psychology books. "I'm not getting emotionally involved with Ellie Stratton."

"Yeah, I've heard that one before. Usually right before the wedding." His smile lit up as he looked past Riley. "Here she comes."

"Did you tell yourself you wouldn't get involved with her?" Riley felt the need to challenge Case.

"I knew I would have that one the minute I saw her. Two minutes later, I knew it was a mistake and I tried to get away. Five minutes after that, I was in bed with her and that was that. Best mistake I ever made. Hey, princess."

Mia was practically glowing as she joined Case. She winked Riley's way. "I'm going to take this guy home. Talk to you tomorrow. And be nice to Ellie. She's really cool."

He watched them walk away hand in hand.

He didn't need Ellie Stratton to be cool. He needed to figure out a way to get her hot.

Case was wrong. When this was over he would walk away and never look back.

Three

Ellie texted her lawyer again. Riley Lang seemed to be avoiding her. She'd called his office to try to reschedule their dinner meeting to a more appropriate time, but his secretary was excellent at deflecting. She'd been told Mr. Lang was in a very important meeting and looked forward to seeing her this evening.

She stared down at her phone. Nothing. The man had said he would be here in about fifteen minutes.

She'd gotten dressed, put on nighttime makeup and stupid heels because it looked like she wasn't getting out of this.

Logic. That was her friend. It wasn't like this was some kind of date. She was meeting with her lawyer. That happened all the time. People met with their lawyers. People had to eat to live. So it was normal to meet with one's lawyer over a meal.

It didn't mean the evening would end with her wrapped in sheets with her superhot lawyer driving into her body and making her scream out his very lawyerlike name.

Nope. Not going to end like that. No matter how much she saw it when she closed her eyes.

It had been a shitty, shitty day.

She'd spent a good hour crying her eyes out because of that clause Riley Lang had found in the contract. Steve Castalano had been more of a father to her than her own pretty-much-evil, did-really-bad-shit dad.

Every time she was forced to think about her father, she went right back to the night he died. To the secret he'd told her.

Now she shared a lawyer with Drew Lawless. It couldn't be coincidence. It was the universe's way of telling her she had some work to do. That she was on the right path. That one day she could explain, and maybe the burden of her father's secret would ease.

She needed to think about this. She wasn't sure she could think around her new lawyer.

Riley Lang was hot as hell, and yes, her nipples seemed to perk up when he walked in a room, but she needed some alone time.

There was a knock at her door. It looked like he was early. She'd hedged her bets on getting him to stay away and gotten dressed. She kind of wished now that she hadn't been so damn thorough when she'd cleaned out her closet the previous week.

She'd tossed out every dowdy suit she'd owned, every heavy blouse and shapeless skirt. Almost every piece of clothing that was black or beige or navy blue.

She'd hidden behind those stupid clothes for years, hoping she wouldn't cause comment from her father about her professionalism. Or worse. Her dad never failed to point out that she'd gotten her mother's penchant to carry a few extra pounds. Her sister, Shari, looked like Dad's side of the family. Blond hair, blue eyes, slender like a supermodel. Ellie had been told time and again that no one would take her seriously in business if she didn't hide her overblown body behind bland suits and a pair of glasses.

Her own husband had told her she should drop a few if she wanted anyone to want her for something other than cash.

The bad news? All of her cash was either gone in the divorce or tied up in the company. She had what she needed to buy out her business partner and not much else.

The good news? She no longer had to listen to her father or her husband.

Tossing out those clothes and buying an entirely new wardrobe had drained the last of her savings, but she'd needed the change. She needed to be the new Ellie.

New Ellie didn't hesitate to open the door to the superhot guy who was her lawyer. New Ellie didn't wish she had a high-necked sweater to hide behind. New Ellie was all about the V-neck.

Her bell chimed again and she wished she was still in a building with a doorman. Or a building in Manhattan at all. Her gorgeous condo had been sold and the money halved, her portion placed in savings to buy her partner out. Her Brooklyn neighborhood was nice and quiet, but she missed the bustle and energy of the Upper West Side.

She glanced at herself in the mirror. She was determined to convince Riley Lang that she didn't need him to take her to dinner to go over the contract. They could do that in the office. She wasn't getting close to someone like him.

She hadn't been able to handle Colin. Riley Lang was a dozen steps ahead of Colin on the sexy-male ladder. She wasn't losing her head over a gorgeous guy who seemed to want to manipulate her somehow.

The girls looked good. They were a nice C cup. They balanced well with her hips. She was always going to be an hourglass. Now she simply dressed to suit her figure. Her makeup was pretty good. She'd left her hair down.

She was ready to face him.

After all, she was kind of manipulating him, too. She needed him for more than a contract. She needed him for his access to Drew Lawless.

Unfortunately, when she opened the door, it was her sister and Colin standing there.

Shari frowned, but then she'd told Ellie once that she never smiled because it caused wrinkles. "Thank God you're here and not at the office. I hate that place. Not that this place is much better. I need to talk to you."

Ellie could feel her blood pressure tick up. Colin walked in behind Shari, his head down.

She thought about railing at her younger sister for selling her stock, but it wouldn't do a bit of good. There were seven years between them and an ocean of issues. Shari had been the indulged second child. After Ellie's mother had died in a car accident, her father had taken up with a sweet but not-so-bright model. Krissy Stratton had overindulged her daughter to the point of rottenness, never seeing what holding her girl to no rules at all was doing to her. After Krissy herself had died of breast cancer, Ellie had tried to take her sister in hand, but the damage had been done.

"What do you want?" There was nothing to do but get to the heart of the matter, and that would always be about what Shari wanted.

Shari rolled her eyes. "Rude much? You could try being nicer to me. After all, I came all the way out here to Brooklyn to see you."

Shari rarely left Manhattan. When she did, it was for some exotic locale like Paris or Milan. She'd worked as a model since she was fifteen, but she spent every dime she had.

And likely a good portion of Ellie's since now she had Colin's half of the money from Ellie's shit-tastic marriage.

"You didn't come to see me. You want something. I have someone coming to pick me up, so make it fast." She would use any excuse to get her sister and ex out of her apartment as quickly as possible.

The last thing she wanted was her lawyer viewing this cozy scene. She needed the man to see her as a professional, in control. She never felt more out of control than when she had to deal with her sister.

"You have a date?" Colin asked, his eyes widening.

When they'd met, he'd been serious about a career in business. He'd been in her accounting class and she'd helped him pass. They'd become friends and then lovers. It had seemed natural to marry him.

She didn't even recognize him now. He'd always been attractive, but now he was dressed like a refugee from a boy band. She wasn't sure how he saw with all that hair flopping in his face.

"I have a date." She wasn't going to tell them that Hottie McHotterson was actually her lawyer. They didn't need to know that.

Shari sighed and resettled her ridiculously expensive Chanel bag over her shoulder. "I don't want to be here to see whatever the Internet spits out as a date these days. Look, I'll get to the point. I need some cash."

"Go to an ATM." Her sister always needed cash.

"I have to have new headshots," Shari explained. "I'm sorry to have to come to you, but I don't have anywhere else to go."

Ellie turned to look at Colin. "She's your girlfriend. Don't you want her to have headshots?"

Colin wouldn't look her in the eyes. "I don't have anything to give her."

She felt her jaw drop. "You had ten million dollars last year."

It was what he'd taken from the divorce. What she'd had to pay him in order to keep her stock.

Shari's portion was sadly locked in a trust fund she couldn't touch until she was twenty-five or finished an undergraduate degree. Ellie wished her father had thought to lock the stock up the same way.

"I . . . well, I made some bad investments. So we need some money. Not a lot. Twenty thousand should do. I can pay you back," Colin insisted.

Colin was an addict, and his drug of choice was the stock market and investing in crazy business schemes. It had been the fight of their marriage. He would have some half-baked idea and expect her to fund him. She'd been forced to keep a tight rein on his spending because he thought nothing of dropping thousands of dollars based on some hot stock tip a guy on the subway had given him. He was gambling, always trying to game the system.

He'd blown through everything she'd worked so hard to build.

She wanted to cry, but she wasn't going to do it in front of them.

"No. I don't have anything liquid right now," she said. "Take out a loan or talk your agent into paying for it. I can't."

It looked like she would spend every dime she had trying to keep her company.

Shari's lips pressed together, her eyes narrowing. "You promised my mother you would take care of me."

Yes, her sister wasn't above using guilt. Ellie had promised her stepmother that she would attempt to look out for Shari. She'd tried. "That was when you were a teenager. It was before you decided to sleep with my husband. So I'm not going to help you anymore."

She was done being everyone's doormat.

"We couldn't help it." Shari's eyes brimmed with tears. She was really good at crying when she needed to. "We were in love. You wouldn't understand because you never loved him. You never loved anyone."

"Ellie, you can't hold this against her forever," Colin said. "She's your sister. She's all the family you have left. You know our marriage was in trouble long before Shari and I fell in love. You spent too much time working and not a second on our marriage or me. Hell, you weren't ever interested in sex. Were you really so surprised I found someone who believed in me? Who truly wanted me?"

"I'm not going through this again." She'd been told time and time again that she was the nag who kept him from really taking off. She wouldn't fund his investments, so his failure was her fault. Shari had made him feel like a man. "You two should leave. I'm not giving either of you a dime."

"I guess I'll have to sell my stock, then," Shari said, her mouth a mulish line.

Colin shrugged. "We can do that, you know. We can sell it whenever we like. That company's all you care about anyway. You won't let us sell it."

Yep, her blood pressure was skyrocketing. Did they think they could con her? They might have been able to if Riley Lang hadn't proven himself to be such a smart man. She'd hated him for being the bearer of bad tidings, but he'd prepared her for this confrontation. "Sure you can. Sell it to me. Let's go. I'll pay you twice what it's worth."

Her sister paled and for a moment didn't speak. "That's all I have left of Daddy. You wouldn't take it from me."

She was about to call her out when there was another knock on the door.

Riley had horrible timing. Damn it. The last thing she wanted was for the entirely too-hot lawyer to find her standing here with her traitorous sister and her ex-husband.

She opened the door, her whole body tense. There he was, dressed more casually than before in slacks and a white dress shirt. He'd ditched the tie, and she could see the hint of golden skin and what looked like a spectacular chest.

"Hi, Ellie. Are you ready? I found a nice Italian place about a block from here." His deep voice went straight to her girl parts, another sure sign that she shouldn't go anywhere alone with this man.

She crowded the door, trying to keep him from seeing inside. "Hello. I have some unexpected company. You're talking about Mario's, right? Why don't I meet you there in ten minutes?"

"Or I could wait for you like a gentleman." He moved into her space, his hand going over hers. He leaned in, and she could smell his aftershave. "Let me in, Ellie. If you've got a problem, I can help. It's what I'm here for. I'm here to make your life easier."

He was speaking softly, as though he'd figured out she didn't want her "guests" to overhear them.

She matched her voice to his. "It's my sister and her boyfriend."

It was too horrible to explain that Shari's boyfriend used to be her husband. She was ashamed enough as it was. She could feel her skin heating with embarrassment at the thought that they would realize very quickly this was a business dinner.

There was no way this guy was dating her. It was ridiculous.

His lips curled into the sexiest grin. "I can handle that. Let's see if we can get rid of them fast. I'm quite hungry."

The way he said *hungry*, almost on a low growl, made her skin heat.

Why couldn't he look like all the other lawyers she'd met? Boring, a bit bland. Way more interested in billable hours than in toning their abs.

No way her sister would buy him as her new boyfriend.

She stepped back and let him in.

He did something completely unexpected. His hands came up, framing her face. One slid behind her neck, cupping her nape and pulling her in close as his mouth hovered above hers.

"It's been the longest couple of hours. The afternoon dragged on after I left your office, and all I've been able to think about is you."

Before she could protest—if she'd thought about protesting—his lips were moving over hers. He didn't ravage her. She wasn't a big fan of kissing because it always felt so messy, but not with Riley. Nope. His kiss was like the rest of him. Smooth as silk and hot as hell. She immediately felt herself soften and she stood there, allowing him to do something she hadn't done since long before her divorce.

He held her, his chest brushing against hers, and there were those pesky, traitorous nipples again.

He broke off the kiss with a chuckle. "Maybe we should order in."

"Who the hell are you?" Colin asked.

She started. For a brief second, she'd forgotten they weren't alone. She turned, but Riley slid an arm around her waist.

His big palm cupped her hip with just enough strength to let her know he wasn't about to let go. "I'm Riley Lang. I'm Ellie's . . . lawyer."

He'd put enough of a twist to the word *lawyer* to make her blush.

"He's helping me with the buyout," she admitted.

"It looks like he's helping you with a lot of things." Shari looked him up and down, obviously liking what she saw. "I might need a lawyer, too."

Riley's arm tightened around her, pulling her close. "Sorry, I think Ellie's going to take all of my time. She's hard to keep up with, if you know what I mean. I'll have to watch her closely. Make sure no one takes advantage of her. Did you come by for a friendly visit, Shari? Can I call you Shari? Or did you perchance decide to borrow more money from your sister because you spent every dime from the stock sale on nightclubs, new shoes, and limo rides?"

Shari gasped. "How did you know that?"

"Because I watch out for your sister's interests. Because my job is to take care of her so she can do hers." He turned his attention to Colin. "You must be the ex. Huh. I thought you'd be taller. She tends to like her men way more athletic than you."

Colin flushed. "You're sleeping with your lawyer? What the hell, Ellie?"

"It's really none of your business." How dare he judge her for something she wasn't even actually doing? It made her stand taller, lean a little more on her superhot fake lover. "Our relationship came about very organically."

Riley turned her way, winking. "That's right, baby. I saw her at work and couldn't keep my hands off her."

Colin shook his head. "You know, I thought you were smart. I thought you were all about being a tough businesswoman. He's making money off you. He's using you. Can't you see that?"

Shari grabbed his hand, her face a nice shade of red. "Let's go. My sister obviously has other plans for the evening. Ellie, this isn't over. Just because I sold that stock doesn't mean I don't have a claim on StratCast. I'll get what I deserve. What our parents would have wanted me to have. Don't think I won't."

They stormed out and Ellie felt her shoulders slump.

Riley let her go, slapping his hands together as though he were proud of himself. "Excellent. Now that we've taken out the trash, let's eat. I'm starving."

Oddly, she'd completely lost her appetite.

Half an hour later, Riley poured Ellie another glass of wine. She still looked slightly shaken. After her waste-of-flesh sister and idiot ex-husband had run out the door, she'd been a very obedient girl. When he'd told her to get her purse, she'd settled it over her shoulder and carefully locked the door behind them. She'd walked with him and answered every question he'd asked in a monotone.

She'd been like a doll, sitting where he wanted her to sit, drinking what he gave her, letting him order for her.

She'd had a hell of a day, and he felt bad using that against her. Not that he would stop, but he was surprised at the gnawing of his conscience.

"Why did you do that?"

It was the first time she'd spoken without being prompted. "Do what?"

Her face flushed the sweetest pink. The color went all the way down that sexy V-neck. Her breasts flushed as well as her face, and it made his damn dick tighten. "Kiss me. Why did you kiss me like that?"

Oh, so many reasons, but he gave her the most compelling one. "I wanted to."

The minute she'd opened the door and he'd seen her standing there looking anxious, he'd known how to calm her down. All he'd had to do was put his hands on her and some odd connection flared between the two of them. She hadn't fought him. He could have gone on kissing her. He'd been the one to pull away.

It was like the minute he walked in, he was the only thing that existed for her. It made him feel ten feet tall, but it also made him want to please her.

It was an unsettling sensation.

Her hands came up, fingers on the sides of the table. "You know what I'm asking. You knew I wasn't alone. Why did you pretend to be my boyfriend?"

It was easy to see she'd wanted him to wait for her at the restaurant so as to avoid his meeting her sister and ex. When she'd opened the door, he'd immediately known something was wrong. He'd gotten a glimpse of her sister and known Ellie had likely needed a hand. It had to be tough on a woman's ego to lose even a pathetic excuse of a husband to a younger sister.

"You were alone with your sister who slept with your husband. Excuse me. Ex-husband."

She shook her head. "At the time, we were definitely married. How did you know he was my ex-husband?"

"He took half your net wealth. I'm your lawyer. At this level, a good lawyer is less legal counsel and more war consultant. I can't properly perform my duties if I don't know everything about you, including the fact that you tend to have terrible taste in men."

She frowned. "I haven't had a ton of boyfriends. I'm not sure what my taste is."

He really wanted to understand why she'd married that obvious prick. "What attracted you to him? Because from where I was standing, he looked like a dickwad desperate to be twenty-one again."

She bit into her bottom lip, her eyes glancing away from him. "He wasn't always like that. I actually met him when he was twenty-one. He was far more mature then."

He liked her candor. "You were in college?"

"Last year of undergrad. We dated for two years and then it seemed like it was time to get married. We'd moved back here to

Manhattan so I could take my place at StratCast. I thought he was going to go to grad school, but he decided on a different path."

"What path was that?"

A single brow rose over her right eye. "You don't know?"

Of course he knew. He knew everything. "Are you referring to your ex-husband's penchant for swinging for the fences? When it comes to investments, that is."

It was what he liked to call "idiots who funded ridiculous ideas." They never wanted a simple profit out of their money. They wanted millions and really fucking fast. They swung for the grand slam when all they needed to do was get on base.

It took a true genius to take a single idea and make millions off it. Drew had.

Her shoulders straightened. "He wanted the easy solution. A get-rich-quick scheme. He wasn't that way at first. At one point he was very intellectual. It's what attracted me to him. He was curious about the world and liked to discuss everything from politics to social justice to movies we saw. He changed. I didn't. In some ways, I blame getting involved with me for what happened to him. He got around my father and real wealth and wanted some of his own. When I met him, he wanted to be a professor. He wanted to teach."

At least he'd gotten her this far. She was talking. Now he needed to get those shoulders down from around her earlobes. For one moment, for that moment when he'd drawn her into his arms and pressed his mouth to hers, she'd relaxed against him, given over to him. Her body had softened and she'd leaned into him, and if he'd pressed her, he didn't know what would have happened. She might have continued kissing him, forgetting all about the other people in the room. He could have cupped her breast, her ass. Put his hands anywhere he liked.

She hadn't given a damn that they hadn't been alone. All she'd cared about was him.

"He never went to grad school. Never taught a single class. I think you're right. He wanted an easy solution. You provided him with one." He'd studied her a little. She was known for certain aspects of her career. "You're quite good at building up an employee's ego. I would suspect you would do the same with a husband."

She was known for being able to take the surliest inventor and make him into a team member. She was the cheerleader, the grand motivator.

It was her gift. He wasn't sure she was the right person to run the business side of StratCast, but there was no question she should be in charge of research and development. From talking to her employees—under the auspices of business—he'd learned they mostly adored her. She coaxed her employees, whereas her father had ruled with an iron fist.

She'd been the one to bring in one of the world's brilliant software engineers to revamp the way StratCast functioned.

She didn't know it, but she'd stolen him right out from under Drew and 4L. He had to admire her for that. It wasn't every day Drew Lawless lost. He was used to winning.

"I tried in the beginning," she admitted. "He's right about one thing. I gave up somewhere along the way. He would get a good job and I would be excited and cheer him on, and then he would quit because he'd come up with something better or he'd argued with the boss. It became easier and easier to stay at the office. I did put a lot of myself into the company. I knew my father was going to retire and then he got sick. I had a lot on my plate."

"He should have understood. A good husband would have worked on the marriage with you." From the way the reports read, the dick had left her in the middle of her father's illness.

He wondered if Colin had known about Shari's trust fund. He would bet not. It would be interesting to see if that couple made it another two years.

He didn't like the thought of Colin getting paid. It might be a fun side project to break them up.

She shrugged and took another sip of the pinot noir he'd ordered. "There are always two sides to every story. In some ways, I think we were too young to get married."

"Why did you? A lot of people these days simply live together."

"I wanted it to start," she explained. "My life, I mean. I was raised in a very isolated fashion. I went to all-girls schools. I was in a very strict boarding school for high school. When I got to college, I wanted my life to start. I wanted something of my own. I've always been impatient. My mother used to tell me to slow down. I wasn't able to do it when I was younger. I would see what I wanted and go for it."

That was surprising. He wondered if the marriage had been the thing to take the confidence out of her. Or perhaps working for her rigid father. "That's not a bad trait. I like to think I do that."

Though sometimes he wondered what he really wanted. He'd spent more than half his life working toward bringing down the people who had ruined his childhood. What would he want when it was all done? What would the world look like to him when he'd finished this path?

"Like you said, I have bad taste in men. It's gotten me into trouble over the years. At that point, I wanted to be an adult. I wanted to work at StratCast and have a family, and I thought I loved Colin. So we got married." She set the glass down and shook her head. "This has got to be boring as hell for you. I'm sure you didn't want a therapy session this evening. Why exactly did you call this meeting?"

"Meeting?" He thought he'd been plain.

The waiter set the salads on the table, his eyes going straight to Ellie's chest. "Is there anything else I can get you right now, miss?"

She smiled up at him, but there was nothing sultry about it. Did she not get that the man was flirting with her? "No, but thank you so much."

The asshole actually winked her way.

"I'm fine, too," Riley said pointedly.

"Of course, sir." The waiter strode off.

She didn't realize how many men were sliding glances her way. She was completely oblivious to her own beauty. She was pretty, though perhaps not in a conventional fashion. She wasn't going to be on the cover of a magazine like her far-too-skinny sister. Shari might have gotten the high cheekbones that photographed gorgeously, but Ellie had an air of innocent sensuality that should draw men to her like flies to honey.

Not virginity. He had zero interest in the state of a woman's hymen. The state of her sexuality was something altogether different. He got the feeling if he could get this woman into bed, she wouldn't be shy. She wouldn't play games—not the mental kind meant to manipulate a man.

She sighed and took another sip of the wine. "This is really good wine. I'm usually a white drinker, but this is lovely."

Yes, she would indulge in sex the same way she did in food. No inhibitions, just purely for the pleasure.

He was hard in the middle of a restaurant. That was a first. He was controlled. Always. He'd learned that in his first years in a group home. *Don't lose your temper. Don't relax. Always be in control of yourself and your surroundings.*

It had only taken one brutal beating to teach him those lessons.

"I'm glad you like it, and this isn't a meeting. It's a date."

Her eyes flared and there was that pretty flush again. This was why she wouldn't make it in the business world. The woman couldn't lie to save her life. He would always be able to tell he was getting to her from the pink stain that illuminated her skin.

"A date?" That cynical brow rose over her right eye. He was starting to get her "tells." "Why on earth would you ask me on a date?"

He got the feeling she would see through any reason with the exception of honesty. "Because I would really like to sleep with you. It's traditional to date first. You see, men take women out usually more than once, though you should feel free to completely ignore societal norms when it comes to that. We go out on a few dates, see if we like each other. Maybe have a really nice make-out session that ends with me taking a cold shower. Then you decide if I'm the man who can bring you multiple, screaming orgasms."

Her eyes had widened, but there was a smile on her face. "Wow, Mr. Lawyer. That is quite a sales pitch."

"I was serious about you picking the timeline. You're a very modern lady. You should go with whatever schedule suits you." It had been a long time since he'd been this flirty with a woman. "Might I also point out that the answer to that last question, the one about the screaming orgasms, is yes. I'm the man."

"Hey, at least you're confident." She eyed him, relaxing into the moment. "Are you always this forward?"

"Yes. I do what you say you're trying not to. I see something I want and go after it. I saw you today and realized you aren't the woman from the press pictures. What was up with the frumpy business suits? And the bun? You're gorgeous this way." He let his eyes slide to the V of her shirt. He didn't want there to be any misconceptions about the fact that he was attracted to her.

It was easy to be attracted to her.

"My father was very strict about what he believed a businesswoman should be. He also thought my weight was a sign of weakness and therefore I should cover up as much of my body as possible." She sat back. "My father was kind of a dick."

He chuckled but his stomach twisted. Her father had been a murdering bastard. "So Daddy died and you came out of your shell?"

"I needed a change. I needed to not be the me who married Colin. I needed to not be the woman who let her father run her life for so long. So I threw out the stuff that I hid behind and bought clothes that made me feel pretty." She frowned, but it was a cute expression, her nose wrinkling sweetly. "I still wish I had those suits sometimes.

They were like armor. On good days, I'm confident. Most of the time, I don't really care what other people think about what I'm wearing. But I'll admit there are times I want to hide again. Like now."

"Why now?" He'd done his absolute best to be charming.

"I don't think it's a particularly good idea to mix business and personal lives."

"Do you have a personal life outside your business?"

"No, not really. I tried some online dating. It didn't work out. Maybe I'm supposed to work on the business for now. A woman doesn't always need a man in her life. She does, however, need a lawyer." She sat back, assessing him. "You're not what I expected."

Because she was used to her father's lawyers. Old men who would likely dismiss her out of hand because they'd seen her in school uniforms and because dismissing smart women was what they'd been taught to do.

"That's good, because you're not what I expected, either. Tell me what bothers you about me."

She paused as though thinking about what to say. She was obviously trying not to act on her impulses, but he needed to strip that layer of caution away. "It worries me that you seem to know so much about me. I don't think my old lawyers remembered my name half the time."

"I have exactly two clients. I have StratCast and 4L Software. I was hired by 4L straight out of law school." No lies there. He'd gone to law school because his brother didn't trust anyone but family. They'd used an old friend of Hatch's in the beginning, but the minute he could, Drew had handed everything over to Riley.

Would he even be able to practice after this?

"Wouldn't he want a more experienced lawyer?" Ellie asked. "After all, the man is one of the richest men in the country. I'm surprised he wanted someone straight out of school."

He had this story in place. "We became friends in college. Drew appreciates loyalty."

"All right. I suppose I can understand that." She put her hands on the table and sat up straighter. "Why do you need StratCast? I'm not anywhere close to 4L's earnings. I'm not even in the same league. I would think 4L would keep you busy. Do you work in billable hours there or for a piece of the company?"

He owned a large piece of the company, but he wasn't about to tell her that. "I don't bill by the hour even for Drew. We have a similar agreement to the one I've offered you. For my services, you give me stock as you've agreed to do. In return for that you have my brain and my experience."

"I haven't signed the paperwork yet. The amount of stock you want isn't insubstantial."

He wasn't a fool. She'd already made her decision. She wouldn't be here with him if she hadn't. The paperwork meant nothing. "But you'll find my services are worth far more than what you're giving up. I meant what I said. My job is to ensure that you can do yours. I have 4L's legal department working like a well-oiled machine now. The boss is finally comfortable with the team I hired, so I can open up a bit. I want a different challenge. The cooling system you're developing has ramifications that go far beyond the computers we use today. Have you thought about what it could mean to quantum computing?"

The faster-than-anything-on-the-market machines had one small issue. They were in experimental stages, but the models calculated and worked so quickly that the machines themselves would only work at near-absolute-zero temperatures.

The person who solved that would make a lot of money.

A grin hit her lips. It was a sexy smirk that told him she knew exactly what she was doing. "I try not to let it out. I've turned away good press because I don't want the word out before we're ready for manufacture, which is likely a year or two off. Yes, I understand the possibilities. We've tried to be quiet about it, but we've obviously used the possibilities to attract investors. We have some tests coming up in the next few weeks that should garner real attention."

"I've done a study of your business," he assured her. "The kind of money that's riding on this type of engineering leap guarantees that you'll have issues. Issues you need someone like me to handle for you. You won't have to get your hands dirty because I'll do it for you."

"And that means you need to know everything about my personal life?"

He was his brother's right hand. He needed to make Ellie see how good that relationship could be for her. She was the kind of executive this type of relationship could really work for—if he were on the up-and-up. "Absolutely. You're about to become the CEO of a major player in communications technology. Everything about you can be used against the company, to manipulate stock, to take you down. I wasn't joking. At this level, business is war, and I don't know that you're ready to play general."

"You don't think I'm tough enough?" The question didn't seem to come with any challenge, as though she already knew the answer.

"I don't think you should have to be. I think you're smart enough to know that a good leader delegates."

Her brow rose again, but this time she took a long sip of wine. "A good leader also knows when something is too good to be true."

"Ah, I'm definitely not that. I'm a ruthless bastard. Don't ever mistake me for less. I'm here as your lawyer because I believe your company is exactly what I need to make it to the next level. I think I'll make a lot of money off StratCast. I'm here as a man because I would really like to get to know you better."

"I thought you knew everything," she said, her eyes steady on him.

"About your business, yes. Like I said, you're not what I expected. And I don't have a personal life outside of business. I work all the time. If I'm going to see someone, she's probably going to be from work. The good news is you can always fire me if it doesn't work out."

"Not according to that contract I can't," Ellie shot back. "If I sign it, I can't let you go unless I want to pay you a god-awful amount of money. Give me one good reason why I shouldn't do this the old-fashioned way. Why shouldn't I simply hire a lawyer and pay him by the hour and not pay him when I don't need him? You're going to cost me a fortune."

Money was the least of her problems. There were issues at StratCast he didn't have to manipulate in order to use. Her employees might adore her, but at the executive level, there were people who thought she had no business running the company. "I've already saved you a fortune. That contract had already been through your legal department and your father's lawyers. Not one of them mentioned the clause. Why?"

Her mouth firmed. "They were very likely paid not to."

He had her. He just had to reel her in. "Now you're thinking like a CEO. Yes. You pay those men by the hour and someone else can buy their loyalty. My pay is directly tied to the best interests of you and the company. I will be your champion. I cannot be bought. You've already purchased me."

"Wow. When you put it like that, I'm reminded of how crappy business can be."

He needed to remind her of that often so she would turn to him when things got rough. So she would trust him over the man she'd known all of her life. "That's why you've got me. You like to do what you do. You like to deal with your people. Let me handle the rest. The buyout is going to be hard. I know you thought it would be a breeze, but that clause in the contract was a clear indication that your partner is going to war."

"I didn't expect him to do that to me." She took a deep breath and stared down at her uneaten salad for a moment. "I thought he cared about me."

"Maybe he does, but Castalano knows that there's no place for emotion in negotiations like these." He reached out and covered her hand with his, his skin warming at the connection. "Let me do my job, Ellie. Let me take care of you."

She looked up, and those fucking eyes were so vulnerable he felt like a hunter about to slaughter a doe. She nodded. "All right, I'll sign the contract, but I have to think about the other part. I still don't know if it's a good idea."

But she picked up her fork. He still had a shot.

He fully intended to take it.

Four

Ellie finished off the last of the cake she hadn't meant to order. They'd brought the dessert cart by at Riley's insistence. She'd tried to turn them away, but Riley had ordered a massive slice of chocolate decadence and then offered her a fork.

God, she loved chocolate. It had been forever since she'd allowed herself to indulge in dessert. She'd worked so much in the last year she usually didn't head home until long past dinnertime and had settled for whatever the team was eating or something she could microwave.

Life, it seemed, had gotten away from her. It hadn't been a conscious thing, really. After the divorce, she'd put everything into her job. She so rarely simply enjoyed anything these days.

She was thinking about enjoying Riley Lang. If she couldn't remember the last time she'd had a great dessert, she really had no recall of even satisfactory sex.

She was pretty sure she even bored her vibrator these days.

"Tell me why you went into your father's business." He sat back, lounging against the booth in his oh-so-casual, I'm-not-a-predator-but-I'm-going-to-eat-you-up way. "It sounds like he wasn't much of a dad."

Why did her lawyer have to be the sexiest man she'd ever encountered? She tried to concentrate on answering his questions rather than staring into those piercing eyes. "He wasn't a good person. It's more about the company than him. I went to boarding school most of the time, but I was home for summers. You have to understand that the boarding school I went to was a little like *The Hunger Games* for mean girls. I was the odd one out. I was bigger than the rest of the girls. Got these babies early." She gestured to her chest. "And wasn't very into fashion and pop music. I liked *Doctor Who* and read Stephen King and romance novels. There was this used bookstore and when we would go into town, I would stock up on cheap paperbacks because despite my father's money, I had limited funds. Everyone else would buy makeup or convince some creepy perv to buy them cigarettes or beer, and I had a stack of books."

"I can see you with your nose behind a book." He finished off the last of the pinot noir. "So you didn't spend a lot of time at home, I take it."

"Nope. My mom died when I was six and then Dad remarried and had Shari. My stepmom was okay. She was nice, but she was very into being a rich man's wife, and that did not include a ton of childcare. So when I came home for the summers, I shared a nanny with my sister. By the time I was ten or so, Dad didn't want to burden Shari's nanny with me, so he took me to work and told me to sit in the mailroom and read."

"For a whole summer?" Riley asked softly.

Poor little rich girl. That was her. "It lasted about a week, and then Steven came down. He decided he needed an assistant and he showed me around. Oddly enough, I ended up in research and development and I kind of became their mascot. I fit in with the geeks. I spoke their language, though let's be plain, I'm not a math genius. They were very kind to a lonely girl, and I started looking forward to spending my summers and Christmas breaks with them."

"You grew to love the company."

There had been times in her youth when she felt so much more at home in the development lab than she did her own room. She'd often cursed the fact that she wasn't gifted in math and science. "I fell in love with the company and what it can be. I went to business school because it was expected of me, but also because I realized that I could contribute something. I can handle the outside world—the never-ending reports to the board, the budget, the advertising and marketing. I can handle that so they can do what they do. They can make the world a better place."

"Holy shit. You're a do-gooder." He shook his head. "Please tell me you don't really think a company like StratCast can help people do anything but spend their hard-earned dollars on better Internet."

She should have guessed he was a cynic. She shrugged. She typically didn't argue with cynics. They couldn't be changed. "Everyone wants better Internet. Are you ready to go?"

He reached for her hand, sliding his around and enveloping her. "Hey, I was teasing you. I want to hear what you have to say."

How could she say it without sounding like an idiot? And why did she care if she sounded like an idiot? It was better that the man understand what he was getting into with her. If he was anything like her father, he would tell her she was naive. She'd been very careful in the last few years to play by her father's rules so he would leave the majority of his stock to her. He'd wanted an heir and she'd played the part. It was time to start shedding that costume.

"We can do better. Corporations owe it to their employees and the people who support them to be better citizens of the world around them. We treat corporations like the be-all, end-all of American existence, so the people who run them have a duty to the world. If I can help make communications cheaper and better and more accessible to everyone, I'll have done my job."

"You really believe that?" Riley asked somberly.

At least he wasn't laughing at her. "My father was rough on his employees. They were cogs in the machine. I spent seven summers interning with this brilliant man. His name was Herbert Simmons. The professor, as we called him."

He'd been one of the single kindest men she'd ever known. Patient. Quiet. He'd taught her more about the tech end of the business than anyone else.

Riley nodded. "Yes, I know his work well. He invented the cable system most high-tech firms now use."

She was impressed. Most suits didn't care about anything but the money involved. The fact that he knew Herb's name and contribution meant he was a cut above the normal bottom-line guy. "Yes, StratCast was built on that system. Higher function, more speed capability, almost indestructible. It made the company billions, which my father promptly wasted buying up other companies in an insane attempt to show what a big dick he had."

"Yes, I remember StratCast almost went into bankruptcy. Probably would have if they hadn't had the cable technology." His fingers played along hers.

She knew she should pull back but couldn't bring herself to do it. "Obviously StratCast owned the patents. Most companies would have rewarded the designer, but my father fired him a few years later because he had terminal cancer and couldn't work anymore. Oh, he made it all look like poor job performance, but Dad was good at that. Herb would have come into an enormous amount of stock if he'd gotten to retirement age. He died in a nursing home. I paid for his burial because he didn't have anyone else. He was brilliant. He changed the world for the better, and he died alone and penniless because my father is excellent at screwing people over."

"That's business, Ellie," he said quietly. "That's what most people call success."

"Then we need to redefine the word. Think about that, Riley. You say you want to be my general, but you don't understand the war I want to fight. It won't always be about money."

"You're an odd one, Eleanor Stratton." His hand slid away from hers.

Yeah, that was the story of her life. She'd never fit in, but she'd managed to make a place for herself at StratCast despite being her father's daughter. "You should think about it. I don't know that I'm the right CEO for you. I don't have your killer instincts. I'll hold off on signing the contract."

"Don't." His eyes came up, catching hers. "Sign the damn contract, Ellie. Our contract, not the other one. I can handle your odd notions about social justice and I think you'll find we'll still make incredible amounts of cash in the process. And if you're planning on making changes at StratCast, you'll need someone like me who can see who'll come after you. Your board could turn on you. No one likes change."

She knew there would be issues. "I'll have to make them see my point."

"And if they won't? You can do all the pretty arguing and I'll handle the real business. I'll get you what you want."

"How will you do that?"

"I don't know that you want the answer to that question, princess. The men on your board will fight dirty. I'll fight dirtier."

It was a tempting proposition. She wasn't foolish. She knew there was a nasty fight ahead of her and she might have to get her hands bloody. She dreaded it. What if Riley was exactly what he said he was? What if he could handle the ruthless parts of the business so she could concentrate on making StratCast everything she thought it could be?

"I'll sleep on it."

"But not with me," Riley surmised.

"I think if we're going to work together, we should keep some distance." Oh, but she didn't want to. She wanted to take him back to her place and forget how shitty the day had been. She wanted to lose herself for a night.

And that would be a terrible mistake. She didn't know this man.

She was likely making a mistake by hiring him, but he'd come recommended and not simply by her father's old lawyers.

The fact that he came from 4L Software made her believe he was as good as he said he was.

She would likely never know about the other stuff. The sex stuff. After all, he only had himself to recommend his talents. It wasn't like he carried around a pamphlet with five-star reviews from his past lovers. He should. It could really help his cause. She could see it in her head. There would be a sexy pic of him on the cover and all his former lovers would talk about his superlative oral techniques.

"What are you grinning about?"

She shook it off. Her mind wandered to the oddest places at times. "Nothing. I should get home. Tomorrow's a long day. I did appreciate dinner. It's been a while since I went out like this."

He took the paid bill from the waiter, who nodded her way. He'd been very kind and attentive. She hoped Riley tipped well.

Riley slid out of his seat and held his hand out, gallantly helping her up. "I intend to force you out more often, then. I know you think we shouldn't have a relationship outside of work, but there's a very good reason people like us end up with coworkers. We don't have personal lives and we need someone who understands when all we talk about is work. You're the boss. Do you really think you're going to hop on the Internet and meet a guy who understands you?"

She was fairly certain no guy would understand her. "Maybe I'm doomed to be married to my company."

"Somehow I doubt it." He held an arm out. "Let me walk you home. I promise to keep my hands to myself. No funny business until you give in."

He was going to kill her. She'd known the man one day, and she was already fairly certain she was going to regret not taking him up on his offer. But she was a businesswoman, and the truth was having a relationship with him could hurt her. She had to think about the goal. Once the buyout was finished and she had the stock she needed in hand, she could think about having a personal life.

Maybe.

She let the first cool blast of spring air slide over her skin as he led her up the stairs and back to the street level. When they'd gone in for dinner, the sun had been setting. Now it was past ten. She'd spent three hours sitting and talking with him. And they'd flown by, mostly with her talking.

It had been nice to be the center of all that attention for once.

She stopped. "It would be easier for you to get a cab here."

He stared at her.

She put her hands up in defeat. "Fine. You're the one who'll be walking a block or two out of your way."

"I don't mind." He settled in beside her, adjusting his longer gait to match hers. "I don't have many nights like this."

"Yeah, I'm sure you don't date much, gorgeous."

She could have sworn he flushed.

"Surprisingly, no. I don't actually date very much. I travel a lot between Austin and here. The very long hours I put in don't leave much time for dating. I had a girlfriend a while back, but it petered out. She started seeing some project manager. I got invited to their wedding," he said with a little huff. "Naturally I was busy that weekend."

She liked casual Riley. Somewhere in the middle of dinner, he'd relaxed. They'd still talked business, but something seemed to have calmed him, and he'd peppered in talk about his favorite sports—football and baseball. "So it hit you pretty hard, huh?"

He thought about that for a moment. "You know, I think what hit me was the fact that most of the people I knew in college are married and breeding like rabbits and I've never even lived with a woman. A bunch of guys from time to time, but never a woman. I barely manage to spend the night at a woman's place."

"I think the whole living-together thing might be overrated," she admitted. "There is a whole lot of compromise. I wish I'd lived with Colin before we got married. I could have saved myself a ton of cash if I'd known he was one of those guys who lets toothpaste go everywhere. Put the cap on, dude."

"Ah, messy, huh? I can see where that would offend."

She rounded the corner that would lead to her building and found herself slowing down. "So did you share a house with a bunch of guys in college?"

She could see him in a frat house. He'd likely been the king of the campus.

"I lived in a group home as a teen. You think your ex-husband was messy. You put twelve basically homeless teenage boys together and see what happens. Not pretty. I think I actually developed some OCD from those days. I'm quite neat."

It took a second for what he'd said to settle in. A group home. Not a frat house. "A group home?"

"Think of it as foster care for the too-old-to-adopt puppies. My parents died when I was twelve. I lived in two different group homes until I was eighteen."

He'd been in foster care? "What happened at eighteen?"

"My brother had aged out before me and he took me in," he explained in a matter-of-fact tone. "I'd been diligent about school and got a scholarship. Managed to avoid most of the pitfalls of our lovely system."

"The pitfalls?" She was still reeling at the idea of him being so vulnerable.

"Drugs, physical abuse. Pretty much anything a desperate kid can do, I've seen happen. But I kept my head down, paid attention to school. My older brother was very insistent about schoolwork. He took his responsibilities very seriously. I'm fairly certain he was harder on my ass than my dad ever would have been. My father was actually kind of a softie. Well, I think he was. It's hard to remember sometimes."

She felt like her whole perception of him had turned around. If she'd been asked, she would have said he'd had a privileged upbringing. All the right manners. All the right schools. His confidence alone made her think he was one of the entitled, though he wasn't as obnoxious as some she knew. Suddenly, instead of simply a gorgeous, sexy guy in front of her she saw the boy he must have been. Alone. Afraid. Determined. "I don't like thinking about you in a group home."

She'd seen sex on a stick, but there was a human being under the beauty. All human beings ached and hurt. Some simply hid it better than others.

He stopped, his hand going to hers, and he looked down at her. "You're far too tenderhearted, Ellie. But I don't like to think about it much, either. I don't know why I'm talking about it. I rarely talk about the past. The present and future are much more interesting."

She glanced at the door. She should go through it, but found she didn't want to leave him. Not like this. And if she kept talking about his past, she might start crying. Not a good thing to do in front of a man who would essentially be her employee. "Speaking of the future. Do you think we can get the buyout contract finished before the board meeting? I want to walk in with all my cards in hand."

Business. She needed to remember to focus on business around him.

"I can try. The board meeting is in a month. Unfortunately, because Castalano tried to shove that clause in there, we'll likely go back to the table. I'll tell his team tomorrow that we won't accept the contract as it is and send back a few demands of our own."

"I don't have any demands except that I give him the money for his stock and his backing of me as CEO." Steven wouldn't be on the board, but they would listen to him. If he went public with his backing, there would be an easy vote.

"We can put that in the contract, but he can always lie unless we hold off on transfer of funds and stock until after the board meeting."

She didn't want to play it that way. If she did it like that, she would look weak, like she'd bought her place, unsure that her partner would back her without a threat hanging over his head.

"No. I want to do it before."

"I'll try," he promised. "But these are delicate negotiations and the press will be watching, so we have to be careful. We're lucky it appears the sale of your sister's stock was a private one or it would have been reported on. It still might be. It depends on who bought it and why."

She could see the story now. If her own family was bailing, how could a young woman ever lead a tech company? The stock would suffer. She could potentially be out.

Damn, but she'd needed her sister's vote. She'd put up with Shari, with everything she'd done, because since the moment she'd known their father was dying, she'd known she needed Shari to back her, and now she had to find someone else.

Of course, if she did sign that contract, Riley Lang became a voting member of the board. Perhaps all wasn't lost.

"Hey, it's going to be all right." He was standing in her space, tilting her chin up to look at him. "No matter what happens, I'm going to take care of it. Try to remember that. Even if something goes wrong, I can make it right eventually."

She wanted to believe him more than anything. She was feeling so alone, and he was offering her company, companionship.

"Tell me I can kiss you," he commanded, his voice going low. "We're off the clock. If you don't want me to touch you at work, I won't. We can keep this thing between us very quiet."

"That would be incredibly unprofessional." She meant the words as an admonishment, but they came out kind of breathy and sultry.

"Yes, but I really wouldn't care. That's what it means to be the boss. You do what you want, when you want it. I learned a very long time ago that if I don't take what I want, someone else will. Take what you want, Ellie." His mouth hovered above hers, so close she could feel the heat of his body, smell the mint on his breath.

It would take so little to go up on her toes and let their mouths meet.

But he didn't understand what it meant to be female in the business world. She was under thirty and a woman. Everyone was watching her. Everyone was waiting for her to screw up so they could take her apart and split the company between them.

She didn't get to follow her instincts.

He took a step back. "I'll be ready when you are. Go upstairs. I'm not leaving until I'm sure you're safely inside. I would walk up with you, but you aren't ready for that."

She wasn't. Not at all. He was too much, too good to be true. She turned and fled like the coward she was.

"I'm surprised to see you." Drew looked up from his laptop, squinting into the darkness that filled the Upper West Side penthouse he'd bought a few months back. "I thought you would be bedding down with her for the night. Did she not take the bait?"

The only lights in the place came from the floor-to-ceiling views of the Hudson and the lights beyond. Much like everything in his brother's world, the penthouse always seemed to be in shadows.

So unlike the cheerful tiny place in Brooklyn Ellie called home. He'd been surprised at how small it was. Nothing but a neat, comfy-looking living room, a tiny kitchen, and a door that led to the bedroom he hadn't managed to get into. He'd only been there for a few moments, but he couldn't help compare it to his brother's multimillion-dollar penthouse. It boasted the best money could buy and it had never once felt like home. Neither did the mansion in Austin.

"She's shy." She was so different from what he'd thought she would be. Not really shy. That was the wrong word. *Cautious* was a better one. "She's well aware how it would look if she starts fucking her lawyer. I'll get around it because she's also very curious."

She was a sensual thing. She'd enjoyed it when he'd touched her, but he might be moving too fast for her. She'd been burned before. It was only natural she be cautious about men.

He'd expected her to be hard, to take what she wanted. He'd expected the daughter of Phillip Stratton to be as ruthless as her father.

She wanted to make corporate America a better place? Who was she fooling? It was a naive thing to do, and it would get her booted out of the CEO spot quicker than she could show her board a business plan.

She needed a keeper, but it wouldn't be him.

"You usually blast through caution." Drew flipped the lid of the laptop down, and Riley noticed he had a glass of Scotch in front of him. It was one of Drew's nighttime rituals. Only one glass. He would never allow himself to be out of control.

Riley bet Ellie would get silly after a few glasses of wine. She'd relaxed after the one she'd had, but if she felt comfortable, she would likely let herself get a little tipsy, a bit playful.

"I can tempt a woman out of a bar. She's not a one-night stand."

Drew sat back, glass in hand. "No, she's not. She's the mark and you would do well to remember it."

"I'm sorry. What have I done in the few hours since we met her to make you believe I view her as anything but the mark?"

Drew took a long drink, draining half the glass before he put it back on the table. "I had dinner with our sister and her husband tonight. Case is an interesting man."

Case was a hard ass for the most part. Case had been the one to train Riley over the course of the last year. He was the reason he was in the best shape of his life and now knew how to handle pretty much every weapon known to mankind. He also, it turned out, was a bit of a philosopher. "Did he give you a lecture on the pitfalls of vengeance?"

"Not at all. It was nothing like that, but he got me thinking. He was attentive to Mia. She practically glows around him. She's happy. I was envious of her. If I'm envious, you and Bran will be, too."

Shit. What the hell had happened to make his brother admit something like that? Drew never admitted weakness. Not once. In all the years he'd been with Drew, he'd never seen him cry. "Mia's different. She didn't go through what the rest of us did. I don't know that I'm capable of being happy the way Mia is."

Drew stood and walked to the bank of windows, his large frame illuminated in the moonlight shining off the river. "Hence the envy, brother. I don't know that any of us can be. I only know that we're too close to turn back now. And I understand her appeal."

"Ellie's?"

"She's lovely and far softer than I would have given a Stratton credit for. In person, she's quite warm. Having read her history, I understand she's been hurt before. You're going to hurt her, Riley. You're going to tear her up. Do you really think you can do it?"

He didn't like hearing it put like that. "She'll have the money at the end of this. Hell, she'll likely still have the company. We're merely going to force the buyout to take longer. Allow Castalano to get desperate. The truth is her company really does have an advantage with the coolant system she's working on. Even if we tank the stock, she should be able to recover."

"Unless someone swoops in and buys the place up," Drew pointed out.

That was always a risk. "We can't think about that. She's a smart woman. I'll be by her side. I'll help defend the company against a hostile takeover if I have to."

Drew turned, pointing a finger his way. "That's what I'm afraid of. You're already thinking about how to save her. You're thinking about fighting by her side. You've known the woman for a fucking day and you're plotting how to help her."

"Do you not feel a moment's guilt, Drew? Are you seriously so fucked up that you can't see she's innocent? Yes, we need to put Castalano in a corner and give him the justice he so richly deserves, but can't we mitigate the damage to her? I'm not backing down. I'll do what it takes, but if I can take some of the sting out of this, I will."

Drew's eyes pinned him. "You can't have a conscience, Riley. Not when it comes to war. Do you think for a second Castalano sat around worried about the four of us? Do you think he worried about what would happen to us? No. He intended to kill us, too. He didn't worry about collateral damage."

"I would like to think we're better than Steven Castalano."

"We don't have the luxury. Go home to Austin, Riley. I'll deal with Stratton myself."

Anger flared through Riley. "Will you stop being such an ass? I have no idea what the fuck has gotten into you tonight, but I'm not going anywhere. I'll be at StratCast tomorrow working on the plan we agreed on years ago. I'm not putting her before you, Drew. I'm not putting her before our parents. If I have to, I'll take her down, too, but if there's any way she doesn't get ripped up, I'll try. Are you finished bitch-slapping me? Because one of us has to go to work in the morning."

"Don't fight. I really hate it when you fight," a soft voice said.

Drew's eyes closed briefly and then he turned. "Bran, I thought you were going out with Hatch."

Bran stood in the doorway, his big frame in shadows. "I came home early."

"He got in a fight." Hatch walked in behind him, scrubbing a hand over his head and sighing. "It's fine. I dealt with the cops."

Drew strode past him, turning on the light and then shaking his head.

Riley felt his fists clench as he got a good look at his youngest brother. "I hope the other guy doesn't look worse. Should you be in a hospital?"

Bran's lip was busted, his left eye swelling. "I'm fine. I've had worse."

That was the problem. Bran had had far worse. Riley thought some of his dreams were shitty, but he had no idea how Bran ever slept.

"What happened?" Drew asked, looking to Hatch.

"What do you think?" Hatch shot the question back. There was no way to miss the splatter of blood on his white dress shirt. Likely it was Bran's. "Some guy got handsy with the stripper Bran had been talking to and Bran threw himself in." He slid a narrowed glance Bran's way. "You know they have bouncers at those places."

To say Bran had anger issues was to put it mildly. He got particularly angry when women were abused.

But then he'd watched a foster sister die. He'd been sixteen, months away from being brought out of the system and under Hatch's legal guardianship, though it was always Drew who had taken care of them. Hatch was simply older and had cleaned up nicely after a stint in rehab that had never completely taken.

Bran never talked about her. Never mentioned her name, but somehow Riley knew she was always in the back of his brother's mind. Drew had forced him to see a shrink for a while, but Bran had begged his way out of it. It was hard to say no to their younger brother.

It was also hard to watch him battling demons no one could see.

"The other guy outweighed him by a hundred pounds and had three friends with him. We're lucky the fucker didn't have a knife," Hatch pointed out. "One of these days, he's not going to be so lucky."

"You can't do things like that." Drew bit off every word as though they hurt him. He put a hand behind his brother's neck. "You have to stop fighting."

Bran's face went mulishly stubborn. "She didn't want him to touch her like that. She's got a right to say no, and don't tell me she's a stripper. She's a woman and she can say no whether she's dressed in a nun's habit or completely naked."

"I know, Bran. I agree with you, but you can't risk yourself like that. You have to stop and think. You have to place some damn value on your own life. We'll talk about it more tomorrow. For now, go clean up." Drew let Bran go as he looked back at Hatch. "Should I expect another lawsuit?"

Bran's fighting had cost Drew more than Riley liked to think about. Often it didn't matter that Bran was trying to save some woman from a belligerent asshole. The asshole got a lawyer and came after him. That was where Riley had to step in. "I'll handle it."

Hatch shook his head. "No. They ran the minute the cops were called, and Bambi vouched for Bran. No charges filed. No one figured out who he was. I'm sure her parents wished they'd rethought that name, though. You know Gladys never ends up on the pole. If I'd had a daughter, she would have been named Gladys."

"She's working her way through med school," Bran said as he walked away.

Hatch's eyes closed. "That boy is going to kill me. I swear. One of these days, I won't be around. It's like he has a damn death wish."

So it had been a crappy night all around.

It had only been shitty when he walked in here. While he'd been with Ellie . . . He couldn't think that way. It was hard because they knew they were almost at the end. They needed to hold on, to not get distracted.

He couldn't let Ellie Stratton distract him. His brothers needed him. His parents needed him.

"I'll try again to get him back into therapy," Drew said, returning to his computer. He slid back into his chair and once again powered it up. This was how Drew retreated, his own private world.

Riley didn't have one. He had work, and right now his work would get him thinking about Ellie Stratton again. "I'll handle Strat-Cast, Drew. Don't worry about anything on that end. You can count on me."

Drew's eyes lifted briefly, and Riley was reminded that this was the boy who'd had to work and save and sacrifice. He'd gone hungry some nights so Riley had food. He'd done everything so he could bring his siblings home.

He couldn't fail Drew.

"I know you will," Drew said softly. "And I'll work from this end."

"And I'll take the rest of that Scotch and try to get some sleep," Hatch quipped.

Drew reached out for the crystal decanter. "There's whiskey in the kitchen. You can't appreciate this."

Hatch frowned. "You are not my son. Lucky for you, I don't like prissy Scotch."

Sometimes Riley wondered what it had been like for Drew and Hatch during that time before they'd gotten Riley and then Bran out of foster care. It had been just the two of them for a while, and it seemed to have bonded them in a way Riley didn't always understand.

Drew smiled a little. "You don't like prissy anything, Hatch. Sleep well."

Hatch shook his head. "If I sleep at all after today. I thought we would be done. Stratton's dead. We've almost got Castalano. Cain's the end. She's supposed to be the end. Once we bring down her Martha Stewart doily–fucking empire . . . damn it, we were supposed to be able to rest."

There had been a fourth. He'd been able to forget that detail Case had sprung on them while he'd been with Ellie. Now it all came flooding back. All these years and they hadn't known a fourth person had been in on the plot to kill their mother and father.

"I'm studying the corporate structure again," Drew replied. "I'll figure out who else would have gained the most money. It's all about money."

Hatch stared down at Drew. "Me. It would have been me, Drew. If you had half the brain I trained you to have, you would throw me out tonight."

"Get some sleep, Hatch. We'll go over everything in the morning." Drew's eyes never left the screen. "And for the record, I never once suspected you. I figured out your secret a long time ago. Even if you had known what Dad was planning, you wouldn't have outed him. You wouldn't have done anything like this."

Hatch didn't back down. "And why is that? Money is a great motivator. I would have lost a fucking bundle had your father blocked the sale of our company."

"Money never meant more to you than she did."

Hatch stilled. "No. No, it didn't."

He turned and walked toward the back of the house.

Riley stared after him. "He didn't know we knew he was in love with Mom?"

"He thinks he's smarter than he is," Drew said with a half smile. "I knew he was in love with our mom before she died. I also know he didn't act on it. He cared as much about Dad as he did about her. It's why he went into that deep decline."

Deep decline was a polite way of saying Hatch found a bottle and hadn't come out of it for years.

Maybe Drew wasn't as cynical as he acted. Riley had wondered earlier if Drew would suspect Hatch.

It had all begun when five friends started a business. Benedict had the vision. Patricia and Hatch had the cash at the time. Steven Castalano and Phillip Stratton had the connections. They'd made a lot of money before the IPO. After the IPO, their father had found out someone had manipulated the stock. He couldn't stand the collusion and had made an appointment to talk to the Federal Trade Commission.

He'd died two days before he could make that meeting.

The company had made millions, none of which the Lawless family saw a dime of.

Hatch had gotten the money, but he'd been so drunk by that time, he'd pissed it away. He hadn't cared when Stratton had come to him with the plan to sell the company for a massive profit.

From what Riley could tell, Hatch had done his deep dive the day after Benedict and Iris Lawless had burned to death. He hadn't come out of it until Drew had found him, forced him to get somewhat clean, and started 4L.

It had given Hatch purpose.

Of course, guilt could have sent him on the same path. If Hatch had made the choice of money over loyalty, it would make sense he'd found solace in the bottom of a bottle.

Riley didn't know Hatch the way Drew did. He moved in, keeping his words low. "The board was small. How can you really dismiss him?"

"I can and I have. I know the man and he couldn't have done this. The answer lies somewhere else. I would really like to get the contents of Stratton's computer. I can't imagine Ellie tossed everything."

"Why don't you use your backdoor?"

"Stratton was paranoid. He kept his personal files off the network. I would bet he taught his daughter to as well. You need to find that system and download as much as you can onto a thumb drive. Maybe that will show us something. I want to know who he talked to back in those days."

"You honestly believe he kept those correspondences?" It wasn't something Riley would do.

"I keep everything. I'm going to go through every employee at Dad's old company and comb through their financials. God, what a fucking mess. How did I miss this?"

"You couldn't have known. It doesn't make any sense. There were five major stockholders in that company. Castalano, Stratton, Cain, Hatch, and Dad. Maybe we need to look outside," Riley offered. "We need to see who bought the stock during the IPO."

"I can try that." Drew's head dropped back, his hand massaging his neck. "I thought it would be over soon, too."

It looked like their collective nightmare still had them in its grip. He sat down across from his brother. It would be a long night.

Five

"That man looks at you like you're a big old buffet and he's been on a diet for years," Lily said as she walked into Ellie's office one week later. "We need to close the shades or he won't get anything done."

Ellie looked up and sent her assistant a stern glare since she wasn't alone. Kyle Castalano walked in beside her.

Still, she caught a glimpse of Riley. His eyes locked with hers for a moment before she forced them away.

Steven's son was a handsome man who always dressed impeccably. If he paid as much attention to his work as he did his clothes, Ellie would have competition for the CEO slot. As it was, Kyle seemed happy to be a vice president and likely spent his afternoons chasing his admin around the desk.

Still, he was Steven's son, so she put up with him. She had to wonder if he was sniffing around Lily. He'd been hanging around her desk a lot lately.

"Who are you talking about?" Kyle had a large stack of papers in his hands as he glanced back through the window that let her see out into the main office and right through to Riley's. "Not the lawyer? You really think he's stupid enough to think sex will work on Ellie? I don't think Ellie's had sex in years."

Yeah, he was obnoxious. "What do you need, Kyle?"

It had been a rough couple of days. She'd fielded calls from her sister. Shari either cried that she was being treated unfairly or screamed that Ellie was a tightwad who wanted her to fail.

Steven hadn't been in the office. He'd checked out weeks before, as though his retirement had already started. Unfortunately, he was still the CEO of the company and she had to have his approval before moving on certain issues.

She still hadn't heard whether Riley had sent back the buyout contract. The lawyer stuff moved far too slow for her.

Not to mention the fact that she got horribly distracted because Riley had moved into the office across from hers. It had been the office she had used before taking over her father's. When her door was open, she could see him moving around. He was on the phone a lot and the man liked to pace, his lean body moving with the grace of a natural predator. Late in the afternoon, he would slip his tie off and roll up his shirtsleeves and she would catch a glimpse of his sun-kissed skin and the muscles underneath.

"We've got a problem in accounting." Kyle placed a thick file on her desk.

"What's the issue?" There had to be a thousand pages sitting there. Did he expect her to go through all of them?

His pretty-boy face screwed up into an expression of ambivalence. "I don't know. They said something about money being earmarked for something and used for something else."

So she would have to handle that, too. Nice. She put a hand on the stack. "I'll take care of it."

"Of course you will," Kyle shot back. He winked Lily's way. "I'll see you later, hot stuff."

Lily rolled her eyes. "Not if I see you first and hide."

"Oh, and Ellie, tell your attack dog to stay out of my business." Kyle gestured toward Riley's office.

So Riley was already hard at work. She'd heard he was asking for reports from department heads. "If he's in your business, he's got a good reason. He's trying to make sure everything is in order for the buyout and the board meeting. Please try to get along with him."

Kyle leaned against the doorjamb. "I'll do whatever he needs to ensure the buyout goes through. He doesn't have to work around me. I want to help you and Daddy Dearest out."

"I would appreciate it if you didn't give Riley too much trouble."

Kyle put a conciliatory hand up. "I wouldn't dream of it. I'll send him a copy of that accounting report, too. I'm sorry I'm being a dick. The head of finance talks over my head. I don't understand half of what he's saying, and I took college-level accounting." He glanced back before continuing. "Hey, as long as I'm here, is there something going on with you and the new guy that I should know about?"

"No, why?"

He shrugged. "People are talking."

"What people?" Ellie asked.

"Hey, you brought in a male-model lawyer. People are going to talk. You've spent more time with him than you have any other male employee."

She felt herself flush but tried to keep her expression perfectly bland. "He's very important right now. He's here to ensure that the buyout and board vote go smoothly, so I'll be spending even more time with him. The gossips need to find something better to do."

"I wouldn't expect that to happen anytime soon." Kyle's eyes softened. "You know I think of you as a sister. I don't want you to get hurt. A guy like that is never going to hang around. If he's sniffing around you, he's likely got ulterior motives."

Yes, Kyle could be a mean sibling. Ever since they'd met as teenagers, he'd always had a nasty edge. "I'll be sure to keep my relationship with him professional. You don't need to worry about me. Like you said before, I can't be controlled with sex. Everyone knows that."

"Hey, you're the boss. There's a reason you're the boss. You're practically perfect, Ellie. Everyone knows that. Lord knows my father's always told me if I want to get anywhere in life, I should be more like you."

Kyle and his father had a tentative relationship. Steven hadn't even known Kyle existed before Kyle was fifteen and his mother showed up demanding support. A paternity test and several court dates later, Steven had found himself paying for private high school and college. He'd given Kyle a job at StratCast and they'd found a decent working relationship.

She was going to have to deal with him after Steven was gone.

There was an explosion waiting and the anticipation was killing her.

Stress was starting to eat her alive. They'd been thrown a curveball with the coolant project. Not anything that her guys wouldn't be able to handle, but it was coming at a bad time. Now this accounting issue, and apparently there was a bunch of gossip.

Little things were falling apart, things that individually wouldn't be an issue but together could cause serious problems. She needed StratCast to look solid.

The vote was coming up. She needed to get the buyout finished before then.

"I certainly don't think we need another me," she finally said, unsure of how exactly to deal with him. "I'm sorry your father said that. I'm sure his intention wasn't to pit us against one another."

"You're right. He simply admires you. I think he thinks of you like a daughter. And I'm sorry to shove the accounting thing your way," Kyle said with a grimace. "I'm awful with numbers and Sharon's on maternity leave for another three weeks. I do have good news, though."

"She could use some," Lily quipped, sitting on the edge of Ellie's desk.

"Not helping," Ellie grumbled under her breath.

Kyle ignored their byplay. "We've got a reporter who wants to do an article on you as an up-and-coming female executive. Something about breaking the glass ceiling in tech."

Ellie groaned. "I'm not CEO yet. That's a tad premature."

"Still, I think good press is good news. I'll leave the number on Lily's desk and she can set up an appointment," Kyle said.

She nodded Kyle's way. He might be obnoxious, but he was quite organized and his direct reports enjoyed working with him. Kyle turned and walked away.

"Now can we talk about the stud across the hall?" Lily asked. "Because if you don't want him, can I have him?"

"He's not a piece of meat, Lily," Ellie protested. Just the sexiest man she'd ever met. That was all.

The sharks were circling. She'd seen them all streaming into his office in their designer suits and sky-high heels. Every woman in the damn building seemed to have found her way to the new guy's office. They'd come bearing coffee or cookies or really big boobs.

He'd taken the coffee, shared the cookies, and thus far turned away all breasts from what she could tell.

It was only a matter of time. StratCast didn't have any dating policies. Riley was free to sample any of the women who offered themselves up.

"Don't you think it's a little unprofessional?" Ellie heard herself ask. She shook her head because she was staring at him again. He was very animated when he talked on the phone. He would pace, his hand gesturing. When he put the person on speakerphone, he would often pull out the putter he kept behind the door and practice golf shots. He hadn't brought much to his office. No pictures of family or friends. Just some books and his putter and a few golf balls.

"They're already gossiping," Lily replied with a shake of her dark hair. "They'll continue to do it whether or not you actually do the deed. You might as well do the crime if you're going to serve the time. That's what I think."

"They really think I'm sleeping with him?" She'd tried so hard to be professional around him.

"The women all know they would be. And the guys are jealous because you never looked at any of them. Don't roll your eyes at me. You don't see it. You're the boss lady. A lot of men find that attractive. They want to see if they can tame you. So yes, they're going to keep talking unless you want to fire Superhottie and bring in someone older and way less hunky. You need to live a little," Lily encouraged. "I'm going to hold your calls while you deal with the accounting nightmare. But you should think about sleeping with him. Someone's going to do it."

It shouldn't be her. She would have to deal with the fact that she would watch some other woman climb into Riley Lang's bed once he got the message that Ellie couldn't do it. He would get bored and move on and then he wouldn't show up at her office door forcing her to eat lunch or take her out to dinner.

She'd eaten at least one meal a day with him for the last week. She'd called it business and they'd discussed their share, but inevitably they'd also talked about more personal things. She knew he liked to read thrillers, though he stayed away from anything legal because he couldn't stand inaccuracies. He loved Indian food and his preferred cocktail was a rum and Coke. He had two brothers and a sister, though he was closest with his oldest brother.

She liked him. It made it so much harder to turn him away.

"Is Kyle hitting on you?" It was easier to ask about Lily's sex life than think about her own deprivation.

Lily shrugged. "He hits on anything in a skirt."

"He's a playboy."

A frown tugged Lily's lips down. "I didn't know you were that close to him. I knew you didn't think much of him, but isn't that a bit harsh?"

She'd never heard that tone from Lily before. Was her supercompetent, always-precise admin falling for someone like Kyle Castalano? "He dates a lot. I wasn't trying to be mean."

Lily seemed to shake it off. "Of course not. You wouldn't do that. I know he's a player, and no, I'm not into him. We're friends. I find him amusing, but he's not getting into my silky undies. I have better things to do with my time. The question is, what's his place here after his father's gone?"

That was a good point. "No idea. He's smart and organized, but I don't know that I would consider him true VP material. He's often late and he dumps things he doesn't understand on other people rather than figuring it out for himself. I'm not sure what I'm going to do. I might let Riley deal with him."

After all, the man claimed he was here to take care of the dirty stuff for her.

Kyle could shape up or ship out. She would give him plenty of time to do it, but she couldn't have an overprivileged playboy on her management staff. Not when there were so many good people who could do the job right.

She had to keep an eye on Kyle and make decisions she could live with.

Lily hopped down and moved to the door. "I'd love to watch that meeting. Are you going to be here or in R&D?"

She stood up. She needed to go down and figure out what the hell was going on. "R&D. I'll be down there a while."

"I'll be here," Lily said. "Watching the lion in his den."

Lily sat down at her desk and sure enough, she turned to watch Riley as he paced.

If Ellie stayed here, that was what she would do, too. Damn it. She would spend the entire afternoon drooling over the man and not dealing with the issues at hand.

She stood but before she could get to the door, it was opening and a familiar face was coming her way.

So apparently the contract had gone back out. She'd avoided Riley this morning, needing some space. It looked like he'd gotten the job done and now she had to deal with it.

"Ellie, I need to talk to you." Steven was dressed in slacks and a golf shirt, a light jacket covering most of both. "It's serious."

She'd hoped to put this off for as long as she could but decided there was no time like the present. Rip the bandage off. "I'd like to talk to you as well. Won't you come in?"

He closed the door behind him. "I was really surprised when I received the contract back with the notes from your lawyer. Do we not talk anymore?"

She'd felt bad about not calling him personally, but Riley had been firm about it. "Of course we can talk, but I think we should separate our business from the personal. I'm trying to do this right."

His face was grave as he stared at her, every line on his face showing. "I didn't put that clause in the contract, Ellie."

She'd wondered how he would handle it. "So you didn't read it before you sent it my way?"

She moved back to her desk, sitting behind it and putting some distance between them.

He pulled the baseball cap off his head and sank down into the seat in front of her. "Do you read every contract that goes out the door? Or do you listen to your lawyers? That's what we pay them to do. Do you honestly believe I would do that to you?"

Somehow he made her feel like a teenager again. Guilt swamped her. Steven had been good to her. Sometimes he'd been better than her own father. "I don't know what to think."

He looked at her, dark circles under his eyes. "Someone is trying to sabotage this buyout, Ellie."

"Who would do that?" The buyout was good for everyone. Steven was retiring. If he sold his stock on the open market, it would weaken the board. It was precisely the reason her father and Steven had put the clause in their partnership in the first place. If the buyout didn't go through, they would be in a holding pattern. As long as she had the money to purchase his shares of the company, he had to sell them to her.

"I don't know." His voice was gravelly, as though he needed a drink. "I talked to legal and they say that's not the contract they sent out, but when I asked them to e-mail me the correct one, it had been replaced on the system."

"Ben delivered it right into my hands, Steven."

He shook his head. "What do I do with the cooling system, Ellie? I don't have the resources to continue the development. Right now it's nothing but a good idea. It's meaningless to a man like me."

But it was a good idea that he could potentially sell. She hated the fact that she was even questioning the man, but she couldn't help but wonder. All of Riley's "business is war" talk had made her paranoid.

Riley wasn't the only one who had believed business was war. Her father had been damn good at it. Sometimes he overreached, but he'd always been looking to prove how smart he was. Could his partner really be so different? Her father wouldn't have hesitated to rip off his partner if he thought he could get away with it.

She'd learned at a young age that because someone was family didn't mean they wouldn't put themselves first.

"The good news is we found the error. Now we can move forward." She tried to put the best possible spin on it.

"I need this buyout to go through." He clutched the sides of the chair, his knuckles white.

"All right. I've got Riley working on it right now." She didn't understand the tension in Steven. "Once your lawyers approve the new contract, I'll look over it myself and send it through."

"That could take weeks and I need the cash, Ellie."

"Why would you need the cash?"

"I owe some people." His eyes slid away from hers. "That's all. Look, it's best for both of us if we get this thing done. I personally think your new lawyer might have something to do with this. That contract was changed. I looked through the one given to me at the beginning of all of this, and it didn't have the clause in it."

"Why would anyone want you to walk away with the coolant project? What would they get out of it?" Money, obviously, but Steven was right. The real money would be in developing the idea.

"I don't know. I'm being set up here. I think we both are. I think someone has been in my house, Ellie."

"Who would do that to you?" She kept the question calm, but was starting to wonder if there wasn't something seriously wrong with Steven's mind.

His jaw tightened, expression blanking from his face. "I don't know. I have enemies. Since your father died, well, let's just say a man starts to think about his mortality, and once he's done that, all he can think about are his sins. Your father wasn't a good man."

She knew that quite well. "No. He wasn't."

"I wasn't always a good man, either. I made decisions I wish I could take back. I can't and I won't allow a stupid mistake to hold me back now. I need the money. Two million as quickly as I can possibly get it."

"Are you asking me for a loan?" Her money was all reserved for the sale.

He stared at her, his eyes colder than she'd ever seen them before. "I'm asking you to give me what I deserve. I hate to do this, but if you don't give me the two million, I'll have to back someone else with the board."

Her stomach dropped. He couldn't be saying what she thought he was saying. "Are you trying to blackmail me?"

"I've got a service to provide. If you don't want it, I'll find someone who does. I know all about Shari selling her stock. Between the loss of her stock and what you had to give to that dipshit male model you hired, you likely can't outvote the rest of the shareholders. If I start talking, they'll find someone else to back for CEO. You'll still have a seat on the board, but until you control my shares, you won't have the job. Sure, you might be able to force your way in next year, but do you really want to wait? Do you want to watch as someone else takes the reins?"

The CEO contract had a minimum of a year attached to it. If the board chose to, they could sign a new leader for as much as five years. She could be locked out for half a decade.

"I don't have liquid cash, Steven. You know that. You're going to have to wait for the buyout."

"We'll have to look at it as a prepayment," he offered, his mouth a flat line.

She took a deep breath. "I'll talk to my lawyer about working up some paperwork."

"No." He leaned forward. "No fucking lawyers. They mess everything up. Get me a check. I need it in a week."

There was a knock on the door and Riley strode in. "I saw there was a meeting going on. I don't think it's good for the two of you to talk right now without counsel present. I know this is friendly, but let's keep up appearances."

It had just gotten so unfriendly. She was still reeling.

Steven stood up, his eyes softening. "I'm sorry, Ellie. If I had other options, I would take them. I'm in a corner."

She could feel Riley's eyes on her but couldn't make herself look at him. Steven's demand felt like a betrayal. Not felt. It was. She needed to stop sugarcoating things. He was blackmailing her. No question about it.

Her cash for his backing and all she had was his word. If he went back on it, there would be no calling the authorities. If anyone ever knew she'd been forced to "buy" her partner's backing, she would be mocked, likely ousted.

She wanted this why?

"Is there something I should know?" Riley asked, looking between the two of them.

She needed time to think. Her initial response was to sit down and cry, because she'd never expected that from him.

Her second, to tell Steven to shove his backing up his ass.

She managed a smile she hoped wasn't too tight. "Not at all. Steven was telling me about his retirement party plans."

Her business partner nodded. "Yes. It's one week away. That would be a very good time to get together again, wouldn't it? I expect a nice gift from you, Ellie. Your mother raised you right. You wouldn't let an old guy leave without a token of affection, huh?"

To the tune of two million dollars. "I'll have to see if I can come up with something."

"I know you will." Steven nodded her way before turning around and striding out.

The door closed behind him.

"What was that about?" Riley asked.

She couldn't talk to him about it. She would end up crying and looking like some spineless creature. She straightened up and stood.

"We were simply talking. Nothing to worry about."

He stared at her, his eyes narrowing. "You're lying to me."

"And you're forgetting who the boss is here." She walked past him. "I need that contract finished. Do what you need to do."

"Yes, ma'am." His tone had gone positively arctic.

There was nothing she could do about that. Maybe it was for the best. She turned and made her way down to R&D without looking back at the man who she'd briefly dreamed about.

It was past time to wake up and smell the gunpowder. Her friendly buyout had become a battle.

Riley stared as she strode away.

What the fuck had happened?

He'd been on the phone with human resources because he utterly disagreed with how a suit was being handled. The head of legal at StratCast was a jackass who thought they were still in the last century. He was going to get the company blasted by women's organizations everywhere. The minute the buyout went through, his ass was so fired. Riley would fire the entire team and bring in his own people.

Of course he had zero intentions of allowing the buyout to go through, and when Ellie figured out what was happening, he would be the one on his way out the door.

She would be left to deal with the ramifications.

Or would she?

"Did you need something?" Ellie's admin was standing in the doorway, her pretty face in a frown. "I can help you if you do."

It was a clear call for him to vacate the premises.

"No, I was coming over to see if anyone needed me." He gave her his best I'm-perfectly-harmless smile. "I'll be across the hall if Ellie needs anything."

"I'll let you know." Her smile was completely bland, and she held the door for him as he moved out of the office.

He noticed she didn't leave the office but closed the door behind him. As he looked back, he watched as she drew the blinds.

What was she up to?

There was a good way to find out. He strode into his office and sank into his chair, watching those closed blinds as he picked up his private cell. It rang in his hands before he could dial a number.

"Bran, what's going on? Something happened between Ellie and Castalano."

"Oh, you should be so glad I was listening in. He's an asshole." Bran sounded delighted.

His brother did have a habit of stating the obvious. "I realize that. Did you hear the conversation, then?"

"Yes. I've taken to keeping it on in the background. Did you know she talks to herself? And sometimes she sings. Mostly pop songs, but she'll throw in a rock ballad every now and then."

"Bran?" Sometimes it was hard to keep Bran on task.

"Sorry," Bran replied. "I like her. She's cool. She's not like a lot of bosses. She actually seems to give a shit."

"Good. I'm glad you like her. Now tell me what Castalano said to her."

There was a short pause on the line, and then Bran's voice had gone hard. "He's blackmailing her. He said he would go to the board and back someone else as CEO if she didn't give him two million dollars."

"That son of a bitch." He should have stopped that asshole and dealt with him then and there.

"Yeah. I think he's feeling the heat. Drew calling in that loan he made him is putting the right amount of pressure on the old bastard. Can we use that tape? Go to the police with it?" Bran asked.

Unfortunately there were so many issues with any kind of tape they could play for the police. "No can do. New York's wire-tapping rules are clear. Unless Ellie would be willing to lie and state that she knew we were listening in, we can't use it. Then there's the issue of what he really said. Unless he threatened to hurt her."

Bran sighed. "Not physically. He was actually really careful about it. Damn it. We didn't expect him to go to Ellie. What happens if Ellie pays him off?"

"She won't." He couldn't allow that to happen. The situation was delicate and if one card fell the wrong way, they wouldn't get what they needed. Castalano had to be without resources. He had to be vulnerable, and paying off his debt would give him a little strength.

"I heard something else," Bran said. "He said something about his health. According to the investigator's report, he's been regularly going to a building that houses several doctors' offices. We didn't want to get too close, but maybe we should figure out what's going on with him. We were right to not get too close. He's already paranoid. He thinks you're against him."

Which proved the man had good survival instincts. "Tell the investigator to follow him more closely. It doesn't matter at this point. If he's already afraid, give him something to be afraid of. Put some pressure on him and see what happens."

"And if Ellie writes him that check?"

His stomach knotted at the idea. "I've got something else in play. It's a short-term solution to the problem."

One he hoped he didn't have to put into play because it had the potential to decimate Ellie and her position.

"All right. I'll let Drew know."

"How are we doing with the stock situation?" Riley asked.

"We're almost where we need to be. I've identified a few minor stockholders who might be willing to part with their shares for the right price. Don't worry about that end. Keep an eye on Ellie Stratton. Make sure she doesn't write that check. I'm not sure what Drew would do if that happened."

Drew might implode. And then StratCast would as well. The way they had it set up, Ellie would still come out of this with either the company or a ton of cash. If Drew really got nasty, she could be left with nothing.

He didn't want that for her. He needed to get her to talk to him, to trust him.

"I'll handle it." Which meant handling her. He glanced across the hall. "Do you hear anything now?"

He wished they could have gotten a video feed.

After a few seconds of quiet, Bran came back on the line. "Nothing. If she's doing something in there, she's being quiet about it."

The door opened and Lily walked back out. She closed the door behind her and strode to her desk. Her eyes found his, and she stared for a moment.

He looked away. "Get me a report on the admin. Something's up."

Case's words came back to him. He'd talked about "complexity." At the time, his brother-in-law had been discussing how Ellie would be more complex than he gave her credit for. That had certainly proven true.

What if the whole situation was more complex than they'd accounted for?

"I will do that. I've got her name. And Riley, I'm sorry about last night." Bran's voice had gone quiet.

"About the fight? You've got to be more careful," he said.

"I know. I'll get someone on Castalano and the admin. See you tonight?"

Unfortunately, the answer to that was likely yes. "See you then."

His pursuit of the lovely Ellie Stratton had reached a damn brick wall, and it didn't look like he would be hopping over it any time soon.

She'd dismissed him like an employee she couldn't be bothered with earlier. She'd given him an icy denial and then walked out like a queen. No looking back, as though she couldn't stand to be bothered by him.

Yeah, he bought that.

He'd thought about following her. She considered Castalano a father figure and the fucker had broken her heart.

She was being stubborn and likely thought that regal act would wound his ego.

His ego was a pretty hearty thing. He was far more concerned with how she was feeling than the damage she'd done to his pride.

She would likely think he would be a dick now. Like most of the men around her. They were an older crowd. Some were genuine and kind, but a few didn't like the idea of a young woman taking over "their" company, and he'd seen her deal with it.

If she followed her schedule, she had a late meeting and then she'd likely come back to her office and eat some piece-of-crap take-out meal. Alone.

So maybe it was time to show the queen that her knight could take care of her.

He looked out and Lily was on her laptop. She didn't stay after with the boss, and that was something he would use to his advantage tonight.

He got on the phone and started making plans. Sometimes a good soldier didn't go over a wall. Sometimes he blasted right through.

It was time to up his game.

Six

Ellie thought seriously about screwing the accounting problem and heading home. She could pick up a bottle of wine along the way and drown her sorrows while taking a hot bath and reading a romance novel, since that was the only action she would see for the rest of her damn life.

You're forgetting who the boss is here.

What the hell had she been thinking? She might as well have slapped him and kicked his ass to the curb.

She stopped as she turned down the hall that led to her office.

She'd simply redefined their proper places. Sure, they'd become very friendly over the last week, but that didn't mean she owed him anything.

And he didn't owe her. All he owed her was his very best work. She would have to be satisfied with that.

Everything was blissfully quiet at this time of night. Oh, downstairs they were still working. Something had gone wrong with the calibrations on the new tests and they were being forced to do them all over again, but up here it was peaceful and quiet. Even the janitorial staff had come and gone. The lights were dim.

And his office was dark. He'd left for the day. He hadn't hung around to see how she was doing or to try to needle the truth out of her. He'd done what he should have done. He'd packed up and headed out to have some kind of a private life.

It was for the best. Tomorrow she would ask him about the contracts and they could get on the professional level they should have stayed on in the first place.

She was so tired. Tired of being professional. Tired of having to play referee for a bunch of engineers who couldn't agree on how to proceed. Tired of everyone she cared about letting her down.

She felt something wet on her cheek and brushed it away. Now she was crying at the office. Way to go.

The light had been left on in her office, but someone had closed the blinds. Lily, likely. She sniffled and grabbed a tissue off Lily's desk. She was glad Lily had her nightly happy hours to go to. She'd texted earlier and asked if she was needed.

It would have been nice to have someone to go through the accounting reports with her, but she would rather be alone. It was her burden to bear. She'd told Lily to have fun.

When was the last time she went to a happy hour? Not since she'd started working in management. When she'd been an intern, she'd gone out plenty of times with the engineers. Even before she could drink, she would sit with them and play trivia and talk about movies. She would listen to them tell weird science jokes and laugh.

Then she'd gotten married and moved into management but she hadn't really fit there. And her dad had been sick, and then she'd been in the middle of a divorce.

It had been a shitty couple of years when she thought about it.

She opened the door and her eyes widened.

Riley was on the couch in the sitting area of her office. He'd brought in a table and it was covered with food. It smelled like heaven and there was a bottle of wine and two coffee mugs from the break room.

"Before you protest, no one saw me, and you need this. You are a very overstimulated executive. I would have put the wine in a sippy cup and gotten you a napping blanket if I could."

He was giving her a stern look and then completely ruined it by smiling. She'd been awful to him and he'd gotten her dinner and wine and stayed behind to keep her company.

He stood, his smile fading. "Say something, Ellie. I don't know what happened between you and Castalano earlier and you don't have to tell me, but I know it upset you. Let me try to help."

He hadn't left. He should have. He should have walked out.

Maybe it was time to stop being worried the man was too good to be true and simply accept what she was being given.

"I'm sorry about earlier."

"It's all right. Do you want to talk about it?"

She didn't want to think about it. Not any of it. The strain of the past few months felt so heavy. She'd worn that worry like a coat, dragging her down. She wanted a few hours where she wasn't the boss, wasn't the executive. Where she was just a woman. "I don't want to talk, Riley. I want you to kiss me. I want you to still want me. Tell me you haven't changed your mind."

If he turned her away, she wasn't sure what she would do.

He didn't even hesitate. He crossed the space between them in two long strides, and then he was in her space, crowding her. "I want you so fucking bad, Ellie. Don't question that for a second."

His hands cupped her face as those sensual lips of his descended, and Ellie made her choice.

It might be wrong. It might be completely unprofessional, but she was going to have him. She was going to sink herself into an affair with him and not worry about the consequences. For once in her life, she was going to do something wild, something for herself.

She gave herself over, letting go of everything but the feel of those lips on hers.

The kiss went wild the minute she parted her lips for him. He wasn't cool and controlled the way he'd been that first day. She'd felt his control that day. Now a wild thrill went through her as his tongue plunged and one hand slid to the nape of her neck. He dragged her against his body, allowing her to feel how much he wanted her.

Ellie's whole body lit up. She felt like a live wire, and she wasn't about to give it up. Sex had been good before. It had been an enjoyable way to spend some time, but it had never been a ticking bomb waiting to go off. It was going to be different with Riley. There wouldn't be any awkwardness.

His mouth pulled back slightly, but his hands ran down to her hips, holding her to his body and letting her feel the hard erection at his core. He was breathing hard, as though his body had gone from resting to a sprint in seconds. As though the idea of being with her had sent him reeling. "Are we just kissing, Ellie? I can handle that. I can. I can keep this wherever you want me to, but I need to set expectations right now."

It would be smart, but she was so far past that. "I want you inside me."

His hands tightened. "Fuck. Don't say that unless you mean it. Once I start, I won't be able to stop. I'm talking about right this second, baby. Anytime you say no, I stop, but if we fuck right now, I'm going to want more. I'm going to need you."

She pressed her cheek to his, a sweet intimacy. She hadn't realized how much she'd longed to be close to this man, to have any part of her skin against his. She let her hands roam. If she said yes to him, she could touch him like this. She would have the right to caress his skin and kiss him with affection, to show him how much he meant.

"I need you, too. I didn't want to. It's not a good time, but I can't hold it back. I'm crazy about you. I need you in my life."

"I'm going to be in your life, Ellie," he replied, passion plain in his voice. "Let me come to your bed. I'm not going to be able to go back to being friends. I'll want you every second of the day."

Then they would be on the same page. "Yes, Riley. Yes."

His mouth came down on hers again. She could feel his hunger, and his hands roamed over the curves of her hips and backside, rubbing himself against her. It fed her own. She'd never felt more wanted, needed by a man. He didn't seem to simply want sex with someone. He seemed to need her—only her.

She wrapped her arms around him and held on, letting him lead.

His mouth moved down, kissing her jaw and ear. "Do you have any idea what I want to do to you?"

A little bit. She'd always been quiet during sex, preferring to concentrate on the sensations, but she wanted to hear him. She wanted to know he was with her. "What do you want to do?"

She shivered with heat as his tongue ran along the shell of her ear, and he nipped the lobe, a thrill shooting through her.

His voice was a low, sexy growl in her ear. "I think about stripping you down all the time."

He turned her suddenly and her back was pressed to his front. She could feel the hard ridge of his erection against her backside. His arms wound around her, keeping her close.

"You want me naked?" She didn't want to stop talking. She could see now that her other sexual encounters had been defined by the walls she'd put up. Though she'd had a partner, she'd been essentially alone in whatever pleasure she'd found. With her ex-husband she would turn off the lights, enjoy the ride, and then sleep in silence, their physicality the only true intimacy between them.

She didn't want that with Riley.

His hands moved up, cupping her breasts through the thin materials of her blouse and bra. The warmth of his mouth and lips moved on her neck. "I'll have you naked. I'll get rid of every single thing that comes between us. I'll strip you and then touch every inch of your body. You might be the boss in the boardroom, but I intend to lead here. I intend to have you every way I can have a woman, Ellie. Once I'm inside you, I won't want to leave."

He was still giving her a way out. She wasn't going to take it. "Yes, Riley. I won't change my mind."

His thumbs rasped over her nipples. "I'll fucking hold you to that. I will."

She had no idea why he sounded so resolute, but his hands were working the buttons of her blouse, dragging it out of the waistband of her skirt and peeling it back.

Cool air hit her skin. Her brain was foggy with lust. Her whole system had softened in a way it never had before. She felt hot, her muscles tight with need, but she let Riley take over. He slipped off her bra and then sighed against her skin as he cupped her breasts again.

"Fuck, that feels so good. These are beautiful, baby. Do you have any idea how long I've wanted to get my hands on these?"

She leaned back against him, her head cradled by the strength of his chest. He was solid all over. His callused hands rubbed against her skin, the feeling of masculinity making her feel more feminine than she'd ever felt before.

His fingers rolled her nipples and for a moment, she couldn't breathe.

"You're going to give me everything I want, aren't you, Ellie? You're going to let me play with this body. You're going to wrap yourself around me and let me have you like I've dreamed of. Without reservations, no thoughts of anything but how we can make each other feel."

Forgetting everything else seemed like the best idea ever. She needed this. Needed to let go of everything and simply be. She hadn't done it in years, maybe never.

But it felt right with Riley. It felt good and true.

"Yes. I don't want to be anywhere but with you. Only you."

His hand fumbled with the button on the back of her skirt and he cursed, finally managing to undo it. "Damn it. I'm not going to last once I get inside you. I'm going to be good for you, Ellie. I promise. I'll make it so fucking good for you."

She loved the growl he got in his voice when he was really aroused. And the way his hands shook. She wasn't in this alone. He was with her, right beside her in his need. She helped him, shoving the skirt down and kicking off her shoes. When she was down to nothing but her undies, she turned in his arms.

She was a little too big, her breasts real. Unlike many women her age, she'd never lifted them or enlarged them. They sagged slightly and she was well aware that her hips were curvier than fashionable. Would he turn her away? Would he see she wasn't as pretty as he'd thought?

He stared, his eyes going right to her breasts. "You're so gorgeous, Ellie. Do you have any idea what I've gone through since that first day? I've never masturbated as much as I have in the last week."

Yep, the man knew what to say to her. She was pretty sure she was glowing. "I've thought about you, too."

"I want you to tell me all about that, but later, baby. Right now, I'm going to do what I've wanted to do since the moment I met you." He leaned over and picked her up like she weighed nothing. He strode across the room to her desk.

Luckily, she kept a neat desk because she was fairly certain if she hadn't, Riley would have run an arm across it, shoving everything to the floor in his haste. He sat her in the middle of the desk.

"Lean back. I'm getting rid of these." His fingers found the sides of her bikini panties.

She did as he'd asked, feeling the smooth leather of her desk protector under her skin. He dragged the panties slowly from her hips and down her thighs. A breath hissed from his mouth as he looked down at her. He loomed over her, and she was well aware that he was still fully clothed. She was laid out like an offering on her desk, her every inch of skin exposed and waiting for him.

Why did that make her so hot? Why did it send her heart rate through the roof, her blood pounding through her system in anticipation of the moment when he would thrust inside her? Her pussy was pulsing with need, softer and wetter than she'd ever been before.

He ran his hands along her thighs, spreading them wide. She stared at him. At his eyes as his fingers skimmed her body. His green eyes heated, warming up as his skin flushed with his own arousal. When she thought he would get to work on his clothes, he pulled her down until her backside was right on the edge of the desk. He dropped to his knees.

She shuddered at the thought of what he was about to do. "Please, Riley."

He looked up her body, their eyes locking as he spread her wide. "This is what I wanted to do about five minutes after I met you. I wanted to taste you. I wanted to put my mouth on you and see if you were every bit as sweet as you looked."

He lowered his head and she felt the heat of his breath on her flesh for a single second before sweet fire seemed to singe her as he put his mouth right on her pussy.

No teasing. No taunting. He wasn't playing around. He meant to make her come and quick. Her body went taut as a bow as his tongue tortured her. Wet heat slid over and around, dipping inside her most sensitive place and making her fight to stay still. She wanted to ride his tongue, but this was his place. She was in control everywhere but here. This was where he ruled, and she loved the power in his hands as he held her down. It only worked because she trusted him, because he wouldn't hurt her. It was all right to let go with him, to give over and let him take the reins.

Pleasure swamped her senses. He groaned against her tender flesh, the sensation sliding over her skin.

"You taste so fucking sweet, Ellie. Nothing ever tasted as good as you do. I'll never get enough." His right hand moved up, and she felt his fingers moving into her channel. "You're going to be so tight. You're going to grip my cock like a vise."

"It's been a long time for me." Even the two fingers he began to work inside her felt big.

He fucked her gently as he stared up from below. "No one since the divorce?"

She shook her head. It felt so good. It was hard to talk, but he needed to know. "I dated some, but no one who moved me. And there wasn't a lot of sex for about a year before."

Two years and all she'd had was her vibrator, and even that had fallen into disuse. She'd put everything she had into cleaning up her father's messes and getting ready to take the company to a completely different place. She'd forgotten about her own needs until this one man made them come roaring back on line.

His fingers caressed as his tongue found her clitoris. He sucked her, gently working as he curled his fingers inside.

Ellie fought to stay still, finally making her hands into fists as she tried so hard not to scream out.

He hit some magic place inside and she couldn't hold back a second more. It didn't matter that they were at the office. It didn't mean a damn thing that someone could still be here. All that mattered was the sensation of his fingers and his lips and tongue. She soared over the edge and before she could come down, he stood and began to fight his belt.

Ellie lay back. Exhaustion made her weak but she loved how her blood thrummed through her system, reminding her of what she'd been missing for so long. Passion. Connection. Intimacy. All of it was wrapped up in Riley Lang.

She looked up as he shoved his slacks and boxers down, freeing his cock. He had a foil packet in his hand. It looked like her new man was a Boy Scout—very prepared. His hands shook as he tore it open. She got a better glimpse of his cock. Thick and long, with a pretty purple head. He sheathed it and then he was back at her core.

"I want to see you."

He was still dressed, with the singular exception of his slacks, which had hit the floor. He pressed his erection in. "I can't wait. I told you what would happen if you said yes."

He was stretching her deliciously, and she couldn't help but smile. Her system was still sparking in a pleasurable way. His hair was mussed, his face a tight mask as he started to press his way inside.

She'd done this to him. He was always so smooth and polished, and now the man looked desperate. Desperate for her. How was it possible? He was a Greek god of a man, but he was pressing inside her, holding her hips and forcing his way in.

"I don't want to hurt you."

She shook her head. "No, baby. You're not. I was just . . . I don't know why you're here with me, but I'm so happy."

He hissed a little and thrust in hard, as though trying to teach her something. "Look at me. I'm here because I fucking can't stand the thought of not having you. You tempt me like no other woman ever has. I don't understand you and I might never, but I'm going to know you, Ellie Stratton. I'm going to know what makes you smile and what makes you scream out my name."

He gritted his teeth and started to fuck her in long passes. So full. He filled her in a way she'd never been before. Though she'd been tired from the orgasm, her body heated all over again. She wrapped her legs around his lean waist and angled herself up. She wanted more of him. She wanted all of him.

He stopped talking, his head dropping forward as he settled in. His hips thrust and she moved to meet him.

"You feel too good, baby." He moved his hand and found her clitoris, rubbing in time to the hard thrust of his body.

She shoved up and went off all over again. It was almost too much, too much pleasure, too much feeling. Tears pricked her eyes and she cried out again as his body lost its rhythm and he pounded into her, holding her tight when he came.

He fell forward, letting his head find her breast.

She held him and wondered if she wasn't in trouble. She wrapped her arms around him because her first thought was that she never wanted to let go.

Her second thought was a bit more practical.

What the hell had she done?

Riley looked at Ellie's curvy form through the opaque glass of the shower and wondered if this woman wasn't his version of freaking Viagra. He'd had her not an hour before and he'd been hard ten minutes later. He could feel the beast straining as he watched her. "Is there room in there for two, baby?"

He'd bundled her up after the mind-blowing episode on the desk. She'd looked up at him, her eyes wide and whole expression so soft, he'd damn near told her everything.

It had been right there on the tip of his tongue to give her every bit of information he had. He thought about holding her and telling her what he was doing and begging her to forgive him. Hell, with Ellie's soft heart, she might understand it all and become his partner.

The fact that he remembered in that moment that his freaking brothers had probably listened in on their sex had shocked the sense back into him.

He'd gotten them both dressed and packed up the food.

Ellie had been quiet during the cab ride to her place, her brain likely going a thousand miles a minute. When the cab had stopped in front of her building, she'd turned to him, but before she could tell him good night or that she needed time to think or other bullshit, he'd kissed her.

That seemed to delay the inevitable recriminations for a few moments.

She'd allowed him in and they'd watched the news while eating the reheated orange chicken, broccoli beef, and dumplings he'd brought them. He'd pressed a glass of wine in her hand and she'd drunk about half of it.

He needed to store a bottle of Scotch over here.

When he'd told her to go take a shower and get ready for bed, she'd shockingly complied.

He should have known that that brain of hers would start working again once the orgasm had worn off. He needed her to concentrate on the fact that it was done. They were in a relationship. Oh, they might not be changing social media statuses, but the deed was done. He wasn't going to sneak away and pretend it hadn't happened.

He finally had her where he wanted her, and he intended to keep her there.

"Um, I'll be out in a second," came the obviously anxious reply. "If you could grab a towel for me, I'll let you have the shower."

Yes, he needed to shut that shit down or she would be waiting for him with his clothes, all buttoned up in some Victorian nightmare gown and showing him the door.

He wasn't about to let that happen. He'd just gotten her naked. He intended to keep her that way for a while. She was simply the loveliest thing he'd ever laid eyes on. Or hands. Or dick.

He was so hard again.

If he didn't want to lose the ground he'd gained, he was going to have to invade. For a few seconds he'd forgotten this was war. He was overdressed for this particular battle.

He shucked his clothes in quick order. He didn't have time to tease her. The fact that she hadn't seen him naked might throw her off long enough for him to get her in his arms again.

If she told him no, he would leave, but he didn't think for a second that was what was best for either of them.

Ellie needed a place where she could go wild. He intended to be that for her.

He would protect her from the fallout. He would keep her safe. She might lose some face, the stock might fall momentarily, but he was being optimistic.

He could do this. He could come out of this with revenge and the girl.

Because he'd decided he really wanted the girl. Fuck, he wanted her so bad.

He opened the shower door and stepped in.

Ellie turned and her mouth opened, likely to order him to leave. She didn't get that command out. Her eyes widened and she was staring at him. "You're naked."

He gave her what he hoped was a high-wattage smile. "I am. So are you, gorgeous. Come here and let me clean you up. After all, I'm the one who got you so dirty."

She seemed to force her eyes away from his dick. He'd closed them into the cozy shower, but she managed to put some distance between them. "I think we might have made a mistake."

He put his hands on his hips and didn't need to affect his emotions. No acting there. He really was sick of this. "I told you to be sure."

Her eyes slid away. "I thought I was. God, Riley, look at you. I'm not an idiot. You're . . . all that muscley stuff and I'm average."

He stared at her, not quite understanding. "You're not average. I think you're beautiful."

"I'm trying to figure out why you're here." She wouldn't look at him. She kept staring at some place over his shoulder. "What do you want from me? You're practically a damn male model. It doesn't make sense."

His blood was starting to boil. He knew it was irrational. He really was here for another reason, but all he wanted from her tonight was sex. And affection. And . . . damn, just her. He just wanted her. "What do I want? I think I've made that plain. I made it plain when I ripped your clothes off and fucked you on top of your damn desk."

She nodded. "Yes, I want to know why you would do that. You could have any woman you wanted. There are many more beautiful women at the office than me. So I have to assume you're with me because I can give you something else."

What was it with women? He could feel his blood pressure ticking up. How could she question the physical charge between them? He'd never had it with anyone else. Did she not feel it, too? His hands were fists at his side. "Ellie? Do you see my dick? Does it think you're average? Is my dick worried about moving up in the business or whether it's fucking the alpha female? Or was it hard again a few minutes after we had sex? Are you really so insecure you're going to force out a man who wants you? I'll walk away right now if you tell me you don't want me, but I'll be damned if I'll let some idiotic insecurity come between us."

For a second, he thought he'd been too harsh. He hadn't thought it through, hadn't planned that speech. Those words had been straight Riley Lawless, as though they were really just two people trying to muddle their way through.

Then she walked to him, her arms going around his torso and those sweet breasts pressing against him. "I'm sorry."

He breathed a sigh of relief and wrapped his arms around her. "I think you're gorgeous, Ellie. I don't care what anyone else thinks. Haven't I been after you since the day we met?"

It might have started as something else, but the attraction was real. The need had turned into something he wasn't sure he could go without.

"I don't understand it. It's never happened to me before."

He forced her head up gently. "Do you think I do this every day? Ellie, I've never pursued a woman the way I have you. I told you before. My relationships have been casual and often random. I have never in my life run after a woman the way I have you. I'm crazy about you."

No lie there. He couldn't remember everything he'd said while he'd been taking her on the desk, but he had to hope his brothers believed he was acting because otherwise he would get some serious lectures about not falling for the mark.

Shit. He might have already fallen for the mark.

He shoved that thought aside. He'd hoped once he'd actually gotten inside her, he would realize that it was simply sex. Yeah, it fucking wasn't, but now wasn't the time to deal with it.

Now was the time to cement the bond. If he had any chance of keeping her after the bomb went off, he needed a strong bond in place.

"I'm crazy about you, Riley." She bit her bottom lip as she looked up at him. "What does it mean?"

Finally she was asking him the right question. He couldn't help himself. He dropped a kiss on those soft lips. When had kissing become something he wanted to sink himself into? Kissing was something he did to get to the sex, but he found himself indulging with Ellie. It meant something more with this one woman. "It means we're together now. I told you I didn't want a one-night stand."

Her hands ran up his back and she moved against him as though trying to get closer. "What about the office?"

He couldn't stop kissing her. He moved to her forehead and that little spot between her eyes. His blood was starting to get hotter than

Lexi Blake

the water. "What about it? There are no rules against dating at StratCast."

"It would look bad."

"Baby, they're already talking about us. It doesn't matter. It simply means that they know we're a team and they have to deal with us. If you look at it in that light, we're actually being aboveboard and honest."

"You think that's the right thing to do?"

"I think I don't want to pretend we're nothing but coworkers. Maybe it would stop Ron from HR and that bastard Greg from sniffing around you constantly."

"You're insane." But this time she settled back against him, obviously letting go of her insecurity.

He might have a fight again in the morning, but tonight it looked like he'd won the battle. "You don't see how men look at you. I suppose I should be grateful because otherwise you might have gotten scooped up. I would bet they looked at you differently when you started wearing those filmy dresses instead of the dowdy suits. And if they saw you naked, they would never leave you alone."

He kissed her, letting his mouth play on hers. He could take his time now that he'd fed the beast. Oh, it was hungry again, but he could handle it now. He could take his time and indulge his senses in her.

In her sweet smell. Citrus and sex. It was a heady combination.

In the touch of her skin. She was so fucking soft and warm. He would regret leaving her at the end of the night.

In the sight of her. He would never forget how gorgeous she'd been spread out for him on her desk. It had been the single most erotic moment of his life, looking down on her and seeing how much she'd wanted him.

And the taste. When he'd put his mouth on her, he'd never wanted to stop. Sweet and sultry. He would never forget what it felt like to put his mouth on her.

He would dream about her for the rest of his damn life.

Without thinking about it, his arms tightened.

"I think I'll pass on the nudity. I would look really funny at meetings if I walked around naked," she murmured.

"You would look gorgeous and no one would get anything done." He wasn't going to think about the fact that she would likely hate him at the end of this endeavor. He was going to concentrate on the time he had. No woman had ever held his attention like Ellie did.

He liked her. He'd liked women before. He wanted her. He'd certainly done that before, too. The problem was he was starting to like who he was when he was around her, and that was a completely new state of being.

He liked being Ellie's protector, advisor, and all-around go-to guy. That was why he'd bristled in a way that had nothing to do with his real purpose. He'd been pissed off that Castalano thought he could get her alone. That fucker thought he could take advantage of her, bully her, scare her.

Kill her?

That was ridiculous, but he'd done it before.

"We should get cleaned up or we'll lose all the hot water." She sighed and cuddled again, either ignoring his possessive hold or not minding it.

Sexually satisfied, Ellie was sweet and affectionate.

"Turn around." He gently moved her so she was back to front with him. He grabbed her soap and worked up a nice lather.

This was an intimacy he'd never performed before. He let his hands work over her shoulders and the back of her neck. She'd already washed her hair, the scent of orange blossoms permeating the room.

Now oranges would likely make him hard because he would think of her.

"I had a shitty day, Riley." She let her head fall back as he moved down, soaping her chest and cupping her breasts.

"I know, baby. If you want to talk about it, I'm willing to listen." He stood there with her, washing down her skin, but more importantly trying to infuse her with his calm.

He didn't want her to worry. It caused him actual physical distress. His stomach knotted at the thought of her being tense and anxious.

"Steven is blackmailing me for two million dollars."

He let the soap drop from his hand. Somehow hearing it from her lips made the righteous indignation he'd felt come roaring back. He turned her around again. "He's doing what?"

She frowned. "Well, if I'd known my bath would stop, I wouldn't have told you."

She knelt down and picked up the soap.

"Ellie, this is serious. What the hell are you talking about?" He wasn't about to allow her to figure out he'd already known. She was talking to him. He was in.

She went to work on his chest, diligently soaping his skin. "He has his endorsement of me as CEO to hold over my head. With my dip-shit sister selling her stock and thereby her voting shares, I'm in a precarious position. I have you now, but I had to use my own stock to fund your seat, so that's not really a gain."

It was as though telling him had calmed her. The tension had left her shoulders and she was simply talking it out.

He'd given her that. She trusted him to work through it with her. He brought his hands up, cupping her face and forcing her to look at him. "I promise I will make sure you get that job, Ellie."

Maybe not exactly as quickly as she wanted it, but he would ensure it.

Her lips curled up slightly. "Nothing is for sure. I have to decide if I trust Steven enough to write him that check. It's like a prebuyout loan. Not loan. It's a small advance."

"Then I'll make him sign a contract." He wasn't about to let her sign that check, but he couldn't overplay his hand. He would make sure that Castalano never saw that money. And he might add a little extra pain because the fucker was messing with Ellie. No one got to mess with Ellie.

Well, no one except him.

She shook her head. "He made it plain that he won't do that. He's in some kind of trouble. I think it might be the illegal-gambling kind of trouble."

He went still under her hands. It was time to herd her toward some inevitable truths. Maybe if she figured some things out on her own, the inevitable blow wouldn't be as rough. "Ellie, do you think he would ever do something really illegal? You said there was an accounting issue. Could he embezzle from the company?"

"I would have said one hundred percent no yesterday. Today, I don't know. I'll look through it tomorrow and talk to accounting."

"I could have a forensic accountant take a look." McKay-Taggart had one.

"I don't think that's a good idea. We have reporters looking at us right now. If word gets out, the stock gets devalued."

"And you owe Castalano less." He didn't see how that was a bad idea. In fact, they were kind of counting on it.

"I'm not going to willingly devalue my company. It's not right. Between the accounting issue and what's going on in R&D, the stock could go into free fall. I'm not going to do that. Not even if Steven's acting like an ass."

Her hands felt so good on his body. She was making it hard to think straight. "Ellie, you can't give him that money without a sound and solid contract. He's trying to steal from you. Let me take the accounting issue. I'll deal with it very quietly."

She worked her way down his arms. "All right. But I only have a few days." She looked up at him, grinning suddenly. "How do you manage to think with that thing? Is there any blood left in your brain?"

He groaned because likely she was right. His dick was throbbing and desperate for attention. "It's not easy. I'm used to being in control. Unfortunately, he is a little in control right now."

The grin turned distinctly sensual. "Really? I kind of thought I was the one in control right now, Counselor."

Her low tone went straight to his cock. He could feel it in his damn balls. That sensation warred with the knot he got in his gut when she mentioned R&D. She couldn't possibly know about his late-night escapades in R&D. He'd done what he'd needed to do two nights before, but he'd been certain he'd gotten away clean. "Ellie, baby, we should talk about this. Tell me what's happening in R&D. You were down there all day. I thought you were avoiding me."

She rubbed the soap along his belly, getting dangerously close to that part of him she really was in control of. He was almost ready to beg her to touch him. "I was, but R&D *is* having trouble. There was an issue with the calibrations on a couple of the machines. It sent out false data. I fixed it. It took me a while. Someone's a dipshit."

Her hand brushed over the head of his cock. She was trying to make him insane. He should stop her. They needed to talk, but something about that saucy smile gave him pause. She was happy now. He found he couldn't deny her that. He also couldn't not ask a few questions.

"So someone screwed up the machines?" He needed to know if she suspected anyone. Prayed she didn't since he'd been the one to do it. It was part of the plan, a part he was certain they wouldn't have to use. It was their nuclear option.

"That about sums it up. Oooo, I think this part is seriously dirty." She dropped to her knees and caressed his cock, taking it in her hand.

Was she really going to do that? Fuck. He needed to concentrate. He needed to make sure she'd fixed what he'd fucked up so the issues didn't become more than he wanted them to. All he wanted was a couple of reports that showed problems with the coolant system. It would be easy for her to fix, but might cause a little chaos that would slow down the buyout.

"Who calibrates the machines?" Getting the words out was a struggle.

She leaned over and licked the head of his cock, and then that was absolutely the only thing that mattered in the entire world.

"They used interns. It's a simple job. I used to do it. Apparently, this intern isn't very good at reading a manual." Her words hummed along his flesh, making his cock tighten. "I fixed it. It was kind of nice. I liked working down there again. It's quiet and I can focus. I like to focus, Riley. I like to do a job properly. I've found that every job requires the proper attention, no matter how small . . . or large the job may be."

He'd known deep down that if he could get her into bed, she would be a sensual thing. He hadn't expected this playful side. Riley relaxed again. She'd done what he'd known she would do. He had his reports on file and she'd fixed the problem. Hopefully, he wouldn't have to use them. It didn't matter now. All that mattered was how good it felt to be with her. "You're known for your attention to detail, Ms. Stratton. It's why you are such an amazing executive."

Her eyes came up, mirth sparking there. "If I didn't have such high self-esteem, I would have a problem with that. As it is, you're right. I'm quite good."

"I make it a point to never argue with the boss." He let the issues with the research and development team float away as she licked the head of his cock.

Fire sizzled along his spine. He looked down and watched that pink tongue begin to work its magic.

"Who the hell are you, Ellie? I don't know if I believe this. Not ten minutes ago you were ready to kick me out because you couldn't accept the fact that I wanted you."

She took his cock in hand and began to stroke him. "You got pissed at me. You're always smooth and easy, like you're managing me. You got mad and let me see it. You were real for a moment. So I have to think the rest of it is real, too. It's just how you are. I'm always thinking about you, but there are moments when I know I'll never stop, when I'm absolutely certain you're important to me for way more than business or pleasure. When you told me about your childhood. When we talked about your brothers and sister. And when you got mad at me for not believing in myself. This is the me I want to be, Riley. If we're going to be lovers, I want to have fun with it. I want you to get the me no one ever sees. I think that's what you gave me in those moments."

He put a hand on her hair and tried really hard to quell the emotion he felt at her words. Too much. He couldn't feel this much about her. He needed to bring it back to where he was comfortable. "I'll give you more than that, Madam Executive. I think we were having fun. I get to be in charge in the shower."

Her eyes lit again and the moment had passed. "I agree to do absolutely anything you require of me in the shower, Counselor. Consider me your girl Friday."

If he hadn't been crazy about her before, playful Ellie would have done it. Her honest, open sexuality made his blood pound. "I'm going to need you to suck me, baby."

"I think I can handle that task. Have I told you how pretty you are naked, Riley?" She leaned forward and took him in her mouth.

No one had ever called him pretty before. Hot. Sexy. Not pretty. He wasn't sure he loved the word, but he damn straight loved hearing it from her.

Her tongue worked over and around his head like a playful butterfly on his skin. Everywhere she touched he felt the connection.

Yes, this was what he needed. He needed to forget about anything but the sex. Need poured through him. He wanted to get a fistful of that soft hair of hers and force her to take him deep, but he was willing to let her play.

He didn't want it to end. When it did, he would have to head home. He couldn't risk sleeping with her. He never slept with a woman. Never rested near anyone.

She rolled her tongue over his cock and then sucked him lightly.

His eyes nearly rolled to the back of his head. He forced himself to focus. Her mouth felt far too good. If he didn't retain control, he would come in her mouth in seconds, and he needed this to last.

"That's what I want. Take more." He let his hips move as she started to devour him.

He watched as his cock disappeared between her lips.

Her hands came up, cupping his balls and rolling them gently.

Over and over, she used her tongue and lips to send him higher. Her hands came up, running over his thighs and around to his ass. Her nails lightly scored him, but all that did was make him hiss and want more.

He was going to come, but he wanted inside more than her mouth.

He twisted a hand in her hair, lightly pulling her. "Stop. I don't want to come unless you're with me. Get up here."

The words came out more harshly than he'd intended, but he was running on pure instinct. She'd given herself to him tonight and he was going to take her any way he wanted, any way that she needed. She didn't want the smooth lover. She wanted the other part of him, the part he didn't share, the part he hadn't really known existed until he'd found her.

The possessive, obsessive lover.

She kissed his cock one last time and then rose to her feet. She moved close to him, her breasts rubbing against his chest. "Riley, I'm on the pill. I didn't stop after the divorce. I suppose I was thinking positive. I haven't had a lover since. And I happen to know you passed the physical you recently took."

He'd thought he couldn't get any harder. The idea of getting inside her with absolutely nothing between them made him pull her close. She was right. He'd passed the physical the company had required before the stock transfer. "I did, but you should know I've never had sex without a condom. Not once in my life."

"Oh." Her mouth formed a little O and she started to nod. "Okay. Do you have another? I don't actually have any here. I wasn't that optimistic."

She'd totally misunderstood him, but he wasn't about to waste time correcting her. She'd given him permission, and he was taking it. He picked her up, shoved her against the wall of the shower, and thrust inside. So tight. She was tight, but wet. She responded so readily to him. "You feel so good. So fucking good."

He wrapped his arms around her and let gravity do its work. She groaned as she sank onto his dick. He gripped the silky cheeks of her ass and moved her up and down.

"You know, I once said I wasn't all that into muscley guys." She gasped as he lifted her up and down. "I would like to totally take that back now."

As long as he was the muscley guy, he was fine with that. "Hold on to me."

Her legs circled his waist and he could feel her nails lightly digging into his back.

He fucked her hard, all thoughts of making it last gone now. He only needed to make it last until she was satisfied. He moved back, pressing her against the shower wall again so he could angle up and hit her clit with his pelvis. He ground against it as his mouth found hers. He needed to be inside her. Mouth to mouth. Arms wound tight. Cock deep inside. He was surrounded by Ellie, and for those brief moments, he blocked out the rest of the world. She was his world.

Her fingernails dug in, her legs squeezing him as he felt her pussy pulse.

"Riley," she breathed. "Oh, how do you do this to me?"

She held on as she came, her orgasm sparking his own.

It raced along his spine, flaring through his system like a wildfire. He utterly lost his cool, slamming into her again and again, drawing out the pleasure.

As he emptied himself deep inside, he wondered how he would ever leave her.

Her legs slowly unwound but she still clung to him. Her eyes were sleepy as she smiled up at him. "I think I'm dirty again, Riley."

He pressed his mouth to hers. Yeah, she was dirty, and he wouldn't have her any other way.

An hour later, he tucked her into bed. She turned toward him, laying her head on his chest.

"So you won't be here in the morning, huh?"

It didn't sound like an accusation to his ears. There was something resigned and a bit sad about the way she said the words. She cuddled against him. He would get up and get dressed after she went to sleep. He didn't want her to show him the door. He wanted her to have the illusion of a man who could be with her all the time. Who could sleep beside her.

"I will. I'll be back here as soon as I wake up. I also think maybe I should look for a place closer by." He sighed and let his fingers play along her skin. He liked the way her hair felt against his chest. So often she put it up in a bun or pulled it back. He loved the way it looked spread out and wild. "I'll pick us up some coffee and donuts."

She shook her head against him. "Don't. I'll make us breakfast. Take my keys and lock up behind you."

"It isn't that I don't want to stay." Despite the fact that she'd accepted his explanation that he didn't sleep well with others, he felt guilty. If she'd fought him on it, it would have been easier. She'd simply kissed him and asked him to hold her until she went to sleep. Why couldn't she be more difficult? Then he wouldn't feel this desperate need to make her understand. "I learned to sleep with one eye open in the group home."

Her head came up, eyes meeting his. "It's all right. I understand."

But she didn't. She couldn't, and suddenly he really wanted her to. He wanted someone to understand him. He smoothed back her hair. He'd never talked about this. He avoided it at all costs, but somehow it was bubbling up tonight. As though his fear and hurt had found a safe haven. "After my brother aged out, I was alone. I asked him if I could run away and be with him, but I had my last year of high school to finish. They don't let homeless kids in. That's pretty shitty of them, I think. So I stayed."

She didn't say anything. She simply put a hand over his and threaded their fingers together.

"My brother had made some enemies there. He's really good at that. Two nights after he left, they decided to take out their anger on me instead. At the time I wasn't as strong as I am now. Like I told you before, I was all about school. I studied. I never worked out. After that night, I worked out. A lot. And I didn't sleep much."

He had nightmares. Nothing like Bran's, from what he could tell, but enough to scare Ellie very likely.

"I want you to rest, Riley," she said quietly. "Whatever you need, that's what you'll get from me. So you go home and sleep and come back to me in the morning."

"I want to be normal." It kind of shocked the hell out of him. He meant that. He'd always tried to look at what had happened to him as a good thing in the long run. It toughened him up for the fight.

He wanted to be able to sleep with his girlfriend.

"There's no such thing, babe," she whispered. "We all want to think there's some magical normal out there that we could achieve if we only did this or believed in that. It's not true. Normal for humans means struggle. We're all out there trying to make it through. We'll find what works for us."

She kissed him again and then he felt her breathing turn normal.

It was a long time before he let her go.

Seven

Ellie had to force the grin off her face as Riley stopped by her door. He leaned against the frame, his gorgeous body encased in a designer suit.

Was there anything sexier than a man in a tailored suit?

Oh, yes. That man naked.

"Good morning, Ms. Stratton," he said in a deep voice.

A week and a half into her relationship with Riley Lang and all he had to do was turn on that deep voice of his to get her motor running. Sleeping with him every night was having an effect on her.

Not sleeping. Making love. Every night. Some mornings. A couple of times in the afternoon in her office or his.

"Good morning, Mr. Lang." She was fairly certain she was blushing.

He stepped inside and shut the door. "I'm sorry I missed you this morning."

The man practically lived at her place since the night they'd first gotten together. With the single exception of the fact that he wouldn't sleep with her. He made love to her over and over again, and then he held her until she fell asleep. She never woke up next to him. A few mornings, he'd made it back to her place before she woke up and then he greeted her with coffee, and once had made her superlate for work, but he slept at his place.

"How did your meeting go?" She tried to put on her business face. It was hard to remember to be Ellie Stratton, future CEO with a plan, when she was around Riley. It was more fun to be goofy Ellie.

And yet she liked working with him. She liked knowing he was across the hall and would be there, waiting with advice or a kiss if she needed one. And when she got tense, the man knew how to make her relax. For the first time in her life, she felt like she had a real partner.

She needed one since things had gotten very tense around Steven.

He closed the door behind him and strode over to her desk, his face going grim. "You're not going to like this."

Her stomach dropped a little. His meeting this morning had to do with her accounting issues. He'd hired a forensic accountant with his own money. She would pay him back, but she couldn't have gossip about a serious cash problem with the company, so they'd decided to keep it quiet.

Four days before, she'd met with the reporter Kyle had introduced her to. Something about the man had made her uncomfortable. Especially his lines of questioning about her father and his business practices. He'd basically insinuated that Phillip Stratton had been a thief. He'd accused her father of stealing intellectual property and then asked her if she intended to do the same when she was CEO.

She'd ended the interview early. She had very little hope the man would write anything positive about her.

"Give me the bad news." It felt like she was in a vise and it was slowly closing around her.

Or she was the frog in the pot. Not thrown in, but placed gently and allowed to get used to the water as the heat turned on. It would be boiling before she knew it was time to jump out.

Was Steven moving her into position? Was this some kind of game she hadn't realized she was playing?

Riley passed her a folder. "Someone has systematically stolen over ten million dollars from the company in the past ten years. It all comes out as R&D expenditures, but Phoebe ensures me she's tried to match them to receipts and they don't exist."

This was bad. She took a deep breath and opened the file. "We don't always have receipts."

"You haven't lost ten million dollars' worth of receipts, Ellie." Riley moved around her desk, getting into her space. "Also, Phoebe found an issue with the purchase of a group of hard drives. The dates claim the company purchased them for over fifty thousand dollars. At the time of purchase, they were out-of-date and not worth more than two grand for the lot."

And no one had caught it until now? How was that possible? "Who signed the orders?"

"The paperwork is gone."

Naturally. "I need to talk to the head of accounting."

Riley shook his head. "Baby, you hired her a year ago and she recently went on maternity leave. She's the one who sent this to you. The man who would have had actual knowledge retired and I can't get hold of him. I have to assume he was in on the game or very bad at his job."

"He was hired by my father." She hadn't talked to Riley about her father and she felt guilty about that. He'd been open and honest with her and she'd held back.

Because he worked for Drew Lawless, and she wasn't ready to look him in the eye and admit what she knew.

"Do you think your father had something to do with this?" Riley asked.

"I don't know." At least that wasn't a lie. "But some of this money went missing after he got sick. Damn. At least a million of it has been in the last six months. That's what tipped off Debra. Did your accountant look at any recent books?"

"I didn't want to pull them in case the gossip started." His hand went to her hair. "It's going to be all right, Ellie. I have an idea where

I would like to look. Every bit of that money went into a set of three accounts Phoebe was able to find. They look like holding companies for the manufacturers the checks were written to."

"And we're sure these aren't real companies?" Maybe there was a mistake.

"They've got LLCs, but I sent someone to the addresses listed. Two were actually shipping centers and one is a PO box. I'm getting everything ready to legally demand the records for who opened those boxes."

She closed her eyes in frustration. He was unfortunately right, but that knowledge would come at a cost. "The minute we get legal, the press will find out."

"Ellie, baby, you know who I think this is."

She did. He'd been working on her for a week with this particular conspiracy theory. "You think it's Steven. You think he's been stealing from the company for years. It couldn't be my father. Not the last two years."

"Yes, I think it's Castalano. I've looked into his other business deals and he's got a very shady reputation."

So had her father, but then business could get messy. There weren't a lot of CEOs out there who were known for their moral and upright standing. They got where they were by being ruthless. "What did you dig up?"

"Did you know he formed a company twenty years ago with your father, Patricia Cain, and a man named Bill Hatchard?"

Her stomach turned at the thought. She knew it all too well. "It was my father's first business. He'd worked his way up the ladder, but he'd never really had anything of his own. They designed a code that allowed more data to be pushed through a stream. It was how he made the money he and Steven based StratCast on. They paid off Patricia Cain and she started her lifestyle website."

Patricia Cain was the authority on everything from cooking to decorating to manners these days. She had a popular television show called *Patricia's Paradise*. She was beloved as a matron of good taste and domesticity.

Ellie's father had called her the most hateful bitch he'd ever met, with the exception of one.

She'd never known the name of the nastier lady, but she'd met Patricia and couldn't believe there was anyone worse than that woman.

She'd never met Bill Hatchard. Her father had told her he was nothing but a drunk with some cash they'd needed.

"There are some people out there who think he stole that code, Ellie," he whispered.

She knew the truth. "I've heard the rumors. Do you think Steven knew about it?"

It was something she wondered more and more lately. Her father had been very intent on confessing his own sins but hadn't talked about the others.

"I do." He stared right at her. "Ellie, I want to talk to you about something."

Before she could reply, the door to her office flew open and Lily was standing there. "Ellie, I think there's something you should see."

Her assistant's eyes were wide and she bit her lower lip.

"What's going on?"

Lily stepped in with the paper in her hands. "This was just delivered."

It was a copy of the *Business Daily Journal* with the important story below the fold but on the front page.

STRATCAST IN DEEP TROUBLE

She gasped as she read through the relevant points. "How do they know this? He's reporting that our coolant system is a complete bust, putting us behind two of our competitors in the race. That's not true."

Riley looked over her shoulder. "What data are they citing?"

Her hands clenched into fists as she read the article. "They apparently have the reports from the miscalibrated tests. How did those get out?"

"I don't know, but I'm going to find out. Is that the worst of it?" Riley already had his phone in hand.

"No." She forced back tears because the humiliation was quite piercing. "They're reporting that I've had numerous affairs with co-workers, starting back when I was an intern all the way through you. I apparently let men influence me on a regular basis."

"I will sue the holy hell out of that rag." Riley's jaw had tightened.

"What they say about me is meaningless. We have to get those reports fixed, Riley. They can affect the stock." Even if she got the real reports out there, it likely wouldn't stop a sell-off.

"I have some contacts. I'll fix this." Riley looked down at her and if they'd been alone, she would have walked into his arms.

But they weren't and she had a job to do. She nodded his way. "I'll make some calls, too."

He strode out, leaving the door open behind him.

At least she wasn't in this alone.

"Is there anything I can do?" Lily asked.

"You can tell me what the gossip around the building sounds like." She'd been avoiding it for a week and a half. Hell, she'd been avoiding everything, especially Steven Castalano. Lily knew all the gossip. She was the fount from which information flowed. Long ago they'd decided to work the grapevine this way. Lily made friends with everyone, even talked to them about the boss sometimes. In return, they felt comfortable around Lily and told her what was going on.

Ellie didn't care if someone didn't like her, but she needed to know if someone was coming after her. Lily could provide that information.

"You want the skinny on you or Steven?" Lily asked.

"Both."

"There are rumors that Steven's sick, but I don't know how much of that I believe. I think he's playing it up to get sympathy."

"Is he getting it?"

"Oh, yes. He's definitely got the upper management in his pocket. They think you're trying to take advantage of a sick old man. Blue collar doesn't trust him as far as they can throw him. He's burned them too many times. He and your dad. In the sections where you've worked—R&D, marketing, and HR—they're solidly in your corner."

"And the ones I didn't intern in?"

"They wonder if you're not a lot like your father," Lily said gravely.

She shouldn't be surprised. Her dad had been a dick to work for. "All right. All I can do is prove that I'm not. I won't get a chance to do that until I'm CEO."

"Some people think that's not going to happen. There are betting pools and right now you're losing."

"Who's winning?" Did she want to know the answer to that question?

"Outside management."

Then Steven really had been talking. He was using the employees to send her a message. He could be the one to put the crown on her head or to take it away altogether.

He'd called and given her a new deadline. He'd told her she had to get him the money by midnight tonight or he would pull his support.

He would do that anyway if the stock price suddenly fell.

He might try to put the blame on her. Even the rumor that she attempted to sway stock prices to devalue the company before a buyout would ruin her. And possibly get her into legal trouble.

If this was a game Steven was playing, what did he expect to get out of it? Money?

"How about the gossip concerning my personal life? I'm sure

there's some of that." She needed to know everything. It was becoming clear to her that there was a puzzle laid out in front of her and she didn't have all the pieces.

Lily frowned. "It's not good. Don't get me wrong. The regular workers adore you. They don't give a crap that you're sleeping with your lawyer."

So they hadn't been discreet enough. "All right. What is management saying about me and Riley?"

"It's only a couple of people, but they're old-school."

"So they're Steven's cronies?"

Lily nodded. "Yes. There's been talk of changing StratCast policy since the new boss . . ."

"Go ahead and complete the sentence." She braced herself for what she knew was coming.

Lily winced. "Can't keep her legs closed."

That was a kick to the gut.

Lily moved in, her palms flat on the desk. "They are hypocrites, Ellie. I happen to know two of those assholes have had affairs with their secretaries. I'm sure there's a lot more. There are rumors that you've slept with Kyle."

"Okay, that might be the worst thing that's happened to me today." The idea that anyone thought she'd slept with Kyle made her sick to her stomach. "Any others lining up to pin a scarlet letter to my chest?"

They were hypocrites and she wasn't about to answer those charges. Still, it let her know where her board would likely be.

"There's some talk that you brought Darvisch on board with a little extra on the side."

"Of course." Darvisch was the brilliant coder she'd hired. Naturally she'd screwed him to bring him on board. "I must have a magical vagina. Really, I missed my calling. I should have gone into prostitution.

Is there anything relevant I should know? Some other piece of gossip that doesn't involve me screwing multiple men?"

"That's where they hit us, isn't it?" Lily slumped back into the seat in front of Ellie's desk. "They go straight for the sex organs. We can't possibly have a brain because we have breasts."

She felt a bitter smile cross her face. "Funny, no one accused me of harlotry back when I wore those buttoned-up suits."

"Yes, they did." Lily sighed. "I never told you, but there were always rumors about you and the nerds."

It was going to be that kind of day. "Nice."

Lily was quiet for a moment before leaning forward. "Are you sure you know Riley?"

"What does that mean?"

Lily's mouth firmed to a stubborn line, and for a second Ellie thought she might shake it off. Instead, she stood up. "It means I think he's lying to you. I think he's been doing it from the day he walked in here."

"Why would he lie? And about what?" She'd gotten the feeling Lily didn't like Riley, but she had no idea why. There was a wariness that rolled off Lily when Riley was around. It was one more worrisome thing she'd ignored in favor of reveling in her relationship with him.

"I don't know, but he's doing something. He had those accounting files before you asked him to look at them. It's why I asked Kyle to talk to Debra. I wanted to know if he'd requested the file and given a reason."

"How do you know he had the accounting files?"

"I broke into his office and found them," she said, seemingly unrepentant.

Ellie stared at her, her jaw agape. "You broke in? You can't do that. Lily, I know you have some out-of-the-box methods of keeping me informed, but I can't have that. The man is negotiating the contracts for my buyout. It makes sense he might want to see the accounting files. He has the right. Hell, he has the responsibility."

"It doesn't make sense," Lily replied stubbornly. "You're wrong about that. You're trying to excuse the behavior. The accounting had already been done. It means nothing to the buyout unless you're going to change your mind. It doesn't affect the price. The only thing that affects the buyout price is the stock price."

She was right about that, but Riley could have had other reasons. He was a thorough man. "If you had questions, you should have come to me."

"There's more. He's shady, Ellie. He's been down at R&D late at night. After even you've gone home. What would he be doing there? No one was working that night."

She could come up with a hundred reasons. Maybe he got lost. He was new at the company. Maybe he liked to walk around after he ate dinner. She often did that when she worked late. She stretched her legs. Maybe he was looking for someone.

Was she looking for excuses?

"I'll talk to him about it." It was really the only thing to do.

"Or you can let me talk to security. It takes a badge to get into R&D."

"He has upper-level clearance."

Lily sighed. "Then I can know what his movements have been. Security wouldn't send us routine reports, but they will have on file what parts of the building he's been in."

It seemed wrong not to trust the man she was sleeping with. "I'll talk to him first."

"And tip him off?"

"You're being paranoid." And very likely she was, too. Steven wanted his money. The buyout couldn't happen until the board meeting, but he wanted the cash now, so he was applying pressure. She could handle it. So what if someone called her a whore? She couldn't stop them. It was something every woman who ran a company had to deal with. Her life would be picked apart and found wanting, and she had to toughen up or get out of the game.

"Please let me talk to security," Lily begged.

"I'm going to ask you a stupid question. Why do you need my permission now? You certainly didn't when you broke into Riley's office."

"You care about him. I care about you. I don't want you to hate me at the end of this, but my every instinct tells me he's bad news. I broke into his office because I needed some proof. Now I don't want to strain our friendship by moving on without you. If you tell me no, I'll stop."

"No." She was going to be an adult about this and ask him.

Lily nodded. "All right, but I want you to know that when all this falls down around you, I'm going to be by your side. I'm going to be your friend. I won't tell you I told you so."

She turned and walked out.

Ellie stared down at the paper and told herself Lily was wrong.

She had to be.

Something was going really fucking wrong. Riley paced as he listened to the phone ring. Three, four times, and then an electronic voice explained the caller he was attempting to contact was not available.

He damn near threw the phone to the ground.

Bran. Bran would pick up. He pressed the button to get his younger brother on the line and was immediately rewarded.

"Hey, you need to stay calm."

Really? "What the fuck is going on and why am I out of the loop? I want to know why Drew used those reports without telling me. Those were our insurance policy if we couldn't get the goods on Castalano."

If they couldn't find a way to imprison the asshole for the money they were sure he'd embezzled, they'd use their doomsday option. They'd tank StratCast and force the bastard to retire with nothing. Or he'd stay at the company and they'd have another shot at him.

But this wasn't supposed to happen. His gut knotted when he remembered the look in Ellie's eyes as she'd read that article. If he could call it that. It was a smear piece, meant to knock her down. He didn't care if Drew had hired the shithead. He was going to make that ass pay.

"The buyout is taking place in a couple of weeks. We're out of time if we want to force the stock down." There was a pause and he was certain Bran was talking to someone. Likely Hatch or Drew, the coward who didn't have the balls to have this discussion himself.

"Put him on the phone." Riley bit every word out like it was a bullet.

"Drew's not here. He's out with Case, checking on something. That accounting chick called, and Case and Drew left like someplace was on fire. I don't even know what the hell is going on. Hang on. Mia's here."

Mia's voice came over the line. "Riley? I think something's going on and so does Case. I tracked Castalano myself the other day. He's been going to doctors' offices, but I don't think he's sick. He was seeing a dermatologist."

"Skin cancer?"

"I don't think so. I think he's planning some work. I talked to the receptionist, and she said he was looking for a good plastic surgeon."

Shit. He was planning on running. "He's going to take off with whatever he can get his hands on."

"I think Case is trying to get eyes on the man right now," Mia said.

"Why did he need Drew to do that?" It was inconvenient since he really wanted to yell at his brother right this instant. He could have done a lot without throwing Ellie under the bus like that.

"I don't know," Mia admitted, exasperation in her voice. "I'm upset, too. I've been trying to get that dick reporter I hired on the phone ever since the paper came out. That is not the story I paid him to report. He was supposed to talk about the coolant system failing the trials and nothing else. That was all we needed for the stock to dive. Then Ellie could have proven the system is still working a few weeks from now, and Castalano would get nothing but a trip to a well-deserved prison cell. He's still embezzling from the company."

"I've given you enough time to prove it. There shouldn't have been a need for this." It had been his only frustration for the past week and a half.

"Apparently the shell companies were hard to track down and now we have to find actual proof. That's what Case and Drew are doing. They said there was some more paperwork somewhere and they found the last company. I don't know. Case's phone is going to voice mail. Hang tight. It's going to be fine. I'm sorry Ellie has to go through this, but once we have the proof that Castalano's been skimming, the company will be hers, free and clear. Well, not free, but cheaper than she thought. This is going to be a good thing, Riley."

Because according to the partnership agreement she signed when she came into her father's stock, if either party was found no longer able to do their duties, the stock would be purchased within the month by the reliable partner. If no partner could be found, it was bought by the company and absorbed.

Ellie had the money ready to go. Despite the news story, she would be the only real choice to keep the company afloat. After she proved that her cornerstone project was running smoothly, she would be settled in as the chief executive and life would go on.

She didn't have to know. She never had to find out the part he'd played.

He had to weather this storm with her, and then he could quietly resign from 4L and be with her. He would be out of the revenge business. He'd have done his part and Patricia Cain could rot for all he cared.

Ellie mattered. Being with Ellie was more meaningful than anything else he could do.

For a second he was transported back, the memory of his father so fresh and keen in his mind it felt like reality. He'd been eight or nine and rushing into his father's office with a completed report he'd been assigned at school. He'd shoved it at his father, proud as he could be. His father had hauled him onto his lap. Though he'd tried to explain that he was too old for hugs and kisses, his dad never let up. And honestly, he'd still liked it. He wished his mom hadn't listened.

"What do you want to be when you grow up? That was your report?" his father had asked.

"Like you. I want to write codes and be smart."

His father had put a hand on his head. "Wrong answer, son. There's only one answer to that question, and I'm going to tell you what it is. This is the secret to life, Riley. When someone asks you what you want to be when you grow up, you tell them this."

He leaned in, ready to hear this magical secret. "What?"

"Happy. You want to be happy." His father had kissed his forehead and started a tickle war.

He wanted to be happy with Ellie. For the first time in his life he understood what his father would have wanted for him. For them all.

Happiness.

"Mia, I don't want Ellie to find out why I was really here."

There was a pause on the line. "That could be hard. How are you going to explain Drew?"

He would work through it. "I'll tell her I don't normally talk about the fact that my brother is one of the world's most successful software executives. She's only met him once. I can easily explain that away. I'm going to stay here with her and get StratCast on its feet again."

"I'm happy to hear that. I like her, Riley. Drew might be a harder sell."

"Don't worry about it." Bran's voice suddenly came over the line. "I'll handle big brother. He'll come around. I'm glad you're going to help her. It didn't feel right hurting that lady."

Bran was ever the gentleman. Even when it came to revenge.

There was a knock on his door. He glanced out. Ellie was standing there. "I've got to go. Call me when you know something. We have to take Castalano down and then make this right for Ellie."

"Will do," Mia replied, and he could practically hear her smiling.

His siblings were going to give him hell. He would never hear the end of it, and that was all right.

He was going to marry Ellie. Not tomorrow. He would have to work her gently toward it, but he would get a ring on that woman's finger eventually.

She would never know how they'd started out. He would leave her the illusion that it had all been smooth sailing from the moment he saw her.

He hung up the phone and went to open the door. As she walked in, he closed the blinds and locked the door behind her.

He'd made the decision to be an optimist. "Are you all right?"

She turned and gave him a tight smile. "I think so. I did a turn around the building. Everyone's on edge. Apparently the stock is already taking a hit. I've got PR working on a statement."

"I can have someone from the *Times* here in an hour." Mia had a vast network of resources that didn't include the motherfucker he was going to beat half to death. He hadn't gotten to the portion of the talk where he explained to Mia that whoever she'd hired to write that story should go into hiding.

Ellie nodded. "That's good."

She looked so tense. He couldn't blame her, but he also couldn't let her stand there looking so damn alone in the world. He reached out and pulled her close. "Baby, this is going to be all right."

"There's going to be talk that I did this myself. That I did this in order to buy Steven's stock cheap."

He put a hand in her hair, stroking her. "We'll get through it. If we need to hold off on the buyout, we'll do it."

As long as Castalano didn't get his hands on the money, it was all right. The longer the man was deprived of funds, the more mistakes he would make. They would catch him. He would be destitute or in jail and that would be justice. It would have to do because he was out.

She was stiff in his arms. "I don't think Steven is going to let us hold out."

"He has to. He won't want to take the offer as it is. He'll need to wait until the stock stabilizes, and then we can move forward exactly like before." With the exception of the fact that the bastard needed the cash and he would take it from the company, and Riley intended to be right there to catch him.

"Riley, I have to ask you something."

"Anything." He would get her through the next few weeks. He would stay right by her side. He would do whatever Drew needed as long as it didn't harm Ellie again. She'd been through enough.

"Did you request files from accounting?"

He went still. Why was she asking that? There was no way she could know he'd gotten those files weeks ago. And yet he had the sudden instinct that this would be a good time to tell some partial truth. He hadn't exactly requested them. He'd liberated the fuckers. "Of course I did. Is there a problem? I'm trying to learn every part of this company. I'm not effective if I'm in the dark. I got those files back when I first joined the company. Not that I understood everything, as obviously proven since I had to hire a forensic accountant. What's going on?"

She looked up at him. "Is there any reason you would go to R&D late at night?"

Shit and shit. "I've gone looking for you a couple of times when you weren't in your office. I got lost once and found myself there. Usually some of the guys are down there. I thought they could help me out, but it was empty."

It was time for a little acting. He hated it, but if he was going to save this, he needed to figure out what was going on. He pulled away, staring down at her. "What's with the third degree, Ellie?"

She seemed uncertain for a moment. "Everything is happening so fast. I'm not sure what's going on, but I feel like it's something I don't understand. I feel like some trap is closing around me."

"And you think I'm doing this?" He feigned indignation. "You think I'm trying to do . . . what? What am I trying to do to you?"

She looked away but not before he saw a sheen of tears in her eyes. Damn it. This wasn't what he wanted.

"I don't know."

He moved in behind her. "Ellie, this isn't the time to fight. Baby, I'm trying to figure out what's happening. I'm trying to find a solution. Please don't fight me, too. I know this is difficult. It's not going the way you thought it would, but you have to put your faith in someone. I want that person to be me."

Her hands came up, cupping his face, and she looked deeply into his eyes. "You mean that, don't you? You want to help me."

No lies here. Not even a tiny fib. "Yes. I told you. I'm crazy about you. There's nothing I want to do more than help you. I fully intend to plant my fist in that reporter's face. Or my loafer up his ass. Whichever comes first."

She sighed and moved into his arms. "I don't know what to do."

At least she was clinging to him. "We'll figure it out."

"I know I should be strong, but I hate the fact that everyone out there is speculating about us. They all think I'm some kind of a slut."

He felt his whole body stiffen. "The first person who says anything like that around me will get fired, and I will personally walk their asses out and ensure they never work again."

She sniffled. "You can't do that. I wish it was different. I'm not going to let it stop me, but I hate the fact that they're talking about us."

"We could stop a lot of the talk."

"I don't see how."

"We could get married." Yeah, he'd planned on waiting to say those words.

She stepped back. "What?"

He put a hand up. "I'm just saying, they would stop talking about us if we were boring married people."

"We've only known each other for a few weeks."

"People have married in less." He wasn't sure why he was pushing it. "It would change the story. Turn something negative into a positive."

"Riley, we can't get married for positive press."

"Then we should do it for the sex."

She rolled her eyes, but she had that half smile that told him she was amused. "We do fine with that on our own. Stop teasing me. We need to go to PR and see what they've come up with."

She was still so tense, so wound up. He wanted to help her forget for a few moments. Selfishly, he needed to be close to her. Those questions she'd asked scared the shit out of him. Where had they come from?

How did she know about the accounting files he'd pulled? About his late-night trip to R&D?

He slid his hand around hers. It was time to pull her close again, to reinforce the bond he'd been strengthening with her.

"Ellie, let me kiss you." When he kissed her he could forget about everything. When they were intimate, there was no deeper play, no con going on. There was only him and her, and it felt better than anything had in his life.

Happy. He felt happy when she was close.

She softened, moving into the cradle of his arms. "I'm sorry about the interrogation. It's been a stressful day."

He kissed her lightly. "I know. It's going to get worse, but I'm here with you. Anything you need from me, you ask."

"Kiss me again." Her eyes took on that dreamy look he loved. She looked at him like he was some kind of magician performing acts of wonder.

She was the amazing one. If she had any idea how much she'd changed his life . . .

He leaned over, brushing against her lips. There was time to show her how he felt. He couldn't say it. He might never be able to say it, but he could show her how much she meant to him.

He held her still for his kiss, his tongue sliding and playing with hers. His body heated.

She pulled away slightly, her eyes glazed over. "Riley, we don't have time for this."

Didn't they? "Just for a second."

He kissed her again, his hands sinking into her hair. She'd worn it partially up, but he could thread his fingers through the length at the back. The kiss went a little wild as she rubbed her body against his and her hands started to explore.

She wasn't shy with him anymore. She touched him when she wanted, where she wanted. He loved it. His body was her playground and the thought of having a few moments with her made his cock hard.

She backed up, pulling him with her. "Be quick. We really do need to get down to PR, but now I won't be able to think about anything except you."

"Same here, baby." He tugged up her skirt as they backed toward his desk. It was the perfect height.

He wouldn't think about anything else until he'd had her again. She clouded his brain with lust, but it was a sweet feeling. The lust he'd felt before had been about getting off, a pure physical need. It meant something different with Ellie. It was communication and connection with her.

Everything meant more with her.

He felt the warmth of her skin under his palms and wished they had the time to get naked.

She shook her head as though she could read his thoughts. "Quickie now. Naked time later. Later on, we can go back to my place and I swear we'll get undressed and not see clothes again until tomorrow. This is just a taste. I'm going to need a full four-course meal tonight, mister."

He hooked his thumbs under her undies and dragged them down her legs, kneeling down to help her out of them. He leaned in close so he could smell her arousal. It was the sweetest scent in the world to him. "I am ready, willing, and able to take care of your every need."

She smiled down at him as she slid her skirt up and hopped on his desk. Her legs spread, giving him a place. "I know you do, Counselor. You're very adept at your job."

A thrill went through him. He wanted to chase her around his desk and play boss and secretary. He was a little afraid he would end up being the secretary in that scenario. His girl had backbone and liked to be in charge. He loved the push and pull of their relationship.

When he stood, she was right there, her hands coming out to find the buckle of his belt.

"How do you do this to me?" She unbuttoned his slacks and slid her hand under the waistband of his boxers. "I should be in my office dealing with a hundred and one problems."

He let his slacks slide to the floor as she gripped his cock. "The other problems will wait. I have an issue that requires your full attention, Madam Executive. Only you can solve this particular problem."

She licked her lips as she looked down at the cock in her hand. "I better be the only one."

She was teasing, but he needed her to understand. He caught her face and forced her to look up at him.

"You're the only one, Ellie. The only one I want. I worry I won't ever want anyone the way I want you."

Her lips curled up. "That's good because I only want you, too. Take me so I can think again."

He moved into the cradle of her thighs, shoving his boxers down. She wasn't joking about wanting him. The minute his cock touched her pussy he could tell she was wet and ready to take him. Her response to him always blew his damn mind, and the fact that he could fuck her without anything between them had become his reason for living. She couldn't think? The minute she entered a room his eyes were on her, his mind running through all the ways he could get his hands on her. He wanted her sitting in his lap during meetings or holding his hand. Anything to touch her, to know she was with him.

He'd become obsessed.

He lined his cock up and pressed in.

"I love the way that feels." She leaned back, giving him a better angle of entry. "I don't think I'll ever get used to it."

He gripped her hips and let her heat suffuse him. He was the one who couldn't get used to it. Her legs wrapped around him. "I love fucking you on my desk. It makes working the rest of the afternoon so much more enjoyable."

She sighed and bit her bottom lip. "Why?"

"Because I'll be able to smell you all damn afternoon and think about you like this."

A chuckle came from the back of her throat, a deeply sexy sound. "Dear God, we won't be having any meetings in here for the rest of the day. It would start more talk."

He thrust in hard and fast. It didn't take much to get him going. Her pussy was so tight around him, her body clinging to his. "Let them talk. It doesn't matter. All that matters is this."

He leaned over and kissed her, his cock doing its work. He could feel her nails biting into him through the thin material of his shirt. He loved how crazy she went when they fucked.

Made love.

Stupid phrase, but he was making love to her. He wouldn't make it into something less. She was the one, and he was going to do his best to make sure she was always satisfied.

Her head fell back and she held on as she came. He fucked her hard, letting go of everything except the feel of her clamping down on him. He groaned as the pleasure took him, jetting into her, giving her everything he had.

He drew her close as he came down from the high.

"Maybe I won't be screaming at our PR people," she said with a lazy smile.

They would both be in infinitely better moods now. "I'll go down with you. I'm going to be by your side all day. Let them talk. Let them know we're a team and they can't bust us up."

She nodded, holding on to him a little tighter. "I'm going to have to go through the rest of the day commando-style. I can't put those things back on. Thank God we have private bathrooms. Kiss me so I can go clean up."

He pressed a sweet kiss to her and stepped back. He was sure he looked like an idiot with his pants around his ankles, but he couldn't work up the will to care. He watched her walk into his private bathroom, already plotting how and when he could have her again.

He straightened up, his brain still pleasantly fuzzy when he heard the knock on the door.

That sobered him up. He straightened out his clothes, hoping he wasn't too wrinkled, and managed to buckle his belt. He grabbed Ellie's undies and shoved them in his pants pocket before glancing around. Everything looked in order.

He opened the door.

Lily was standing there, a frown on her face.

"You and Ellie are needed in the boardroom. Castalano called an emergency meeting." She leaned in. "I swear to God I will rip your balls off if you've gotten her in some kind of trouble."

He forced himself to breathe because he had the sudden thought that they were all in trouble.

Eight

Ellie walked beside Lily, Riley on her other side.

As they walked down the hall, she could feel eyes on her. It looked like the employees of StratCast could feel the tension in the air. Ellie schooled her expression and smiled brightly, nodding as she walked past.

She was going to have to gather them all together and have a talk. The last thing she needed was the troops getting anxious. They would be worried, too. They might not have millions of dollars in stock, but many of her employees had invested and some got stock as incentives. They depended on it for their retirement since her father and Castalano hadn't seen fit to give out bonuses or match 401(k)s.

That would change when she took over. She intended to have employees heavily invested in StratCast's future. It was one thing she and Riley saw eye to eye on. An employee who made more money when the company succeeded was an employee who worked harder. They had to have skin in the game or it was simply another job and not a commitment.

"Lily, put together a company-wide meeting for three thirty." She wanted them to go home with their worries eased.

Lily nodded. "I think that's a good idea. People are scared. I think they're more scared now that Steven's dragged board members in."

"Any ideas about what he's planning?" Ellie asked.

Lily shook her head as they made their way toward the board-room. "No idea. I was making a few calls and Castalano's admin walked up with a shit-eating grin on her face and told me I better have you and Lover Boy here in the boardroom asap."

"Lily," she ground out.

Lily waved her off. "Sorry. Everyone knows what you're doing when he closes the blinds and locks the door in the middle of the day. And you suddenly don't have panty lines. I've told you time and time again to wear a damn thong."

She hated thongs. Could everyone really tell she'd recently had a mind-blowing orgasm? She squared her shoulders because she wasn't about to apologize for that.

"You look perfectly respectable," Riley murmured. "I wish I had a couple of minutes to figure out what this is about."

He'd argued that they should take their time, figure out what Casta-lano wanted before they walked in. She was sick of waiting and game playing. She wanted to get through this so she could deal with the fallout. If she was about to get raked over the coals because of that ar-ticle and the problems with the coolant trials, she would rather it hap-pened sooner than later. Worrying about it wouldn't help anything.

"It's fine. They're pissed and think I mishandled the situation. They probably don't understand that the new trials are going to prove that everything is proceeding exactly the way it should. I'll explain it and we'll all move on so much faster. I can set up a new trial this afternoon if that helps."

Confidence was required in situations like these. Never let them see you sweat. It was one of the few helpful things her father had taught her.

Lily stood back, frowning. "I want to know everything the minute you get out. I'm going to talk to some of the other admins. I swear if

I find out they've been holding out on me, I'll be dealing with a couple of those women myself."

Ellie glanced up at Riley. She wished she could hold his hand, but she had to look like the toughest bitch in the room. And tough bitches didn't hold hands with their boyfriends in the middle of board meetings.

She pushed through the doors and had to stop herself from gaping.

Steven Castalano was in a three-piece suit, sitting at the head of the table. He looked every inch the elder captain of industry. She hadn't seen him looking so strong and put together in two years. Since her father had passed and it was decided she would buy Castalano out, he'd taken to dressing for the golf course, not the boardroom. He'd become almost docile in the way he handled things right up until the blackmail attempt.

He stared out at her in a way she'd never seen him before. Cold. Calculating. Ruthless.

What the hell was happening?

"Kind of you to join us, Ms. Stratton, Mr. Lang." He gestured to the two seats he'd left for them. They were off to the side, a deliberate insult to her place in the company. She should be at the head of the table or in a place of power.

Unfortunately, to get there, she would have to evict her partner or the elderly board member at his side, which would make her look either weak or nasty. Her position was always a delicate balance. Unlike her male counterparts, she was judged for social graces as well as her business acumen. Castalano knew that, and it looked like he was placing her in an untenable position.

"Please, Mr. Garner, don't get up," she said, even though the man had made no move to stand. "I can sit here. I'm sure I can still make myself heard from this seat."

Riley held the chair out for her. "As this isn't a formal meeting, I don't think it matters where you sit, Ms. Stratton."

Garner had flushed. If they used her femininity against her, she could call them out for not being gentlemen. Castalano merely smiled, his eyes watching them as she settled in and Riley took the seat beside her.

"I'd like to know what's going on." She looked around and recognized the six most important members of her board. They didn't form the majority of the shareholders, but they came damn close. An enormous amount of StratCast stock was currently sitting in the room, looking at her with judgmental eyes.

"I would as well." Riley was looking around, obviously seeing the same thing she was seeing. "There isn't a quorum here. There can't be a vote. And I don't know who those two are."

He gestured toward the two people she didn't recognize. A man and a woman sitting across the table and to her left. She didn't have time to truly think about them however as Steven was pressing on.

Castalano sat back. "I'll get to that in a moment. I don't need a quorum. I only called in some longtime board members because they were very disturbed by the turn of events around the company lately."

So this was a dressing-down and very likely the start of a nasty fight. There were fifteen board members. Six of them were sitting in this room. These were the men on Castalano's side. Along with Castalano's own vote, he had seven. That left her and Riley, and four others she was sure were on her side. That was likely the reason they weren't here. That left two votes unaccounted for—a woman who had bought Patricia Cain's stock in the company and whoever had purchased her sister's stock. Riley was looking into that. He'd put a call in to the company that had bought it but hadn't gotten a call back yet. She needed to feel out the new investor. Whoever it was would have a voting share. She needed to get to that person before Castalano could.

This was likely Castalano's way of showing her he still had the muscle in this world.

"I understand we've had a setback with the reports about the coolant system's issues. I'm very happy to tell you that those reports are false and I've got someone looking into them right now." She'd set a couple of her best managers on it early this week. They would figure out who had leaked the reports on the faulty systems.

"I've discovered who leaked those reports." Castalano sat back, looking over the table.

"Excellent. I'd love to hear who it was." If he'd done the job, she would thank him profusely. It would have been better had she been the one to take care of things, but she would make the best of it.

Riley was on his phone, texting someone. "And if you'll wait a moment or two, we can have the new reports up here. I'll bring the head designer in to explain what went wrong and how it has no meaning at all to where the project is right now. Which is on time and under budget."

It was a perfect solution. She had them here. She could get her best guys to truly explain the situation.

"I think we can skip the scientific drivel." Steven nodded to his admin, who was standing in the back with a stack of file folders in her hands. "Jane, if you will. Gentlemen and Ms. Stratton, as you know, an article came out today questioning leadership here at StratCast and calling our cornerstone project an abject failure."

A low grumble went through the room as Jane began to pass out copies of the article. They'd worked very quickly to get everything together. Steven must have been desperate to make her look bad.

Had she made a mistake in not paying him off? She'd gone back and forth but finally decided that she'd brought Riley in for a reason. She was paying him handsomely and, given their relationship, he wouldn't steer her the wrong way. After all, he had a stake in StratCast as well.

"Do you expect me to answer the charges one by one or to simply give you all my opinion of this guy's hatchet job? I apparently pissed him off at some point in time." She was trying to figure out who the extra people were.

One man, one woman. Both in suits. Both very buttoned up, but not in a corporate way. They looked somehow tougher than executives.

Neither one looked down at the reports. Every now and then they spoke to each other or looked at their phones.

Riley was staring at them, but she didn't think it was a good plan to lean over and have a private conversation.

"I have to question why you thought it was a good idea to talk to reporters when we were having trouble with a product as important as the coolant system," Steven said pointedly.

Deep breath. It wouldn't do to show how angry she was with the man who was supposed to be her partner. "That's the point. We're not actually having problems with the coolant system. Those reports were based on miscalibrated machines. I got the go-ahead from PR. I would never have talked to anyone from the press without clearing it with public relations. The story was supposed to be about me taking the reins as one of the few female executives in telecom. It was never supposed to be about the coolant project. It is not my fault the reporter had an axe to grind."

"Did he have an axe to grind or did he ask very pertinent questions?" Castalano asked.

"What is that supposed to mean?" Riley sat up straight beside her, his irritation obvious.

Castalano shook his head. "I'm not talking to you. I'm talking to Ms. Stratton. She is the one whose decision making is in question here. You're simply one of those decisions that I call into question."

Riley's eyes narrowed. "I'm sure you wish she'd stayed with a lawyer you could buy off. Did you get upset that I refused to allow her to sign away the coolant system?"

Castalano sat back, obviously unmoved. "I believe you're the one who added that clause to the contract in an effort to make me look bad. You're the one who has tried time and time again to discredit me with Ms. Stratton."

She was so aware of the fact that they were doing the one thing she knew they shouldn't—air their dirty laundry in public. Every eye was on her.

Riley leaned forward. "I've done my best to protect her from you."

This was the last thing she needed. Riley needed to be her lawyer, not her lover. "Steven, why are we here and not talking about this in private?"

"We're here because the stock has already dropped twenty percent."

Her stomach clenched. Twenty percent? It had only been a few hours. How low would it go before the end of the day? Before she could get those corrected reports out? Oftentimes the media pre-ferred to report bad news over good. It could be days before the word spread. "You know as well as I do the stock will come back up once the real reports get out."

"That will take time." Her partner stared right at her, accusation in his eyes.

Where was this coming from? He'd never once looked at her like that.

"We have time. We're a few years away from actually manufactur-ing. A few weeks means nothing."

He nodded regally. "Yes, you're right about that. I've brought some worried members of our board in to reassure them that our stock won't stay down for very long. The company will survive this unfor-tunate incident, and it will be all the stronger for flushing out the employees who caused the problems."

Shit. Had he figured out who had messed up the calibrations on the machines? That had been her job. She handled R&D. Always. It was her baby. Even when her father had been in control, he'd ceded R&D to her.

She wasn't about to let go of her place. "I think we need to talk about any possible staff changes, and we don't need to do that in front of the board. I'm sure they have much more important things to do with their time. I assure you all that we can handle this situation. The stock will come back up in a few weeks. It's unfortunate, but I will get the correct information out as soon as possible. My PR people are contacting the big financial networks and informing them of the issues we're having. We'll show them the correct reports, perhaps invite a couple of trusted reporters to witness our tests. This is going to pass, and we'll be stronger for it."

"We still have the issue of your image and poor decision-making process," Castalano explained.

"You can't possibly believe what that article said. Steven, you've known me all of my life. I'm certainly not the woman portrayed in that article."

"Are you having an affair with Riley Lang?"

Riley shook his head. "That's absolutely none of your business."

She wasn't hiding behind half-truths. "*Affair* is a ridiculous word to use. Do I have a personal relationship with Mr. Lang? Yes. Does it affect my decision-making process? No. I still do what's best for this company, and as a fellow stockholder, so does Mr. Lang. This isn't a case of having a relationship with someone working against us. It also isn't the first time an executive has had a serious relationship with a coworker. I'd rather not list them all, but it's happened many times. There's nothing in the company codes about fraternization."

"That's something we intend to fix," Garner said righteously. He slapped at the table. "You young people think you can sleep with anyone at any time. By God, when I was working here, we were businessmen. What would your father think?"

"My father didn't give a crap about my personal life and neither should any of you. Let's not be hypocritical, Bill. We all know about the affair you had with your secretary when you worked here." If they wanted to play hardball, she could throw them a few sliders. "And you, Steven. Should I get into your relationship with the head of HR a few years back? You were married at the time. I'm not married and who I sleep with is my own business."

"Not when you use him to do your dirty work," Castalano said.

"He's my lawyer. Doing my dirty work is his job," she shot back.

"Is devaluing the stock so you can buy me out at a bargain-basement price his job, Ms. Stratton?" Steven's question dropped and the whole room went silent.

He was really going to play this for everything it's worth. "Steven, I suggest we delay the buyout. Obviously it's not in your best interest for me to buy you out now. We wait until the price comes back up. I know you're eager to start your retirement, but I'm not trying to cheat you."

Riley had gone still beside her. "I don't like the accusations you're making, Castalano."

"Then you really won't like this." He nodded to his assistant, who turned on her laptop. With a few keystrokes, she threw the feed up onto the media screen.

Ellie was confused. Had he planned a multimedia campaign to humiliate her? She felt her skin heat. If someone had caught them getting physical and put it on tape, she was going to sue the shit out of them.

The camera came into focus. She leaned in, trying to figure out exactly what she was seeing. It looked like someone had left the camera on their computer on. The shot was very narrow, but she could see the wide tables that they used in R&D. Everyone had a desk, but the middle of the "lab," as they called it, was a grouping of big tables with the testing engines on it along with the machines they used to measure the function of the coolant engine.

The lights were low, only every third one on, so it was likely late at night or early in the morning. The building was never dark, but the lights were on a timer to go to one-third power after eleven for con-servation's sake. That told her even the cleaning staff had gone home when this was taken.

"I want to know what's going on." Riley turned to Castalano.

"I think you know," came the smug reply. "This was taken over a week ago. The night before the testing was done."

"Before the tests that were improperly measured? Is this about the calibrations? Because I was told it was an intern mistake," Ellie said.

Steven's head shook. "There was no mistake, Eleanor. The only mistake that was made was that you thought I wouldn't find out. One of your interns left his camera on. He'd been using company equip-ment to video chat with his parents. He caught this. He likely would have gone to you, but he was well aware of your relationship by then and came to me instead."

"What does my relationship have to do with any of this?" But then she understood because a familiar figure moved into camera range.

Riley had his jacket off, shirtsleeves rolled up. He was obvi-ously unaware the camera was on him. He looked around and then a smile crossed his face as he found what he needed. He pulled out his phone and seemed to be speaking to someone. He picked up the first of the testing devices and popped off the back to get to the inside of the machine.

The whole room went cold.

"Ellie, I can explain."

She heard Riley, but she couldn't take her eyes off the screen. He seemed to be talking to someone. Likely he'd placed his phone on speaker. It was sitting on the table as he reworked the calibration machines. All three of them. He seemed very intent on what he was doing and he'd come prepared. When he needed a screwdriver to get inside the system, he pulled one out of his pocket.

He'd waited until everyone had gone home and then made his way down to the department and deliberately changed the calibrations so her tests would fail.

So she would fail.

A numbness wound through her system, like someone was pouring ice through her veins. It was good because that meant she couldn't feel the pain.

"Ellie, there's an explanation for all of this." Riley put a hand on her arm.

She very calmly pulled away. She wasn't going to make a further fool of herself over this man. He was playing some kind of game and she wasn't sure what it was. She only knew she'd lost.

She had to keep whatever dignity she had left intact. In a low monotone, she spoke to her former lover. "Mr. Lang, you're fired. I'll have security escort you out. You'll find there was a criminal clause in your contract. Had you managed to stay more than a year, I would be forced to purchase your stock at current value."

Riley turned her chair around. His face had gone tight. "Ellie, I need to talk to you."

She had very little left to say. "As that is not the case, your stock reverts back to me. I'll let you know if I decide to file criminal charges against you."

A low chuckle made her turn. Castalano applauded lightly. "Is that how you're playing it, then? He must not have been too good in bed if you're willing to throw him to the wolves at the first chance. As it happens, no criminal charges will be brought against Mr. Lang. You know that the press would be all over that kind of thing. It wouldn't look good. I'll let Mr. Lang go with the warning that he really should know his enemies from now on. I can't say the same for you, dear."

The door opened and suddenly there were two police officers standing there.

What the hell was going on? He'd just said he wasn't going to prosecute Riley, though he damn straight should have talked to her about that. That should be a decision between them, security, legal, and PR.

"Having security escort Riley out is enough. I scarcely think he's going to require a police escort." She turned to him, looking at Riley for the first time. "Or are you going to humiliate me further by causing a scene?"

His eyes were on Castalano. "Ellie, baby, I don't think this is about me. Whatever he's done, know that I'm going to get you out of this."

He was so serious it caused Ellie to look around. Everyone was looking directly at her. And the man and woman in business suits had stood up.

"Ms. Stratton, my name is Special Agent Charles Cooper. It is my duty to inform you that you are being placed under arrest," the gentleman said.

So this was what it felt like when a person was stuck in a dream, figured out it was a dream, and still couldn't wake up.

"Arrested for what?" It was ludicrous.

Castalano stood, buttoning his suit jacket. "We discovered how you and your father managed to embezzle ten million dollars. Did you think we wouldn't figure it out eventually? The holding companies were cleverly hidden, but they're all in your name. We can't find the actual money, but I suspect that's the bureau's job. You will also be charged with fraud for manipulating the company stock for personal gain."

This was a dream. It had to be. Nightmare, really. Except she felt really awake.

Riley's hand found hers and he leaned in close. "You hold your head up. I'm not letting you go down for this. I swear to God, Ellie, I will get you out of this."

For a second, she held on. She threaded her fingers through his because she so needed his warmth. The whole world seemed to have gone cold.

The words the officers were saying didn't quite process. She knew them. Anyone who watched television knew their rights. Miranda rights. She was being Mirandized because the FBI had decided she was the one who'd stolen from the company.

And they would book her for fraud as well. For attempting to manipulate the stock market because they had proof her right-hand man had screwed with those machines.

Had Riley been the one to give the press the reports? Had he been the one to tank StratCast stock?

There was a hand on her elbow, hauling her up. Her fingers slipped from his.

"Do you have to do that? She's going with you willingly." Riley's voice sounded like it was coming from far away. It was muffled by a roaring sound in her ears.

She felt like a rag doll. She was there, but she wasn't. This couldn't be happening to her. Her feet felt wobbly under her, but somehow she was upright and the police officer was pulling her hands behind her back, cold metal snapping against her skin.

"You're lucky we're not bringing you in, too," she heard the cop say.

"Eleanor, I'm sorry it's come to this."

She turned at the sound of Castalano's voice. He was standing there, a smug look on his face. He certainly didn't look sorry. He looked triumphant.

Why was he doing this to her? Why was he standing there in his thousand-dollar suit? All he'd wanted to do was retire.

Or had she been a fool all along? He'd never planned to do anything but this. She knew what her contract stated. She knew what would happen now. She would lose everything.

If something looks too good to be true, it always is. Always. She should have remembered that lesson from her father, too.

Riley had been too perfect for her because he'd never been here for her. She'd been a pawn in this game.

Steven Castalano's game.

"You son of a bitch," she said, finally figuring it out. "You never intended to let me buy you out. This was your play to get rid of me and take it all for yourself."

He shook his head. "Not at all. I was so looking forward to the golf course, my dear. Please escort her off the property. Let me know what you need to ensure she's prosecuted to the fullest extent of the law."

"Ellie, I'll be right behind you," Riley promised.

She looked at him. He'd been too beautiful. Too sexy. Too good. Too perfect. "Don't ever talk to me again."

It was almost a relief when they led her out. At least she wouldn't have to see him again.

Riley felt like the ceiling and the floor had flipped places. What the hell had happened? They were taking Ellie out in handcuffs. They were leading her to some goddamn detention cell like she was a criminal.

All around him people were shaking hands and encouraging each other that it was all for the best. That getting rid of Ellie solved their problems.

He turned on Castalano. What a fool he'd been. He'd fallen into a trap. How had that happened? He'd been the one laying the trap.

He didn't believe for a single second that Ellie was the one behind the embezzlement scheme. His gut told him there was no way Ellie was involved. His brain was still working though. When he really thought about it, they had zero proof it was Steven Castalano. They'd simply seen what they'd wanted to see. They'd known Castalano was a criminal and seen criminal activity and ascribed it to him.

If he had half a brain, he would look into the situation. He would withhold judgment until he had absolute proof that Ellie was innocent.

He didn't need a brain. He had a fucking heart and he knew beyond any shadow of a doubt that Ellie hadn't done this. He could walk into a room and find her knee-deep in cash and ask her where she'd gotten it. He would never question her integrity. He knew that woman inside and out, and she was rock solid.

It was sad that everyone around her was such a deceiving prick. Including himself.

His mind worked, seeing the con from the other side now that it had played out. Oh, that he'd had some foresight. It would have saved them all.

He stared at Castalano. "You did this so you could purchase Ellie's stock cheap."

Castalano sighed. "Gentlemen, I think I could use a moment with Mr. Lang. He doesn't understand how the world works and I need to explain a few things to him. If you wouldn't mind going to my office. I believe you'll find a very nice bottle of Scotch for us to work our way through this afternoon. My son is waiting there for all of you."

To celebrate his victory over sweet, smart, save-the-world Ellie. She had crazy ideas about justice and what was right and how the world should work.

The world had just taken a nice chunk out of her flesh.

He was supposed to be the one to protect her. He was supposed to be the white fucking knight who took all the hits so she never had to know how shitty the world really was. He'd failed her utterly. He was the reason her world had crumbled.

How could he have missed that camera? He'd been on the phone with Bran that night. He'd needed his brother to explain how to fuck with the calibration on the testing machines. He'd actually been talking about Ellie at the time. Like he wasn't messing with her company, her livelihood, her life. He'd been talking about how he'd had dinner with her and then sneaked back into the building to grab some contracts. He hadn't noticed the open laptop and camera.

All his fault. It was all coming down around them, and it was his fault. Everything—the plan to avenge their father, all of Ellie's hopes and dreams—they were dying because he'd been a dumb fuck.

Where would they take her? Which precinct? The feds had allowed the police to arrest her so she would go to a local jail. They often did that to give local authorities the arrest on their docket. They would likely question her and then move her to a federal facility.

They might leave her in a city jail until she'd made bail.

God, they were going to put Ellie in jail. Pure panic began to thrum through his system.

Castalano was going to try to put her in jail for years, and all so he could take the company from her.

"So this was all about a cheap stock buyout?" The door closed behind the men Castalano had brought in to witness Ellie's downfall. Riley would have run after her, but they wouldn't let him go with her. They likely wouldn't allow him anywhere near her.

Castalano smiled. "Oh, I think we both know it's more than that. You know, the funny thing is I thought I would only get her on the embezzlement charges."

She'd had nothing to do with those charges, but it brought into question some of Castalano's recent actions. "What the hell was the request for two million dollars about? You tried to blackmail her."

He couldn't go into why. He knew Castalano owed millions to a mobster, but he wasn't going to give up his cover at this point. He needed every advantage he had.

"What? Me? Why would I ask Ellie for two million? I was about to retire. She was going to buy me out. Now, had I gone to her in order to confront her about the embezzlement, I likely would have requested that she begin to make some restitution on her part. Twenty percent would have been an excellent start."

That told him everything he needed to know. That check would have sealed her fate if he hadn't. To the feds, it would have been an admission of guilt. To Castalano, it was a down payment.

"Holy shit, you intended to buy her out with her own fucking cash. You son of a bitch." They'd walked into one long setup. Castalano had never intended to retire. He'd played the elderly gentleman. Talked up his doctor's appointments. He'd done the rounds so everyone knew how happy he was to be leaving it all to the next generation.

He'd even had his son tip Ellie off to the accounting issues.

He hadn't had the money to buy her out. So he'd waited patiently, telling her they would get the deal done.

"And you put the clause in the contract," Riley surmised. "I should have seen it. I should have known no one would be that stupid."

Complexity. His brother-in-law had talked about it. Case had told him they were ignoring the fact that any situation they walked into was complex and fluid. He'd been so right. They'd been arrogant to think they could stalk in as the only predators in the game.

Castalano had that smile on his face. It made Riley want to cut it off his fucking body. "I don't know what you're talking about. I do know that the anger and confusion from it being there likely set us back by weeks. I feel for Ellie. I really do. I've known the girl all her life. In some ways she was like a daughter to me. If only it had simply been the issue of money, I would have bought her out and we could have moved on. I would have done that for her father's sake. Nasty bastard, but he was my partner. He couldn't have known she was taking all that money from the company."

"The embezzlement began when she was seventeen. Are you telling me she formed holding companies and managed to steal from StratCast without being caught when she was a teenaged intern?" The idea was ridiculous.

"Well, everyone knows Ellie was a business prodigy. She was practically running R&D in high school. Certainly she had some people on the inside. If we find out who they are, we'll send them to jail as well. It was really your perfidy that did her in. I was willing to settle for the stock at a reasonable price."

"You were going to force her to pay you so she could stay out of jail." It was so obvious now.

"Now I'll get both. You gave me the means to make a true power play. Do you have any idea how long I've waited to take true control of my company?" He gestured to the door where two uniformed guards were now standing. "I believe your escort is here, Mr. Lang."

"I am not going to let you get away with this. You took that money." And Castalano's company was built on his father's murder. He wasn't going to get away with that, either.

"That is not what the evidence proves." Castalano was cool as a cucumber. "It clearly proves that Ellie was behind everything."

"You faked it. I'll prove that and I swear when I'm done, you'll be the one left with nothing." He felt a beefy hand wrap around his elbow.

They weren't leaving anything to chance. The other guard was right beside him.

"We need you to leave now, Mr. Lang," a deep, gruff voice said. "Don't make us call the police back."

"They'll be back here one day. Count on it." He couldn't take his eyes off Castalano. The snake.

The guard to his right pulled on his arm and he found himself being hauled out of the conference room.

"I will sue every single one of you." He knew it was a douchebag lawyer thing to say, but at that moment, he meant it. He would burn this place down. He would cover it in kerosene and light the match to make them pay for what they'd done to Ellie.

He would never forget the blank look on her face when she'd looked at him.

Don't ever talk to me again.

He had so much work to do. He let them lead him out because his mind was whirling.

She had to feel so alone. They would be putting her in a squad car. It would have been kinder to have the feds arrest her. They would have likely given her some dignity. The fact that they'd allowed the police to take her into custody meant they thought she was a big fish. They were allowing the locals to take credit. They would eventually move her to a federal facility, or they might allow a local judge to oversee her bail hearing.

He had to get her out as soon as possible. He had to get her out now.

His whole body felt tight. His throat had practically closed and he couldn't see straight as they led him down the hall.

It didn't look like a single person was left in a cubicle. They were all up on their feet, all talking and a few women crying. The tension was palpable. They would be worried about their jobs, their futures.

Yeah, he'd done that, too.

He should have been the one being walked out in handcuffs. They'd all watched her humiliation.

"You bastard."

He looked around, expecting to see Ellie. They were in front of his office somehow. How had he gotten here?

Lily was standing there, tears flowing down her cheeks.

Lily, who hated him. Lily, who had figured him out way before Ellie had.

He looked up at his escort. "May I grab my things?"

The larger of the guards nodded. "But you keep that door open."

He gestured for Lily to join him. He wasn't surprised when she practically ran into the office. She was begging for a moment alone with him. She likely wanted to flay him alive.

He didn't have time for that.

Lily looked back at the guards. "Please, Carl. Please let me have a minute alone with him. For Ellie's sake."

The shorter of the guards looked up at Carl. "Do you honestly believe Ms. Stratton stole from the company?"

"No," Carl replied, his eyes on Riley. "But I believe that motherfucker is the reason she's in trouble."

So everyone loved him.

Lily didn't give him a chance to defend himself. She softened and turned big eyes on Carl. "Please. We're the only chance she has. She made sure you got paid paternity leave when your wife and baby were so sick after the birth."

Carl held up a hand. "Two minutes."

He would take it. Riley slammed the door and turned on her. "Stay quiet. We have two minutes before they shove me out the door. I need you to find out everything you can. Work whatever magic you have and call me."

"I would rather rip your balls straight off your body and feed them to my cat. How could you? How could you hurt her like that?"

He went to his desk and grabbed what he needed. He'd kept most of his information on a single thumb drive, and then there was his personal laptop. He left the company one behind. All the good information they'd gotten had come from hacking anyway, with the exception of that accounting info that he'd copied a long time ago. His cell was trilling, but he didn't have time to answer it.

"I know you hate me, but I'm the only one who can save Ellie right now. Unless you have a multibillion-dollar corporation backing you."

Lily frowned, crossing her arms over her chest. "Why would I believe a word you say at this point? I saw that tape. All the admins have, you bastard. They kept it from me until a few minutes ago."

And she likely hated that fact. Lily liked being in a position of power and she loved Ellie. He had to use that because she might be the only ally he had left.

"I love her." He said it. It didn't matter now how stupid he sounded.

Stupid? He loved Ellie Stratton. That wasn't stupid. That was everything. Yes, it made him vulnerable. Yes, it made him weak when it came to her. But he loved her. He would trade anything to make sure she was all right. He finally understood what that damn word meant. Love. It meant he would sacrifice himself for her. It meant it didn't matter that she never wanted to speak to him again. He loved her. He would do anything to save her.

Lily stopped, her eyes going wide. "Are you serious?"

So she understood. He moved to her, trying to show her how damn serious he was. "I love Ellie. I came here under false pretenses, but she's all that matters now. I will do anything to make sure she's safe."

Lily's jaw turned stubborn, tilting up. "Even if it means hurting yourself?"

Even if it meant giving up the revenge he'd dreamed of since he was a child. He finally saw the future his father had wanted for him and it didn't include hate—though he hated that fucker Castalano now more than ever. "I promise if I can trade myself for her, I will. I'll do anything. I love her more than my own life. More than anything."

Lily moved in, scooping up the files on his desk. "Take it all. I'll steal whatever I can before they walk me out. I have allies here, too. And Ellie is loved. If I can get the truth in the ears of the right people, we might still be able to sway things. I'll get on the phone to the board members who are close to Ellie. I swear if you're playing me, I'll find you and my cat will feast. Do you understand?"

Apparently, Lily's cat really had a taste for testicles. "Yes. Get as much information as you can. Try not to get walked out. Play dumb. You had no idea. You're shocked. You're a true StratCast girl. Throw us under a bus if you have to, but try to keep your job. We need eyes and ears here."

He needed something. How had it gone so wrong? How had he underestimated Castalano? Ten years. Castalano had been planning this for ten years. They'd known he was skimming, but they hadn't suspected he'd had a fall guy in place.

Fall girl. His girl.

God, she hated Riley. She hated him and he loved her.

He shoved it all aside. All that mattered was getting her out of lockup.

"She can't stay in jail." Lily handed him the file folders to stuff in his briefcase.

There was a knock on the door. "It's time to go."

They needed to move.

"I'll have her out in a few hours. As soon as I can. I'll call a defense lawyer as soon as I walk out the door."

"Maybe I should do that," Lily offered. "Ellie can afford it."

He needed Lily to understand. "She can't. They're freezing her assets as we speak. She has nothing. She won't be able to make her mortgage next month. Castalano will take everything from her."

Lily stifled a cry.

He put his hands on her shoulders. "I'm going to take care of her. Stay here. Be our eyes and ears. I will make them all pay."

She nodded.

He grabbed his briefcase and laptop and nodded as the door came open. "I'm ready. Lily, get the fuck out of here. I don't want to hear your bitching anymore."

Lily seemed to understand. "I hate you both. I can't believe you did this."

He strode out with his head held high. Until he saw Castalano. He stood in the hallway, watching everything.

The guard reached out and held Riley's arm. "It's time to go."

He was led past Castalano. Hatred welled. He wanted to stab the man through the heart and watch him bleed.

Castalano merely watched him, a smirk on his face. "Good-bye, Lang. You know, you have your mother's eyes."

Riley stopped, his whole body suddenly a live wire. What had he said?

But he was dragged to the door.

Castalano had played them all.

Nine

Ellie straightened her skirt as they walked her out of the holding cell. She'd been processed hours before and then left in a cell with five other women. She'd sat there, looking at her hands, fingers stained with ink because that tissue they'd given her didn't get rid of the residue left from her fingerprints being taken. She'd been booked, and that would follow her to her dying day. There would be a picture of her holding up a police sign with her name and number on it.

It would likely be in the news tomorrow since the bastard had reporters waiting on her as she'd been hauled out of the building.

The better to report on you, my dear. The better to send the stock price tanking...

"Your lawyer is here, Stratton," the dour-faced guard explained.

For the first time in hours she felt something. Anger. It hummed through her like a fire warming her icy blood. Her lawyer? Had he really come here? Did he think she was so stupid she would keep him on?

Or had he come to explain himself? She didn't need an explanation from him. She'd already figured it all out. The funny thing was he'd told her the first time they'd met. There was no real loyalty in the world that couldn't be bought. He'd been Castalano's man from the beginning. He'd been sent to seduce her and make her look like a fool. To give his boss the tools he needed to easily wrest the company from her because she was weak.

That was what her father had called her. Weak. Pathetic. If he'd had anyone else to leave his place to, he would have. She was a waste.

Maybe he had been right all those years.

"Tell him to go away."

The guard's brow rose. "Are you that stupid? You get one shot at talking to this guy and then you have to face that judge on your own. You really going to send his ass away? Because from where I'm standing, princess, you need all the help you can get."

She stared at the door she was supposed to walk through. "I didn't ask for my lawyer to come here. My lawyer is kind of the reason I am here."

The guard frowned. "Seriously? Because Henry Garrison is known for getting rich people out of jail. Not putting them in."

Henry Garrison? "Not Riley Lang?"

"Princess, I don't know who that is. I do know that the most expensive criminal defense attorney in Manhattan is sitting inside that room waiting for you and you're out here. Do you like bologna sandwiches that much?"

She didn't need any more prompting. Lily must have done it. Oh, she was so going to get a raise when they got out of this.

Because she was going to get out of this.

As she'd sat in her cell she'd realized she had two choices. She could give in and let that man take everything from her. She could be the weak-willed girl her father had always seen. Soft and too compassionate for her own good. She could likely give Steven what he wanted and pray she could cut a deal.

Or she could fight like hell and let the chips fall where they may. She could burn his house down around him.

She felt like lighting a match.

As for Riley, well, he really didn't matter anymore. He'd been a mistake. One she didn't intend to make twice.

She steeled herself and walked in.

Henry Garrison was a shockingly handsome man in a three-piece suit, his jet-black hair slicked back, with piercing blue eyes behind a set of designer glasses. He looked a little like Clark Kent.

She might need Superman.

"Ms. Stratton, my name is Henry Garrison. I've been hired to defend you against these charges." He held out a hand.

She looked down at hers. "I don't think you want to do that."

He reached over and took her hand. "I'm surprisingly resilient."

He was made-for-TV handsome and known as a shark who could get a murderer off even if he was found with a smoking gun in his hand and a body at his feet.

Lily had done well, but Ellie wasn't sure she would be able to afford him. She would have to sell the condo in Brooklyn. She would have to sell everything.

She sat down in front of him. "I know you probably hear this all the time, but I didn't do this."

He shrugged. "I don't care. My job is merely to represent you to the best of my ability. It doesn't matter if you did it or not, but don't ever tell me you did. It's best if we'll be entering a plea of not guilty that you continue to affirm your innocence."

This was the world she'd landed in. Or maybe it was the world she'd been in all along. It didn't matter that she was innocent. All that mattered was the game and winning it at all costs.

"When am I going to be arraigned?" While she'd sat in that cell, she'd made her decision. In the end, she was alone. She needed allies. As much as she loved Lily and needed her, she was going to require more firepower if she was going to engage in this war Castalano had started.

There was only one person she could go to, and he might take one look at her and tell her to get the fuck out.

Did he know the truth? Had he been as much Riley Lang's victim as she'd been?

No. The enemy was Steven Castalano. She had to stop thinking of Riley as anything but a weapon that had been used against her. He was meaningless.

She missed him. She missed his hand in hers, the way he would look at her and she would know that everything was going to be all right. The way he would smile right before he kissed her as though he was so happy to be close. His joy had fed hers.

He'd been very good at his job.

Her lawyer glanced down at his phone. "I've pulled a few strings and I'm getting you on the docket in the next two hours. The police are eager to get rid of you. They didn't think you would get the kind of press coverage you're getting."

"Everyone likes to see a failure." She'd been reduced to a train wreck. *Female executive can't keep her panties on or her hands out of the cookie jar.* She could read the headlines now.

"Unfortunately, that's only the beginning of the process. You understand these charges are serious. After the local judge releases you, you're not going home. You're going to be released to FBI custody and we'll appear before a federal judge in the morning. It's the best I can do. You're lucky, because most of the time this is at least a seventy-two-hour process."

She would have to spend the night here. "I don't even have my purse."

"You'll be given anything you require. I have the phone number for a Lily Gallo. I was told she'll bring your purse. My assistant will have some things waiting for you after the arraignment."

"What kind of bail are we looking at?" She probably didn't want to know.

"I'm not sure. Likely fairly high. With the press watching the case, the judge won't want to look weak on crime, and especially on a one-percenter."

She snorted. "Yes, I'm so wealthy. Everything I have was wrapped up in that stock and the liquid I was going to use to buy out my partner."

"The bad news is your bank accounts are frozen and will remain frozen until the trial is over."

"I don't understand."

Garrison's eyes bore through her. "You're being accused of skimming more than ten million from your company coffers. Everything you have is going to be frozen until such time as you're exonerated or found guilty. They won't allow you to spend what could be company funds."

"How am I supposed to live?"

"I'm sure arrangements will be made. I'll need to ask you a few questions, but we'll have time after I've gotten you out on bail."

"I can't make bail if I don't have money."

"As I said before, arrangements have already been made."

So he'd found a bail bondsman. God, she needed a bail bondsman.

She had no cash. She would likely have no home very soon since she wouldn't be allowed to sell her condo and she couldn't make the mortgage because she had no cash. She had no job and zero prospects for one.

Her trial could take years.

What was she going to do?

"Ms. Stratton?"

No parents. No boyfriend. For a moment, she'd really felt like everything had come together. She had him. Riley. She'd seen herself the way he'd seen her and she'd been beautiful.

"Ms. Stratton?"

Of all the things Steven had done to her, Riley had really been the cruelest. It all could have been achieved without him, really. Certainly without the seduction routine.

"Ellie?"

She shook her head. "Yes?"

"You're crying. Do you need some time?" He was holding out a small package of tissues. Likely he kept them in his briefcase for overly emotional clients.

She took it, pulling one out and drying her eyes. This wasn't going to help her. "No. What do you need from me? Besides money, which I apparently don't have any of."

He stopped for a moment. "My fee has been taken care of."

That sent a shiver through her. "By who? I thought my admin had called you."

"I was contacted by Riley Lang. I was given carte blanche when it comes to your defense and paid extra for dropping everything to, as he put it, get my expensive ass down here."

She shook her head. "Why would he do that?"

Garrison shrugged, the gesture oddly elegant. "I was under the impression the two of you were in a serious relationship. According to the articles I read on the way over, your relationship with Mr. Lang is part of the problems you're facing, though from what I understand, there was no code of conduct that forbade you from fraternizing."

"We're not in a relationship. He was working against me."

"Then why would he have hired me?"

She remembered Riley's eyes in those last few moments, how panicked he'd seemed. She'd thought at the time he'd been panicked because he'd gotten caught, but wouldn't he have known he would get caught? Shouldn't that have been the plan all along?

"He used up a lot of clout to get me here, Ms. Stratton," the lawyer said softly. "I don't work for cheap, and I don't normally take cases like this because rich people stealing money from other rich people bores me."

"But making a lot of money is exciting, huh?"

"Having the right people in my back pocket excites me." Garrison sat back, studying her for a moment. "Do I find myself in the middle of a lovers' spat? Because I would find that even more boring."

She made the only decision she could. "He means nothing to me, but I'm in a corner. If he feels guilty about what he's done, then I'll use that guilt for as long as I can. Has he asked to see me?"

"He's asked to be kept apprised of the situation. I assumed he would be in court this afternoon, but I was told that I am your attorney and I answer to you and you alone."

"Yes, of course. And he can cut off funding the minute he likes," she murmured, wondering what he was up to now. Was this some other clever plan? What more could the man want from her?

"You don't understand," Garrison said. "He wired me a million dollars an hour ago. When that runs out, I reach out for more. He merely wants to know what's happening with the case, but if you tell me I can't talk to him, I'm your attorney. I won't talk to him with the singular exception of asking for more money if I need it."

She shook her head. "Why would he do that?"

"Again, I don't care. Now if you don't mind, my time really is his money. I'd like to go over a few things before we appear in court."

Her ridiculously hot but cold-as-ice lawyer began talking about her arraignment and the bond Riley had also stated he would pay for. She listened, but in the back of her mind she had to wonder who she'd been sleeping with.

Who the hell had she fallen in love with?

Riley stormed into the penthouse. He should be at the station. He should have gone in with Henry Garrison, but the lawyer had talked him out of it. He'd told Riley there was no way he would be allowed to see her, and he was doing everything he could to get her out as soon as possible.

But she would still spend the night. His Ellie would spend the night in a dank prison cell with God only knew who inside with her.

He'd been by 4L's "office" only to be told that everyone was back here at the penthouse.

"Drew!" He tossed his briefcase aside.

Mia ran out from the kitchen. "Riley, you're home early! The boys are all plotting in the kitchen. Apparently StratCast stock is doing a deep dive. That makes them happy and me worried about their karma banks."

"Have they heard the news about Ellie? Are you watching TV?"

"How did you know about that? What's on TV? Did someone from McKay-Taggart call you?" Mia's eyes went wide. "She's in trouble, Riley. Apparently Phoebe gave Case the names and accounts of where all that money from StratCast went, and he and Drew traced it back. Ellie's name is all over it. Someone's trying to frame her."

"Someone already did." He loved his sister, but he had to talk to Drew. He'd gone straight from getting kicked to the curb to Garrison's office, where he'd given the man a million-dollar war chest in exchange for taking care of Ellie.

He hadn't talked to his brother yet. He'd wanted to do that in person.

Drew stepped out, followed by Case and Bran.

Riley eyed his eldest brother. "How the fuck could you do that to her?"

Drew's shoulders squared. "I told you why we ran that article. I already explained this to you."

"About the testing on the coolant system. You never said one fucking word about calling her a slut." He felt his hands fist, the need to hit something—someone—nearly overwhelming him. "Everyone in the business world is going to read that hatchet piece."

Hatch strode out of the kitchen, frowning at all of them. "Don't blame Drew. I okayed the article. It did exactly what I needed it to do."

"Humiliate her? Make her look like a whore?"

"No. I didn't do it to hurt her. I did it to get your damn attention." Hatch's eyes narrowed. "It seems to have worked, since you're here. You're not with her. You've spent every spare second with that woman and she's making you soft. That article made you think for two seconds with your brain and not your dick. At least that was what I hoped it would do. Riley, have you forgotten why we're here?"

"I didn't like the tone of that article, either," Mia said, standing beside him. "I should have been the one to write it, but Drew and Hatch refused. And I think this whole thing is going to blow up in our faces."

"It's working," Drew stated plainly. "Will you relax? This is exactly what we wanted to happen. I'm watching the Dow, and the stock is dropping like a rocket. By the end of the day, Castalano's stock will be cheap and Ellie can buy it. Hell, apparently she's got lots of cash."

He felt his jaw drop at the implication of those words. "What are you saying?"

Drew's eyes had gone cold. "I'm saying your girl is dirty as hell. She's skimmed over ten million from the company. I told you to watch yourself with her."

Case shook his head. "And I told you this is all some kind of plan of Castalano's. I've studied her. I know you think your IQ trumps mine, and it probably does, but I've worked more cases like this than you have. There's no way she's done this. Mia doesn't think so, either."

"All you have to do is look at her financials," Bran interjected. "If she's got ten million, where is it?"

"What happened to you knowing Castalano did this?" Riley couldn't believe what he was hearing. Drew really thought Ellie had stolen from her own company? From her people?

Drew shrugged unapologetically. "I think she's in on it. After the dirt the reporter dug up on her affair with Castalano's son, I think she's very likely helping that family out. We didn't pay the reporter to write a complete fiction. We paid him to dig up dirt and he found it. She's in deep with that family."

"Then why the fuck was she arrested not three hours ago?"

The whole room went still.

Case sighed. "I'll get on the phone and see if I can figure out where they've taken her."

Riley shook his head. "Don't bother. Henry Garrison already told me I can't get her out tonight because they're moving her to a fucking federal facility. She's being accused of embezzlement, fraud, and manipulating publicly held stocks."

Drew's eyes had gone wide. It was the first time in a long time that he'd seen his brother shocked. "Manipulating stock?"

That was the cruelest part of all. It hadn't even been Castalano who'd done the most damage. The embezzlement likely would have been dealt with by restitution and possibly parole. The stock manipulation would get her serious time. "They have a tape of me screwing with the test systems, and I'm sure they'll find out I was the one who leaked the false reports to the press. They believe I was working under her orders, and we all know that Castalano can make shit up. He's probably got false e-mails from her to me by now. She's being accused of tanking the stock so she could buy Castalano out for cheap. While you guys were celebrating, she was taking the fall for something we did."

Mia gasped. "Poor Ellie."

Bran closed his eyes briefly before shaking his head. "I'll find out everything I can about what they're saying in the press."

Riley didn't need any help there. "I can tell you what they're saying. They're saying the whore of StratCast is also a thief. She won't be able to work again. And you're wrong. I don't care what the rumors say. She wouldn't have touched Kyle Castalano with a twelve-foot pole. She hasn't had sex with anyone since her divorce. Anyone except me."

Hatch pointed Riley's way. "I told you he was in too deep with her."

Drew held out a hand. "Stop. It doesn't matter now. What matters now is how Castalano reacts. I assume he's the one who pulled the trigger."

"With a gleam in his eyes, brother," Riley replied. "This has been his plan all along. He was going to make it look like Ellie embezzled the money he took. He's had years to plan it. His first plan was to buy her out with her own money."

Drew nodded as though catching on. "He would force her to pay him back and he could use that to buy her out. Obviously he's going to use the criminal clause in the partnership contract to force her to sell."

Riley nodded. "Now he can bank the money because we tanked the stock. He's going to reap the benefits of our plan and Ellie could go to prison. Her assets have already been frozen. When I drove by her place, there were feds there, combing through every aspect of her life. And reporters. She won't be able to go home. Do you understand what we've done to her?"

"It's unfortunate, but we need to focus on Castalano," Drew replied. "This is a setback. I agree with that, but it doesn't mean it's the end of the game."

What the hell was his brother trying to say? "This isn't a game. It's Ellie's life."

Drew waved that idea away. "She's meaningless now. She'll be too busy fighting the charges against her to come after us, though I can't imagine she's happy with you. If she's as docile as you say she is, she won't be out for revenge. You said she'd gotten a good lawyer. That's all she can do."

"How did she pay for Garrison?" Hatch asked. "He's a thousand-dollar-an-hour lawyer and her assets are going to be frozen for a long time."

Bran looked up from his computer. "How do you think? He's paying for it. He's doing the right thing. I'll help out, too."

Drew stood in front of him. "Riley, I need you focused on taking down Castalano. Ellie Stratton is a diversion. If what you're saying about Castalano is true, then he might have been planning this all along. He used what we did to his own good. We've got to fix this."

Riley was going to piss everyone off. Drew was going to be so disappointed in him, but he had to make a decision, and he was making the one his father would have wanted. He knew it deep in his soul. "I'm going to take care of Ellie. I'm out unless it's in her best interests."

Drew used the two inches he had on Riley to loom over him. "You're choosing this woman over your family? She's Phillip Stratton's daughter. You're choosing the daughter of the man who killed our parents over your family?"

He couldn't think of her in that way anymore. She wasn't someone's daughter. She wasn't a thing to be used. She was Ellie. She was the woman who smiled and lit up a room, who cared about the people around her, who made him a better man than he'd ever been before. "I'm hoping I don't have to choose her or my family. I'm hoping my family loves me more than they need to punish someone, but in the end, yes. I'm choosing Ellie because I love her. I'm choosing her because she's my family now."

"Damn, I really should have bet more. Princess, I'll take that hundred you owe me in sexual favors," Case said with a wink toward Mia.

Mia hugged Riley, squeezing him tight. "I'm happy for you. I really like your Ellie. I'm glad someone has figured out that revenge isn't worth selling our souls for." She let go and looked back at her husband. "And my sexual favors are very expensive, so that hundred ain't getting what you think it will."

Case simply smiled. "I got more cash where that came from."

"Role-play somewhere else, you two." Drew had gone a little white. "Riley, you understand that I can cut you off from every dime you have."

"I already gave Henry Garrison a million. That should handle a good deal of her defense." He didn't like to think about what he would do without access to 4L's coffers, but Drew had been the brains behind the company. Riley had just been a lawyer. He wasn't sure Castalano wouldn't come after his license. He could be disbarred, and then he and Ellie would both be jobless and homeless. "I'll deal with the rest of it. Hey, it's not like I haven't been dealt a crap hand before. I'll figure out what to do."

"I'm going to cut your income off, Riley," Drew insisted. "And then I'll make sure you don't work again. Do you understand me?"

He stood up to his big brother for what felt like the first time in his life. For years Drew had been his rock, the man he could turn to. When Drew told him to get a law degree, he'd gone to law school and graduated top of his class because he didn't want to let Drew down. When Drew asked him to focus all his skill on 4L, he'd gone to work. When Drew asked him to seduce the daughter of an enemy, he'd done that, too.

He'd owed Drew, but he owed Ellie more.

"I do understand. I'm still choosing Ellie." He loved his brother, and he realized what he was doing would change the relationship between them forever. It was irrevocable. He was splitting from Drew in a way he couldn't take back.

And Ellie might never speak to him again. It could all be for nothing. He could lose everything, but then he'd taken everything from her.

Drew nodded. "All right. 4L is at your disposal. Anything you need, it's yours."

Riley stared at him. "Are you serious?"

"I had to know you were really in love with her," Drew replied, his face grim. "If you're willing to give everything up, then yes, I'll back you."

"We're really going to help Phillip Stratton's daughter?" Hatch asked.

Drew sighed and ran a hand over his head. "No, I'm going to help my future sister-in-law. I'm not going to lose family over this. I didn't keep us all together so I could end up being the dick who cuts off my own brother because he fell for the wrong girl. I assume you're planning on marrying this woman."

Absolutely. Something eased inside him the minute he realized Drew wasn't going to fight him. He didn't have to pick. "Yes. If I can convince her I'm not an asshole. That's going to be harder than you think. She really hates me right now."

"She needs you, too," Drew shot back. "Be ruthless. Don't let up. Get her back and don't let anything stop you. I'm not going to lie. I don't like the idea of having a Stratton in my family, but I'll learn to deal. But I need you to compromise, too. Help me get Castalano."

"He hurt Ellie. He's trying to destroy her and he couldn't care less. So yes, I'll help. You have to know that she comes first." Now was the really bad part. He'd kind of buried the lede, but now that he was coming down from his anger and fear, he had something else to tell his brother. "Castalano made me. He probably figured it out fairly early on."

Drew's jaw dropped. "He made you? As in figured out who you are?"

"He said I had my mother's eyes." He would never forget the smirk that had crossed Castalano's face. He wondered if his father had seen that same smirk before he died.

"That bastard," Hatch bit off. "I'll kill him. We can save ourselves a shit-ton of trouble and headaches if you let me hire an assassin and get rid of them all."

"I'm getting a drink. I need to think about this," Drew said. "I hadn't planned on this."

"Smartest thing anyone's said all damn day." Hatch followed Drew into the kitchen.

"So where's Ellie now?" Mia asked. "Is there anything we can do?"

"Garrison's with her right now. She'll be moved to a federal facility and likely released on bond tomorrow." And she didn't want to see him. Garrison had been plain about that. He wasn't invited to court.

She didn't want to talk to him. She needed time. He could give her some. A little. But they had to talk. He had to explain things to her.

She needed him. Ellie wasn't so stubborn that she would allow herself to go to jail because she hated him.

He could win her back. He had to.

He settled in for what was likely to be the longest night of his life.

Ten

"They'll be everywhere by now," Henry Garrison said, allowing his driver to shut the door to the limo. "I'll take you out back so we don't get mobbed. Niles doesn't like to be mobbed."

The grim-looking, had-to-be-ex-military driver nodded shortly and spoke in a crisp British accent. "Not at all, sir. I rather hate the buggers. I could handle them for you, of course."

"Let's keep you out of jail," Garrison said with the closest thing she'd seen to a smile, as though his driver's penchant for violence amused him. "But if they find us and you happen to run over a couple of feet, I've got an emergency fund for those kinds of payouts."

"You're the best, sir." The window rolled up and she and Garrison were alone as the limo pulled out of the courthouse where she'd been let out on a bond of one million dollars of Riley Lang's money.

That was two million he'd spent on her in the last two days. How the hell had her lawyer gotten his hands on that much money in such a short period of time?

"Is he talking about reporters?" The night before had been one of the longest she'd ever endured. She'd sat there in the FBI detention cell and thought about how many pictures they'd gotten of her being moved from city to federal facilities. They'd been waiting, and though kept at a distance, she was sure that particular humiliation had been captured by long-range lenses.

"Of course." Garrison the Grim, as she'd decided to call him, stared down at his phone for a moment and cursed. "As a matter of fact, they're waiting at your condo. We need to talk about the fact that the press is going to play a big role in your trial."

Her trial. The words still made her head spin. When was she going to wake from this nightmare?

She needed a shower. She needed to sleep. It looked like she would also need a hotel.

"Where should I go?" Security in her building wasn't the best. She'd downgraded so she could afford the buyout.

"I have a suggestion but you're not going to like it."

"I don't like anything that's happened to me in the last twenty-four hours."

"I don't think you should go home," Garrison explained. "The press is annihilating you. This is a juicy story. Hot lawyer has affair with upcoming CEO and they try to defraud an old man."

"Steven Castalano is a shark. He is not an old man. He's the one who defrauded me."

"That's not what the story is right now. Right now the story is Ellie Stratton is a woman who got to the top through nepotism and sleeping with the right people. You look like everything people hate about the upper classes, and if you do an interview, they'll tear you up."

"I don't think I should do an interview. I should keep my head down." The last thing she wanted to do was talk to the press.

"That's the worst thing you could do. That makes you look weak. I'm simply saying we need to change the story. We need to dig up every tiny granule of dirt we can on Castalano and turn this around. I want 'powerful man seeks to steal from nice young couple in love.'"

Now he was talking. She could get into taking down Steven. "I've got some dirt on the man. I can't prove it, but I might be able to . . . young couple?"

Garrison sat back. "Yes. If you want to flip the story, you need Riley Lang."

There was that rage she felt at the sound of his name. She might want to forget the man, to deny he meant anything, but she was angry. Hurt. That was what she was really denying. She could cloak it in anger because that felt better, but deep inside she had a ragged hole because of his betrayal. A hole she wasn't sure she would be able to close again. "I'm never seeing that man again."

Garrison sighed, a deeply disappointed sound. "I doubt that. You're being stubborn and you don't know the whole story. I can promise you the man wasn't working for Steven Castalano."

"How do you know?"

"Because I do know the whole story."

"All right, I'm listening."

"Attorney-client privilege, my dear." He gave her a half grin. "If you don't want me talking about your case, I certainly can't talk about his. I can and will give you advice. Talk to the man who is the only reason your sweet ass isn't still sitting in prison next to a prostitute named Sweetie Pie who may or may not have shivved her last john."

"I want nothing to do with the man." She would never speak to him again.

"Well, he certainly wants you. I've found that men that powerful tend to get what they want. You're in a position to use his attraction against him."

"I don't like the way you talk about using people."

Garrison's head shook. "He told me you were naive. I expected Phillip the Horrible's daughter to have a modicum of common sense. This is the way the world works, sweetheart. You had money and privilege. Someone bigger and badder than you came along and took it all away. You can cry or you can fight back. If you choose to do the former, tell me so I can find you some pissant, do-gooder lawyer to hold your hand while you walk into a federal pen and discover that orange is the new black. In that scenario, I really suggest you find your sexuality fluid because someone is going to snap you up as her bitch very quickly."

She kind of hated him. "I told you. I'm going to fight back."

"Then use every tool in your arsenal. Riley Lang is a major weapon. He's got money and clout and he can get things done. Announce your engagement. Be seen holding hands. Hell, actually marry the guy. That would be my advice. Marry him as soon as possible and then get in front of the press and tell your side of the story."

The whole idea horrified her. "I'm not speaking to the man again, much less marrying him."

"Think about it," Garrison insisted. "It flips the story around. But, of course, you're the client. I'm merely the ridiculously expensive lawyer who knows how to get a criminal out of jail and back in power."

"I'm not a criminal."

"Yes, you would be so much more reasonable if you were."

"Does that mean you believe me?"

Cool blue eyes rolled. "Like I said to you yesterday, your guilt or innocence is meaningless to my defense. As it happens, I've come to the conclusion that I do believe you. You're exactly the kind of wide-eyed innocent who could find herself in the middle of this shit storm. You don't even really know what's happening and yet you're plowing on like everything will work out in the end because you're innocent. The prosecutor doesn't care. All he cares about is keeping his job and moving up the ranks. You're a big story. He'll take you down any way he possibly can. He's Castalano's big gun."

She didn't want to listen to a word this man was saying. "Riley Lang isn't a big gun. He's an asshole who apparently feels guilty."

"Use it. He's an asshole who can bring some firepower to this fight."

It wasn't fair. It should matter that she was innocent. It should mean something. The court system shouldn't be about money and power and big guns. It should be about justice.

Maybe she really was naive. She looked out at the street and wondered how long it would be before she was there. She couldn't go home. Couldn't afford a hotel. Wasn't allowed to leave the city.

She only had one other play she could make. She'd thought about it all night long. It was time to finally meet with the man her father had sinned against. "I'd like to make an appointment with someone who might be able to help me."

Garrison's eyebrow rose. "All right. I can manage that."

"I hope you can. I need to meet with Riley's other client. I need to meet with Drew Lawless."

He might hear her name and kick her out.

Or he might listen to her. He might have no idea that her father and very likely Steven Castalano had killed his father and mother, had stolen from him.

Garrison looked at her, a surprised expression on his face. "Oh, I'm sure I can arrange something, but first I need to get you settled somewhere." He pushed a button on the side of his door. "Niles, we'll be heading uptown."

Uptown. Where she would find an ally or a brand-new enemy.

She stared out the window and tried not to think about Riley.

An hour later, Ellie wished she'd changed clothes. She was back in the same clothes she'd worn the day she'd been arrested.

It was too risky for Lily to bring her something. She would have been seen and then likely walked out of StratCast. She still might, but it seemed like Lily had kept her job thanks to a long talk with Kyle Castalano.

She prayed Lily didn't take things too far. She didn't trust the son any more than she did the father.

Henry Garrison had dropped her off at a gorgeous apartment building right across from Central Park. He'd explained that he'd made arrangements for her to stay here with a friend of his, and her things were upstairs.

Apparently his friend was incredibly wealthy.

She looked at the doorman and frowned. Maybe she should leave, go back to her place and damn the reporters.

She wasn't even wearing undies. She'd let Riley take them off her the day she'd been arrested. After they'd gone at it on his desk, she'd left them off.

It struck her that she'd shed a lot more than simply clothes for that man. She'd shed her inhibitions and given him a piece of her soul she could never get back.

"Ellie Stratton?"

She looked at the entrance and a massive hunk of pure American male was standing there in jeans and a T-shirt that couldn't hide the fact that this boy worked out. A lot. Holy hotness. He had to be six foot five with a body to die for.

And he knew her name.

"I'm Ellie."

He strode forward, and she noticed he was wearing cowboy boots. "Hi, I'm Case Taggart."

The name sparked a memory. "Of McKay-Taggart? That's the security firm Riley hired to check into our accounting problem."

He nodded and gave her a grin that would likely make most women melt. "Yes, and if we'd been about two hours faster, we would have saved you a lot of trouble. Well, maybe not a ton of trouble, but at least we would have gotten you out of there before the cops and press got there. Please, come with me. I want to get you off the street before someone recognizes you."

She reluctantly allowed herself to be led inside. Garrison was going to call her back after he'd arranged the meeting with Drew

Lawless. She thought seriously about simply heading to the 4L Software offices, but she wasn't sure where they were. They were somewhere in Upper Manhattan, but without her phone, she couldn't access the address. Without money she couldn't get a cab.

Would her credit cards still work?

She was in a horrible position. She couldn't work, couldn't access her money. If the case took very long, she would lose her condo and everything she had because she couldn't pay her bills.

Bankruptcy was calling her name, and even then she would have bills to pay. Garrison would be gone the minute his million ran out. At his rate, that might not take long. She'd be left with a public defender.

Or she could cut a deal, which was exactly what Castalano was planning on.

He wanted her in the worst situation so she couldn't fight. She would need what little cash she could get from the buyout.

"We have a room ready for you." Case Taggart led her to an elevator.

She hesitated. "I don't know you."

He held the door open. "No. But I know you. I know you didn't ask for this and you didn't deserve it. I know that my firm and I will do anything we can to help you, and that includes getting you out of any situation you find uncomfortable. Even if it runs counter to my brother-in-law's wishes."

"You're married to Riley's sister."

He smiled and nearly lit up the entire building. Oh, that man loved someone. "Mia. She's a ball of trouble. I think you'll like her."

"Is Riley upstairs?"

Case nodded. "Yes. If you don't want to go up there, I'll take you somewhere else. I'll arrange for a hotel room. You can't leave the city, but I assure you I can put you somewhere no one's going to find you."

"Why would you do that?" His kindness was getting to her. She'd had so little of it in the last two days.

"Because you deserve some control, Ellie. If you don't want to talk to him, I won't force you. This is all about you now, but there are things you should know. Things only he can tell you."

She stared at the elevator that would take her to her ex-lover. "So you think I should go upstairs and face him."

"I think you should go upstairs and give him hell. He deserves it." The big guy's Southern accent deepened and he winked her way.

Mia Taggart was a lucky woman.

The gorgeous cowboy was right. Why should she hide? She hadn't done anything wrong. Riley Lang should be quaking in his overpriced loafers at the thought of seeing her again. It was obvious he wasn't. He was trying to force this confrontation, likely because he thought he would say a few words and she would melt like she always did for him.

She was trying to pretend like he didn't matter, but he did. He'd betrayed her horribly. Should he get away with it? Or should she look for closure? For some final encounter that might bring her some measure of peace?

She could see him again, let him know how she felt. Hurt him a tiny bit.

See if there was any way to save the relationship?

She jumped away from that thought like it was a fireball about to exterminate her. She didn't want a relationship with that dickhead. Whether or not he was in bed with Castalano, she wasn't going to try to salvage their relationship.

He'd betrayed her. That was forever.

She stepped inside the elevator. "I don't know what he expects from me."

She could see him. One last time. She could stand in front of him and let him know he hadn't broken her. He mattered not at all.

He'd reached for her in that final moment. He'd tangled their fingers together and squeezed her like he couldn't let go. Shouldn't he have gloated? Have let her know he'd beaten her?

He shouldn't have held her hand like she was precious. That was the cruelest bit of all.

"I think he expects to get his ass kicked." Case pressed the button for the top floor.

"Does he actually think I'm going to stay here with him?" She couldn't. No matter how comfy he tried to make her because his conscience was aching, she had to say her piece and walk away.

"In this case, he really is trying to protect you."

"He's trying to protect himself. I'm sure I'll be forced to sign some kind of document saying I won't report him to the bar." It made sense. He needed her to stay quiet. Castalano likely didn't have solid proof that Riley had done things under her orders. Since he hadn't. Of course, she also hadn't stolen ten million dollars and that didn't seem to matter at all.

Taggart chuckled. "I'm sure he would love it if you didn't get him disbarred. He will likely make a hearty argument against that. But you should think before you tell him to screw himself. He's spent all night and most of today getting a room ready for you. You've got all your books and a computer and all your toiletries. He had shoes and jewelry and clothes delivered. Everything you need to be comfortable is right here. You can accept it and not accept Riley back in your bed. I would make him work for that."

"He can't work enough to ever get back there." She couldn't let him back in. She could never trust him again.

"See, this is where I wish I wasn't alone up here. Mia won't go high-dollar with me. I need Adam. Adam is always willing to take a thousand-dollar bet and he inevitably loses."

Before she could ask him what he was talking about, the elevator door slid open, and she walked into the foyer of what Riley Lang apparently called "his little place." Yeah, that had been a lie, too.

He'd told her there wasn't enough room at his place and that was why he always came to hers. This place was huge. Apparently, he hadn't wanted her to know the scope of his wealth.

What else had he been hiding from her?

She walked down the marbled hall and into what looked like the living room. To her right was a spectacular view of Central Park. She was surrounded by floor-to-ceiling windows and leather furniture that likely cost a fortune.

This place in this part of town was worth twenty million easy. Why the hell had he needed a job as her lawyer?

Maybe she really did need to start asking the right questions. He hadn't been at StratCast for money. He obviously didn't need her as a client. Why had he needed her?

Why would he work for Castalano if he had this kind of wealth at his fingertips? Garrison had told her she didn't know the real story. This was the first time she believed him.

"I think everyone's in the conference room," Taggart said, walking in beside her. "It's kind of like a war room right now. And yes, some families have game rooms. My family tends to have playrooms—and those are not for the children. But this family has a flipping war room. I wish I'd known that before I agreed to marry into it."

"It wouldn't have changed a thing." A petite blonde stepped into the room.

A familiar-looking blonde. "Do I know you?"

The blonde smiled. "Ellie! I'm so glad you're here. We met a few weeks ago."

Now she remembered. "At the coffee shop on Fifth. Riley sent you? That was before he started working for me. I take it he sent you there."

Mia shook her head, a wealth of thick hair curling around her shoulders. "Oh, no. He was really pissed about it. I wanted to get to know you. You were important to all the planning and stuff."

"The planning? Planning what?"

Mia started to open her mouth, but her husband's massive hand closed over it before she could speak.

"I think you should talk to Riley about that," Case said. "And my wife should stay out of it. She makes a habit of inserting herself into situations she really shouldn't be in. It's her hobby. Princess, you put that tongue all over my hand. I don't mind at all, but you should know the minute you bite me, I'm going to bite back."

Mia harrumphed and crossed her arms over her chest.

But it no longer mattered because Riley had walked into the room. He was dressed as casually as she'd ever seen him in slacks and a button-down, his sleeves rolled up.

Not as casually as she'd ever seen him. She'd seen him with nothing on at all. She'd seen him as he worked over her, his face a mask of pure pleasure.

"Ellie." He barely breathed her name and then he was crossing the space between them, his arms out as though it was his right to catch her up and hold her close.

She knew what her right was. She hauled her fist back and punched the bastard.

Hard.

Riley reeled back, his hand going to his jaw as Case bit back a laugh and Mia gasped.

"Oh, I take back everything I said about her," a new voice said. "She's welcome in our family."

She looked up and the man who had come to her office with Riley the first day was standing there. He was a good two inches taller than Riley and broader, though she preferred Riley's lean frame. Andy, as Riley had called him, intimidated her with his massive size. He was closer to Case Taggart than Riley.

Riley shook his head as though shaking off the pain. "Don't tease her, Drew. Ellie, I deserved that. Will you come in and let me explain everything to you?"

Drew? "I thought his name was Andy."

The other man loomed over Riley, his eyes suddenly finding hers. "It's Andrew, though with friends and family I go by Drew."

Tears filled her eyes because she really was a fool. Now she knew why Riley was so surrounded by wealth. "Drew Lawless. Of course. The last card I had in my hand. He's your brother, isn't he?"

Riley nodded. "I can explain."

She looked at three of the Lawless siblings. They were orphans because of what her father had done.

This was why Henry Garrison had practically been laughing as he'd dropped her off. Everyone had been in on the joke except her.

The last card in her hand turned out to be a dud. She'd never had a chance. Not one.

She turned, tears pouring down her face, and walked toward the elevator.

"Ellie," Riley said.

She'd almost made it when she felt a hand on her arm. She was pulled around.

"Ellie, baby, talk to me."

The horror of the last few days welled up inside her. She had nothing left. Nothing. There was no Andrew Lawless waiting out there for her story and offer of an alliance to bring down the man who had likely hurt them both.

Maybe it was really her fault for not going to him when she'd first found out. She'd been greedy, worried that he'd take the company from her and ruin all the plans she had for the employees. She hadn't wanted them caught up in a powerful man's revenge.

It had happened anyway.

"Ellie?"

She heard him, but she didn't really care now. When she thought about it, she'd always been alone. From the moment her mother died. Her father wanted a son and got two daughters he'd never really cared about.

Her husband had changed. It was what people did. They changed, with the exception of her.

She would change now because there wasn't a way out of the trap.

She felt his arms go around her, hugging her tight. When he picked her up and hauled her close, she didn't care. Her misery was all that mattered now.

In the distance she heard someone crying, wailing. Someone screamed out in pain, but Ellie no longer cared.

Riley felt years older when he walked out of Ellie's bedroom. It was hers because she was staying here. With him.

God, what had he done to her?

He might never forget the sound of her crying out in pain, the sound so broken it had almost made him drop to his knees and join her. She'd been so heartbroken. How was he ever going to fix this mess he'd gotten her in?

He had to find a way, and it started with talking to Drew. He needed Drew firmly on his side because he had a plan that might get them all into trouble.

"Is she all right?" Hatch stood in the hallway, his face weary.

"No. She's asleep. She cried herself to sleep." She'd been in his arms, but vacant. He'd felt the horrible distance between them. She'd allowed him to touch her, to stroke her hair and rock with her, but she'd been like a doll in his arms.

Ellie had pulled into herself, and he wasn't sure he could make her come back out.

Hatch looked over at the door Riley had closed. "Your brother is having a hard time with this. You know he never meant to hurt her."

"That's not true, Hatch. He didn't care and I know that because in the beginning, I felt the same way he did. I thought she'd be vile and privileged, and I was ready to take her down a peg or two because she's Phillip Stratton's daughter and we can't get to him. He died and she was a convenient target." His gut was in knots. "We all went into this knowing we would hurt her. We told ourselves it didn't matter. She would get back on her feet."

"No one thought Castalano was planning this. This is really his damn fault."

"No. We put her in this position. We gave him all the ammo he needed to fuck her over for years. And guess what? She's nothing like her father. She's an optimist. Do you know what she wanted to do with StratCast? She wanted to make the corporation accountable to the employees, to the public. It's so stupid. It wouldn't work, but she was going to do it."

Hatch sighed. "She's not like Stratton. Damn it, Riley, she's like your father."

Because his father had been a dreamer. His father had wanted to change the world and it had cost him his life. The way it could cost Ellie hers.

He'd watched her for a long time after she'd fallen asleep. He'd dragged her skirt and blouse off and dressed her in one of the nightgowns the personal shopper he'd hired had brought in earlier in the day. She hadn't been wearing panties because he'd taken them from her.

He'd left her without the shield of a pair of damn underwear. How had she felt sitting there knowing if they made her change into prison overalls, that she would have to ask for underwear. It was silly but he felt so fucking guilty about that.

She'd been alone. He hadn't been able to be there to defend her, to protect her. He'd left her in that place.

"I can't let her go." She would try to leave. There was no question in his mind that she would be on her feet as soon as she woke up.

Hatch shook his head. "I think she's already broken, son."

He disagreed. Nothing could really break Ellie. Maybe she could be down for a moment, but he knew her. She would rise again. "No. She hadn't really let herself cry. I don't know why seeing Drew did that to her, but she needed this. She needed to let it all out, but you should know when she wakes up, she's going to try to kick my balls up into my body cavity and then she'll shoot me the finger and try to walk out. I can't let that happen. She'll be alone out there, and that would be the worst thing in the world for her."

"She's got a sister."

"Who is useless. She needs me. She needs someone who is willing to put her first." He started down the hall. He suspected her sister would be thrilled with the turn of events. "Unfortunately, I suspect I'm going to have to fight like hell to get her to stay here."

He'd called Lily after Ellie had fallen asleep to let her know Ellie was safe. Even Lily thought she'd leave him. She'd offered a place for Ellie to stay, but that might not be for the best.

Lily had already been working the younger Castalano. She'd been assured she had some time before they decided what to do with her. She might be able to stay on and be Riley's eyes and ears.

There was no way she could do that if Ellie was staying at her place. The press would find out and Lily's loyalties would be unquestionable.

Ellie needed to stay here. Ellie needed his protection and his family's money. She needed to be a Lawless.

Hatch followed him. "Or you could give her a reason to stay."

How far would he go to protect her? It was a question he'd been asking himself since the moment they dragged her away. He was already the villain. How much further would he have to go to ensure her safety? "I already have. She knows I'm paying for Garrison."

He'd hoped that would be enough, but that punch she'd greeted him with had told him otherwise. She'd turned and started walking for the door.

He couldn't allow her to walk through it.

"Yeah, she also knows you'll keep paying for him," Hatch said as they turned down the hallway.

Drew would be in the conference room. Why couldn't they have a damn game room or family room? No. They all gathered in the conference room like being a family was a business.

It was for them. And their real business was revenge. It had been since the day their parents had died and they'd been splintered and broken.

What if they could be more?

"I'm not going to hold that over her head," he replied as they entered the conference room. "If she insists on walking out, I'm still going to help her. I won't leave her with no resources."

Drew looked up from his computer. "Henry Garrison thinks that would be a mistake."

Riley stared at his older brother. "You talked to Ellie's attorney? He talked to you about her case? He told me he wouldn't do that unless she agreed."

It had been a thirty-minute argument that he'd only given in on when Garrison had explained time was running out. She'd been arrested on a Thursday. If she wasn't moved to the federal facility by Friday morning, she would likely remain in custody all weekend long. He'd conceded because he couldn't stand the thought.

He rather thought Garrison liked that he'd conceded. The man was an asshole, but he was the best in the business and nothing else would do for Ellie's defense.

"Money talks, brother," Drew said. "When I explained to him that 4L would retain him for Ellie, he was more than happy to give me some advice."

Thank God. Offering Garrison his bank account was one thing. Offering up 4L's was like opening the gates of heaven and asking the defense attorney to come in and take what he liked. Drew had ensured that Ellie was the defense attorney's absolute top priority. "You're serious?"

Drew sat back. "I didn't expect her to hurt like that. The way she cried out . . . well, it turns out I'm more human than I thought I was."

Riley put a hand on his brother's shoulder. "Thank you. You won't regret it. She's a good person, Drew. You'll like her if you get to know her."

She was utterly lovable. She was competent when it came to work, silly when it came to play. Ellie was real. She changed with the moment, with her emotions, but there was a core set of values to her that didn't change. She was always kind. Always loyal. Always seeking to do what was right.

He couldn't be the person who broke her. He loved her. Somehow she'd made him whole, and now he had to do the same for her.

"She has a good right hook. I already like that," Drew replied, but sobered quickly. "She had a reaction to finding out who I was. Garrison told me she'd asked for a meeting with me. Not the Andy she thought was your fellow lawyer. She wanted a meeting with Drew Lawless. She put it all together when I walked out. Why would she do that?"

"I don't know," Hatch said. "It was obvious to me she had no idea Riley was a Lawless."

"I'll ask her about it when she wakes up, but I would like for her to sleep through the night. She's been through a lot." He glanced at the clock. It was already after seven. She could easily sleep until morning.

He wouldn't, though. He would watch over her.

He'd already ensured that when she woke up she would have her purse and all her favorite toiletries to use. He'd made sure her bathroom was stocked. She wouldn't have to ask for a toothbrush or soap or makeup. He'd filled her closet with clothes. If she didn't like them, he would toss them all out and let her buy more.

Anything she wanted was hers, with the singular exception of a door that would take her away from him.

It was wrong, but he couldn't let her walk away. Not when he was the only person in the world who could make certain she didn't go to jail.

After her trial was over, if she wanted to leave, he would still get on his knees and beg for a second chance.

"So how do we keep her here?" Hatch asked. "Because I think that girl is going to want to leave. It's obvious to me she didn't really expect that you would be here."

"I'll lock the stairs," Bran said with a smile. He walked in carrying a couple of pizza boxes. "She won't be able to use the elevator because she doesn't know the code. Unless you think Case gave her the code."

"He didn't," Drew replied. "But you should know that our heroic brother-in-law has offered to take her wherever she would like to go. He's apparently not into kidnapping."

"Mia married him, why?" Bran asked, opening the first box and pulling out a slice of pepperoni.

Drew shuddered. "Don't ask her that question. Seriously, she will tell you all about her husband's apparently really big schlong."

Hatch frowned. "I blame her adoptive parents. I would really think a lesbian couple would be more averse to teaching Mia to talk about her hetero sex life. She was telling me about Case and how good he is with a crop. I pray to God she was talking about his farming skills."

Riley was pretty sure she wasn't. Mia had a very interesting relationship with her husband.

Somehow, Mia had come out of their wretched nightmare whole and loved, and he worshipped the ground her mothers walked on for it. Those women had been supportive of all of them. They'd patiently allowed Drew and Riley to visit and taken Bran any time they could.

He wanted what Mia had. He wanted that one person in the world he could count on, he could find himself with. He wouldn't say be himself. He was fairly certain he didn't know who the hell he was. Ellie was his chance to find out. Loving Ellie would define him, enhance him. Make him better.

"We should listen to Mia more."

"I always thought she was weak because she hadn't gone through what we had. Maybe you're right," Drew admitted. "But we have to deal with the fact that Castalano has us all by the balls now. He's laughing somewhere and we can't let it stand."

No, they couldn't. He had StratCast, and that belonged to Ellie. Maybe at one point it should have been theirs, but now Riley knew where that company belonged. God, his father would have loved Ellie. They would have been partners in crime. "So what's the plan? Ellie didn't steal that money."

Drew held up a hand. "I understand that. I'm ceding this argument to you. If you say she's clean, we'll go with it. So we have to figure out a way to prove he's behind all of this, but we also have to keep Ellie close. We need to figure out a way to control the optics on this one because she's not coming out well right now."

Because they'd paid a reporter to work her over in print. Still, she wasn't a Kardashian. She was a tech executive. "It will blow over by tomorrow."

"Have you watched the news? I don't think it's blowing over," Hatch said. "She's all over the news, and not only on the business channels. The press is treating it as a rich-girl-gone-wrong story. Castalano comes off as a sick, sad old man. He's playing this to the hilt. There's no doubt they're tainting the potential jury pool against her. For now our names are out of it, but the minute she starts talking, we're all screwed."

"Why would she talk?" Ellie didn't love media. She wasn't one of those executives who lived to aggrandize themselves. She was shy about the press.

"Garrison will put her out there," Drew said. "Whether I want him to or not. He's going to fight this in the press. He needs to make her look innocent, and one way of doing that is to throw your ass under a bus. It won't take long before your connections to me come up, and then 4L, and all of us will be out there."

He hadn't thought about that. He'd changed his name long ago so he could blend in. For all the good it had done him. "Castalano already knows. Why wouldn't he talk?"

Hatch took that one. "Do you really think he wants to bring those rumors up? He might have handled the cops back then, but there was always the theory out there that they stole your father's code. If he brings the Lawless name up, it brings back bad memories for him. It's very likely why he went hands off with you. Otherwise, you would have found yourself in a cell beside Ellie's."

Drew's eyes hooded, staring up at Riley. "Is there any way Ellie knows? Maybe her father told her at some point. Could she possibly have access to the source code? They built their entire business on Dad's work."

No way. If Ellie had any idea her whole company was based on a lie, she would have come forward. "She thinks it all came from this elderly scientist who was nice to her as a kid. She has no idea, though now I wonder why she knew who you were. I mean as anything but a competitor. She was really proud she managed to snag Darvisch away from you."

Drew growled a little. "Yeah, I want to know how she managed that. I offered him way above what I should have."

"Ellie knows how to soothe the angriest geek." His girl was good at making a man believe in himself. He was sure it was her own sweet soul and not money that made Darvisch choose her. "He'll likely be looking to leave without her."

"I'll scoop him up if I can. We do have a few things in our favor. I've managed to keep quiet about some of my moves. What neither she nor Castalano knows is I'm the new board member. We're not out of this yet," Drew said.

Because not only did they have the stock they'd bought, they still had Ellie's, if they could bring her around to their way of thinking. "Until Castalano forces a sale, we've got a chance."

"Unless Ellie hates you more than she wants revenge," Bran mused.

"Is there any way we can convince her to stay here? I think if she gets to know us, hears the truth about this thing, she'll probably be on our side."

Riley looked at Bran. "I thought you were all about female empowerment."

"Only when it's good for her. She's being stubborn. You love her. You'll take care of her. That kind of trumps her anger." Bran gave him a bright smile. "I'm a happily-ever-after kind of guy. I blame Mia. She made me watch a bunch of chick flicks when I got to stay with her. I associate them with happiness. So I say a little kidnapping is nothing in the face of what she'll get out of it."

Drew's eyes finally lit. "She'll get a shitload of family issues. But we'll also stand behind her. I don't know. It's a hard sell on our end."

"Not if I'm ruthless. Not if I make it so there's really only one choice." Him. It was a dick move, but it was the only one he could make if he wanted to have half a shot with her. "I have a plan, but it's risky."

"Nothing that's worth anything is safe," Drew said.

No, it wasn't. Riley leaned in and told his brothers his plan.

Eleven

Ellie smoothed her palm over the Chanel dress she'd selected out of the massive closet she'd discovered when she'd awakened. She'd slept like the dead the night before.

It was morning and she needed to make a few decisions, the first being the decision to take at least a few of the clothes Riley had bought. It looked like he'd hired a personal shopper and given her unlimited resources. She would think they belonged to someone else if every piece hadn't still had a tag on it. Despite the fact that she'd been a rich man's daughter all her life, she'd never bought designer clothes. They rarely actually fit her well given her curves, and her father's version of an allowance hadn't left much for designer outfits. He'd told her once that she didn't need nice clothes. She got all the brains while Shari got the looks. She'd had to decide if she wanted to use her limited resources on Wharton or plastic surgery because that was what it would take to make her look good according to her father.

Lily had taught her how to dress for her figure.

Riley seemed to have that part down. Every single outfit looked like it would flatter her curves. And the man had a serious shoe fetish. There had to be twenty boxes of shoes waiting for her. Jimmy Choo, Christian Louboutin, Prada.

He did kind of owe her. When she left this place, she would take what she needed and not feel guilty about it.

"If you don't like the clothes, I can have more sent. Although that looks beautiful on you."

She looked up and Riley was standing behind her. He was already dressed for the day in slacks, a white dress shirt, and a tie that brought out his eyes. He was simply the most beautiful man she'd ever met, and it killed her that he hadn't been real.

She'd had her head in the clouds.

"I brought you coffee." He set a mug on the counter. "A little cream, one sugar."

He'd gotten to know her quite well, but then that had been the point of their relationship.

She wanted to throw the coffee in his face and walk out, but she'd decided it was time to stop reacting and start thinking.

She needed a place to stay, needed money, needed so many things she couldn't count them. Lily was her only friend in the world right now. If Riley Lawless felt guilty about what he'd done, she needed to use that to her advantage.

"Thank you." She took a sip of the coffee. Naturally it was delicious. Her stomach growled. Yes, she needed food, too.

"If you're hungry, I can get you some breakfast. Mia's probably cooking right now. Her husband eats a lot. Apparently two hundred twenty pounds of muscle requires a lot of calories."

"I'm fine for now." She was starving, but he didn't have to know that. "I would rather talk. I think we should have a discussion, don't you?"

She was pleased with the even tone of her voice.

He moved in behind her. "Yes, we need to talk. I want to explain it all to you. Ellie, I know it seems bad right now, but I'm going to get you out of this. I'm going to make sure you don't go to jail."

"We'll see about that." Somehow she felt better, calmer after sleep and a shower. She turned, facing him fully for the first time since she'd cried in his arms the night before. It had taken every ounce of will she had to not hold on to him. "So you're really Riley Lawless."

"That's my birth name. I go by Lang professionally. I changed it so I wouldn't be connected to Drew. We do need to talk, baby. There are things I have to tell you. I don't know how much you understand about the way our families are connected."

It was obvious now that her big secret wasn't such a secret. She'd been the only one in the dark. "My father had your parents killed."

His eyes widened. "You knew?"

There was zero reason to keep her secrets now. "I've known since the night my father died. He told me. I think he was confessing his sins. He killed your father because Benedict wouldn't sell him the code he needed to make the fiber optics work. Your father wanted to offer it for free because he thought the information was too important to keep to himself. He was a dreamer and my father murdered him for it."

That was as baldly as she could put it.

"You knew and you didn't come forward?"

Good, she liked the accusation in his voice. It meant he wouldn't be playing nice. She didn't want to play nice. "I had employees to think of. Had I blown up StratCast they would have been out of jobs, had their pensions caught up in a legal battle. I intended to go to your brother after I bought out Steven. I was going to do what I could to see your father's vision through."

She waited for him to scoff at the idea.

He softened instead. "Yes, I can see you doing that. You very likely didn't tell me because you didn't want to put me in the middle. You didn't want me to have to make the same decision you did. Ellie, I'm so sorry."

She walked past him. "Really, I would think you would be far more suspicious, Riley."

"Not about you." There was a longing in his voice she didn't want to think about.

"So my very clever plan after yesterday's debacle was to find Drew Lawless and ask him for help. I was going to trade my knowledge of what my father did for his help in getting StratCast back, but surprise. You were already there. Is he the one who's been buying up stock?" She was done being a fool. She'd thought about it in the shower. It made sense. She'd been a pawn in a war she hadn't known was being fought. "How did you convince my sister to sell?"

Riley frowned. "We gave her several opportunities to spend a whole lot of money and get into debt with the wrong people. She had to sell. She would have found her way there anyway."

"Sure. Tell yourself that. Anything you need to do to sleep at night."

"I don't, baby. I don't sleep at all anymore. And I don't feel bad about what I did to your sister. She deserved it. You, on the other hand, did not, and that's why we're going to do whatever it takes to get StratCast back in your hands."

He was likely right about Shari. Ellie was afraid her sister was in a slow slide to drug addiction. She knew Shari spent her evenings in nightclubs and liked to relax with a few recreational drugs. No amount of talking to her about it changed anything. For a while, being with Colin had pulled her back from it, but it seemed now that Colin was along for the ride. Still, Riley didn't have to help them along. It didn't matter because the deed was done and they had other considerations.

"You have to keep me out of jail first. And I'm not sure getting StratCast back is possible. Steven's going to force me to sell in the next week or so. He'll find a way to do it quickly since he'll want to take advantage of how low our stock has sunk."

"I did that. I'm not going to lie to you or try to get around it. I tanked the reports and the reporter was hired by my brother. I had no idea the reporter would talk about you that way or I wouldn't have allowed it."

"Do you allow or disallow things, Riley?" She needed to understand how the siblings worked. "Or is it all about Drew?"

Drew Lawless was an enigma in the business world. In an age where tech CEOs tended to be treated like rock stars, Drew was reclusive. He allowed the head of his publicity to handle all media relations and very rarely allowed himself to be photographed.

The rumor was he was a shut-in, an agoraphobic. Ellie now had her own thoughts on the matter. He didn't allow himself to be seen so he could play out his revenge.

"Drew doesn't control me." Riley's jaw tightened. "I wouldn't have allowed it and now that Drew fully understands your place here, he won't do it again."

"I don't have a place here, but I would like to understand why you thought tanking StratCast stock would do anything but cost us all money."

He started to pace, the large room allowing him plenty of space. "Castalano likes to play deep. He's got a gambling problem. I think that's where the ten million actually went. Recently he went in deep to a man with a certain reputation for not accepting IOUs, if you know what I mean."

"You wanted a mobster to take care of the situation for you?"

"We wanted to apply pressure and see where it led."

She held her hands out. "It led us right here. Now Steven has all the money he could want, and I'm sure he'll use it to pay off your incidental hit man."

Riley frowned, deep lines marking his face. He did look like he hadn't slept in a while. "Yes, I'm certain he's already done it."

"Was that all you were supposed to do?" She wanted to know the whole of his perfidy.

"I was supposed to see if I could find anything that might implicate your father and Castalano in our parents' deaths. We believe they paid someone to do it. Along with Patricia Cain."

"My father wouldn't say anything when I asked him if Steven was involved. He said Steven's sins were his own." She remembered how tortured her father had seemed in those last few days. The drugs had made him incoherent much of the time.

Riley crossed his arms over his chest, his face turning hard. "He was involved, Ellie. I know it. So was Patricia Cain. We're going to take them all down."

"So I'm merely collateral damage, huh?"

"You're more than that and you know it."

"I don't know anything, Riley." She braced herself but she had to ask. She had to know the truth. She needed to hear it from his lips. "Did you have to seduce me? I was willing to be your friend, your coworker. I gave you access to anything you needed. You didn't have to get into bed with me."

His arms came down and he crossed to the bed, sitting where he could still see her. "No, I didn't. I did that because I wanted you."

"So the plan wasn't to seduce me."

His hesitation told her what she needed to know. "Ellie, what I feel for you is real. It doesn't matter how it started. It's real now. I'm in love with you."

She laughed at the thought. "What is this act supposed to buy you? I don't have anything left for you to steal."

"I told you. I want you. I'm going to make this right for both of us."

"I'm going to make a deal with you." She had to bite the bullet and compromise, though what she really wanted was to rake him over the coals. "In exchange for paying for my lawyer, I won't go to the bar association and demand your license."

The sympathy in his eyes nearly made her scream. "You won't do that anyway, Ellie."

"You think I'm not capable of rage?" Maybe he didn't know her as well as she thought he did. Yesterday, she'd thought of any number of ways she could hurt him back.

"I know you are, but you love me, too," he said quietly. "Underneath all that ache, you still love me. You aren't capable of hurting someone you love."

"I don't love you." She was going to do anything she needed to in order to make those words true. "You killed any love I had for you when you betrayed me."

"I don't think so," he replied in an all too even tone. "I think it's still there and it's going to be there forever. All I have to do is hold on and you'll reach the proper conclusions. You know we're good together."

She really wanted to shake him up. His calm was annoying her and she couldn't believe a word the man said. What was his angle now? "I know I've been the idiot who slept with her enemy."

"You are not my enemy." He didn't take his eyes off her. "You're the woman I love and I'm going to make it all up to you."

Yep, he was getting on her very last nerve. "By buying me things? You think I care about designer labels? You think I can be bought off so cheaply?"

"No, those are all for show. If you're going to the press, you're going to have to look the part. I know you don't care that I can buy anything you want. You don't measure someone's worth by their wealth. It's one of the things I love about you."

"Then how are you going to magically make things between us better?"

"Not magically." He stood and moved toward her. "I'm going to work my ass off to make sure you're safe, and I'm going to be the man who stands behind you after all this is over. I'm going to do everything in my power to make your dreams come true because I finally figured out what I was born to do, what I want to be when I grow up. It's stupid, but I've been thinking about it a lot lately."

"Don't say it." It was easier when she thought he was going to fight her. "Don't you dare say it."

"All right, but we both know what I mean." He grimaced. "Is it because it's really corny?"

"It's because it's all another lie."

He moved in, standing far too close for her comfort, but she wasn't about to give him the satisfaction of moving away. "It's not, but the only thing that will improve our situation is time and care. I'm not going away and I'm not giving up on us. I love you, Ellie. I'm going to say it until you understand that I mean it. This started out as a job, as a path I've been on since the night my parents died. But it led me to you, and though I wish my mom and dad were here with me, I have to be happy that I found you."

Son of a bitch. She wasn't going to buy what he was selling. Maybe he was saying it out of guilt or some misguided affection, but she couldn't fall for this again.

"It's not going to work."

He brought a hand up, almost touching her. With obvious reluctance, he pulled back. "It will. Now let's get breakfast. We have a big day ahead of us. Case and Mia are going to take a harder look at the embezzlement case against you, and we have to be at the courthouse at noon."

He stepped back and walked to the door.

"Garrison didn't tell me I had to be in court." Her next hearing wasn't for months. At least that was what the judge at the arraignment had said. The idea of having to go back in there made her stomach knot.

"Not in court. At the courthouse. I made arrangements. That blue is perfect. You look every inch the gorgeous bride. We're getting married this afternoon, baby."

He strode out and she was left staring after him.

He walked into the kitchen because he might need witnesses. Ellie might not take his head off in front of witnesses.

Cool. He needed to stay cool and collected because his almost-wife was about to lose her shit. If he thought it would make a difference, he would get down on his knees and beg, but all that would do was likely give Ellie a better target. His jaw still ached from yesterday. Luckily he hadn't bruised because explaining that away to the press on his wedding day would have been tricky.

"Hey, you want an omelet?" Mia asked. "I bought enough eggs to feed an army. And there are bagels, too."

"I ate the last one." Case sat at the small bistro table beside Bran and Drew, who looked to be plowing through omelets and bowls of fruit.

Bran always ate so quickly, a remnant of years of not having enough.

"Where does he put it all?" Bran asked, pointing at their brother-in-law. "If I ate like him I would weigh five hundred pounds."

"It's because of his job. He runs a lot," Mia explained.

"Dodging bullets burns calories, as my brother would say. As for you, you're going to start hitting the gym with me. We'll get some serious muscle on your frame." Case patted Bran on the back.

"I'd like that." Bran smiled suddenly. "Hey, Ellie. You look really lovely today."

Ellie stopped and it was easy to see that her polite heart was aching to reply. The beginnings of a smile started before he watched her shove it down. "How I look is irrelevant. You must be the other brother. It's very nice to meet you, but I am not marrying Riley."

Bran grinned her way as though enjoying the drama. "I'm Bran. I'm the youngest of the brothers and also the most handsome. Really, you're marrying the wrong Lawless."

He thought seriously about smacking his brother.

Ellie flushed. "I'm not marrying any Lawless at all."

"Oh my gosh, that blue is gorgeous on you!" Mia ignored the denial completely. "I knew it would be. You should totally wear the white Pradas. Unless you think that's too matchy-matchy with the belt. It might be."

"I don't get it," Case said. "I thought matching was good. You're always telling me my concert T-shirts don't match my jeans."

Mia shook her head sadly. "Baby, your faded Luke Bryan T-shirts don't match anything. Anything at all. It's very sad."

"I'm not getting married." Ellie strode up to Riley. "Do you think Garrison didn't already run this past me? I said no."

"Ellie, it's for the best," he said calmly. "You'll have the protection of the family, and marrying is the best way to quash the rumors that you're promiscuous."

"I thought almost never having sex was the way to not be known as promiscuous."

He'd put her in a horrible position. "I don't want anyone talking about you that way."

"Then you shouldn't have hired a reporter to rip me apart," she snarled back.

"That was my fault," Drew said, standing. "As far as Riley knew, the reporter was going to write a complimentary story on you and then talk about the fact that the tests on the coolant system had gone poorly."

Ellie turned, seeming to find a new target. "Do you know how illegal that was?"

"Are you going to turn him in?" Drew asked.

"I could." She straightened her shoulders. "I was talking to Riley about making a deal with him. In exchange for my silence about the testing, I would like you to pay my lawyer fees."

Drew seemed to consider it for a moment. "This is Riley's whole career we're talking about here. You sure you don't want to ask for more, because this lawyer thing is really all he's got going. He'll be scrubbing toilets if you get him disbarred."

"Thanks a lot." His brother's humor came out at the oddest times.

Ellie didn't crack a smile. "I don't care what he does after this. If you'll pay my legal fees, I'll agree to not prosecute any of you."

"Or you can marry into the family and we take care of everything, and you can't be forced to testify against your husband," Drew countered.

"The crimes in question happened before the marriage," Riley pointed out. "It wouldn't work. See, I paid attention in school. This really is all about ensuring Ellie is safe."

"I would still feel infinitely more secure if Ms. Stratton here changed her name. I think then I could safely pay for any and all legal fees and use every power I have to ensure she doesn't go to prison." Drew picked up his coffee. "You have to agree to live here, though. We need to keep up appearances."

"Appearances?" Ellie kind of choked out the word.

Mia had a spatula in her hand as she turned. "It's only for a little while, Ellie. And Riley doesn't expect anything physical from you."

Oh, he was going to try. The easiest way to get her back was to get her in bed. She craved love and affection and he would do his damnedest to give her plenty of both. She also craved family. She was a woman who needed to be needed, and his brothers could give her that, too.

Ellie wouldn't be able to hold out for long. Mia and Case had to go back to Texas soon and Ellie would be the only female among a group of sad-sack, needy men who were deeply grateful for any kindness a woman gave them. Hell, Bran thought the housekeeper walked on water because she did her job. Bran was like an overgrown Labrador retriever. Once Ellie figured that out, she wouldn't be able to deny him affection. She would slowly become important to all of them and then she wouldn't be able to leave.

"I'm not marrying the man who screwed me over," she said, her hands fisted at her sides. "If that means I have to get a public defender, then so be it."

He stepped in front of her to stop her from leaving. "Ellie, the lawyer is yours no matter what you choose to do, but please think about this. Marrying me gets the press off your back. It gets people talking about our marriage instead of our affair. Married people are boring."

Her brown eyes met his. "What do you get out of it?"

"Time to convince you that we belong together."

She shook her head. "No."

"Ellie, I understand how angry you are with Riley, with all of us," Drew said quietly. "You got caught in a war you never wanted, but you're here and you aren't going to be able to get out of the line of fire unless you choose to make a plea deal and give up your company."

"I'm never going to do that," she said.

"Of course not." Riley put his hands on her shoulders and was so grateful when she didn't push him away. "Marry me. It can be in name only unless you decide otherwise. We'll make nice for the cameras and then you can go to your room and I'll go to mine. When this is all over, we'll divorce if that's your choice, but Castalano will understand that you have the full support of this family behind you. Everyone he could use against you will understand that, too."

"You changed your name. I don't think he knows who you are," she shot back.

"He does. He made sure I knew it," he replied. "As he had me walked out, he told me I had my mother's eyes."

The same mother Castalano had murdered.

Ellie gasped, and there was the sympathy, the sweet nature he'd come to crave.

"Ellie, if you agree to marry Riley, I'll come out as the newest board member and I'll throw my full support behind you," Drew explained. "And when this is over, I'll sign over my stock to you and ensure that you're in a position where no one can take the company away from you again. All you have to do is go to the courthouse and sign some papers."

"I have to be Riley's wife." Her stare nearly burned a hole through him.

"On paper, yes." He intended to make it so much more.

"Why are you doing this?" The question came out as a tortured whisper.

"Because I love you and if I let you go now, you won't ever give us a chance. You're mad right now and you have every right to be, but you won't always be so angry with me. I'm going to be sitting by your side when that day comes and I will grovel and beg and get on my knees and pray you let me back into your life. I don't want my own life. I want ours. I want what we had."

"It was all a lie."

"No, it wasn't." He was going to have to get used to saying those words. He would say them until she believed it. "Baby, I asked you to marry me before Castalano pulled the rug out from under us. I meant that. I wasn't trying to trick you. I thought if I could get you to marry me, if I could get that ring on your finger, you would have to think about kicking me to the curb when you found out the truth. I would have done anything to keep you with me. I was willing to walk away from 4L and my family because I need to be with you."

Her eyes had a sheen of tears and she shook her head, moving away from him. "I don't want to hear this. After what you did, I can't. What you did was criminal, Riley. All of you. Do you even care that you could have cost those workers everything?"

"I wasn't going to let it come to that," Drew insisted. "I wasn't going to stiff some old guy out of his pension."

"No, but you were willing to commit a crime to get your way," she shot back, the argument giving her fire.

Arguing wasn't the way to win with Ellie. "We didn't want to commit a crime, but we needed time to prove that Castalano is guilty of something."

"So you took it on yourselves to do whatever it took. That's not fair to the other people you hurt," she replied.

"There's no such thing as fair. We couldn't let that man walk away with millions. He would have disappeared and lived out his life happily." Bran's voice had gone to a low growl. Sometimes the happy retriever remembered how long he'd been a stray. Bran's typical demeanor was so easygoing that Riley often forgot how violent his brother could become. "That wasn't fair, either. It wasn't fair that we grew up in foster homes or that our dad and mom died screaming."

Bran's jaw was tense, his body shaking slightly.

Ellie's whole being seemed to soften. She moved to Bran and knelt down beside him. "I'm so sorry about that. I'm very sorry for what my father did to yours. I wish it hadn't happened."

Bran sighed and put a hand over hers, his anger deflating in a second. He never could keep his rage around a woman. "I know you didn't have anything to do with it. I do. I don't blame you in any way, but I can't sleep knowing he's got everything that should have been my father's. He gets to retire. He gets to have grandkids. He gets this whole life and all because he took my father's code."

"None of us sleep very well," Drew admitted.

Ellie sat down beside Bran, putting her free hand on his back. "I'm sorry things got so heated. I wish I could make it right. I'm afraid Castalano's going to walk through the company taking whatever he wants and screwing everyone over. Somewhere along the way, my father started thinking about the company as his legacy. He was a horrible man, but he wanted his name to live on. It's why he left the majority of his stock to me. He thought I could maybe do something important with StratCast. I don't think Steven cares about anything but his own bank accounts."

"You can help." Bran took a long breath. "You can help us and yourself and all those employees. You can take it back."

His brother was sometimes a genius because Riley saw the moment Ellie knew she was caught.

She was still for a moment. "I want it in writing that you'll give up the stock or allow me to buy it back when we divorce."

They weren't ever divorcing if he had his way. "You'll get 4L stock the minute we're married."

"Part of the prenup I've had drawn up is that we divest ourselves of each other's stock should you two divorce. You'll get the StratCast stock. The 4L stock comes back to us." Drew strode over and refilled his coffee mug. "I also promise to vote with you on your board. You could use allies."

"I intend to fight my firing so I can keep those voting shares," Riley explained to her. "I've already filed a wrongful termination suit. I can drag this out. We can catch him, Ellie."

"And after we do, we divorce," she said, but there was way more uncertainty in her voice than had been there before.

"If that's what you want." He kept his own tone calm, not wanting her to hear the satisfaction he was feeling. All he needed was time. She wouldn't be able to hold on to her anger forever. If she was living here with them, she would inevitably come to care about them. Bran and Mia were completely lovable. Drew was an enigma, but one Ellie's soft heart would likely want to help.

Did he want her to stay with him because she fell in love with being part of a family? Did it matter as long as she stayed?

"All right, then." She glanced over at Mia. "Is there any way I could get something to eat?"

"Of course," Mia said with smile. "Omelet? I've got every ingredient known to man. I swear Case would eat gummy bears with his if I let him."

"Hey, gummy bears go with everything," her husband insisted.

And there was that smile that brightened his life. Ellie shook her head. "I will skip the gummy bears but go heavy on the veggies, please."

"See, someone who doesn't eat like a seven-year-old." Mia hummed as she began prepping.

"Thank you," Ellie said as she settled in next to Bran.

When Riley sat down across from her, the table finally felt right.

Twelve

She was making a horrible mistake. She stood in the reasonably clean bathroom at the courthouse and stared at herself in the mirror, grateful for the few moments alone. This was not how she'd thought her wedding day would go.

Her second wedding day. It seemed like she was forever on the raw end of the wedding stick. Now she was actively going into a marriage with the full knowledge it would fail. Because she wasn't going to get her happily ever after with a man who could betray her like that. No matter what he said.

There was no question about it. She thought briefly about running. She could take off and run as far and fast as her Prada heels would carry her.

Which wouldn't be far. She rather suspected the Lawless clan knew that. Designer shoes were really a trick by men to slow women down. Put a chick in four-inch heels and suddenly she couldn't sprint away and find a new life as a mole person underground. Ellie had thought about it on the ride over. She could rule there. She could be queen of the mole people. She would take care of them and they wouldn't ever turn on her. She could happily live out her life being the queen of the sewer because no one would try to steal that from her.

What the hell was she doing?

"Are you all right?" Mia stepped inside. She'd changed into a lovely pink sheath dress that likely cost more than most people made in a month.

The whole clan was in designer duds, including Mia's hunky husband. They were too gorgeous, too much.

"I don't belong here." She meant that on so many levels. She shouldn't be marrying a man so she could stay out of jail. She shouldn't be selling herself for protection.

She should be marrying Riley because she loved him. Unfortunately, that love was in the past tense. She could never trust the man again.

"In the courthouse?" Mia asked. "I wish we could do it someplace nicer, too."

"No, I meant here with all of you." How would she function in the penthouse? Should she view herself as an employee? Or an ally? She'd been on her own most of her life. Suddenly being around so many people was odd. "Did you have to come? Riley and I can sign some papers on our own."

"It's my brother's wedding," she said with a quizzical half smile. "Where else would I be? Drew doesn't like to be photographed, but the rest of us will stand beside you when the inevitable reporters show up."

Ellie groaned. "Will they?"

She could be yesterday's news. Literally. It would be a relief.

"Oh, they'll show up. Garrison's here, too, and trust me, that man only shows up when the cameras are around. He's got a statement and everything. I know this marriage isn't what you planned, but you're one of us for a while. You should get used to being intrusively supported. I think it's because we got split up so young. We're doing the obnoxious-sibling thing now. And if you think this is bad, you should meet Case's family. They're twice as bad, twice as many, and they're all heavily armed. His oldest brother makes Drew look like a soft little kitten."

She couldn't imagine anyone making Drew Lawless look weak. The man oozed power and pure will.

She straightened her skirt. "Well, I'll try not to get too used to it. I've been married before. This is more people than who attended my first wedding."

"Just you and your family, huh?"

Ellie scoffed. "More like me and Colin and a slightly drunk pastor in Vegas. My father couldn't be bothered and my sister didn't care until later when she decided Colin was the perfect man for her."

"Did you invite your father?"

"I wanted a big wedding." It was silly, but she'd wanted a white dress and all the trappings. She'd thought she was starting her own family and wanted everything to be perfect. "He gave us the tickets to Vegas since he was using the company jet that week. He told me to be back at work on Monday or I was fired. Gosh, I don't miss my father."

"Well, he was a murderer. So no fatherly affection. Here, let me fix the back of your hair. The wind did a number on it." Mia moved in behind her.

Ellie stayed still as Mia began smoothing down her twist. It was odd to think of it, but this woman was about to be her sister-in-law. Mia had already done more for her than Shari ever had. "My dad wasn't big on affection. He viewed me as the smart one, though, so I got placed at StratCast young. The only time my father seemed willing to spend much time with me was at the end. I think once it sank in that he was really dying, he became afraid of being alone. That was when he told me the secret."

"But he didn't mention Castalano or Patricia Cain?"

She watched Mia in the mirror. The other woman's jaw had tightened, but her hands remained gentle. There was nothing about Mia's demeanor that told Ellie she was angry. "No. I asked because obviously they'd been there in the beginning. Patricia sold out her shares when she got her television show, but she had a major stake in the beginning."

"He didn't tell you they had anything to do with my parents' murders?"

"He was a little out of it by the end." She tried not to think about those last days. She'd sat by his hospital bed, the dutiful daughter to a father who had never loved her. She'd figured out long ago that she couldn't measure her life by how other people treated her. It was how she treated them that made her Ellie. She hadn't been able to abandon her father. "Sometimes I wonder if he knew it was me he was talking to. He said he could only speak for himself. And then he talked about a cave where all the sins were kept. That was when I knew the drugs had kicked in."

Mia chuckled. "I think it's a good thing you were with him. You would have regretted it. No matter what he did, he was your father. I worry I'm going to feel that way about my brothers one day."

"What do you mean?"

She finished up and moved away. "I love them so much, but I think revenge is more important to them than family or love or anything. Drew's become single-minded. Why am I saying *become*? He always was. Now that single-minded focus has shifted from how to keep us together to how to tear apart the people who hurt us. I know he thinks he can handle it, but if getting to them means giving up a piece of his soul? I don't want that for him."

"This isn't only about what Steven did to your parents, though that would be enough. I always meant to go to Drew and tell him what I knew."

"But you were going to wait until after the buyout so your people were out of the line of fire."

Mia seemed to understand her. "Yes. Steven didn't care. All that mattered was taking what he needed. He'll strip the company bare. He'll take everything my developers have worked so hard on and sell it for parts like a stolen vehicle, never understanding or caring about what it could have been, could have done for the world."

"If you think about it, he's really trying to do it again. He stole my father's code and built a company. Now he's trying to steal from your developers. Do you really think he won't let the project play out?"

She shrugged. "I think this particular project won't really start making money for a decade or more. He might have that or he might not. It would be far easier for him to sell the project to someone else under the table. A bit of corporate espionage from the top of the food chain."

"That would be nice to prove," Mia mentioned.

"I'm sure they've done lots we would love to prove." She was stalling. Drew had managed to find a friendly judge who had waived the twenty-four-hour waiting period and would marry them on a weekend. "I want you to know I'm going to do my best to be unobtrusive around the condo. Riley's already told me he doesn't want me to find an apartment. Apparently our cover is important now. I don't want you to think I'm going to take advantage of your family."

Mia nodded. "And you should know I'm going to do everything in my power to draw you in and make you love us because it's a sausage fest in there and I need some estrogen to hang with, sister. At least when we're with Case's family there are plenty of women around."

"Armed women." Apparently. Now she was curious about the Taggart side of the family.

"You have no idea. I'll give you a couple of minutes, but don't take too long. Riley's worried you'll run away. I told him no one can run in those shoes." Mia winked, and Ellie was left alone again.

Her second marriage. Soon it would be her second divorce. All that mattered was getting her company back. She would let the Lawless brothers deal with Castalano and the rest.

Her cell trilled and she looked down. Steven. That bastard had the balls to call her?

She didn't even think about ignoring him. She swiped her finger across the screen. "What do you want?"

"I hear you've gotten yourself out of jail. That was very quick. Tell me something. How are you going to afford Henry Garrison, dear? He might take you on for the publicity, but he's going to want to be paid in the end."

Why was he calling her? Taunting her? Was this how the man got his jollies? "I don't think that's any of your business. You should know that I've already put a legal team on the partnership agreement. I'm not selling my stock to you."

A humorless chuckle came over the line. "You will. The only question is how much you get for it. If I force your hand right now you'll get nothing. Or you could play ball with me and come out of this with half a future. The man you think of as Riley Lang is the son of an old adversary of mine."

"Benedict Lawless."

"Excellent. So I was right and they're the ones paying Garrison."

She winced. So this was information gathering. She couldn't feel too bad about it. They were talking to the press in an hour or so. He would have found out anyway. "It's really none of your business."

He ignored her. "Yes, I see they've likely told you the tale. Naturally you won't care to hear my side. I think if you go to Riley, he'll try to protect you. He can't. All that's going to happen is I'll have to take down the entire family one by one. I won't hesitate. If you care about them in any way, you'll convince them to give this up. I suspect that will be impossible, so you should protect yourself, Ellie."

Anger burned inside her. "What makes you think you can touch them?"

"I can touch anyone. You certainly didn't see me coming. I'll take them out, but if you back off and give me what I need, I'll think about going easy on your lover."

"On the man who betrayed me?"

"Is that how you're playing it? Don't be ridiculous. I saw him after you were hauled out. He didn't care about his revenge then. I expected more from him. I thought for a moment I might have found a worthy adversary. He's more like his father than I gave him credit for. Apparently Benedict's ridiculous softness has found its way to the new generation. You looked quite pathetic on the news, by the way. The camera added far more than ten pounds. You know the truth is you're actually lovely in person. If you hadn't been so very prudish, I might have considered you for myself."

The idea made her flush with anger. "Now you just want to make me sick."

"No, I want you to understand that the man you knew for all those years doesn't exist. I'm far worse than your father ever thought of being, so you should back down now while you still have something to live for. Get out of this fight. It's between me and the big dogs. You'll only get hurt."

"What is the purpose of this call, Steven? I know you didn't call for my health and well-being."

There was a low chuckle over the line. "Your father left me something. I want it. It was to come to me upon his death."

Her father had left a lot of things behind, but nothing that would interest Steven Castalano that she could think of. With the singular exception of StratCast stock, and he almost had his hands on that. "There was nothing left to you in his will."

"This was a gentlemen's agreement and it has nothing at all to do with legalities. StratCast made its fortune from the original source code we based the company on."

"The code you stole from Benedict Lawless."

He sighed. "Ah, they've been telling tales. No matter what they say, they can prove nothing. Your father took the original code and held it hostage over my head all these years. I want it back. Find it and I'll stop the prosecution. I'll purchase your stock when it comes back up by, say, twenty percent. Then you'll be out of this war you find yourself in. You can take the money and enjoy your life."

Twenty percent was still less than half of what she should have been owed. "It seems to me that source code would be worth more."

"More than your freedom? More than their lives? If you don't get me that source code, something terrible could happen to that lover of yours. Not that I would have anything to do with it, of course. Or your sister. I know she's a bitch of the highest order, but she's your only blood. Perhaps I'll start firing all your friends here. I think I'll start with dear Lily. My son likes her, but I am less enthralled."

A chill went through her. This man was capable of anything. "So if I find this source code, why wouldn't I give it to Drew Lawless?"

"The code itself proves nothing," he replied in an even tone. "He can drag my name through the mud, but it won't mean a thing. I would like to avoid that. I would like to avoid all-out war with them. I simply wish to retire in the near future with as much cash as possible. You're going to be tempted to choose them over me."

"Oh, *tempted* is a silly word." She wouldn't choose him if he was the last person on earth.

"Nonetheless, they'll never care about you. You have to start thinking with something other than your sadly underused lady parts. They're using you. You'll always be Phillip Stratton's daughter to them. They hate us, Ellie. They hate all of us. They would do anything to bring down this company. They'll say anything to get you on their side. I know what I did was brutal, but it's nothing compared to what Drew Lawless will do to you. Take my deal. Get yourself and your loved ones out of the line of fire. You could start again if I convince the prosecutors that I was wrong. I can pin this on someone else. I can give you back your life. You can come back to StratCast and take care of research and development. You were never suited for an executive position anyway."

"I'm supposed to marry him in a few minutes."

A pause came over the line. "They're willing to go very far to bring you in. Perhaps you'll have an accident soon and then Drew

Lawless will have what he needs. His brother will have your stock. He could fight the contract. It's what he's been trained to do. Think about it. Every single one of them has given up their own hopes and dreams so they can be soldiers. Do you really think they would welcome the daughter of their enemy into their home without having a plan to get rid of you?"

Could they be plotting? Absolutely. Riley was ruthless. His whole family was. Mia's sweetness and sunshine could all be an act. Her husband's stoic routine could be there to make Ellie feel comfortable. Would Case Taggart really help her? Maybe not. All of Drew's offers could be complete shit.

Marriage would give Riley her stock. Her stock might or might not be worth anything, but he couldn't play at all if she wasn't in the game.

If he married her he had access to anything she owned, anything her father had left her. He might be hunting for this source code. He'd gotten into her bed in order to screw with Castalano. He could go this far, too.

"Think about it," Castalano said over the line, his voice smooth as silk. "This doesn't have to end poorly for you. Why don't you come by and we'll talk about it. We can have dinner and discuss how we can help each other."

If she went through with this marriage, she was taking the biggest risk of her life. She could actually be risking her life.

"Fuck you."

She hung up the phone. He didn't get to take one more thing from her. He sure as hell wasn't taking away her chance to fight. He might think she was soft, but she knew when it came time to take a risk.

She strode out to where her almost-husband stood, surrounded by family.

"Are you planning on offing me in order to take control of my stock?"

Riley went white. "What? Ellie, I'm doing this to protect you. What-

ever else has happened between us, know that I would never hurt you."
He took her shoulders in his hands, looking her right in the eyes. "I will
do my best, try my hardest to never hurt you again."

He could be the world's best actor, but she had three choices. Him
or Castalano or going it alone. She'd been alone for far too long.

"Let's do this thing."

Riley looked out over the darkened park and wondered when his
blood pressure would tick down again. It was hours after his wedding,
hours after they'd greeted the press together, and Ellie had just now
thought to drop her bomb. Talk about burying the lede.

"He threatened you."

Ellie had changed clothes, getting into a pair of jeans that showed
off her every curve and a black T-shirt that clung to her breasts. She
sat on the sofa looking completely delicious.

It was their wedding night. She was his wife. He had the paperwork and everything. He'd never planned on getting married. Never
really thought about it.

Damn, but he wanted to fuck his wife. He wanted to get her in bed
and not leave again for a few days. He wanted to be getting on a plane
to someplace tropical where he could keep her naked and sated and
happy.

And he wanted to shake her a little since she hadn't bothered to
mention this situation earlier.

"Did he directly threaten you?" Drew asked.

"Oh, yeah. He was practically twirling his evil-villain mustache."
Ellie sighed as she took a sip of the wine she and Mia were enjoying.
"I hung up on his ass before he could give me the *mwah-ha-ha* laugh."

"This is serious," Riley complained.

At some point in time Ellie had relaxed. She'd held his hand during the interview and managed to look like a bride. Now she seemed

fairly happy. She'd sat with Mia and Case and talked for the longest time. She wouldn't hold his hand again, though.

"Of course it is." Bran walked in and started passing out beers. "But we'll handle it. We're the good guys."

Riley was certain his wife would argue about that. He wasn't going to give her the chance to. "I want to know everything he said to you, and I damn straight want to know why I'm only hearing about it now."

She sat back. "Because I was fairly certain you would throw a hissy fit and then all of it would have been for nothing. We were supposed to look like star-crossed lovers, not like you were about to change into the Hulk. Should your eyebrow be twitching like that?"

Mia leaned over. "It does that when he throws a hissy fit."

"I am not throwing a hissy fit. I am very reasonably pissed off that the man who killed my parents is now making threatening phone calls to my wife." He put a hand over his left eye in a vain attempt to stop the stupid twitch that happened when he got truly enraged.

"She's right, though. You look psychotic, bro." Bran sat down with the women.

"Calm down." Hatch sat to Drew's left, still in the clothes he'd worn to the wedding.

His wedding. He'd stood in the judge's office and promised to love, honor, and cherish Ellie Stratton until the day she died. It was wrong to put it like that. She could die first and he was fairly certain he would still love her, still honor and cherish her. He was wretchedly sure there would be no other woman for him, and he'd screwed it all up.

He needed to stay calm or he could lose any shot he might have with her. If she thought he was a crazed maniac, she might run sooner than later. He took a deep breath and tried to go for a smile. "Baby, why don't you tell me what he said. I think we would all appreciate knowing about that conversation."

A grin appeared on Ellie's face. "Wow. Now you look like a psycho who's trying to pass for normal. It's actually creepier than the first."

"Damn it, Ellie." So much for staying calm.

"Fine." She set her glass down and crossed her legs. "He called to tell me that he would stop the prosecution if I play ball with him. He wants me to stay away from you and to turn over the source code my father stole."

He stopped, her words chilling him. "Your father had the source code?"

"Apparently. He said it was supposed to come to him on my father's death, but it didn't. Either my dad screwed him over or something went wrong. I got the feeling it was something dear old Dad held over his head." She turned to Drew. "He told me it wouldn't prove anything."

Drew's eyes narrowed. "It might not, but I would love to get hold of it."

"He doesn't know that I have a copy of that code. The code itself didn't belong to the company. That was something Benedict was working on in his spare time. The code that eventually became the foundation of StratCast is something your father claimed he and Castalano worked on over the years. We didn't have auto backups back then that were as good as they are today. We really could lose things. Ben would back up to a hard disk. The odd thing was about a week before he died, he asked me to keep a copy, too," Hatch explained.

"Why didn't you put that out there when StratCast first formed?" Ellie asked.

The room went quiet.

Riley tried to figure out a way to explain without throwing Hatch under a bus. "He wasn't in a very good place back then."

"I was drunk," Hatch corrected. "By the time I was sober enough to deal with it, the patents had already been filed and there wasn't a lot we could do. But I was smart enough to keep the original code. I'm sure they thought they burned all the backups in the fire. I wasn't capable of doing a goddamn thing. I didn't even realize you kids had gone into foster care until weeks later and what did I do? I drank some more and told myself there wasn't anything I could do."

"It's all right, Hatch," Drew said, his voice calm. "It's all in the past. I don't know that you could have done anything. The police had closed the case. It's highly unlikely we would have gotten a judge to force them to open their source code. Our father was a little naive. He hadn't put in for a patent. StratCast did that quite quickly. We were kids and you didn't have the best reputation even before they died. You need to let it go. No one blames you."

"So if I could find the source code, we could potentially use it against him? Could we prove it was your father's?" Ellie asked.

There were several problems with that scenario. "It would be difficult to prove it at this point. Castalano will very likely say that it was his partner's code. Your father is dead. My father is dead."

"But code is its own language." Ellie sat up straight. "My father never wrote a ton of code, but I might be able to find it. Code is like any language. We all speak it differently. At this point, the code we use has been rewritten about a thousand times, but that source code would show the truth."

"And then Castalano would say Stratton did it and fooled him or that Dad was in business with them, so it did belong to them. The problems are endless, but if Castalano wants it, I think we should make sure he doesn't get it." He wasn't about to allow Ellie to hand over anything to Castalano. He wasn't going to let her be in the same room with that fucker. He hated the fact that she'd been on the phone with him.

"But I don't know where it is," Ellie admitted. "I packed up my father's office. There wasn't anything like that. He'd gotten rid of most of his old material long ago. I went through his laptop and everything I could find. I've been in his office for over a year now. If it was there, it's long gone."

"Was there anyone he would have left it with?" As far as Riley was aware, Phillip Stratton had outlived his two wives and there hadn't been a girlfriend he'd seemed close to. His last six months had played out at his home or in a hospital where his daughters had been the only regular visitors.

Ellie shook her head. "He didn't have any friends. Not any he trusted, and now anything I might have had at my house has likely been taken into custody. I can try to get in touch with his admin. She retired when he got sick."

"Give me her name and I'll get us all the relevant information," Case offered.

"What did he threaten you with?" Mia asked.

"Her life, of course." Riley had done nothing but think about all the ways Castalano could hurt her since yesterday.

Ellie pushed her hair back. She'd taken it down after they'd gotten home and now it flowed around her shoulders. "No, that was you, according to him. He told me you would marry me to get my stock and then I would have a convenient accident. He said none of you would ever accept Phillip Stratton's daughter into your family."

"Well, we definitely wouldn't take the other one. I read the write-up on her," Bran said with a shake of his head. "Sorry, but your sister's a skank. You're perfectly welcome. You make Riley less obnoxious. He also masturbates way less."

"Dude!" His brother's humor was often lost on Riley.

Ellie's throaty laugh filled the room. "I think he's going to have to go back to that." She turned to Case. "Speaking of my skanky sister, he did threaten her and all of you." She sobered a bit. "I think he was going to try to hurt you whether I did as he asked or not. He's going to come after you all. I was hoping Case could help me with Shari. She's a horrible person, but she's my sister."

"What can I do?" Case asked.

"If Steven kidnapped her, he would have a decent hold on me. I was hoping I could use my newfound Lawless fortune to hire you to kidnap her first," Ellie said.

"What?" Riley had to have heard her wrong.

"I think that can be arranged," Case said with an easy smile.

"Did you just ask someone to kidnap your sister? Who the hell are you?" He couldn't stop himself.

She glanced back at Riley. "Hey, we're married now so I can let my freak flag fly. You know what they say, Counselor. It's all sweatpants and ponytails and kidnappings after the wedding."

Case held up a hand. "I can handle the sister. We'll make sure she goes somewhere safe and quiet for a month or two."

"Pay her," Drew said. "That woman goes through money like it's water. Tell her if she'll stay at my place near Bali for a month, we'll give her a million dollars."

"She would go for that," Ellie allowed. "But she gets bored easily and she loves attention. I saw that she gave an interview yesterday defending me. I was surprised at that. Oh, she talked about how I would never survive in prison because I wasn't pretty enough, but she seemed genuinely concerned."

"Not a problem. It's a private island. I'll cut cell access and she won't have a boat," Drew explained. "She'll be out of our hair. Should I send the boyfriend with her?"

"Let Castalano have him." He didn't want that fucker to get a nice vacation. "We'll let Castalano torture him. It'll give the asshole something to do."

Ellie merely nodded Drew's way. "Yes, please. Maybe after a month of being alone together they'll see if they're really suited. I'd love to see how they do without Internet. It's its own form of torture for those two. Well, that's one problem settled. According to Garrison, I don't have to deal with appearing in court for a while, so I can focus on trying to figure out where my father might have stored that source code. My only other worry is my friend Lily."

"She won't want to come out." He'd talked to Lily several times. Not since Castalano had started threatening people, but he doubted that would change her mind. Lily Gallo wasn't the kind of woman who wilted in the heat.

Ellie looked over at Case.

"And you can't have her kidnapped." What the hell was going on with his wife? "Is that your go-to now?"

Ellie shrugged him off. "It seems like an easy solution. I'll call her in a while. But if it gets really dangerous, I'm having her yanked. I'm not allowing that man to kill someone I care about. So has anyone figured out how Castalano managed to frame me? I still don't understand all of that."

"The holding companies were in your name." Drew set down his beer. "It's easy enough to do. All they needed was to register the LLCs to you and have someone forge your signature."

"I've got the auditor's name. StratCast would have gone through several audits that should have caught something," Case explained.

Bran shook his head. "It was a nice, sneaky thing. I've gone through some of it. Corporations as big as StratCast make large purchases. It's inevitable. He kept most of them under ten grand, and I suspect some of them were viable purchases. They simply overpaid for the materials and the money kicked back to Castalano."

"How can I prove it wasn't me?" Ellie asked.

"We open your personal books." He'd been thinking this through all day. He intended to go over her defense with Garrison with a fine-tooth comb. He wouldn't leave any stone unturned. He didn't want this to go to trial. He would find a way to get it thrown out before then. "I'm going to start looking at the dates of the purchase orders to prove that you weren't even working at StratCast at the time."

"They'll blame my father and say I took over for him." Ellie easily figured that out.

"We find the accounts. He's likely using offshore accounts, but he's got to get that money laundered somewhere. And someone's been filing tax returns for the shell companies. We figure out who that is and maybe we have some leverage." He'd already put Case's team on that. "The good news is, he didn't pull this off alone. Someone's helping him, and we'll figure out who it is. Once we've got a name, we'll apply pressure and see what happens."

"I've got some thoughts on it, too." Hatch began a spirited debate about how they were going to save Ellie from the big house.

Three hours later he stood in front of the room he'd slept in every time he came to New York. He'd given it up to her. He liked the idea that her clothes were in his closet. Even when his were no longer there.

He wanted to take her down to Austin. He had his own place there. He'd bought the three-bedroom house because Drew had told him it was a good investment. He wanted to share it with Ellie.

Or they could find their own place here.

"Is the room all right? I don't have an apartment in the city because it always seemed easier to stay with Drew when we were up here."

"It's fine." Her hand was on the doorknob.

He was standing in front of her like an idiot, hoping he could get so much as a good-night smile from his wife. "If there's anything I can do to make it better . . ."

She stopped with her hand on the door. "Riley, you can't seriously expect me to sleep with you tonight. Tell me that's not why you're here and not going to your own room. You do have a room, right?"

"No. Of course not." Although a man could hope. "I wanted to make sure you have everything you need."

She stared at him, her eyes meeting his. "You know I do. You were thorough about stocking the bathroom and the closet."

"I tried to make sure of it. I tried to remember the things you like."

"Did you search my apartment?"

He'd promised her he wouldn't lie. Damn, but he wished she hadn't gone there. "Yes."

She turned to him, leaning against the closed door. "All right. I suspected that. Oh, not when it would have done me any good, but when I was in jail I had a lot of time to think, and I realized you had very likely used the time after I went to sleep to search my place."

"I'm sorry."

"It was a waste of your time and talents. Unless you wanted to find my stash of sadly underused sex toys and discover that I have a hidden love of tabloid rags, you were likely disappointed."

"I'm still sorry. It was a violation of your trust."

Her face was a careful blank. "Would you do it again?"

He knew the answer to that question. Not that she would likely believe him. "No. I would come to you and ask you to help me, but I didn't know you then."

She smiled, but there wasn't any humor in it. "You didn't have an opportunity to search my place until after we slept together, Riley. That was the majority of our relationship. You didn't know me by then? Because I thought I knew you. It's why I went to bed with you. I thought I'd finally found the guy who got me. The guy who wouldn't be scared off by my long hours. The one who understood the business but didn't think I was an idiot for what I wanted to do. You did get me. You got me good."

He hated the cynicism in her voice. Of all the things he could have done, turning her hard and jaded seemed like the worst thing he could do. Ellie viewed the world differently. It was made brighter by her beliefs. "I made a mistake, Ellie. I made a horrible mistake and I should have trusted you. I should have told you everything, but I wasn't programmed for this. This is completely new to me. Growing up I was taught one thing and one thing only. I could trust my siblings. No one else. They were all I had and we had one thing in life we needed to do."

"Get revenge on my father."

How could he make her understand? "Justice. If the courts wouldn't give it to us, then we had to take it. We had to completely rebuild our world and we had to do it from nothing. I couldn't take the chance that you would go to Castalano. I thought you wouldn't, but I owed it to my parents to do anything I could to bring him down. Hell, Ellie, can't you see what we were doing was for the best? Look at what's happened. He would have done this whether or not I'd been here."

"He wouldn't have been able to tank the stock without you," she pointed out.

"But he would have put you in jail and taken the company, and no one would have been here to save you." That had to get him some points with her.

"That's true, and yes, I would have been in a horrible position. I would have gone to your brother for help and we would have met. And you wouldn't have given me a second look."

How could she possibly believe that? "That's not true."

She stared at him, her eyes so focused. "Have you ever gone out with a woman like me, Riley?"

"What is that supposed to mean?"

"It means I looked you up. I found some pictures in the Austin social pages."

Shit. He'd had a thing for tall blondes. He'd dated a few models. None of it mattered. "I've never felt this way about another woman. I've never told a woman I loved her. Not once. Only you."

"It won't last," she said sadly. "I think what you're feeling right now is guilt. Things didn't go as you planned and you didn't expect to feel such guilt over how it worked out for me. So let that go. We'll work together and we'll do whatever we can to make it right. But you don't love me. I would have done it, by the way. I would have done anything you asked of me because I did love you. You think I got the good end of everything, but I didn't have siblings I could count on. I don't have any memory of my parents loving me. I even knew deep down that it wouldn't work with Colin. I never opened myself up to him. Not really. It's why I can't leave him to Castalano any more than I would my sister. I didn't have anyone I could trust. Anyone except you. Good night, Riley. We'll get to work in the morning."

She opened the door and it closed between them. He heard the small snick of the lock bolting him out and realized he might have lost her forever.

Thirteen

Ellie walked as softly as she could through the hallway. She couldn't sleep. The clock beside her bed read three forty-five, but it seemed so much later.

Which room was Riley staying in? The penthouse was massive. It seemed to have entire wings. She kind of wanted to explore, but the day had been taken up with marriage and threats and all the juicy parts of a really good novel. Well, with the exception of sex, because she wasn't going to do that anymore. Sex got her in trouble.

She glanced at the door to her right. Riley could be anywhere.

Not that it mattered. She kept telling herself that, but when she closed her eyes all she could see was Riley with his gorgeous eyes and that square jaw that softened when she made him smile. She would have sworn as she lay there that she could still feel his hands on her, sliding along her skin as he kissed every inch of her. The man always seemed so hungry, so ready to devour her.

How could she already miss him?

She'd only had a few weeks with him. How could so little time have left such an ache in her body?

She moved toward the kitchen, intent on grabbing a bottle of water.

It was quite ridiculous that she couldn't sleep because she couldn't get her mind off Riley. She had so many other lovely things to worry about. Prison time for crimes she didn't commit. The potential murders of her friends and family. The fact that she'd lost her company and reputation and might never get either back.

But what was she thinking about? She was thinking about how Riley made her feel in bed and how much she was going to miss him. Her girl parts were apparently way more important than her dignity or financial status.

At least one of her problems was leaving. Her sister was heading to Drew's place in the islands tomorrow afternoon. She'd been more than happy to accept the vacation from her new in-laws.

She stopped at the sight of the city at night. The massive bank of windows made a magnificent mural of light and dark.

"It's beautiful, isn't it?"

She gasped and turned. Bran was on the sofa, his head resting on his hand, his body lying on his side. Despite what they'd said this morning at breakfast, Bran actually had quite a bit of muscle on him, as evidenced by the very cut chest he had on display. It looked like he had a sheet wrapped around his lean waist and nothing more.

"Tell me you're not naked under there. And why are you on the couch?"

Bran sat straight up. "Hey, no nudity. It's not that kind of place. PJ bottoms." He flashed flannel bottoms. "As for why I'm out here, I like the view. It feels like I'm the only person in the world and this show is all for me. Us now, since you're here and I'm no longer the only person in the world. I would actually hate that, by the way. I know the shrinks will all tell you that I have several personality disorders, but I quite like most people. I'm simply very active about the ones I don't like. I think that makes me honest. They like to use words like *anger issues*. We agree to disagree."

Her new brother-in-law was odd, but likable. "You like to sleep on the couch?"

Bran ran his hand over his head. He looked slightly younger than his twenty-eight years, with thick hair and all-American good looks. Like his brothers, he could have been on the cover of a magazine. "I like this couch better than the one in the game room. The media room chairs all lie back, but without a movie or something playing, it's got a tomblike vibe and that's kind of Riley's thing, not mine. When Mia and Chase head back to Texas, he'll move into their room."

"He took your room?" She sighed and sat on the chair across from him. "I take it I'm in his."

"I don't mind. Riley needs a room. I don't. I could bunk with Hatch or Drew, but Drew snores and Hatch talks in his sleep. He says some weird shit. I have no idea what goes on in his dream world, but it's crazy. So I came out here. It looks so peaceful at this time of night."

"The city? Yes, it's lovely at night. Of course, it helps to be forty stories up. It's a little different on the ground."

"It's still beautiful in its way. That's what I've really learned. It's all about how you look at things. We often choose to make something ugly or beautiful."

She couldn't see anything good in her current situation, but she didn't want to talk about that now. She knew she should get her water and go, but she found herself curious. "Why would he take your room? I understand that I'm in his, but shouldn't he be the one out here on the couch?"

"He can't sleep in an unlocked room." Bran turned to her, his skin lit by the city lights. "I thought he told you."

"All he ever said was he couldn't sleep with another person in the room." If Bran was willing to talk, she would count this early-morning session as a win.

Despite the fact that she knew there was nothing between her and Riley now, she still found herself hungry for information about him.

"He got the shit kicked out of him once," Bran explained with a shrug, as though that was something that happened every day. "It was bad. A couple of broken ribs and one of his legs. He got a trip to the hospital. They jumped him in his bed one night. He was in the hospital for a while and then in rehab for the broken leg and then Drew got custody of him because he'd managed to sober Hatch up, and they'd gotten a place to live. Still, Riley can't sleep with anyone else in the room and he really needs the door locked. I worry that something will happen to him and we'll have to break the damn door down because I'm fairly certain that he puts a chair under the door handle, too."

He'd been a boy. Alone. Scared. How bad must the incident have been that he still felt the need to protect himself to this day? "I was surprised when he told me he wouldn't sleep with me."

But he'd been so earnest about it, she hadn't thought to be offended. He'd looked sad, as though he wanted so badly to be normal.

There's no such thing as normal, she'd told him.

"I wondered how you would take that. I totally offered to seduce you, by the way," he said with a grin. "I thought I was the better choice. I would have stayed in bed with you all night. I'm a cuddler."

He was a charmer. Unfortunately, she'd already been caught by one Lawless. She wasn't falling for another. "I don't think that would have worked unless you're a lawyer."

"Nope. MBA."

"You don't look like an MBA to me." She'd hired many an MBA. They tended to be type A personalities. All buttoned up and strait-laced. Bran Lawless looked like he should be hanging out on a movie set.

"I did it for 4L," he admitted.

"For 4L or for The Plan?" She'd come to think of the Lawless siblings' revenge plots as The Plan. It seemed to need that extra-special capitalization since according to what she'd heard and seen, it had been something they'd worked toward most of their lives. They'd plotted revenge with the single-mindeness most people used on seducing their beloveds.

"Both, I guess. It's hard to think about other things when there's a hole inside you. I'm not as sure as Drew and Riley that it can be filled with some magical vengeance, but they need it."

"You don't?" That wasn't how he'd sounded this morning.

"No, I do. I need to know that the people who killed my parents can't do it to anyone else. I do owe them that justice. But Drew and Riley rarely think past it. I wonder what any of us is going to have left when we're done. Will we still be this close? Will we find out the thing that was missing all along was something different?"

"See, MBAs don't tend to think like that."

He smiled, an open, happy expression that dialed his charm way up. "I have a minor in psychology. I would have likely tried to be a therapist or a social worker if I hadn't needed the MBA. But if I'd been the one going into StratCast, I would have been a good hire. I was going to try for one of the project management jobs. And then I would have romanced the boss."

She was glad to get back to the issue at hand. Getting to know Bran was a bit unsettling. Still, it was hard to get mad at him when he looked so damn cute. "Then we wouldn't have worked in the same department, and I have to say that proximity really helped your brother. Despite what I'm sure he believed would happen, I didn't fall into bed with him the first day I met him. I suppose he won the Ellie lottery because of his law degree."

Bran sat back. "Drew could have done it. He offered to hire on in R&D. After looking at the way my brother works, you would have hired him in a heartbeat. We discussed all the possible scenarios. Riley insisted on taking the job and I think that was more about you than he'll even admit to himself. We all studied up on you, read the reports. Riley got a bit obsessed. He read all the articles about you."

She just bet he had. "Know your enemy."

He stared at her for a moment. "See, that's what I'm talking about. I tell you one thing and you put your spin on it. I'm utterly fascinated by how human beings ever manage to communicate when we so obviously don't speak the same language ever."

So Bran was a philosopher. "I'm not sure what you mean by that."

"I said something. You heard something else. I spend all day working in an industry that claims to truly connect human beings. The Internet, social media, it's supposed to bring us closer together. That's the job, right?"

All of this pain had begun because apparently Benedict Lawless had believed he could do that. His code had helped to make the Internet faster, more reliable. "That's what we're trying to do."

"All it does is make me understand that we can't ever be connected," Bran countered. "Not really. Our lives are lived in these meat suits, and no one else can know what it means to me or you. We can empathize, but at the end all that information isn't pure. It's filtered through our experiences, and the information that went in gets distorted, mangled by what we lived through before. I told you Riley became obsessed with a beautiful woman he saw, but you heard that he was studying an enemy."

Something about the wistfulness in his voice opened a well inside her. "I never felt pretty until I was with him. Not really. It's stupid, isn't it? I'm a twenty-seven-year-old woman. I was going to run a major tech company and I still want to feel pretty. Shouldn't I be beyond that now?"

"No one ever gets past that. Not really, I think. Do you think you'll ever be able to forgive him?"

"Sure." In some ways she had. "I understand why he felt the need to do what he did. Losing your parents like that had to be horrible."

Bran looked back at her, and she had the feeling he saw more than she would like. This nighttime view of Bran was changing her opinion of him. He saw more than he told his siblings, likely felt more, too. "There's understanding and then there's forgiveness."

"Are you asking me if I'll give your brother another chance to savage me?"

Bran laughed, but it sounded more ironic than anything else. "Well, that answers my question."

"Would you?" She didn't like how she felt about this conversation. It made her antsy. She was the victim, but Bran made her feel like she was doing something wrong. "Would you walk right back into a relationship with someone who hurt you the way Riley hurt me?"

"It would depend on whether or not I loved the girl. It would depend on whether or not she really knew what she was doing."

"He knew exactly what he was doing."

"None of us knew how badly it would hurt you. We thought it would put you through a few days of discomfort—which Riley would have been there to support you through—and then you would have the company. Not once was it discussed that we should take StratCast. Never."

Though it had been their father's brilliance and blood the company had been built on. She supposed she'd never thought of it. They could have come after her company in a way that she could never have taken it back. Drew Lawless could have bought up stock until he could claim the board and fire her. He could have bought them out and casually dismantled the place like a lion enjoying a light snack.

"You should think about that when you consider how much to punish Riley," Bran offered. "As to your question, yes. I think if I loved her, I would. I think my pride would mean less than my love. At least I hope it would because I have found that love is very rare. It's not something you toss away because it didn't come in the package you thought it would."

"Well, you don't understand, then." Everything Riley had told her was a lie. He'd come into her life on false pretenses and then even when he'd known he had her, he'd continued to lie. If he'd told her what he was doing even up to a few minutes before Castalano had sprung his trap, she could have dealt with it. The only reason he'd told was because he'd gotten caught. It wasn't the same as confessing.

She got up to go because it was obvious Bran was going to plead his brother's case and make her question what she knew was true and false.

That was the true danger of staying in this house. It wasn't curiosity. It was familiarity. How would she feel a couple of weeks from now when she'd really gotten to know these people? When they were more than simply the ruthless bastards who had run a wrecking ball through her life? When they were men who smiled and laughed and joked and she wanted to be one of them?

This was Riley's play. He was betting she couldn't hold herself apart and that one morning she would wake up and realize she didn't want to leave.

It was all still a game to him, and this was his latest move.

"I really do understand why he felt like he needed revenge," she said. "I'm sure what you all went through was horrible, but I'm out of all of this the minute I get my company back. I'm sure you'll go after Patricia next. Good luck with that."

She would grab her water and go back to her room. She wasn't playing this game with Riley. She didn't need any of these people. He'd supplied her with a laptop. Tomorrow she would spend her day researching the situation she found herself in. She needed to find a way to keep her stock. Could Castalano take it from her when she hadn't been found guilty yet? She would go over that contract until she found a loophole.

She would leave her room to grab some food and meet with her attorney. That was all. She wouldn't fall into the obvious trap.

"We were there, you know."

Bran's words made her stop. "There?"

"We were in the house that night. Drew and Riley don't talk about it. Mia doesn't remember it. I get it in flashes. Sometimes I wake up and I can feel the heat. I can hear Drew whispering. He should have been shouting, but he was scared because he thought they could still be there. He doesn't say it, but I think he saw something that night. He had Mia in his arms when he came for me and Riley. We shared a room back then. He wouldn't let us cry or talk until we got out through a window in the bathroom."

She knew she should walk away, but her feet wouldn't do the job. "Why not one of the doors?"

"Because someone was waiting for us. We tried the back door and they'd done something to it. We couldn't get it to open. I guess the fire took care of that because the cops said they didn't find anything." He stared out at the city again. "I think we were supposed to die, too."

The horror of it all washed over her. She'd known, but hearing about it from Bran made it more real than her father's admission. Her father had done that. He'd paid someone to do it. He'd paid someone to stand outside the door and keep those children inside. How had he sentenced a whole family to death over some code? Over cash?

"That's why it can't work." It was good to be reminded. Every time she thought about what her father had done, a pit opened in her gut. "I'll always be Phillip Stratton's daughter. I'll always have had a life built on your family's suffering."

Bran looked up at her quizzically. "Yes, you're your father's daughter. Absolutely. You've proven it time and time again. You likely would have helped him. Would you have done it? Would you have blocked the door? Would you do it now? If I was standing between you and Strat-Cast and all you had to do was take me out." His voice dropped to a whisper. "No one would know. Pull one trigger and everything you want is yours."

She couldn't help the tears that made the world watery and ill defined. "I would never do that."

Bran stood. "Because you might have his name, but your soul is your own, Ellie. Riley knows that. I'm sorry. I was harsh with you."

He put his arms around her and it was easy to take his affection.

How long had it been since someone offered simple kindness and she was able to take it? She laid her head on Bran's warm shoulder. There was nothing sexual about his comfort.

"You're not Phillip Stratton and we all know that. You think this was some play to keep you close to Riley, but I need you, too. I need to know that one of us can find some happiness," Bran whispered. "I'm pulling for you and Riley, but it's selfish. If Riley can make you love him, maybe there's someone for me."

She wrapped her arms around her brother-in-law. He was so sweet and smart and lost. Was it right to hold herself apart from him because she was scared? Her father had done such damage.

Could she undo some of it?

"I suppose it's good to know you don't hate all of us," a dark voice said.

The hands on her back suddenly came up and Bran took a step back. "It's only a hug, brother. She was crying because of something I said."

She turned and Riley was standing there. Apparently none of the Lawless men wore shirts. Of course, if she looked as good as they did, she might go around half naked, too. Riley was staring at his brother, his eyes fierce.

"What did you say to her?"

He was a little dramatic. She needed to shut him down now. "We were talking. I got emotional. He pointed out a few things to me."

"I might have mentioned that she's not anything like her father," Bran confessed.

"Of course she's not. I think I've told her that a few hundred times." Riley's eyes went between them.

"Are you seriously wondering if I have a thing for your brother? You have got to be kidding. I can't handle one of you much less start up a group." She huffed and stalked away into the kitchen.

The simple sight of the man set her on edge and she wasn't sure why. She'd come to terms with their nonmarriage. It didn't have to be acrimonious, but he'd stared at her like he was jealous.

How much of his act was she supposed to believe? What the hell was she going to do if it wasn't an act?

She opened the fridge and found a bottle of water.

"I'm sorry. I didn't like walking in and finding you with Bran."

She closed the fridge but didn't turn. "I kind of thought spending time with your family was one of the points of keeping me here."

He winced. "Maybe, but he's also younger than me and nicer than me and probably more attractive. It bothered me seeing you with him."

She couldn't help but roll her eyes. She turned and leaned against the fridge, needing as much space between them as she could get. "You're the hottest man in this condo and you know it."

"I really don't. I'm not as big and muscular as Drew or Case."

"They're too overwhelming. You're lean and muscular. Like a jaguar." His body was sleekly muscled, every single inch of him toned and perfect. Even the scars he had made him seem more real to her. She loved how warm his skin felt under her palm and how he shuddered when she touched him. He loved to be stroked.

"Bran's got a nose that's never been broken." He stepped in, his feet bare on the marble.

Even the man's feet were sexy. And she couldn't quite take her eyes off the way the pajama bottoms clung to his waist, showing off the cut notches at his hips. "Bran's too pretty for me."

"But he was the one you were hugging. I didn't even get a kiss today." He was close enough for her to smell the scent of sandalwood. He used it when he shaved.

Being this close to the man was something like a drug, his presence drowning her good intentions. Like she intended to walk off now. "I kissed you in the judge's office."

When the judge had proclaimed them man and wife, Riley had leaned over. His hands had gone to her waist and she'd seen that look in his eyes that let her know he was determined. He would have made that kiss last. He would have shown her what she was missing.

So she'd lightly brushed his lips and stepped back, making it awkward for him to do anything but let her go.

He put a hand on the fridge behind her, caging her. "That was a peck. That was nothing. I dream about kissing you, Ellie."

Again she intended to duck under him and walk away, but instead she stared at his lips. Too sensual and plump for a man. She liked to run her tongue across his bottom lip because it always made him sigh and pull her closer. "It's only been a few days since the last time you fucked me."

"Made love to you," he corrected. "And that's way too long."

She shook her head, well aware she was forcing herself not to touch him. "It was for show, Riley. I'm not going to kiss you again."

"Why not?" His voice lowered to a tortured whisper. "You're planning on leaving. I know that. So what's the problem with using me while you're here? We're good in bed together. We're married. There's zero reason for you to stay away from me physically, Ellie."

"Except I don't want you anymore."

His hand came up, sliding over her neck. His thumb traced the line of her jaw. "If I really thought you meant that, I would want to die, Ellie. I can't stand the thought of you hating me forever."

"And I can't stand thinking about what you did to me."

"I know. All I can do is try to make it better. Tell me and I'll do anything. You want me to walk away from this? I will. I'll go right now and pack everything we need and leave it all behind."

"You would never leave your family." He was lying again, telling her what he thought she wanted to hear.

"It would hurt, but you're my family now. You're my wife. You might not take it seriously, but I considered you my wife before I married you. I'll think of you that way even if you leave me. Baby, don't think for a while. Let me show you how I feel. Remember how good we are together."

His words rolled over her. They had been good together. Why wasn't she using him the way he'd used her? It didn't have to mean anything. It didn't have to truly bind them. She could be whole and still walk away from him.

Maybe it wouldn't be as good now that she really knew who he was.

It could just be sex this time.

His mouth brushed over hers and he moved in, his body making contact.

Her skin felt alive again, her system flaring with need.

This man knew how to make her feel. He knew how to take her to a place where nothing mattered but the pleasure he could give her. She needed this. The days since the last time she'd touched him seemed like weeks of pain and ache, but this was respite.

She didn't have to love him to take comfort from him.

As though he sensed her acquiescence, his arms circled her, bringing her close.

"God, Ellie, I've never wanted a woman the way I want you. I can't stop thinking about you." He whispered the words against her skin. "I couldn't sleep knowing you were next door. All I could think about was coming to your bed and sinking inside you."

His hips moved restlessly against hers, his hardness rubbing like a cat seeking affection. A big predator who needed her to pet him.

He licked along the shell of her ear, causing her to shiver in his arms.

No one else in the world could get her to respond the way he did. He'd taught her in the nights he'd spent in her bed. He'd taught her to expect pleasure from him, and her body jumped at the chance.

"Touch me." She needed his hands everywhere. She wouldn't think beyond the moment, beyond her need.

His hand slid up the tank top she was wearing and covered her breast. She breathed into the sensation, her chest swelling against his hand. He cupped her and palmed her breast as his mouth claimed hers.

"Come to bed with me. Let me make you forget everything else," he whispered.

She knew it was a mistake, but she was going to make it anyway. "Yes."

He lifted her into his arms and strode out of the kitchen.

Riley practically ran down the hallway. He needed to get her somewhere private and get his mouth and hands on her. He needed to take away her ability to think before she changed her mind.

He hadn't been able to sleep. He'd felt like shit when Bran insisted on giving him his room. He'd tried to explain to his brother that he wouldn't sleep at all, but Bran wouldn't listen.

When he'd walked out and seen his wife wrapped in Bran's strong arms, he'd nearly exploded with rage. He'd forced himself to stop and think. Bran wouldn't hurt him that way and Ellie . . . God, his sweet Ellie wouldn't do that.

But his every insecurity had welled, making it nearly impossible to stop himself from forcing the two apart.

Thank God he hadn't, or he wouldn't be carrying his bride back to consummate his marriage.

He strode past Bran, who was politely looking away as though he'd known what would happen.

It was inevitable. He and Ellie had too much chemistry to deny themselves for too long.

"It doesn't mean anything," she said, her voice soft.

"It only means we need each other in bed." He would give her every illusion she needed. "I understand this isn't forgiveness."

"I don't know that I can forgive you," she admitted. "Riley, this isn't fair to you."

Nope. She was thinking again. He managed to get the door to her bedroom open. "I don't care about fair. I told you, use me. Take what you need from me. I'll give it all to you."

"You'll expect me to stay."

"I'll beg you to stay, but I won't expect it. Let me have you. Ellie, give me one month to prove this marriage can work. You don't have to do anything at all but sleep with me when you want to. I'll do the rest. If you still don't want the marriage at the end of the month, I'll move you into your own place and we'll communicate through lawyers."

She stared up at him as he laid her out on the bed. "I can't trust you."

"I'll put it in writing in the morning. It can be a postnup." He was willing to do anything to get this precious time with her. One month. Thirty days. If he couldn't win her, he would lose her. "I promise."

"I'm going to leave, Riley," she said, but she sat up and tugged the tank top off, her gorgeous breasts came into view.

"I'll let you go if that's what you want." He couldn't take his eyes off her. She was so stunning.

"But as long as I'm here, I can't lie to you. I do want you physically."

He would take whatever he could get. He had to bet that Ellie would come back to herself. She'd had a horrible shock to her system. Everyone had let her down. She'd managed to come through a lonely childhood whole and filled with love. He couldn't be the one who put out her light. "I want you so badly."

He let his hands find the bottom of her pants and pulled them down, leaving her in nothing but a pair of underwear. It was too much. He dragged them down and fell to his knees.

"Please." She lay back and let him spread her legs.

She didn't need to plead with him. She was all he wanted and it had been far too long since he'd made a meal of her. He pulled her down the bed until she was in the perfect position for what he wanted to do.

"I will never get enough of you. If all I have is a month, I'll make sure it's a month neither one of us will forget." He could already smell the sweet scent of her arousal. He touched her, parting her labia. She was already slick and wet and ready for him. He would never get used to this, always need it.

He leaned over and put his mouth on her, his tongue going deep. He didn't have to warm her up. She was already hot as hell. He fucked her with his tongue long and slow, not leaving an inch of her untouched.

She writhed beneath him, the little moans going straight to his cock. His body pulsed with need, but he continued his feast. He licked and nipped at her. He let his finger slide against her as he settled over the pearl of her clit. It was already swollen and needy. He pulled back her hood and was thoroughly satisfied by the shudder that went through her body when he dragged his tongue over her.

"How can you do this to me?" Her voice was breathless, the words exhaled with a throaty groan. "Why is it only you?"

Because they belonged together. Because she was the only woman in the world for him. "You do the same to me."

She shook her head. He watched her, his eyes staring up the length of her body. "No. You've had so many women."

He kept up the slow motion of his hand. "You seem to think I'm much more of a player than I am."

"I've seen the pictures. I looked you up in the Austin papers."

"Those were dates because I didn't want to go to functions alone. They weren't girlfriends. I didn't have time for a girlfriend. I told myself that at the time, but now I know the truth. I didn't want to make time for them. They weren't the right girl. For the right woman, I'll change my whole life. There's no question of making time. There's only how much of your time I can have."

"Don't talk. I can't. I can't talk about this with you. Not now."

He knew what she wanted, needed. And he definitely liked the fact that she hadn't said *not ever*. It was what he counted on. He would use every charm he had, every trick he could think of to make sure that in one month she was right here in his bed and his life.

He settled in and suckled her clit. His whole body was tight, ready to take her. His wife.

She gasped, tightening like a bowstring, her head thrashing back and forth as she came.

He stood, shoving off his pajama bottoms, freeing his cock.

He stood between her legs, making a place for himself. She was laid out for him, her body languid, and for the first time in days she looked relaxed and sated. Her hair was spread out on the sheets. She glanced up at him, her eyes soft and her smile lazy, and for a second it was like nothing had come between them. Just for a heartbeat, they were together and his Ellie was back to her happy, loving self.

He would do anything to get her back there. To get them back.

"What's wrong?" Wariness replaced the sweet glow in her eyes.

"I don't want you to take me because you think you owe me for the orgasm."

She groaned and moved up on the bed. "I was kind of hoping for round two. If I'm going to use you, I'm going to use you well. Don't hold out on me, Lawless. I admitted I want you. I'm not giving you anything else."

He practically jumped on her. He settled his body on hers, giving her every ounce of his weight. She wasn't holding back. Her legs went around his waist, trapping him and squeezing him tight.

"I need this." He thrust in. He needed her. The last two days had been marred by misery, but it all fell away when he was with her. His cock drove deep, as deep as he could go, so he could feel their connection.

"You feel so good." She was wrapped around him, not letting go.

She never held back during sex. She didn't play coy or make him work harder for her affection. Ellie gave and he soaked it all up like a sponge denied for far too long.

He let go, the primitive need to mark his wife too overwhelming to resist. His wife. His. He'd never been possessive before. He'd always known the things he cared about could be stolen or lost or tossed away like they were trash. He'd seen everything he loved lost at one point or another, but she was different.

He couldn't lose her.

Over and over he drove into her, pushing them both along. She tightened around him and he felt her come.

He couldn't hold out and let go, pouring himself deep inside her.

He fell to her side, holding her close.

For one blissful moment, she lay in his arms. And then she took a deep breath and moved, disentangling herself and rolling over.

"Can you hand me the blanket before you go?" She took the left side of the bed, moving her head to the pillow.

He didn't want to go.

He didn't want to leave her. He wanted to sleep with his wife.

"Can I stay?"

She rolled over again, her eyes steady on him. "You don't sleep with anyone."

"I want to sleep with you. I know I don't deserve it, but if I only have a month, I want to spend it with you."

She sighed. "It won't work. I can't trust you."

He would have to work on it. She didn't trust him and she had good reason. He had to pray that time and proximity would fix what was wrong between them. He would try this every time she let him in her bed. Eventually she would give in.

And what? And he would wake up screaming or simply lie next to her all night, not sleeping at all. Maybe it was better she told him no.

He started to get off the bed to get his pants.

"Lock the door, turn out the light, and come to bed, Riley," she said quietly.

He rushed over to lock the door. He wasn't going to move the chair under the door handle. The lock was enough. He wasn't going to show Ellie he was a complete freak.

"You should use the vanity chair. It looks like it's the right height."

He stopped. How had she known about that? Probably Bran had been talking, explaining why he was on the couch and Riley in his room. He took a deep breath. "I don't need it."

"One thing at a time, Riley. I'm falling asleep, so get the door secure and come to bed or go to your own room."

This was his room, technically. He grabbed the chair and placed it where he needed it. Once he'd turned out the lights, he climbed into bed with Ellie, dragging a blanket over them.

He'd never done this. Not once in his life. He lay in bed, staring up at the ceiling. He was going to get through the night. Maybe tomorrow it would be easier. Or he could take a nap. Yeah, he could take a nap during the afternoon.

She turned and her arm went around him.

Warmth suffused him and he was surrounded by her scent. He relaxed a bit and let his skin settle against hers.

"I owe you, too, Lawless. I can't stand the thought of you never sleeping with another human being. My father took that from you. Maybe I can give it back. Don't think this means more than that."

It sure felt like more than recompense. It felt like love and affection and comfort.

"Gotcha, Lawless." He wasn't going to let her forget that she'd married him. "This is a sympathy cuddle."

He felt her chuckle against him. "Damn straight."

It wasn't long before he felt her breathing even out. Her head was on his chest, her legs tangled with his and after a while, he drifted off, too.

At first, it didn't register. He felt the flare of pain, but he couldn't tell where it was coming from. They stuffed something in his mouth, something filthy. He tried to spit it out, but they held it in.

Not so tough without your brother around, are you?

He couldn't see. It was too dark, but he knew that voice. Donny. Asshole. He and Drew had been enemies for the past two years. When they'd come into this group home, Donny had been the bullying fucker everyone was scared of. Then Drew had kicked his ass and left him a crying mess.

Drew was gone. He'd left earlier in the day. He had a full ride at the University of Texas and he'd moved into a dorm. He'd promised it wouldn't be long. He intended to find their dad's old business partner, get a job, and bring them all back together.

Four months tops, Ri. Survive for four months and I'll get you out of there.

He couldn't breathe, couldn't shout. He felt a punch to his gut and all the air he had in his lungs was gone. The pain seemed to be everywhere as more than one kid used their fists on him. When he fell to the floor, they started to kick him. Donny held down his hands.

Yeah, this should let your brother know who the real king is.

He tried to scream again.

"Babe, you're having a nightmare."

A hand moved over his chest but this wasn't the same. Soft. Warm. Gentle.

He came awake with a shock.

Ellie. He was in bed with Ellie. He dragged air into his body.

Had he hurt her?

"Are you okay? Did I hit you?"

She snorted a little and yawned. Early-morning light streamed in, but she made no move to get up. "Is that what you thought would happen? You thought you would hit me in your sleep?"

"It's a violent dream." He tried to shake it off. It was easier this time because she was cuddling against him.

He couldn't mistake her for some sweaty, awful gang of boys. She wasn't ever going to hurt him. Not intentionally. She would lock herself in a room with the crazy guy on the off chance she might help him.

"You're not a violent man, Lawless. Hush and go back to sleep. I was having a good dream. Prison was actually a five-star all-inclusive resort and all the guards looked like Chris Hemsworth."

He was still shaking a bit, but it didn't matter because she was here with him. "I'm definitely keeping you out of that jail."

"Spoilsport," she muttered before turning over.

He turned with her, spooning her as she went back to sleep. Her backside cuddled his cock and he discovered the real problem of sleeping with Ellie. He got hard fast.

He kissed her cheek. She needed sleep. He let go of the dream and held on to her.

Fourteen

Two weeks later, Ellie looked down at a grainy photo.

Fourteen days into her marriage to Riley and she felt different. She wasn't sure that was a good thing. She was calm. She had a hearing coming up, but she wasn't crying herself to sleep every night like she'd thought she would.

She was crying, all right. Crying out Riley's name, screaming in passion. The man was getting creative and now that he'd proven he could manage to sleep with another person, he seemed to have forgotten how to sleep not wrapped around her.

"I managed to get this from a security camera across from the bank in the Bahamas where the account was set up." Case stood behind her, the rest of the family sitting around what she now called the war council table. It was a heavy wood table that easily could have graced the war room of Winston Churchill or FDR. She wouldn't be surprised if Drew had found and purchased an antique. The man had a flair for the dramatic.

"I can't see her." It was obviously a woman, but she was wearing a wide-brimmed hat and sunglasses. There were three photos and none of them really showed the woman's face. She couldn't even tell what color the woman's hair was.

"Is this really the best we have?" Hatch asked with a shake of his head. "This could easily be Ellie."

"She's too thin to be Ellie," Bran argued.

Ellie briefly glanced up to see Riley watching her intently.

The man always seemed to be watching her. She would look up and his piercing eyes would be on her, waiting for her to need something, to ask for something. He was always close. She'd nearly tripped on a step the other day and Riley had shown up out of nowhere to catch her and set her back on her feet.

"Of course it's not Ellie. We need to look at the women in Castalano's circle and figure out who he would use," Riley said with a sad smile.

Yeah, that sad smile was starting to get to her.

Two weeks into her marriage to the man and she felt like the clock was ticking down. According to their agreement, she had two weeks left before she could move out on her own. She could go back to her place. The cops had taken everything they were going to take. Riley would pay her mortgage as long as her accounts were frozen. She could move back in and try to rebuild her life.

She'd gotten used to not being alone. She'd gotten used to walking into the kitchen at all hours of the day and finding someone to talk to or playing strategy games with her brothers-in-law at night.

Everything was likely happening the way Riley wanted it to happen. But she had a surprise for him.

She was still going to leave. She wasn't going to be the woman who built a life with someone who could betray her. As much as she'd come to care for these people, she couldn't forget that they were the reason she was here in the first place. They had a job to do and damn anyone who got in the way.

"We know it's not Ellie," Drew said with a sigh. "The problem is the authorities aren't going to accept our belief in Ellie's good heart as an acceptable defense. Someone had to open the account in her name."

"And this is as close as I could get to a picture of the woman who did it." Case rubbed between his eyes. She was fairly certain the man had been working overtime on more than one issue. "I sent someone down to the Bahamas to look into it. We even paid the bank rep to talk to us, and it didn't come cheap. She didn't remember much since it was several years ago. The woman had the proper identification. She hasn't been back since. They don't take photos or keep video footage. Like many of these types of banks, they make their living off confidentiality."

"And tax evasion." That would likely be another fun charge she would deal with. She looked at the photo, trying to figure out anyone it could be. "His admin is sixty-two. This looks like a much younger woman."

"Yes, I wouldn't say she was middle aged," Mia agreed. "And we can't count on this being someone from his office. He's a wily one. This particular account was opened before Ellie's father died, right after she came to StratCast. Have we considered that he could have opened the account? He and Castalano were partners for a very long time. They committed one crime together. Why not two?"

She hated to think of her father setting her up, but she had to be reasonable. "It's possible that he and Castalano were in on it. They are the types of men to view a publicly held company as their own private money source. And he wouldn't have minded setting me up for the fall."

Riley frowned as he pointed at the picture. "Is there any way this is your sister?"

Tears welled, but she shoved them back. Nothing mattered except the truth. "Anything is possible. I was actually shocked when Dad left her the stock he did. It was all supposed to be held by me. He didn't trust her with it any more than he did her trust fund. Dad might have had more affection for Shari, but he was also honest about who she was."

"You think the stock was a payoff for pretending to be you?" Bran asked, sympathy in his voice. "Because I don't know that your sister's smart enough to see that as a proper bribe. Designer shoes, maybe."

"Cut the sarcasm, Bran," Hatch ordered.

Bran shrugged. "Well, I met her. I'm the one who had to take her and douchebag to the airport. She's dumb as a post. Like, man, Ellie got all the brains and all the sweet curves. Chick needs to eat a burger."

"How about you stop commenting on my wife's curves," Riley shot back. "But you're right about her sister. I'm not sure anyone in their right mind would use her to cover up a crime."

Yes, realism was important. "My father might have done something like this, but Shari would definitely have said something to me. She can't help but say mean shit, and this would be something that would hurt me. She's a bitch, but she's a predictable bitch."

Drew sat up. "All right. We're no closer to figuring out where the source code is than we were before. I've even hacked into StratCast and can't find anything resembling my father's code."

"It's morphed over the last twenty years, though I'm sure you know that. Some companies keep their code, building on the last and changing, but about seven years ago we upgraded to something completely new. Tech changes so quickly. I can hand over the code we were using then."

Drew dismissed the idea. "I've already studied it. You're right. It morphed to the point I can barely see my father's hand in it. Twenty years in tech is like a hundred."

It was like the body had degraded to the point that no one could make an identification. She could practically feel the frustration rolling off them.

Riley's hand came out, covering her own. If she'd grown to be able to sense her in-laws' stronger emotions, then Riley seemed to have become an expert on her. He read her so easily. He knew when to hold her hand and when to lead her someplace private because she couldn't stand another second alone with her thoughts and she needed to be outside herself for a while. That was when he would give her his body, the comfort of his skin against hers.

She pulled her hand away.

How was she going to live without him?

"I'm going to my sister's." She'd thought about this long and hard. "I have a happy hour date with Lily and then I'm going to Shari's. I know she took some stuff from Dad's. Maybe I can find something. Her being out of the country means I can snoop without her hanging around. If she knew for a second I was looking for something, she would hold it over our heads forever."

"I thought she lived with your father until he died." Case started looking through his notes as if he was shocked he'd missed something.

"She did, but shortly after she moved in with Colin, they used her half from the sale of Dad's place to buy a condo on the Upper West Side. She took anything of value she could get her hands on." Her sister hadn't asked if she wanted to split anything. She'd simply had the movers take it all.

She'd likely been selling it off a piece at a time.

"Well, I hope we come up with something because Case and I are at a dead end," Mia admitted. "Your father didn't have a mistress at the end of his life. So no one to talk to. His will left everything to you and your sister."

"And we can't find a place where he rented a storage unit or a safe-deposit box. We've tried everything I can think of," Case concluded. "If he hid the source code somewhere, he did a damn fine job of it."

"Why wouldn't Castalano know where it is?" Bran asked. "They were partners. Shouldn't they have both had a copy?"

"My father handled the majority of the tech end of StratCast while Steven and Patricia dealt with getting investment and start-up money. After Patricia left, they divided the roles and I suspect at some point my father likely took the source code to hold over everyone's heads." It was a scenario that made sense to her knowing her father's love of power and his deep belief in having a backup plan.

She'd thought he was paranoid, but knowing what she knew now, she had to give it to the old goat. He'd been right about Steven.

He'll come after you. Always coming after us. Can't get away from what I did. But he can't, either. His sins would fill a cave. A dark cave. Do you understand? You're the only one smart enough to understand.

She shivered as she remembered the words her father had spoken. He'd been so far gone. The cancer had eaten him up and he'd been on morphine, but he'd kept talking.

Did it for her. Hate her now. That bitch led us all into hell and then waltzed away. Kill her. Should have killed her.

Her father really hated Patricia Cain.

"I think my dad had an affair with Patricia," she said. "I don't know if that helps anything, but when he was dying he talked about the fact that he'd done what he did for a woman and she left him."

Hatch grimaced. "I can't imagine Phil touching Pat. I know she looks nice on the outside, but that's the single coldest woman I've ever met in my life."

"She's been married three times," Riley pointed out. "Someone didn't think she was cold."

"Those were carefully selected spouses," Hatch countered. "Even her first husband was married for his connections. Are you saying Phil might have given the source code to her?"

"No," she conceded. "He hated her. I'm just trying to figure this out. He was more open and honest with me in those last days than he'd ever been. Unfortunately, he was also heavily medicated, so it doesn't all make sense."

"Write down as much as you can," Drew said as he stood up. "Riley and I have a call with Garrison concerning your and his StratCast stock. Garrison's found an expert who thinks he's got a loophole that could buy us another month or so."

"Not that it means anything," Riley replied glumly. "Castalano has found new ways to keep the stock low. He's leaked a report that Strat-Cast is about to lay off twenty percent of its workforce."

Ellie's blood heated. There was no reason to do that. If anything they should be in a hiring mode. "That bastard. He's doing that to get to me."

"He's already gotten rid of Darvisch," Drew said with no small amount of sympathy. "He was walked out early this morning."

Ellie felt her hands fist. "That will set us back months. I'll never find someone who can do what he can."

"I had a limo meet him. He's being offered a job at 4L with the knowledge that should you take back over as CEO, he'll be allowed to return to his position at StratCast. He was quite adamant that he preferred to work for you," Drew explained.

"She's the nerd whisperer." Bran nodded her way.

"Apparently, that's not far from the truth," Hatch seconded. "Has anyone told her yet?"

"Oh, God." Her mind went to the worst possible scenario. "Did the entire R&D team quit?"

"Oh, no, though you should expect them to be fired if Castalano finds out what they've done," Riley explained. "I wanted to save the good news for the end. We get so little of it these days. That tape Castalano had of me messing with the calibration on the equipment has mysteriously disappeared from the FBI and from StratCast. Everything is digital these days. The agent was lazy. He'd backed up to a local network but nothing else."

Mia turned to her husband. "Unless Case did it. McKay-Taggart has some hella good hackers on their team. Look for a line item under *communications expert charge*."

"I know nothing." Case's face was a complete blank. "But something like that could potentially happen if someone on Ellie's old R&D team perhaps called and tried to help, because apparently there are entire sections of StratCast who are trying their hardest to make things difficult for Castalano. Not that I can confirm or deny anything."

She blinked back tears but for a different reason. She did still have friends. When she left here, she could have a life. She didn't need this group of people.

She simply wanted them.

Ellie took a deep breath and banished the thought. Two more weeks and then she would go to her own place and figure everything out. She couldn't make any decisions while she was locked in the Lawless bat cave. She was too close to the situation to really understand it.

Take a step back. Look at the problem from all angles and allow the solution to find its way to you.

Her old mentor used to tell her there wasn't a problem she couldn't solve, given time and distance and intellectual processing.

She wasn't capable of that when she was close to Riley. She would move on and maybe someday she could call him again and see if there was anything left between them.

"Are you all right?" Riley asked.

She nodded. "Yes, I'm happy I still have friends there, but I'm worried Steven is going to ruin the company. This is his way of challenging me. I might be able to wiggle out of the worst charges, but I can't come back to work. He can do whatever he wants. I might fight like hell and get my company back only to discover I no longer have a company."

Steven could basically rape and pillage at will with her gone.

"We'll figure something out," Drew said. "Riley, it's time."

Riley looked over at her, obviously reluctant to leave. "Case and Mia are heading back to Texas for a few weeks. Their plane leaves soon."

Case had been her shadow when Riley wasn't with her. She was going to miss the big cowboy, but he had things to do at home. She hugged him and then Mia. The sister she wished she'd had.

"We'll be back soon. Take care of my boys," Mia whispered. "They need a level head like yours. I'm so glad we're sisters now."

Ellie simply nodded. She couldn't bring herself to tell Mia or anyone about her agreement with Riley. They likely thought that since she and Riley were sleeping together again, they were good.

"Bran, do you mind?" Riley asked. "I can't leave right now and she's going to want to go out."

Bran gave his brother a thumbs-up. "I'm on Ellie-watching duty."

"I don't need someone to watch me," she argued.

Drew stopped her. "Steven Castalano killed our parents. If you walk out there alone right now, every single one of us will be worried out of his or her mind. Please take Bran. He acts like an idiot most of the time, but he's quite effective when he wants to be."

They really would worry and they had cause. She hadn't been allowed out on her own since Castalano had made his threats. Another thing that would change in two weeks. "All right. I've got a key to my sister's place; we'll go there after the meeting with Lily. She said she's got some information, but she doesn't want to tell me over the phone. You'll have to be discreet. She doesn't like any of you."

Riley frowned. "She thinks we kidnapped you."

Lily couldn't believe she'd married Riley willingly. She'd called and tried to get Ellie to leave him, offered to help her with money, anything to get her away from the man who had ruined her life.

If she hadn't been forced to stay with Riley, forced to talk to him and see how he actually worked, would she feel the same way? Would she have gotten bitter and angry?

She was still mad when she really thought about it, but if she'd been raised as he had, she might have behaved in the same way. Riley thought there was no life but avenging his parents. It was everything he'd worked toward.

He could say he would leave it all he liked, but she couldn't trust him. He would pick his family in the end. He would choose revenge over her as he had before.

"I'll try to convince her otherwise," Ellie promised. "I'll talk to you when I get back."

She had a mission, too. And when it was all over, they could finally go their separate ways.

Riley sat in the meeting, staring down at his notes but not really seeing them. Thank God he'd written everything pertinent out for Drew and the contract lawyer since he was incapable of logical thought.

They talked around him and every now and then he found the concentration to interject a point, but how was he supposed to care about stock and holding on to his position when all that mattered was Ellie?

He wasn't a fool. She was still planning on leaving him.

The thought of Ellie walking out the door panicked him. It was his new nightmare. Somehow the beating-at-the-group-home nightmare had been replaced with Ellie fading away. She would leave and they might talk every now and then, but she would drift away from him. If she walked out the door, he would lose his wife.

For her it was a marriage of convenience. For him it was a whole new world. Things seemed brighter since he'd married Ellie. He was happier. He thought about the future in a way he never had before. His life didn't have to be an endless round of revenge and then proving himself. He could have more.

He loved her. How was he going to let her go?

"You're very helpful these days," Drew said as he disconnected the call.

"I try," he replied absently. Maybe if he hurried he could catch her before she left for her meeting with Lily.

Drew groaned. "I was being sarcastic. You suck at everything lately. Unless maybe you're going to start writing love songs to your girlfriend. I'm sure you would be awesome at that. That's how I see you now. Sitting somewhere writing love poetry."

He ignored the sarcasm. It was the way Drew communicated best. "She's not my girlfriend. She's my wife."

Drew lost his grin. "See, that's what I'm worried about. *Is* she your wife?"

"I sleep with her every night. I think we can call the marriage consummated." He didn't like where this conversation was going. He'd been careful to act like everything was good between him and Ellie. It was good. When they were in bed together, she didn't hold back. She let him hold her all night.

The distance came in the morning when he felt her pull away from him. She could smile all she liked, but it wasn't the same open, brilliant grin she used to give him. It was the polite expression she used on everyone.

"Just because you're fucking her doesn't mean she intends to stay," Drew replied. "You should protect yourself. I don't think she has any intention of trying to make this thing work."

"Why would you say that?" He wasn't sure he wanted the answer.

"Because I overheard her talking to her building manager. She was telling him she was moving back in soon. I take it she hasn't told you."

He'd known she was thinking about it, but she'd actually called? She'd made plans? Was she giving them any kind of a chance?

Drew stared at him. "I'm going to take that as a no."

He felt like he'd gotten punched in the gut. "No. I didn't know she was making arrangements already."

Drew's brow arched. "Already? Then you knew she would make them at some point? I thought we had a plan. She agreed to stay here with us until she gets her company back. Is she getting her company back in two weeks? You really should have told me about this amazing new talent of yours. You now can tell the future."

He didn't need this. "Of course not."

"Then why does she think she's leaving here in two weeks?"

"I'm not going to keep her here if she doesn't want to stay." Then he became her kidnapper as well as the man who had ruined her life. She didn't need more reasons to hate him. He was sure she woke up every day, realized she wasn't going to do the thing she loved, and blamed the man sleeping next to her.

"We had made a very plain arrangement." Every word came out of Drew's mouth with a chill to it. "We can't have her out there. Castalano could get to her. We need her where we can watch her. It's the only way this plan works."

He hated hearing his marriage referred to as "the plan." "What do you think she's going to do if she moves back to her place?"

Drew huffed as though frustrated. "I think Castalano can get to her more easily. He can move in and start talking in her ear and guess what? Now she's got 4L stock to play with because we gave it to her. All Castalano has to do is convince her he's the better bet and we've got a serious problem. So I want to know why she thinks she's leaving here in two weeks."

"I made a deal with her."

Drew's head fell back. "Let me guess. You get to sleep with her. She gets her freedom after an agreed-upon number of orgasms."

"It wasn't like that."

Drew's head came back up and his gaze narrowed. "Really? What was it then?"

"I asked her to give us a month. I thought if we were intimate, she would see how much I really care about her. I thought she would see that we should be together."

"Well, you should really have tried harder, brother," Drew said with a nasty twist of his mouth. "Because you're only two weeks in and she's got her exit plan in place. She'll be taking StratCast meetings before you know it."

"You honestly believe she's going to go in with Castalano? You think she'll have him over for dinner?" He was worried about a lot of things should Ellie actually move out at the end of their deal, but the last thing on his mind was Ellie turning on them all. It wasn't in her.

"I think anyone can go dark given the right circumstances, and we've given her plenty. She's not over what we did. She can sleep with you all she likes, but she hasn't forgiven you. Until she does, she needs to stay here where I can watch over her."

Riley stood up. "No."

Drew's eyes widened. "No?"

Riley knew that wasn't a word Drew heard often. "I love you, brother, and I can't thank you enough for everything you've done for me, but no. Ellie is my wife and until we sign the divorce papers, I'm going to do whatever it takes to ensure that she's happy. I think I'm going about this all wrong. I've worried and made bargains with her. I've put her on timelines and I've done it because that's kind of how I grew up. Everything was always about the next part of the plan. The next step we had to take. There is no next step. Ellie is the end of the road for me. I'm playing her like a game when she is so much more. My marriage is not a negotiation, Drew, and I not only ask that you stay out of it, I demand it."

Drew stood up. "This is about more than your marriage, Riley. This is about everything we've worked so hard to achieve."

He'd thought about that a lot lately, too. "What? Are we really looking for Dad and Mom's killers or are we trying to put a Band-Aid over a gaping wound? Do you honestly believe that putting Steven Castalano in jail is going to make you feel better? Is it going to take away the ache? Because I figured out what takes it away."

"So you're going to throw it all away because some chick gets you off better than the others? Does she have a magical vagina? Is that it? She can heal you with the power of her clit?"

He didn't think about it. He popped his brother. Right in the jaw.

Fucker had a strong jaw. It hurt like hell, and it didn't fix the problem. He stepped back. "Don't talk about my wife like that."

Drew couldn't understand. It was like asking his brother to translate a language he didn't speak. Riley could tell him all day long what Ellie meant to him and Drew's brain would somehow make it about sex. He couldn't understand love because he'd never experienced it.

Might never experience it.

"I'm sorry for hitting you." He'd never hit his brother.

Drew ran a hand across his jaw. "I'm sorry for offending you. I don't get this thing. Don't get me wrong. I like Ellie. She's a nice woman, but I don't think she loves you. I think you're going to get hurt and it bothers me to stand here and watch it."

Control freak. Drew had been looking out for them for so long he didn't know another way. "Some things are worth getting hurt over. And she does love me. I know she does. She's a little like that story Mom used to read us. You remember? The one with the dragon."

"'Sleeping Beauty.' I always wanted the dragon to win."

Because the dragon was the coolest part for a bunch of boys. Mia had loved the princess. "Ellie's asleep right now. She's buried this integral part of herself because I hurt her. I hurt her badly. She's got her defenses up, but eventually she'll let them go because that's who she is. Some prince will come and kiss her and wake her up again. I'm the fucking dragon who will scare all of them off and kiss her myself. Prince Charming was a wimp. She needs a dragon to protect her."

That got Drew smiling. "You think you can convince her in two weeks?"

"No. That was a mistake." He finally realized what he'd done to her. He was the one who kept placing boundaries on them. He was putting them in horrible positions and it had to stop.

"She could take us all down, Riley."

Poor Drew. All he had to cling to was his never-ending plan. "She won't. She's not one of us, not in that way. You look at her and think she had everything you didn't. Her background is more similar to ours than you would think. She grew up alone. She had a father who barely could be considered a guardian much less a loving dad. She didn't have a mom. She grew up in boarding schools."

"Which is a far cry from a damn group home," Drew shot back.

"She didn't have anyone and somehow she still figured out how to give a damn about the people around her. Don't think for a second she's the enemy. She's who we should be trying to be. I thank God Mia found Case before we dragged her fully into our misery."

"It's not misery, damn it. It's justice."

"No, it's revenge." He could see it so clearly now. "Justice would be proving that man killed our father, not this righteous takedown of him and everyone around him. We get Ellie's company back and then I'm out."

"You don't care who the fourth person was?" Drew asked, righteous indignation in his voice. "You don't even give a crap about finding out the name of the other person who killed them?"

"I do, and if we can connect Patricia Cain and the mystery person to our parents' murders, I'm all in for taking that to the right authorities. But other than that, I'm going to do what our father would want me to do. I'm going to live a life. I'm going to be good to the people around me. God, Drew, do you even remember him anymore?"

"I remember them both." Drew's eyes were red, his hands fists at his sides. "I remember how they screamed."

He turned and walked out.

Riley ached for his brother. Those last moments were all Drew seemed able to remember. Had he forgotten how loved they'd all been? How their mom would bake them cakes and call them little monsters? How their father had scooped them up and twirled them around and told them the world was a magnificent adventure?

He caught sight of his wife walking by.

He was on his feet in an instant.

Bran followed Ellie, grabbing a light jacket. Riley managed to catch them as the elevator opened.

"Ellie, can I have three minutes?"

Ellie nodded and looked to Bran. "I'll meet you in the lobby." After the doors closed on Bran, she turned to Riley. "What do you need? You know eventually you're going to have to let me walk around the city without a bodyguard."

"Not while Castalano's after you." He couldn't help but smile. She was wearing a yellow skirt with a pretty white top and a black belt that cinched her waist in and made her look sexy and sweet.

"Why are you smiling?"

"Because looking at you makes me happy."

Her eyes turned down. "Riley, I should tell you something."

"You've already called your building manager about moving back in."

"How did you know that?"

"Drew overheard you. It doesn't matter. I was a fool to give you that deal."

Her chin came up, a stubborn expression on her face. "So you're going to block me?"

"No. I'm going to find an apartment in your building and I'm going to court you all over again, baby. I'll start at the beginning. I'll introduce myself because I saw you walking in and I couldn't take my eyes off you. I'll help you with your groceries, but you should know I'm doing it all because I'm praying you'll go out with me and give me a chance."

She shook her head. "It can't work."

It had to. "I'll wait for you. That's what I didn't tell you before. I was impatient and tried to push you into something you're not ready for and that's not my job."

"Your job as my husband?"

He shook his head. "No. I might not be that for long. I'm talking about my job as the man who loves you, the man who places you above all others. I won't ever walk away from you, Ellie. Not two weeks from now. Not twenty years from now. If you can't ever love me again, then I'll be the best friend you've ever had. I'll be the dependable one, the one who looks out for you. I'm going to spend the rest of my life loving you, Ellie. One way or another."

There were tears in her eyes, but she didn't move to him.

Time. He had to give it to her with no threats or promises beyond the fact that he would be here.

"Have a good day, sweetheart, and if you need anything, call me. I'll be there." He stepped back and gave her room.

When the elevator came, she moved into it, but her eyes were on him right until the door closed.

He walked away lighter than he'd been before.

Fifteen

I don't understand how you can sleep with that man," Lily said, her mouth tight.

"He's really good in bed." Ellie looked down at the menu. She felt bad, but she kind of wished she'd ignored Lily's request for a happy hour meeting. She had so much to think about, but Lily seemed to mostly want to remind her of all the reasons she should hate her husband. She definitely shouldn't have told Lily she was still sleeping with Riley.

Lily's eyes widened. "Have you forgotten what that man did to you?"

Ellie put the menu down, her eyes on her friend. "Not at all. I think about it every single day."

And she wondered what she was going to do about it. She had two weeks left and she was no closer to finding a way back into her proper place.

Riley knew she'd made arrangements to keep her apartment. What he didn't know was how torn she was at the thought of leaving the penthouse.

His plan had worked beautifully. She loved the penthouse and sitting down with the entire clan for meals and talking and arguing over pot roast and a couple of bottles of wine.

It was everything she'd missed when she was growing up. The

Lawless siblings were a family. Drew was the authority figure. Mia, the one who made everyone laugh. Bran was the quiet, thoughtful one. Hatch was the crazy uncle. And Riley worked his ass off. He was Drew's strong right hand.

She'd rapidly discovered she had a place in this crew. She argued with Drew and Riley and made them think about something beyond making a dollar or plotting revenge. They'd had several serious political discussions and she'd managed to make her brothers-in-law think about their positions. Drew was considering implementing some of her worker-friendly ideas at 4L.

"Ellie, he destroyed your career."

She glanced over. Bran was sitting at the bar, smiling at the waitress. Her brother-in-law had a serious soft spot when it came to women. She actually worried about him. There was something in his past. Something no one would talk about. Bran had a weakness and it was any woman with a sob story. He looked back her way and gave her an encouraging smile.

Damn it. She already loved Bran. Not the way she loved Riley. She wished she didn't love Riley.

"I thought you said the workers were still behind me." She'd been thinking a lot about what Riley had or hadn't thought would happen when he did what he'd done. He really could have thought she would easily move through it.

Lily took a sip of her wine. "Some of them are, but they're risking everything by taking your side. Riley did that. He used you."

"And he's trying to make it up to me."

"By marrying you and taking your stock?"

"Which is worth next to nothing right now." When she really thought about it, Riley didn't have to offer her marriage. It would have been easier for him not to. Drew had been forced to give her stock in his company. That had required an enormous amount of trust on his part. She could use the stock to put Drew and 4L in a bad position.

Should she look at his words or his actions? His actions told a very specific tale. Every move he'd made since Castalano had dropped the hammer on them had been to help her. He'd done everything he could to save her.

Had he done it strictly out of guilt?

"It's going to come back up," Lily said.

They were sitting in the back of the small restaurant. Lily had insisted on subterfuge. She'd come in the back way and planned to leave through the kitchen. They were far from StratCast, so no one would likely wander in and find them together. It was all getting to be too much.

"Lily, I think it's time for you to get out of StratCast."

Her friend's eyes widened and she sat back as though she'd never thought of the idea herself. "Why would I do that? Has he convinced you to give up the fight? Are you so happy with him that you've forgotten the rest of us?"

Guilt weighed her down. "No, I haven't forgotten. I'm simply worried about you. You don't know what Castalano is really capable of."

"I think I do. I've taken over as Kyle's admin. He talks about his father like he's some kind of evil genius. He says if we wait the old man out, everything will come to him."

"Lily, tell me you're not seeing him." Kyle was bad news.

"I can handle him," Lily assured her. "And he's really not so bad. His father is awful, but Kyle will protect me. I'm far more worried about you. Kyle explained the situation with the Lawless family to me, and you're in real danger. They play deep games."

"Oh, I would love to hear how Kyle explained it."

Lily leaned over as though she thought Bran could hear her from across the bar. "They think your father and Steven stole some kind of code from their dad. They're even crazy enough to think Steven and your father and Patricia Cain murdered their parents. Can you imagine Patricia Cain as a killer? Would she do a segment on the proper etiquette of murder and what to serve your guests afterward?"

Actually, the woman was cold enough to do it. "My father told me the truth before he died."

Lily nodded. "Kyle knows it all. That code was always your father's. Benedict Lawless was the one who tried to steal it."

"No. My father killed Benedict, took the code, and that's how he, Steven, and Patricia formed StratCast. He told me himself. My husband's family is right. Steven even called me a few weeks ago and threatened to hurt everyone I love if I don't find the source code my father kept from him. I think he's afraid it will prove his crimes." Drew wasn't so sure, but he wanted to see it. If she could find that code, she would hand it over to him and hope to be done with the whole mess.

Would Riley do what he'd said? Would he try to start over? Would she let him?

She tried to picture herself turning him down, and somehow the image wouldn't form. What if they could meet with none of this between them? Would they do it right this time?

Lily sat back in her chair. "I can't see Steven really murdering someone. I know what he did was awful, but going all the way to murder . . ."

She needed to make Lily believe. "He did. My father was in a bad place when he confessed. He also told me something I've been thinking more and more about lately."

"The code? I know Steven is all up in arms about something your dad took. He says it belongs to the company, but your dad took it so he could hold it over Steven's head." Lily's lips turned up in a wry grin. "Naturally your father is the villain in his version of the tale. Steven told Kyle that if you turned over the code to him, he would take some of the heat off you."

So many lies. "Then he's lying. He told me if I turned over the code, he wouldn't hurt you."

Lily frowned. "Me? He's holding me over your head? I can handle myself."

Lily would try, but Ellie wasn't sure her friend was capable of doing what it would take to truly defend herself. "Watch your back. I would feel better if you walked away."

"I can't. Someone has to watch them. Kyle has fired three people because he didn't like them. These are good people, Ellie."

"Yes and you weren't able to stop him. They don't talk around you. I don't think it's worth risking your life when we're not getting anything out of it."

"Well, I'm sorry I haven't been great at the spy thing." Lily seemed to blink back tears. "Maybe I can help you find this code."

She didn't want to involve Lily more than she had to. "I have an idea of where he might have hidden it."

"But you're not going to give in, are you? I know you, Ellie. He made a mistake when he threatened you like that."

She reached out and put a hand on Lily's. "That's why I need you to walk away. If he doesn't have someone to hold over my head, then everything else is simply business. I have to trust that the man still wants something out of StratCast. He can fire anyone he likes, but he needs the money the company can bring in."

"You're going to give the code to your husband." Lily said it with an almost fatalistic acceptance of the situation.

Ellie nodded. "I believe what my father told me. I believe that code or whatever it is belongs to the Lawless clan. But, Lily, I don't know that Riley is going to be my husband for long. I'm moving back to my place in two weeks. We'll see where we go from there."

"Why are you moving? I thought the point was to keep you safe. Did he throw you out?"

Wow. Her friend immediately went to the worst possible scenario

where Riley was concerned. "No, I'm choosing to get back to a normal life. They'll support me while I figure out what to do. And who
knows? Maybe we can see each other. The point is I'll be out of this
war with the exception of wanting my job and my company back."

"So you think you'll be able to find it?"

She wasn't so sure about that. "I think I've figured out where to
look."

"And you want me to get the hell out of there."

"I do. The minute Steven figures out I have what he wants, he'll
use you against me. He knows how much I care about you."

Lily squeezed her hand. "I care about you, too. And I'll go easier
on your guy. I suppose I should. We all make bad decisions and sometimes they put the people we love in awful positions. I guess I never
considered that you would forgive him."

"I'm not totally there yet. I can forgive him, but it's hard to forget.
I do understand that he thought he was doing the right thing for his
family. I'm not sure we work as a couple, though. They won't be done
even if they manage to get Steven behind bars."

Lily's well-shaped brows rose in obvious surprise. "They want
to take down Patricia Cain? How are they going to do that? She's not
in the tech business anymore. Are they going to poison her fall pies
or find some porn she did as a young woman? Because that would be
cool."

She'd tried to stay out of their business when it came to that
woman. "I don't know, but if they think Steven is a monster, I don't
know what they would call Patricia."

"You never call her Auntie Patty."

"Never." She shuddered at the idea. "My father hated her. She's not
a 'Pat' and no matter how much she tries to be America's homemaker,
that woman is a shark. I don't like the idea of them going after her.
Someone's going to get hurt."

She wasn't sure it would be Patricia.

Who would be the voice of reason if she left? Mia and Case were needed back in Dallas. Mia couldn't leave her husband right now.

If Ellie left, it would be the men of the family and they didn't always make the best decisions.

She looked over at Bran, who was quietly talking to the bartender. He glanced Ellie's way and then gave her an open smile.

Would he be the one they sent into Patricia Cain's den? Or would Riley go since he didn't really have a lot else to do in New York?

She'd found her place in the family. Was she ready to leave it now?

"So I'll go back to the office and pack up my things. I'll leave Kyle a fuck-you note." Lily gave her a smile. "Think there's an admin job for me at 4L?"

"I think my brother-in-law can pay your salary until I get my job back." Drew could handle it, and it would be nice to have Lily around again. She could get back into business mode.

Lily gave her a little salute. "I'm your girl."

The waitress came by and they ordered another round. All the while Ellie contemplated her future.

Two hours later, Ellie looked around her sister's apartment, wondering if she was going to get her mind off Riley anytime soon.

How the hell was she supposed to deal with him now? She couldn't get her mind off his last speech to her. What guy said that? What was his game now?

What was she going to do if he wasn't playing a game?

Bran whistled as he walked around, looking at the space. "This place is nice. Wow. Modeling pays well."

"Not the way Shari does it. She started out well, but she struggles to get jobs now because she's so difficult to work with. She doesn't believe call times should apply to her."

"Well, someone's doing well. This place isn't cheap."

She'd had a massive fight with her sister when Shari had bought this place. "They bought it with Colin's half of our old place and his half of everything I earned during our marriage along with Shari's half of our inheritance. I argued that they shouldn't spend everything they had, but Shari claimed she needed the best to keep up appearances. They'll be lucky if they're still here in a year."

"That sucks." He picked up a picture that was sitting on the hallway table. "Is this your ex?"

She glanced over. Sure enough, there was a picture of Shari and Colin. "Yep. They had those done last Christmas and sent them out as Christmas cards."

"He doesn't look like your type." Bran set the frame back down.

"I suppose Riley looks like my type."

Bran strolled around the apartment. "Sure. He's solid. Masculine. That dude in the picture spends way too much time on his hair. Riley might dress well, but that's because of his job. He works out because he needs to be strong, not to show off his six-pack."

"Colin wasn't always like that." She looked around the apartment. The trouble was almost everything here had come from her dad's old place. The elegant sofas, the prewar tables. Shari might be an idiot, but she knew good furniture when she saw it.

Why would she have taken anything from their father's office?

"Oh, that's the problem. See, talking about shit really does work. I can't convince Drew of that. He thinks he's going to be all stoic. I personally think it's best to put it all out there. Sure it's cost me a bunch of women I would have liked, but hey, if they weren't built for the long haul, why start the ride?"

She turned to her brother-in-law. "What on earth are you talking about?"

"I'm talking about the fact that a lot of your anger at Riley isn't really anger. It's fear that another man you care about is going to turn on you." Bran looked back at her, his eyes soft. "He won't, you know.

He's not coming from the same place your first husband was. He'll need you more than you can know, more than he'll likely ever say. Definitely more than that asshat in the picture there."

"I'm not still wounded by my divorce, Bran." That was ridiculous. "I'm pissed off that your brother lied to me and used me."

"Then why are you still sleeping with him?"

Case never asked those kinds of questions. When the big cowboy had been her babysitter, he'd talked about football and where to get the best burger. She really preferred Case. Maybe honesty would shut him up. "Not that it's any of your business, but your brother is incredibly good in bed."

Bran simply grinned. "It runs in the family. But I also have to call bullshit on that. You're not the type of woman who sleeps with a man for pure pleasure. There has to be something else involved."

"I can't want an orgasm?"

"For you an orgasm means more than simple physical release. You need more and you found it with Riley, but because you thought you found it once before, you're afraid to trust it."

She let out a long sigh. "Go psychoanalyze someone else, Bran. I have a . . ." She didn't even really know what she was looking for. "Something to look for."

She strode down the hall. She was sure Colin had an office somewhere in here. Despite his recent retreat from the academic world, he'd made it a habit of keeping an office. Now that he was "managing" Shari's largely nonexistent career, he wouldn't stop his former habits.

She found it down the hallway. It was a lovely wood-paneled room with a wall of beautifully stacked books.

He'd loved books. She looked at the shelves. She'd given him many of the books left there. Shari had never met a book she liked.

Bitterness. She could taste it in her mouth.

She didn't love Colin. Not at all. She actually wondered if she'd ever loved him, but she felt the anger well.

Was Bran right? Could a person let go of love but hold fear and anger close? Could she be pushing Riley away because she was worried he would change on her?

He'd lied about his reasons for meeting her, for becoming her lawyer. Did that mean he'd lied about who he was? About his feelings for her?

Could she believe a word he said? Ah, that was the real question.

She'd believed Colin. She'd brought him home and showed him off and planned a whole life around him, and her feelings for him hadn't been half of what she felt for Riley. She'd been hurt when Colin left. How would she feel when Riley decided he'd been punished enough for what he'd done to her?

Oh God. She was thinking that way. When he'd offered her a month, she'd taken it with the full knowledge that she would leave because he wouldn't last a month with her. She should walk away before he did.

"Hey, El." Bran was standing in the doorway, his big body taking up all the space. "I'm sorry. I shouldn't push. I can only say I'm worried you're going to leave. I don't want you to leave. I like having you around."

"You might not be wrong about me thinking Riley will change on me. Colin did. He was the first person I really brought into my life, and he changed very quickly."

"Riley won't. He's not the same as Colin. He's constant. Ellie, he's had one goal for twenty years. Nothing has been able to change that goal with the exception of you. He loves you. He needs you. I know that because I need someone like you. Do you have any idea what I would do to have what Riley has?"

She sniffled. Was he being serious? "He has a woman who won't commit to him."

Bran took a deep breath, and she felt a well of emotion from him. "He has a woman he loves. Yes, I want that. I want to love someone.

It's the big mistake people make. They think they need someone who loves them. But loving someone is way more important. It says more about who we are that we can love. I want to love, Ellie."

Damn it. He was getting to her again. "I don't know if that's going to happen for me and Riley."

"It doesn't matter. He will have loved you. Loving someone is so much more important than being loved. I think my brother loves you and that will make the difference in his life. He can spend it in this cave of revenge we've built, or he can walk in the light."

Her father had lived in a cave with no one to love or care about. No one who loved him.

He'd spoken often about his cave.

He'd said he was safe in the cave. He'd said he needed no one, so his cave was safe. He'd said he'd buried all the sins in the cave.

What if he'd been making sense? She'd thought the morphine had been talking, but what if her father had been rationally trying to tell her something?

His cave. He'd called his office his cave.

"We could be in trouble here."

"How so?" Bran asked.

"I think we're looking for something from my father's office."

"Okay. We can do that."

He didn't understand the inherent problem. "But I know for a fact that Shari has sold off a lot of stuff."

Bran's face fell. "Shit. So it could be anywhere. Well, take a look around. You think he hid it, don't you? Where would your father hide his secrets?"

"I don't know. Let me think. Look through those books. Some of them are from my father's library." Shari had sold some of their father's stuff through a Christie's auction, and a bunch more had simply been sold on eBay.

She searched through Colin's desk, finding nothing but notes on Shari's meetings and the parties she needed to attend. Apparently her sister was attempting to make the move into acting and it wasn't going well.

There was nothing in the desk. No false drawers or hidey-holes she could find.

She walked back through the apartment, finding absolutely nothing. An hour passed and her frustration nearly reached the breaking point.

Bran found her in the living room, silently cursing her sister.

"It's gone," she said. "Someone from Minnesota or some buyer from Finland likely has it."

Bran put a hand on her shoulder. "I'm sorry, Ellie. We'll find another way. Say, if there's anything you want from here, you should take it. She'll probably sell everything after she gets the money from my brother. Any chance you want that portrait of you as a girl?"

She stopped. He wouldn't. Her father had kept a portrait her stepmother had commissioned. It was of Ellie as a young girl, holding her toddler sister in her lap. They looked angelic in the painting. Her father had said he'd placed it behind his desk because it gave him cover for his own misdeeds. Who, he'd asked, could see such tiny angels and think of their father as the devil?

It would be exactly like her father to hide his secrets there.

"I need you to help me get that picture off the wall." She walked back to the living room, which had been decorated in Shari. There were pictures of her all over the space, including the large portrait of her as a toddler in her sister's arms. It was the only sign that Shari even had a family.

Bran moved in, his height making the portrait takedown easy. He lifted it off its anchor and brought it down. "What exactly are we looking for? Do you think it's behind the canvas?"

"No idea." She disregarded the front. The artist had a light hand with the oil. Everything was smooth on the front of the canvas. She turned it around and inspected the back.

The canvas had been stretched over wood. From what she could tell it hadn't been redone. Looking at it told her nothing. It seemed perfectly normal.

"Ellie, there's something under the upper right corner," Bran said quietly. "It's hard to see because the color masks it, but I think something has been shoved under the frame."

Ellie ran her hand under the wood and sure enough, something was there. She had to wiggle her fingers under, but she pulled out the small thumb drive.

There it was.

Bran looked at her and smiled. "I hope that's what we think it is."

"We won't know until we try. Did you happen to see a computer in that office?" She wanted to boot this sucker up and make sure it was real.

"No computer. I think they took it with them to the South Pacific, where they're likely figuring out that they have no Internet. I voted for cutting off all their power and not sending them any food. We can see who eats the other first. My bet's on the dude. Your sister doesn't look like she eats."

Ellie felt unaccountably optimistic all of a sudden. She'd found it. Whatever was on this thumb drive was important. "She doesn't, but neither one of them would ever get their hands bloody."

"Neither would you, and that's a good thing."

That was where he was wrong. She was way stronger than any of them gave her credit for. "I will get my hands completely bloody for the right cause. I'm ready for a little of Castalano's blood."

She might have a chance to make this all right. Maybe not all, but she could start working to right her father's wrongs.

First things were first. She pulled out her cell and texted Lily.

Come back to the penthouse. Found the info.

She wanted her family around her when they opened the package. Lily was as close as she had to a family left. She needed Lily to get along with her new relatives.

"You ready? I'll try to hail us a cab." Bran winked as he left her to lock up.

Her cell phone trilled as Bran closed the door. When she answered it her entire world went straight to hell.

Sixteen

Riley flipped through the data the McKay-Taggart specialist had sent him a few moments earlier. He was glad he could use the whole "Taggart as an in-law" connection like a blunt instrument. He'd gotten someone named Adam on the phone and once he'd explained that he was Mia's brother, his two-to-three-day turnaround had become roughly thirty minutes. Riley was fairly certain the guy had been on his way out the door, but apparently everyone adored Mia.

"Did I miss anyone?" Adam Miles asked over the speaker.

"I don't think so. It's just a mega shit-ton of names." There were a lot of workers at StratCast. The year the last bank account was opened, there were almost a thousand workers employed by Strat-Cast. A whole bunch of them had gone to the Bahamas.

It was an easy winter getaway from the city. He should have known.

"You've got some additional issues," Adam pointed out. Adam was a McKay-Taggart "communications specialist." Or as Case liked to call it—dude who knew how to hack a system.

He glanced down the list, recognizing a couple of names. "What kinds of issues?"

He'd had the idea after Ellie and Bran had left. He didn't recognize the woman in the picture Case had found, so he needed to narrow down the prospects. Castalano didn't have a large group of friends. He wouldn't trust many people. It was possible he'd hired someone to "play" Ellie, but he was betting Castalano would keep that woman fairly close. He would have something on her.

He kind of hoped Castalano hadn't offed the girl.

"Besides the fact that your bad guy might have used someone not connected with the company, your main issue is cruise ships. If this guy is really smart, he sent her via cruise ship because while they do check passports, they don't stamp them," Adam explained. "If she flew in, we'll have a record. If she went in for a day through a cruise ship, you are shit out of luck."

"Or you could look through cruise ship rolls for that week." It seemed fairly simple.

There was a long pause. "You suck, asshole."

McKay-Taggart wasn't known for their customer service. They were known for getting shit done. Also, he'd likely thrown out professionalism when he'd told Adam there was Taggart sperm in his family tree. Well, it was certainly in his sister's tree by now, or very soon, since those two seemed to go at it twenty-four seven.

He wished he had the same happy arrangement with Ellie. Their lovemaking only happened at night when they went to bed. It made it seem almost dirty when it was anything but. It was the best part of his day, the only part that made him feel truly alive. He wanted the right to take her hand and make love to her the way he had before she'd discovered the truth.

"I'm sorry. It's important."

A long sigh came over the line. "This is about your wife, right?"

"Yes. She's the one in trouble." He found he couldn't lie to Mia's new family. "But she only married me because I kind of forced her."

"So it's a marriage in name only?"

"Not in my mind. This marriage is forever. I'm pretty sure she doesn't think the same way."

"Hey, you've got her name on a document that states that you belong to each other. You've got more than most people do. Get that woman into bed. Give her something special. It's seriously so much easier when there are two of you. Jake and I can tag-team our wife and she never gets a chance to think too hard."

Yeah, he'd heard McKay-Taggart had some crazy sex stuff going on. "I'm going to have to handle it on my own." He skipped through the names. "Hey, there's no Lily Gallo here."

"You asked me to look through the employees working for Strat-Cast that year. If she's not there, she wasn't on the payroll."

Something about the girl in the picture made him think of Lily. It could be that he wanted it to be her. She hated him.

But finding out that Lily was a plant would kill Ellie.

"Of course," he replied. "I'm sure it's fine."

"Give me two seconds to pull her passport records," Adam said.

"Don't," Riley began, but the Muzak on the line had started up. At McKay-Taggart there was only one song played over and over again. The crazy elevator version of "Sweet Child o' Mine." It was enough to make a person insane.

Who thought to do that? Who took classic rock and made it elevator music?

And why was he humming along?

Castalano's wife. He'd thought about it and discarded the notion. She was too thin to be the girl in the picture. She was sixty according to her records, and though she'd had an enormous amount of work done, she wasn't as young as the woman in question. He would place her age as late twenties to early thirties. Not anywhere close to Castalano's wife or his mistress, who was in her late forties.

There were other women, but none Riley thought had enough at stake in the game to be used. Castalano would have something over this woman, something important.

The GNR song kept playing and he wondered where Ellie was. She should be home fairly soon. Bran had texted him a while back that they'd finished up with Lily and were on their way to Shari's apartment.

Shari. Waste of flesh. He didn't understand any sibling who could treat a sister or brother the way she had. Maybe if their parents hadn't been brutally murdered, he and Drew and Bran and Mia would have been normal and seen each other every Thanksgiving and Christmas and barely known what was really going on in each other's lives, but that wasn't what had happened. They were all they had. Even Mia, who'd found happiness, gave her brothers everything she had.

And Ellie had a place in this family. Maybe she didn't know it, but she'd already become integral to the Lawless clan. She challenged every single one of them. They needed that more than any of them would admit. Well, Mia would happily admit it. She was Ellie's biggest champion. She loved having another woman in the house, especially one who questioned the Lawless authority.

Ellie was perfectly happy to go after Drew. She would argue with him on everything from politics to religion to what he was doing to make the world a better place. In Ellie's mind that wasn't much. She wasn't a big proponent of revenge as world healer.

"Hey, any word when Bran's coming back?" Hatch stuck his head in. He was dressed for going out in a pair of slacks and a collared shirt. "We're supposed to meet up with a couple of very nice ladies tonight."

Jesus. "By nice ladies you mean strippers?"

Hatch's eyes narrowed. "I mean lovely women who might or might not spend some time on the pole. They're artists. Do you really want to be a judgmental asshole here?"

He never wanted to be a judgmental asshole, but he wished his brother would get out of his stripper phase. "I think Bran should get more serious."

Hatch stepped into the room. "It's hard for him. He was serious once and it went really damn poorly from what I can tell. He's worried about getting serious again."

This was the first he'd heard of that. Bran refused to talk about his time in foster care. Drew had pulled him out when he was almost seventeen, but it had been years and Bran hadn't been as successful at finding a permanent home as Mia. Bran had gone from house to house. He'd never stayed anywhere for more than a year, but Riley didn't know a damn thing beyond the names of the foster parents he'd stayed with. There had been several instances of bad behavior during Bran's adolescence. Most of them committed by Bran.

"He talks about it?"

"Only when he's seriously drunk. Is that 'Sweet Child o' Mine'? It's awful. Who does that to a classic?"

The music had recycled back through. McKay-Taggart needed to seriously reconsider their wait time entertainment. "Don't worry about that. What does Bran say?"

Hatch sighed. "He talks about a girl when he was sixteen. He tried to save her and couldn't. That's all I know, all he talks about. When he's sober he acts like nothing ever happened. I've tried to get a name out of him, but he never gives that out. Bran is more damaged than he lets on."

There was no question about that fact. Bran had too many run-ins, his anger far too volatile to be normal. He worried about Bran's anger as much as he worried about Drew's arctic chill. Whereas Bran had gone red hot, Drew was icy cold. They were both bad things to be.

Ellie was warm. She made him warm and happy. That was where a man needed to be. He was rapidly coming to the conclusion that the only way a man ever made it there was through the right woman.

Or dude. If said dude was into other dudes, he would need the right one. No man could be complete without a soul mate.

"Bran should be home any minute." He went back to looking through names. He needed to match them up to pictures, and maybe he could eliminate most of them. Once he'd gotten it down to a reasonable number he could start really investigating. If he didn't find anything from this batch, he would open the list wider.

"Any word from your girl on the source code?" Hatch asked. "Though I think it's odd Phil would want to hide it."

Riley didn't look back, simply kept sorting through the names Miles had sent him. "It's stolen. He wants to hide it."

"Why? Does anyone honestly care at this point? There's too much money involved for the cops to really prosecute. Don't think it doesn't matter. When there's no way to truly compensate the victims, justice tends to be thrown to the side. It's the entire reason we went about this the way we did. We knew we couldn't get Stratton and Castalano and Cain for stealing the source code."

Hatch was making way too much sense. "All right. Let's say what you're saying is true. Why would Castalano deliberately send her after the code?"

"Because there's something else he wants more. Look, I know how these people work because I was one of them once. Castalano wouldn't have gone in on anything without having mutually assured destruction. He wouldn't have taken a partner, much less two without it."

"Tell me something," Riley began. "Did he approach you?"

It was something he'd always wondered about. Hatch had been in the original investors. He'd been involved in the company before StratCast.

Hatch shook his head. "No. It was as much a shock to me as it was to you, but then I was always pretty plain about where my loyalties lay. I don't think they would have been stupid enough to try to bring me in, but I understand fully why you would question me. I don't think Drew has questioned me enough."

He wasn't sure why Drew had so much faith in Hatch. He simply knew he did. Drew had trusted Hatch with everything from 4L to watching over Bran, and for a few years after they'd gotten custody of his younger brother that had been a big job. It still was sometimes.

"We know you're not the fourth, Hatch."

Hatch seemed to shut down. "And how the hell do you know that?"

He gave him the only answer he had. "Because none of us wants to live in that world."

Hatch's shoulders slumped. "It wasn't me. I loved your father like a brother, and as for Iris . . ."

"You just loved her." Iris Lawless had been a stunning woman. He could remember how lovely she had been when she would get ready for an outing. She would sit at her vanity and put on makeup and smile at him as he watched her. She would be putting on blush with a huge brush and reach out to rub his nose with it. He would giggle and run away.

He could also remember his mother crying and swearing nothing was wrong.

"I did," Hatch admitted. "But I never made a move on her. It's hard to understand that your parents are human beings, too. They make mistakes and missteps like the rest of the world. I know I'm not your parent . . ."

"You've been my father figure longer than my biological dad." It was hard to acknowledge sometimes, but it was true. And Hatch was right. He'd had to come to terms with the fact that the two father figures he'd gotten were imperfect. Likely he would have been forced to face the same facts about his mother and father had they lived.

"Well, I wish like hell your father had been the one to talk to Bran about sex. That boy has some weird ideas, and he's not afraid to share."

Riley grinned. He wasn't sure that by sixteen or seventeen Bran had needed much of a talk.

His cell buzzed and he looked down. Luckily Adam Miles had called on the landline. He could still hear the hold music as he answered his cell. "Hey, buddy. How is it going with Ellie? Did she and Lily have a good time?"

"She ditched me, man. I swear to God I walked downstairs to hail a cab and she never showed. I looked everywhere," Bran explained.

"What do you mean she ditched you? Why the hell would she ditch you?" His heart started racing.

"I mean I talked to one of the building attendants, and he saw her leaving through the staff entrance. She knew what she was doing. She was trying to get away from me."

"Why would she do that?" His mind played through a hundred scenarios.

"I don't know, but she has the source code. At least we think it's the source code. It's something her father left for her, but we didn't get a chance to open it."

"What's going on?" Hatch put both his hands on the table and stared at Riley. "Is there a problem with Ellie?"

He put the phone on speaker. "Are you absolutely sure Ellie isn't in the building?"

"He lost Ellie?" Hatch nearly shouted. He was on his phone in a heartbeat. He would be getting in touch with Drew, no doubt about it.

"I'm sure. I've looked all over. The man I talked to said she was alone," Bran explained.

It was a little surreal. "Sweet Child o' Mine" was still playing in the background, an odd soundtrack to his life disintegrating around him. She'd walked out. She'd found the source code and then sent his brother off.

Or had she?

"Did she tell you to go get the cab?"

"No. I offered."

He quickly turned to his laptop. "She didn't send you away. She wouldn't have. Something happened. Someone got to her."

Hatch put the phone he was holding to his shoulder. "Are you serious? You think about this for two seconds. She has the source code and then she ditches Bran. Obviously either she's taking it to Castalano in exchange for him not prosecuting her or she's going to hold it over your brother's head. She's going to contact us very soon and ask for a ridiculous amount of money."

What Hatch said made total sense. It really did. Except he knew Ellie. He knew that woman deep down to her soul. "No. Someone got to her. She's in trouble."

"We're all in trouble, damn it." Hatch put the phone back to his ear. "Riley's thinking with his dick again."

He was thinking with his soul. It sounded stupid but he couldn't even contemplate that Ellie could betray him.

"I'm worried about her," Bran said.

A beep came across the line. He pulled the phone away. Ellie was calling.

"Bran, it's her. I have to go." Without waiting for his brother's response, he answered Ellie's call. "Baby, are you all right? What's going on? Please tell me where you are so I can come get you."

Hatch was getting in his space. "Tell her we won't give her a damn dime."

"Riley, I have the code, but I can't give it to you." Her voice sounded strained, like she'd been crying.

"What's going on? Whatever it is, it's going to be all right." If she wasn't giving the code to him, something had gone horribly wrong.

"It's not going to be all right. We'll sue her if she doesn't hand it over," Hatch said.

"Stay out of this." He strode away, trying to focus on her.

"I'm about to walk into StratCast," she said. "I know you're going to hate me forever, but I have to give it to Steven."

There was only one reason she would do that and it had nothing to do with money or power or even getting even with a husband who had betrayed her. "I understand. He has Lily. Baby, is there any way you can wait for me to get there?"

He was already grabbing his wallet.

"He does have her. How can you believe that? I ran away from Bran because I thought he would take it from me."

"I would have kicked his ass for doing it and gotten it back to you." He had to get to her. "I can be there in fifteen minutes, Ellie. Please wait."

He needed a gun. Why didn't he have a gun?

He heard her gasp over the line. "I can't wait, but I wanted you to know. I wish . . . Everyone in your family is going to hate me, Riley. I can't come back."

He gripped the phone, wishing he could see her. "I don't hate you, baby. I'll be there as soon as I can."

"I'm sorry, Riley. You'll never know how much."

The line went dead and he was left breathless and terrified.

"Riley?" Adam's voice came back on the landline, ending the Guns N' Roses cycle. "You won't believe this. Lily Gallo was in the Bahamas that day. I just put it together. I'm sorry I took a while but one thing led to the other and I think she's your girl. It looks like her father used to work for StratCast. They don't share the same last name. He was arrested for insider trading a couple of years back and Castalano is the one who paid his bail."

Ellie was walking into a trap. Riley turned to Hatch.

"I need a gun."

Hatch's eyes widened. "I might be able to help you with that."

Ellie's hands were shaking as she turned off her phone. Riley would call back. He would try to convince her to give up the thumb drive.

Except he hadn't.

She'd called because she'd found she couldn't hand it over to Castalano without telling Riley what she was doing. She'd resisted the urge until she'd stood outside the building.

"Miss Stratton?" The guard on duty stood up at his station.

She wasn't Miss Stratton anymore. Of course, she might be soon. "Hello, Thomas. Could you please tell Mr. Castalano that I'm here to see him."

She had to request access to her own building. She hated that man. Hated him with a searing passion. In that moment, she understood why her brothers-in-law had sought their revenge. Steven was evil.

Thomas picked up the phone and did as she'd requested. When he put it back down, he frowned her way. "Are you sure you want to go up there? Everyone's gone for the day. From what I can tell, you'll be pretty much alone with him."

And that was how he wanted it. Castalano wanted her alone and vulnerable. "I'll be fine."

Thomas pushed the button that gave her access. "I don't believe a word he says about you. Almost none of us do. You stay strong. We all want you back here. You need anything, you call me."

She might need one thing. "Thomas, I know it might get you in trouble, but my husband is likely on his way down here right now. I know he's banned from the building."

"He's a smart guy. I'm sure he's pretty sneaky, too. Man like that can get right past a guard." Thomas nodded. "I'll probably hear something I have to go and check out right about that time."

So she might not be alone the whole time.

"Thank you." She walked to the elevator and pressed the button, her hand shaking.

Riley hadn't yelled at her. Oh, she'd heard Hatch. He'd reacted the way she'd thought Riley would.

I don't hate you, baby. I'll be there as soon as I can.

He hadn't accused her of trying to steal from his family. He'd immediately known what the problem was, as though he'd known she would never do anything to hurt him if she could help it.

Riley trusted her. He trusted her almost without thought.

And she knew deep in her heart that he would be coming for her.

He would have fought to get to her if Thomas had proven to be more loyal to Castalano.

She stepped into the elevator and let the doors close behind her before she hit the button for the top floor.

She trusted Riley with her life. She might need to throw out the notion of punishment and take another look at forgiveness.

What was she doing? The floors ticked by. She should have called the police despite what Castalano had said.

You have very little time to get here and save your friend. If you're not here in twenty minutes or if I get a hint that you've called the police, Miss Gallo will be found dead in the ladies' room. She's already written out a note. Turns out she was involved in your crimes and can't stand the thought of going to jail. It's so easy to get pills these days. Isn't that sad?

Had he already had Lily when Ellie had texted her? Or had the bastard duped her phone and he'd been waiting for a chance like this?

She should have gone straight home, handed everything over to Riley, and been done with it. But no. She'd had to text her friend. She needed Lily to know she'd gotten one thing right.

Now Lily was in danger and her in-laws would likely never speak to her again.

She had to do it. She knew damn well that Castalano wouldn't hesitate to go through with his plan. And he would do it up right. If he said it would look like suicide, then it likely would.

After all, he'd managed a "murder-suicide" once.

The doors came open and Kyle stood there. He was dressed in a suit, all dapper for his villainy. Excellent. At least she elicited some fashion from the criminals who had taken over her life.

She squared her shoulders. "You're not getting a thing from me until I see that Lily is alive and well."

Kyle's eyes rolled. "God, you're really going to play this out to the end, aren't you? Noble Ellie, everyone's savior. It's actually quite sickening and exactly why you've lost this particular game."

He had a hand on the elevator door, holding it open.

"I might lose a few battles," she admitted. "But this war is likely to continue."

Kyle smirked her way. "Honey, you don't even understand the rules of this particular war. Come on. They're waiting for you. And I could take it from you, if I wanted to, but this is going to be infinitely more fun for me."

She stepped out of the elevator and looked up, noticing the cameras were on. A tiny green light blinked. There wouldn't be any security cameras once she got to Steven's office. Her father and Castalano had decided privacy was far more important. But he might have had to drag Lily down the hall. If they got that on tape, maybe they would have a chance with the police.

Lily would testify.

Which was why it didn't make any sense for Castalano to give her up.

She stopped in the middle of the hallway. Why would he give Lily up? Why would he let her walk out?

Kyle's fingers wound around her elbow. "Is there a problem, Ellie?"

Oh, so many problems. She hadn't thought the situation through. Kyle was right about that. She'd run the minute someone had needed saving.

Please let Riley be on his way.

"Is Lily still alive?" Twenty minutes was more than enough time to get rid of a witness. They'd likely known she would follow their rules. Why on earth would she think for a second this could go any way but poorly?

"Of course she's still alive." Kyle hauled her along.

"But she won't stay that way, will she?" She had one card left to play. "My husband knows where I am."

"Good for old Riley." Kyle turned down the hall past her own office. He nodded toward her door. "That's mine now. It always should have been mine. Your father was weak, and God knows you're completely pathetic. You're not cut out for this level of the business world. I always knew that."

"Yes, you're so much more suited. You couldn't even finish college. If you think you can really run this company, you're high. I suppose you can run it into the ground, but I'm starting to suspect that's your father's plan."

"His plan is to pass the company on to his son, as it always should have been. Why do you think he's done all of this? It's been for me."

"Now you're delusional." She had to hurry to keep up with him. She glanced around, hoping someone, anyone was still at the office. "He's going to sell off all the important research and pocket the money for himself. Or he'll simply take as much money as he can and get the hell out. If StratCast lasts another five years, we'll all be lucky. I would bet he's got plans for his retirement."

Kyle kept right on walking, dragging her along. "Of course he does. That's the point. He's going to retire and I'm taking over. He bought a nice place in Europe and I'll be appointed the CEO in less than two years."

"Where?"

"Why do you care?"

She had a suspicion. "I do. Where is this retirement home?"

"It's in Saint Petersburg. He's made all the arrangements. My stepmother's family is from that part of the world. The Venice of the north. Dad is going to be happy there and I'll take care of things here."

"Russia. He's retiring to Russia? Do you know who retires to Russia, you moron? People who don't want to get extradited to the U.S." She might not have been thinking before, but Kyle was proving he never thought. Not once in his damn life. "Do you really believe the board is going to back you as CEO? You have almost no management experience and no college degree."

That seemed to make an impact. Kyle stopped briefly before his jaw went hard and he started walking her toward his father's office. The door was closed ahead.

"They'll do it because my father will tell them to and he wouldn't do that to me. He wouldn't lie. I'm his only son."

"And he worked his hardest to not pay child support."

"My mother was a whore," Kyle replied with a frown. "He was right not to pay her a dime. She would have spent it on drugs. That's another reason he's leaving me the company. He left me there with her."

"You think your father is capable of feeling guilty? Do you understand why he wants this thumb drive? It proves that he stole the whole basis of StratCast from Benedict Lawless. He had my husband's parents killed."

"Sure he did. Now who's the delusional one?"

"It's all true." She wasn't sure why she was trying to convince him, but she kept on.

"No. Your father was the thief." He opened the door and shoved her through. "My dad is protecting me and this company."

Castalano stood behind his desk. "That's right, son. I'm protecting your legacy from my former partner."

Lily sat in a chair in front of the desk. She turned, her eyes red from crying. "Ellie, I'm so sorry."

She nodded. There was nothing to do now except try to brazen her way through. "It's all right. I'll give you the thumb drive downstairs. Walk down with us and we can be done with this."

"Or Kyle can take it from you." He nodded to his son.

Kyle grabbed her bag off her shoulder and turned it upside down. He quickly found the thumb drive. "Got it. And you're an idiot, Ellie. Haven't you figured it out? How did we find out you had this? Who do you think turned you in?"

She looked back at Castalano. "You bugged Lily's phone."

Lily's skin was a pale white. "Ellie . . ."

Castalano put a hand on her shoulder. "Lily's worked for me for years. I saw this coming a long time ago. Who do you think opened the accounts under your name?"

Ellie felt a hole open inside her. Lily had been her friend for years and yet she'd carefully herded her, leading the lamb to slaughter. Lily had been her only friend.

"Ellie, I had to do it to save my father," Lily said. "I never meant to hurt you."

Ellie had always come second. Second to her father's business. Second to her sister. She always would be.

Except Riley hadn't seemed to care that she was throwing away his best shot at revenge. Riley seemed to be trying to put her first.

Nothing mattered except getting back to Riley.

"You have your source code and you let me know that you've taken everything from me." She wasn't going to give any one of them her tears. They didn't deserve her tears. She would save those for later, when she was wrapped up in her husband's arms and he would hold her tight. She would definitely save them for Drew, who would likely yell at her, and Hatch, who would absolutely yell at her. Tears might work on them.

She could handle their anger. The certainty came over her. She could handle Drew and Hatch being pissed because they wouldn't kick her out. They would yell for a while and then force her to sit down with them and solve this next problem as a family.

The one thing she'd never had.

"I'm going home. You can sit here and fool these two all night." She turned, but Kyle was there blocking her path.

"There is something I can still take," Castalano said.

That was when she noticed he was holding a gun, pointing straight at her.

She stood firm. "How exactly are you going to explain killing me?"

"Well, dear, you came here to kill me. When you showed up—uninvited, might I add—and tried to convince me to stop the prosecution of your case, I explained that I wouldn't. That was when you got violent. Wasn't it, Kyle?"

Kyle chuckled. "She did. I saw the whole thing. Didn't you, Lily?" He leaned in. "By the way, she's been my mistress for years. Do you know how we laugh about you?"

Lily stood. "That's not true, Ellie. I slept with him because I pretty much had no choice, but I would never laugh about you. I love you. I admire you. I hate myself for what I've done."

"But you'll continue to do it, won't you, dear?" Castalano asked in a silky smooth voice. "You'll be the one to tell the police that your friend was corrupt, that you saw everything."

Lily looked back and tears rolled down her face. She stared for a moment and then turned back to her boss. "No. I won't help you kill Ellie. And Kyle, he's been selling technology to the Russians for years. He's going to gut the company and flee the country. He never intended to leave you a damn thing."

"That is unfortunate." Castalano turned the gun and shot Lily in the head.

Ellie stared in stark silence. She couldn't breathe. What had happened? Her dear friend, the woman who had betrayed her, fell to the ground dead.

"Why did you do that?" Kyle screamed the question as he moved toward Lily's body.

Ellie wanted to scream, wanted to charge Castalano, but she now had a shot. She turned and bolted out of the office, leaving everything behind.

He heart was racing. He'd killed Lily. He'd shot her and Lily wasn't here anymore. No matter what she'd done, Ellie hadn't wanted her dead. She couldn't even process it at this point.

She had seconds. She couldn't wait for the elevator. She wasn't sure she could get to the stairs. There was a bank of cubicles in front of her. She dipped down behind the first one as she heard a second shot.

Her heart pounded, adrenaline flowing through her system in a great rush. What had happened? Had he shot his own son?

"Ellie, dear, this won't do. Why did you kill your friend? And my boy. I can't believe you were so jealous of their love. But then you had to have him, didn't you? Could you thank your husband for sending the reporter our way? He's made this very simple. Everyone knows you had an affair with Kyle. I didn't mean to kill Kyle yet, but it does wrap all of this up in a neat bundle."

Naturally, he intended to play it that way. She kept her mouth closed and listened. He moved from his carpeted office to the marbled floor. His shoes tapped against the marble and then went silent again as he hit the carpet the cubicles sat on.

She didn't hear Kyle at all. Castalano could be lying. It could be a ruse, but she didn't think so. She thought he'd really done it. He'd gotten rid of all the witnesses who could speak of his crimes.

"I never actually thought the boy was mine anyway. Like that bitch couldn't have paid off someone in the lab." His footsteps moved ever closer.

Ellie crawled to the next row, staying as close as she could to the cubicle walls. She had to get to the stairs someway. Or she could run down the hall toward the back stairs.

"You're going to make this hard on me." Castalano sighed. "I had all the cameras taken offline. When the police ask, I'll tell them I didn't want your begging and pleading broadcast. After all, you're the daughter of my partner. I knew you as a little girl. I assure you, I'm ready for the questions."

She heard something, a squeaking sound that caught her attention. She went still and Castalano was silent for a moment.

"No one's coming to save you. I've given instructions that no one is allowed in the building. It's just you and me. Why don't you come out and have some dignity?"

He didn't realize how much some people hated him. Maybe the guard wouldn't let Riley through, but maybe he would.

Then what? Riley would walk right into an ambush. He would likely take the elevator and Castalano would hear it. He would shoot her husband like he'd shot his own son and Lily.

She had to get him away from the hall. Where Castalano was likely standing, he would see Riley right away.

"My husband won't let you get away with it." She moved quickly to the next row, keeping her head down. The cubicle walls were nice and high. He shouldn't be able to see her unless he jumped on top of a desk—despite his obvious decent health, he was still an almost-seventy-five-year-old man with one hip replacement behind him.

She heard him moving, trying to track her and getting farther from the bank of elevators. That might give Riley a chance, though she was no longer sure she wanted him to come after her.

The thought of him dying was worse than anything. A world without Riley Lawless wouldn't be her world.

"I'm sure he'll try, but I'll be gone in a few weeks. I've made my last deal."

"You're selling the coolant project to the Russians." She moved again, edging toward the stairs. She could outrun him. All she needed was a few seconds and a little distraction. She would get to the stairs and run one floor down. She wouldn't let him pick her off from above. One floor and then she would cut over and call the police. She would hide in R&D.

"Your coolant project is netting me both twenty million and the assurance that I won't be extradited. I really will get my retirement out of this place, and poor Benedict's children will be left with nothing. Again. That thumb drive wasn't the source code. We destroyed that long ago. No, it's much worse. It's your father's burn file on me. It's everything I've ever done. I had one on him as well and Patricia. Mutually assured destruction. It's the only way to go. He was supposed to leave it to me in his will, but your father was a giant ass. He sent Patricia hers, but left me hanging. I think he figured out I'd set you up at some point. He loved you in his own way."

"Is there proof that you killed Benedict and Iris Lawless?" She was almost there. A few more desks and she would have to be ready.

"I should think not. We buried that. There is no proof. Well, there might be a bit, but only Patricia has that information. Why we left it with that bitch, I'll never understand, but our friend trusted her more than the rest."

Friend?

Was he talking about the fourth person who was in on the conspiracy? She'd learned everything about the night the Lawless parents had died. She'd made a study of them over the last two weeks. Iris's body had been found next to her husband, a bullet through her head. The police had claimed it was murder-suicide. It had really been an assassination.

She needed to get that stupid thumb drive back. Maybe her father had left her more than Castalano thought.

She heard the doors to the elevator slide open.

"Ellie?" Riley's voice floated through the space.

"He's got a gun!" Ellie screamed, no longer caring if she gave up her position.

Gunfire boomed through the room and she heard someone grunt.

"Ellie, you stay where you are!" Riley shouted.

"Oh, poor Ellie. I hit your husband. I might be old, but I'm quick," Castalano said.

Riley was hit? She couldn't stay down. She stood and ran toward the hall. She felt something burn as Castalano shot at her, but she didn't pay attention, merely kept running because Riley was on the floor. He was behind a wall of cubicles, but Castalano was moving in. She dove to get to Riley, her knees banging on the carpet and pain flaring through her system.

Bright red blood stained his white shirt. Where was it coming from? It seemed to be everywhere.

"I told you to stay where you were," he said. He still had a gun in his hand, but he was shaking.

Tears blurred her vision. "Where are you hit?"

He shook his head. "Doesn't matter. Take this gun and get the hell out. I'll keep the pistol and I'll distract the bastard. Drew's coming up the stairs. He'll protect you. Find Drew. Bran is with him, too."

"Why aren't you with them?"

He looked over at her, those glorious lips of his turning up. "Too impatient. Had to get to you, baby. Love you."

He was turning a ghastly pale, his skin graying before her eyes.

He pressed something into her hand. Cold metal brushed her palm. It was a gun. Apparently her husband had come fully armed and ready for battle.

She'd never used a gun before, never held one in her hands.

"Ah, what a lovely couple." Castalano stood over them.

Riley tried to bring his gun up, but his hand shook and then his shoulder jerked back as Castalano shot him.

"He should have known better. You don't have the stomach for real business, Ellie. Let me tell you how this is going to go."

She didn't care. She was done living in his world. Without another thought except to pray Riley had taken the safety off, she raised the gun and fired and fired and fired.

An acrid smell hit her nose and she watched as Castalano looked down. He put his hands to his stomach and fell to his knees.

Ellie stood and moved to him, kicking his gun out of the way.

"Ellie! Riley!" Drew ran in looking far too competent with a gun in his hand. Bran was behind him.

Thank God they were here, because she didn't want to stand over her enemy. She had more important things to do.

She dropped to her knees beside her husband. "Riley, where are you hit?"

"Feels like everywhere." He slumped down, but his hand found hers. "Did I ever tell you how pretty you are?" His eyes were glassy as he looked at her. "So damn pretty. My Ellie."

She couldn't lose him. Not now.

Bran dropped down beside her. "Ambulance is on its way."

"Don't let him." Riley groaned as he tried to sit up.

"Stay down and don't move," she ordered.

"Drew, no." The words slurred from Riley's mouth.

Ellie looked over and Drew was kneeling by Castalano.

"Please don't let him," Riley begged.

She stood because she couldn't let her husband down. He'd come for her, taken a bullet for her. There was nothing left in her heart for him but love, and she needed to stop his brother from making a horrible mistake.

"Drew, don't."

Drew's face was completely blank, his hands circling the man's throat. Castalano was still breathing, though he was unconscious. "All it takes is one twist, Ellie. One little twist."

"And then you'll be as bad as he is." She put a hand on her brother-in-law's shoulder.

"I already am."

"No." She knelt beside him. He hadn't closed his hands around the older man's throat, but the potential was right there. "You're not."

"You have no idea the things I've done," he replied.

"You saved your family. Don't leave them now. Please, Drew. Let the court handle him. Let justice take care of him. Please."

Drew cursed and finally stood and turned back to his brothers.

"You know that's a flesh wound, Riley." He shook his head. "And we got everything on tape. The guard agreed to turn the cameras all back on once Bran and I explained the situation."

"He confessed," Ellie explained, getting close to her husband again. "He confessed everything to me. And it's not a flesh wound. It's serious."

Riley grinned, a drunken look. "Chicks dig scars."

The elevator opened and the room was suddenly filled with EMTs and NYPD.

She watched as they rushed her husband out, Bran and Drew holding her hands.

Seventeen

Riley stepped into the elevator and brushed off his brother's help. Bran had turned into a meddlesome thing, always standing over him and watching. "I'm fine."

"Dude, you just got out of the hospital where you went through multiple surgeries."

He had some serious new scars. He really did hope his particular chick dug scars.

Although his wife hadn't come to the hospital to collect him. She'd come to visit him and she'd held his hand, but she'd treated him so gingerly he wasn't sure if it had been about love or guilt.

Bran pressed the button to take them up to the penthouse.

"Are you going to tell me if Ellie's moved out or not?" He didn't look his brother's way, merely stared straight ahead.

Bran sighed. "Yes. I'm sorry, Riley. She moved out a few days ago."

He nodded to himself. "All right."

It wouldn't make a difference. As soon as he could pack, he would find a place as close to her as possible. He would start over and do it right this time.

"She said to tell you she was sorry she didn't come to the hospital. She was surprised you were getting out today," Bran explained.

"I know. I got the text." She'd texted him that she wished him a happy trip home. He should have known then and there she wasn't going to be waiting for him. "I also saw the news."

"Yeah, I was going to get to that."

"You can't keep me out of the loop forever." Bran, Drew, and Hatch had all been tight-lipped about Castalano and what happened after Ellie had shot him. He vaguely remembered Drew over Castalano's body and prayed he wasn't finishing the old bastard off. Not that he didn't deserve it, but Riley didn't want Drew to have that kind of blood on his hands.

He could still remember how Ellie hadn't hesitated. She'd used up the gun when he'd no longer had the strength. She hadn't fled as he'd asked her to. She'd stayed at his side and taken out that son of a bitch.

Who had managed to survive the three bullets she'd placed in him only to have a heart attack yesterday. The day before he was set to finally talk to police. His lawyer had wanted a plea deal in exchange for full disclosure of Castalano's activities and his partners.

"I want to know everyone who went into and out of his hospital room," Riley said.

"Case is already on it," Bran replied. "Of course you know what Drew thinks."

"Likely he thinks exactly what I do. Patricia Cain and whoever is left got to Castalano before he could talk. She knew there wasn't anything about her on Stratton's thumb drive since someone from the police department leaked what was on the drive."

A systematic record of Castalano's deals with foreign companies and governments to sell technology. He'd made millions. Unfortunately, he'd also spent it.

Lily Gallo had left proof behind, too. She'd left a document on her computer detailing everything she'd done to aid in setting up her boss. It was left to send out to Ellie and the police if she didn't check in on her server every thirty-six hours.

Ellie was free and clear. And gone.

"You know she's had a lot to do these last couple of weeks," Bran said as though reading his mind.

The trip to the top of the building seemed endless. He would be going back down as soon as he could. He would march himself to her condo and ask her out. If she said no, he'd do it all over again tomorrow.

He couldn't lose his wife. She was the most important person in the world to him.

"I know she's needed to be at StratCast."

"The whole company was in chaos and there were a ton of legal issues to deal with and her lawyer was on pain meds."

"I still could have done it," he argued.

"No." Bran shook his head. "You're the stubbornest man I know and that's saying quite a bit. It used to be Drew, but now it is definitely you. Garrison's friend did an excellent job. The stock has all been transferred to Ellie via the partnership agreement between Castalano and her father. It all came to her in case he died and had no heirs. Despite the fact that she doesn't have to since he was under investigation for crimes at the time of his death, she wrote a substantial check to his widow."

"That's my Ellie." She wouldn't be able to stand the idea of the wife being impoverished. She'd always seemed mousy and quiet, like the kind of woman who had been ground down by life and a horrible husband.

"And she paid for Lily's funeral," Bran said quietly.

He was mad at Lily Gallo, but his anger meant nothing in the face of Ellie's pain. "I wish I'd been there to hold her hand."

"Drew and I took care of her."

"I'm a little surprised she let you do that." He'd expected she would pull away from them all.

The doors opened and Bran put a hand out to hold them. "She's been very nice and more than a bit bossy about things. Drew got pissy at first, but then she pointed out that she kind of was the woman of the house. He might have said it was his damn house. That was when she threatened to take you and her amazing chocolate chip cookies with her. And that was when Drew decided he didn't need to call it a war room anymore."

Riley shook his head. "What?"

Drew was standing in the hallway, a wry smile on his face. "She took exception to the war room. She said she wasn't allowing her children to be brought up in a home where there was a war room. So now my damn war room is being renovated."

Bran held his hand up for a high five. "We're getting a real live game room. Ellie's geeking the whole place out."

"Your wife is a pain in my ass," Drew complained. "But I suppose she's family so we'll keep her. And you need to heal fast because her board is also a pain in my ass. I've signed over every share of my stock to you. You can deal with the fact that she's decided to change the world through better management or some shit."

Riley stopped, staring at Bran. "You told me she moved out."

"Bran, you're a mean shit," Hatch said as he walked toward the elevator.

Bran grinned. "I am. Hey, I'm the little brother who never got to torture his older brothers. I have to make up for some seriously lost time. And the car is waiting for us. I have some amazing strip clubs on the menu for us tonight."

Drew rolled his eyes as Hatch joined Bran. "I'll be down in a minute. And we're not going to a strip club. We're going to a baseball game."

"Oh, we'll see what happens after," Bran said with a mischievous grin.

The elevator doors closed and Drew put a hand on his shoulder. "You good?"

"I'm spectacular if my wife is still here and she's fighting you on renovations. You know we can move."

Drew shook his head. "Don't. I've asked her to please stay. You two will be living here more often than the rest of us. Consider this place a wedding gift. I know eventually you'll all move on, so let me have a little more time with my family. She did, however, move out of your room. I gave you two the master suite. She had that sucker redone in a week. I've never seen contractors work so fast. Apparently I like to live in a cave. Ellie likes the light. I think she's going to be very good for you, brother."

"For all of us if you let her. Have you thought about settling down?"

Drew stepped away. "Don't. Don't try to go there. I like Ellie, but you need to know I'm not getting married. I'm not having children."

"Why?" He knew if he'd been asked the same question two months before he likely would have said the same thing Drew had. But now, with Ellie, the possibility of the future dangled in front of him like a ripe fruit he wasn't about to let go of. "You can have a future, Drew."

"Only if I let go of the past, and I'll never do that." The elevator doors opened again. "I'm going to take down Patricia Cain. I'll leave all of you out of it, but I won't rest until she's in jail or dead. And I will find out who betrayed us."

The doors closed and he was left alone. Except he was never really alone. Not ever again.

Though he ached for his brother, he needed to see her. She was the light in his life.

He turned down the hallway that led to the master suite.

When he stepped inside, he could see that Ellie had transformed his brother's brooding masculine cave into something bright and lovely. The living area of the suite was now a beautiful yellow. It was sunny. Like his Ellie.

"They told me you wouldn't be here for another hour." She was dressed in a pair of jeans that hugged her curves and a T-shirt, her feet bare. It was obvious she'd been moving things around, trying to get everything perfect.

For him. How could he tell her that the simple fact she was in a room made it perfect?

"My brothers lied. They told me you had moved out."

She stopped in front of him, her hands coming up to cup his face. "Now, why would I do that?"

He could think of a few reasons. "I lied to you. I betrayed you."

"You used to be a different man. Now you're better. You were a bit of a fixer-upper, but then my own father was a murderous tyrant, so you're really a step up for me."

"Say it." He needed to hear the words. He loved how sassy she was, how funny and smart, but now he simply needed to hear the words from her mouth. "Please."

"I love you, Riley."

He leaned over to kiss her. "I love you, Ellie. I'll spend the rest of my life proving it. Starting with christening this room. I don't think this room has seen action in forever."

Because big brother hadn't figured out that there were more important things to life than revenge.

"Whoa," she protested. "Did you forget the surgeries?"

No way she was getting out of this. He kissed her again, fully satisfied when she sagged against him. "You'll have to be gentle with me, then. After all, you are the boss, Madam CEO. I'm a lowly lawyer."

She laughed and went on her toes. "I think you know I have a gentle hand. Let's see what we can do."

He let her lead him back to the bedroom. It was past time to get started on a new generation of Lawless kids.

That was a plan he was sure his father would approve of.

Epilogue

Bran looked at the girl as she sat in the outdoor dining area of the small Italian restaurant. She was supposed to be on a date.

Carly Fisher was putting her toe back into the dating field after a spectacularly bad marriage. Her ex-husband was now doing time in the state pen, and pretty Carly was trying her hand at Internet dating.

Yeah, that probably wasn't going to work out for her. Unfortunately, her date was his brother Drew. He was planning on walking in and charming the woman and likely taking her to bed—all so he could get close to her boss.

Carly seemed to be a magnet for abusive shitheads. She worked for America's leading lifestyle expert, Patricia Cain, who also happened to be one of the people who'd paid to have Bran's parents assassinated.

Life hadn't been particularly fair to the lovely Carly. She was a fluffy little thing, and by little, he simply meant smaller than him. He'd never once had a thing for tiny women. Tiny women broke. Though he was the smallest of his brothers, he was still six two and had packed on some serious muscle. He liked women he could hold on to. Women who could keep him warm because sometimes the world was really fucking cold.

"Is she in place?" Hatch asked over his earphone.

They were doing all kinds of spy shit. They had three different people watching the poor girl. "She's settling in."

"Good, we'll let her stew for ten minutes or so," Hatch explained. "Then I'll send in Drew."

They wanted her vulnerable, on edge. They wanted her insecure. She would likely look at Drew and wonder why he'd picked her, and Drew would lie and say he'd wanted her the minute he'd seen her picture.

Bran wasn't sure he'd go that far, but she intrigued him. She didn't dress for her body type. She was far too covered up. It was hot outside, but she'd worn jeans and a black shirt, likely because she'd been told black was slimming. She didn't need to be slimmed. Her dark hair was pulled up in a ponytail. She frowned and looked down at the menu.

From what he'd read about her, he knew that Carly Fisher was twenty-eight years old. She'd grown up taking care of her younger sister. She'd put her sweet self through college and landed a job with the superawful Patricia Cain. She'd married and then found out her husband had only married her to get his hands in Patricia Cain's cookie jar. Ah, embezzlement. It had been the end of her marriage but somehow not the end of her career.

Would she see Drew as her life finally turning around? Would she welcome him into her bed and her heart only to have it shattered when she realized the truth? She would lose her job and her lover. Would that be the final nail in the coffin of her optimism?

She didn't look so optimistic. She bit her bottom lip and looked around as though ready to run.

Then the waiter stepped up and asked her a question.

When that girl smiled, the whole world lit up. He sat there for a moment staring at her because she was gorgeous when she smiled.

"Drew, you ready?" Hatch asked.

"I'm ready when you are," Drew replied, his voice chilly.

Not when she was. Carly Fisher didn't matter. Not to his brother.

Bran moved across the street, walking straight to the little outdoor café.

"Bran, what are you doing?" Drew asked.

The right thing. He tugged his earpiece free and tossed it away. Sometimes a man had to change up the game plan.

He pulled out the chair across from Carly. "Hey, my name is Brandon Lawless."

She looked around like she was trying to figure out who was watching her. "Um, you have the wrong girl."

He smiled at her. "Nope. I've got the right girl. Carly, your boss murdered my parents twenty years ago. What do you say you help me bring her to justice?"

"Are you insane?"

Yeah, he got that reaction a lot.

THE STORY CONTINUES
IN THE NEXT LAWLESS NOVEL

Satisfaction

COMING SOON FROM BERKLEY.

TURN THE PAGE FOR A SNEAK PEEK . . .

LOS ANGELES, CA

Carly sat back and took a deep breath. It was over. Almost. One last thing and then she could go home and figure out exactly what to do with the rest of her life.

She could sell the car. It was the only viable asset she had. The house would go back to the bank. That hurt. She'd turned that little town house into something beautiful. She would be lucky to find an apartment building that would rent to her. Very likely she would end up working retail or at some fast food restaurant. Everything she'd worked for was one big steaming pile of crap.

That's what happened when a girl fell for a slick con artist.

She'd lost her husband. She was about to lose her job, the domino that would send all the others falling—house, status, car. No more nice shoes for Carly. She would be lucky to have the money to buy secondhand, much less the Manolos and Prada she'd worn for the last few years because her boss insisted she look the part of Patricia Cain's right arm. She'd learned really fast that Patricia Cain's right arm wore some expensive shit. But then so did her left arm, ankle, knee, and every other part of her.

She was about to lose a job millions of women would kill for.

Thank God.

She tidied up her desk and prepared for the confrontation. Ever since that moment when the police had hauled Roger off in handcuffs, she'd known this was coming. Carly glanced down the hallway. She wished it could have happened while they were in Saint Augustine, where she wouldn't have to find a way back home, but Los Angeles was as good a place as any to make her final stand.

The door to the office opened and Emily's eyes flared as she took in the sight of Carly at her desk. "Kyle from accounting said you were here. I didn't believe him. What are you doing?"

She was being brave for once. "I'm waiting to speak with Patricia."

"Because you're going to murder her?" Emily let the door slam behind her. "Oh God, you're going to do it, aren't you? Everyone's always said one day her assistant would shoot her. I knew you would be the one to do it. You're not an evil sheep like the rest of them."

"I'm not going to shoot her." Though she'd often thought about it.

Emily shot her a sympathetic look. "She had your husband arrested. No one would blame you."

"The police would. Also the DA. Probably a jury of my peers, too. Roger embezzled a million dollars from Cain Corp. He deserves to go to jail." She believed every single accusation leveled at her soon-to-be ex-husband. She would throw in a couple more. Cheating. Lying. Gambling. Running up her credit cards, which she soon would have no way to pay for. And she'd bought it all for two years. She'd been the one to get him the job here, where he'd managed to embezzle all that lovely money he'd spent on God knew what.

Now it was time to pay the piper. Or the righteous bitch, in this case. Patricia Cain would never pipe. Far below her dignity.

Emily worked on the magazine side of the business as a copy editor. She was a nice girl, one Carly always had lunch with when they were in LA. "Seriously, you should walk out. She's going to be so mean to you."

And that was different how? "I'm going to give her my letter of resignation and leave with some dignity."

She had the cheapest ticket she could find in her purse. She left LAX for Jacksonville at eight tonight. She would find the cheapest wine she could and drown her sorrows.

And celebrate a little because she never had to see Patricia Cain's cosmetically enhanced face again. She never had to deal with another of that woman's issues. She was getting out right as the Queen of Domestic Bliss was planning her own wedding to a disgusting billionaire whose greatest talent seemed to be his ability to leer at women half his age and younger without a single ounce of shame.

Freedom. This was the one good thing Roger had done for her. She was going to be free.

What she'd never worked up the nerve to do was finally out of her hands. She'd worked for Patricia Cain for three hellish years, all the while telling herself it was only a matter of time before she was rewarded for all the ridiculously late nights and degrading tasks. She would do her time, make her connections, and then move on in the world. Everyone knew Patricia never kept an assistant for more than five years, and then she moved them out into the vast network of TV and publishing and home goods businesses that paid her considerable rent. A shiny new assistant would be brought in and the old one put to happier pastures.

She couldn't hold out that long. Two more years of working for that bitch would kill her no matter what was waiting at the end of the rainbow. Some things weren't worth the price she had to pay.

Now it was over, and she could find a life free of Patricia Cain and Roger. She was going to be broke with zero prospects, and that suddenly seemed pretty damn fine to her.

The door opened again and Patricia entered. She was dressed in a Chanel business suit, her icy blond hair in a bun. When she filmed her highly rated television show, *Patricia's Paradise*, she wore denim and even T-shirts, her hair down and flowing, her makeup under-stated. She was the face of new American domesticity. Elegant, but casual. Inviting.

This was the real Patricia. A shark in a designer suit. She turned her cold eyes Emily's way. "Out."

Without another word, Emily scurried away and Carly was left alone.

There was nothing to do but get this over with. She'd been terri-fied of this woman for long enough.

"Ms. Cain, I waited because I wanted to give this to you person-ally." She held up her well thought-out resignation letter.

Patricia looked at it like it was something diseased. "No, thank you. I think we should have this discussion in my office. Where is my coffee?"

She started her day with a triple-shot vanilla latte, no foam, no sugar. Every day without fail for the last three years, Carly had it waiting for her. Not today.

"This is my resignation letter, Ms. Cain. I'm no longer your as-sistant. You'll have to find someone else to get your coffee. I'll leave this here for you, but I've also sent you an e-copy of the letter as well. Good luck finding someone new."

She wouldn't need it. There would be a line of applicants a mile long once word got out Carly had quit. After the news from last night, there might already be one forming. Roger's arrest had been all over the news, so there was no doubt people would be talking.

The never-ending backbiting and gossip—one more thing she wouldn't miss.

Patricia stared at her, cold snakelike eyes assessing. "I think you should come to my office, Carly. I have a few things I need to say to you. Legal things."

She thought about running out the door and not looking back. It would be easy since Patricia had turned and strode into her office, her heels thudding along the tasteful hardwood floors. Something about the way her boss had said the word "legal" made her follow.

She'd signed a contract when she'd first become Patricia's assistant. Carly's brain worked overtime thinking about what all she'd agreed to in exchange for a halfway decent salary, clothing allowance, and travel budget. All she'd had to sign away was her soul.

There had been a ton of nondisclosure stuff, which, given some of her boss's proclivities, was a damn fine idea. No tell-all books would be written about Patricia Cain by one of her assistants without a nice long legal battle. She'd been required to live within fifteen minutes of her boss's Saint Augustine mansion. There had been a ton of blah blah legal stuff, but she couldn't remember anything about a requirement that she stay for a certain length of time or there would be penalties. She was fairly certain that wasn't even legal. Patricia couldn't keep her here, so she followed along.

One last battle.

"Close the door behind you," Patricia said without turning around.

Carly shut it and faced Patricia as she lowered herself into her antique chair behind a desk Carly was fairly certain had once had a place at Versailles. "Did you need more than the resignation? I could give you a week or two, but after last night I thought you would want me gone."

Patricia settled back, crossing her long legs one over the other. "Last night was about your husband. Not you. I certainly don't think you were either smart enough or ballsy enough to try to steal from me."

Yes, there was the wit she'd come to love so much. "Still, I was dumb enough to marry him and bring him into the company. I think it's best we sever ties. I'm in the middle of divorcing him, but I'll still likely have to spend time dealing with the fallout of his arrest."

"Yes, timing is a problem, is it not? I've got the fall TV launch and there's the issue of my wedding to Kenneth. Having to break in a new assistant would be difficult."

Her stomach dropped. "I'm sure you can find one who will work."

"But I think you'll work nicely. You see, there's something you don't know, dear. Something I've kept from my legal team and will continue to keep from them. Your husband stole two million dollars. Not one. He was quite intelligent but I'm smarter. Well, the people I pay for these types of things are smarter. Would you like to know whose name the second account was in?"

Her belly was now in complete free fall. "He wouldn't."

A laugh came from Patricia's mouth, but it was somehow sinister. "Not you, dear. That would have been far too easy. No. He asked your sweet sister to open an account. I believe he told her it was so he could buy you an anniversary present without you knowing about it."

Anger flared through her. She would kill Roger. She could actually see herself doing it. Meri was in college. She had her whole life ahead of her. There was nothing on the planet Carly loved more than her little sister, and she could easily see Meri getting scammed into thinking she was doing something good. "She didn't have anything to do with this."

"Oh, but she did. That money was in her name before your husband withdrew it," Patricia said slowly. She sighed and sat back. "I've thought long and hard about this. You see, I realize I'm a difficult woman to work for. I like things certain ways, and you're quite good at following orders. I let the other assistants go because I needed them in other areas of the business. They form a network of sorts."

"They feed you information." What did any of this have to do with her sister? She would have to find a lawyer. She would fight this. There was no way she was letting her sister take the fall for Roger's greed.

"Yes, they spy for me. They tell me who's screwing who and who's meeting with my competitors. They take care of people I need taken care of. I realized about six months into your employment that you would never be good at that type of work. You have an air of innocence about you that's quite cloying."

No, she wouldn't spy on her fellow employees. It was easy to see she'd been incredibly naive. "All very good reasons to let me go. But Meredith didn't touch that money, Ms. Cain."

"Yes, as I said, I know that. But it does make very good leverage. I'm tired of training new assistants. I want one who is completely loyal to me. If I can't have that then I'll have one who is so afraid of what I can do to her that she'll fall in line. I decided long ago that it's better to be feared than loved. You've read Machiavelli, I presume."

It made complete sense to her that Patricia would quote Renaissance philosophy about how to rule the peasants to her. After all, this woman truly believed she was a queen, the type who took her crown by force. "Of course."

"Well then you understand where I'm coming from. I have plenty of spies. I need a mouse who'll do anything I say. I've got all the documentation, and your husband was more than willing to sign a statement saying your sister was involved. Eventually the statute of limitations on prosecution will run out, but I think until then, you and I will get along fine."

"What is this really about?" It couldn't be about having an employee who was certain to hate her.

The slightest smile curved her lips up. "You'll also go on public record as being deeply grateful to me for allowing you to keep your job after the horrible thing your husband did. I will pay for the lawyer and your divorce. You'll discuss how kind I am and how you were certain you would be out in the cold."

Shit. It all fell into place. Three weeks before, the *New York Times* had run a story on Cain Corp using Third World sweatshops to make cheap home goods. They'd found she'd paid pennies to young women who worked in the most terrible of conditions. "The network thinks your image is ruined and you're trying to rehab it."

"They think I could use a shine, and you're going to do it for me. Like I said, you have an air of innocence. It's what attracted that man to you in the first place. He knew he could use you. Now I'm going to use you. We're doing a special with one of the morning shows. We'll be flying to Cambodia and visiting the women who were horribly taken advantage of. Naturally I knew nothing about the conditions. It's certainly my responsibility, but I am horrified. After all, I do everything I can to lift other women up."

And drop them off the roof. "I won't do it. You knew exactly what was happening in those factories. You signed the papers authorizing a pay cut and longer hours."

"Did I? I doubt you'll be able to find that. No, I was foolish and taken advantage of as well. Now, you should decide if you're going to stay and do your job or if you would prefer for your sister to go to jail."

Her hands were shaking. Actually shaking. There was zero doubt in her mind that Patricia would do it. She never bluffed. The devil didn't have to. The devil always won. "I'll go get your coffee."

"And Carly?"

She turned. "Yes, ma'am?"

"Drop some weight before we go to Cambodia. I can't have you looking like a cow on screen."

Carly walked out, wondering if she'd ever feel whole again.

Lexi Blake is the *New York Times* bestselling author of the Masters and Mercenaries series, including *Master No*, *You Only Love Twice*, and *A View to a Thrill*, and coauthor with Shayla Black of the Perfect Gentlemen series, including *Big Easy Temptation* and *Seduction in Session*, and the Masters of Ménage series, including *Their Virgin Mistress* and *Their Virgin Secretary*. She lives in North Texas with her family. Visit her online at lexiblake.net.